# LAST SEEN IN HAVANA

# LAST SEEN IN HAVANA

TERESA DOVALPAGE

Published by
Soho Press, Inc.
227 W 17th Street
New York, NY 10011

Library of Congress Cataloging-in-Publication Data

Names: Dovalpage, Teresa, author.
Title: Last seen in Havana / Teresa Dovalpage.
Description: New York, NY : Soho Crime, 2024. | Identifiers: LCCN 2023025383

ISBN 978-1-64129-539-0
eISBN 978-1-64129-540-6

Subjects: LCSH: Cuban Americans—Fiction. | Mothers and daughters—Fiction. Women—Cuba—Fiction. | Family secrets—Fiction. | Havana (Cuba)—History—21st century—Fiction. | LCGFT: Detective and mystery fiction. Novels. Classification: LCC PS3604.O936 L37 2024 | DDC 813/.6—dc23/eng/20230530
LC record available at https://lccn.loc.gov/2023025383

Interior design by Janine Agro, Soho Press, Inc.

Printed in the United States of America

10 9 8 7 6 5 4 3 2 1

# LAST
# SEEN
# IN
# HAVANA

# THE ASHEN HOUR

At the ashen hour, that peculiar time of the day when night hasn't fallen yet but you can't see the edge of things, when the whole world seems to have gone underwater, my mother sometimes came to me. It wasn't a dream, for I kept my eyes open the whole time, nor a childhood fantasy. It was a betwixt and between state, a rip in the fabric of reality, the glimpse of a mirage.

I remember one evening when the house felt quieter and emptier than usual. The blue glare of the television was the only light in the living room. I tiptoed outside and sat in the back-yard under a mango tree while Mamina, my grandmother, busied herself in the kitchen. She was making *congrí*—black beans and rice, cooked together, with cumin and tiny pieces of bacon. I smelled fried chicken too (fried in lard, of course!) and my mouth watered.

I was getting hungry but soon forgot about the food. My mother approached quietly, her feet not quite touching the gravel path. I looked up and knew instantly that it was her, though I could not remember her face.

"*¡Mamá!*"

She knelt by my side and caressed my hair. A smell of roses engulfed me. I waited for her to explain those years of absence, to apologize and say that she loved me. But Mamina's voice always broke the spell.

"Merceditas, where are you?"

My mother never came. The ghost of my nine-year-old self stayed under the tree, waiting for her.

# CHAPTER ONE

*January 29th, 1986*

*Dear Rob,*

*Yesterday, I had the privilege of meeting Fidel. He visited the army unit where Joaquín works and went around inspecting the headquarters, mingling with everybody and shaking hands. Yes, El Comandante is so close to his people! And he had minimal security. A Barbados delegation had come with him, and I was asked to be their interpreter. A great honor indeed, but I got nervous and fumbled my words so many times that Fidel ended up talking to them directly. (His English is much better than my Spanish.) He was very gracious about it. Today's paper ran a photo of the visit, which I'm enclosing. You'll see me close to El Caballo. "The Horse" is one of many nicknames people use for Fidel, some more respectful than others.*

THE LONG-LEGGED BLONDE CROSSED the street toward a house with the name VILLA SANTA MARTA displayed in wrought-iron letters over the gate. Her chin-length bob framed a slightly square pretty face. She wore blue jeans and a tie-dye T-shirt. Two men who lingered outside the grocery store broke off a discussion of the Industriales team batting average to observe her. Three women interrupted their dissection of a friend's divorce to watch her as well. All eyes followed the blonde as she walked through Villa Santa Marta's front yard and until the house's heavy door closed behind her.

"Who's that chick?" asked the oldest woman, her nose high in the air like a hound picking up a fresh scent. "First time I've seen her."

"Joaquín's new girlfriend," another woman answered officiously. "She's been living here for a week."

"Eh! What about Berta?"

"That's over, *chica*. But this one . . . she doesn't look Cuban, does she?"

"She looks Russian."

"That would be right down Joaquín's alley," a guy spoke up. Everyone nodded.

Inside the house, the blonde stood under a blue pendant lamp in the middle of a huge living room. The faded grandeur of the place still impressed her as it had the first day. She approached an upright piano and played the first chords of "London Bridge."

Though the piano needed tuning, it had a rich, warm sound. There was a blue vase on top, next to the portrait of a dark-haired woman with a pearl necklace. The frame, heavy and ornate, looked like tarnished silver. The wall behind the piano was covered in paintings. The landscapes of marinas and countryside scenes didn't impress the blonde, but she examined the portraits trying to discover a resemblance between their faces and Joaquín's. If there was any, it eluded her.

Through the picture window, she saw people waiting in line across the street—the same people who had stared at her when she passed them. Her new neighbors. In due time she would join them at the grocery store queue, and they would get to know her.

She smiled and two dimples appeared on her cheeks. How fast things had moved! Less than a month ago she had been a guest at Hotel Colina in El Vedado, thinking of the handsome lieutenant who had swept her off her feet after the Triumph of the Revolution parade on January first, but not believing that their relationship (if you could call it a relationship) had any future. After all, she was an American—a "Yankee," as they said here—who had come to Havana for eight days. But the days had turned into weeks. And the weeks would turn, hopefully, into months, and the months into years . . .

She remembered the first time she had locked eyes with Joaquín. He was still wearing his full-dress uniform and approached her as she wandered near Revolution Square, having just watched the parade. He had approached her and said something she didn't understand—her Spanish wasn't that good, and there was a lot of noise with so many people around. But she instinctively knew it was something sweet and smiled at him. Later, he had offered her a ride in his jeep. When they said goodbye at the Hotel Colina entrance, he had kissed her hand. He had returned the following day with a big bouquet of roses and invited her to Coppelia, the ice cream parlor that was only a few blocks away.

"If you could just stay . . ." he had said over a chocolate sundae, taking her hands in his.

At first it sounded absurd, but as days passed, she realized she was falling in love with him. As for staying, why not? She could start a new life here, seeing that she wasn't too happy with the one she had led at home. When the day she was supposed to leave came, she simply tore up the return ticket. Joaquín had taken her to his house and promised to move heaven and earth so they could be together.

Oh, Rob, the friend who had invited her to Cuba, had been

so horrified! He was part of a San Diego–based anti-embargo group called Compañeros de Cuba and had always wanted to visit the island. When he found out that it was possible to fly from Tijuana and skip the State Department's lengthy permit process to travel to a communist country, he planned to spend the winter break in Havana. "They don't celebrate Christmas, so it'll be a different kind of holiday," he had said. She had decided to go with him on a whim, and look where it had taken her! But when she announced her intention to stay, Rob had been beside himself: *This is crazy! I can't go back home without you. What are your parents going to say?* She shrugged. Some people simply didn't get it. And Rob wasn't in love, was he? Of course he wouldn't understand, but he had sworn eternal silence. She knew that he would never betray her.

She had promised him to write every week. That morning she had started a letter about her amazing meeting with Castro. Well, the meeting hadn't turned out too amazing after all. Actually, it had been quite embarrassing. But still. Rob would appreciate the story.

She walked through the dining room and stopped to peer inside the china cabinet. It wasn't locked, but she didn't feel comfortable opening it. She admired from afar the porcelain dishes with golden rims and the baccarat wine glasses. A fifteen-branch chandelier with a solid bronze ring hung from a detailed, decorated chain. Tarnished as it was, the lamp looked stunning and cast a soft glow over a dovetail oak table long enough to sit twelve people. The matching chairs had curved legs. Despite the beautiful furniture, the room wasn't inviting. It was too big and had no natural light.

The phone rang. It took her a while to locate it on a marble-top credenza that occupied a corner of the living room. The phone had a rotary dial. On the gray circle in the middle, a number, now illegible, had been scrawled in black ink. She lifted the heavy handset.

"Hello."

"How are you doing, Sarita?"

It was comforting to hear Joaquín's voice, though she winced at being called Sarita. The ending -*ita* meant "little," which didn't fit her, at almost six feet tall. She preferred when he used Spanish pet names like *mi amor* and *corazón*.

"Fine." She thought of saying she had been snooping around but didn't. "Are you coming home soon?"

"No, I'm sorry. I have a meeting at six but will get there before seven, I promise. I'll take the jeep. Is everything okay?"

"Oh, yes. I took a nice walk around the neighborhood."

"That's great. See you soon, *mi amor*. I just didn't want you to get concerned."

They said their goodbyes, and Sarah studied the handset before putting it back in the cradle. Everything in the house was ancient, likely made before she was born, but she found a special kind of beauty in those items from bygone times.

The kitchen, located at the other end of the building, was the most hospitable area. Big, like all the other rooms, but not oppressively so. It was painted white, farmhouse style, with granite countertops. The breakfast nook was furnished with a solid-wood scallop-edged square table, also white with a hint of gray, and four chairs with chunky legs. A green capsule Frigidaire purred in a corner. The countertops were granite, not Formica like in her parents' house. The place reminded Sarah of her grandmother Pauline's kitchen and made her feel at ease.

Had her grandma been alive, Sarah would have told her about her Cuban adventure. Instinctively, she touched the locket with Pauline's picture that hung from a chain around her neck. Her grandma would have approved. Her parents,

sadly, wouldn't. How mad they would be if they found out
. . . They had monitored her constantly during the last few
months, and she was now worried about them. Or rather,
worried about them worrying about her. She had given them
so much trouble lately, more so after her involvement with
the Sanctuary movement. But it was trouble for a good cause,
she reminded herself, even if they didn't see it that way.

She drank a glass of water and ate the leftovers of the
previous night's supper—rice, beans and fried tilapia. A
salad would have been a good addition, but she didn't know
where to find vegetables, which weren't sold at the bodega
across the street. Still hungry, she ate two slices of bread
with butter.

An old cuckoo clock read 3:55. Three more hours until
Joaquín came back! Sarah looked for something to do, but
she had cleaned the house the day before. Supper—rice and
beans again—was ready on the stove. She would make two
omelets later. She stepped out to the backyard.

Villa Santa Marta (a fancy-schmancy name, she thought)
was nothing if not massive. The backyard looked like a neighborhood park, with mango trees, a stone fountain crowned
by a statue of the Greek goddess Athena and rustic benches
scattered around. It didn't have any lights, though, which
made it a scary place at night. Fortunately, a tall wrought-
iron fence surrounded Villa Santa Marta, and Joaquín had
assured her that Miramar was a safe neighborhood. Nearby
was a smaller square building that was also part of the
property. It stood like a lonely sentry between nothing and
nowhere.

Sarah walked under the trees, but soon felt tired and
sleepy. She had been up since 6 A.M., when Joaquín had left
for work. She returned to the house and crossed the somber
dining room toward the marble staircase. Joaquín's family

must have had a lot of money, she had assumed, but it felt intrusive to ask.

She was halfway up the stairs when a current of cold air engulfed her. She tried to remember if she had left a window open on the second floor. Then her right foot slipped, her ankle twisted and she fell down as if someone had pushed her.

# CHAPTER TWO

Last time I took one of those silly personality tests, the results said I was a "craftsperson." Though I don't believe in online surveys, I had to agree on that. I like doing things with my hands: repairing furniture, grooming dogs and, above all, cooking. In fact, it was my job as a chef at La Bakería Cubana that helped me through a hard, dark time in my life.

La Bakería Cubana had started as a no-frills bakery in 2010. Nine years later, it had turned into a popular full-fledged restaurant featured in *Bon Appetit*. Marlene Martínez, a former Cuban cop who now lived in Miami, had opened it, and I partnered with her in 2018.

Getting involved with the restaurant was my way of dealing with loss and heartache. My husband, Nolan, had died in 2017, killed while we were together in Havana. I couldn't help but blame myself, at least partially, and the tragic episode had almost unhinged me. I moved from Gainesville to Miami, invested most of my money into La Bakería Cubana and began cooking and baking, tasting this recipe and twisting that one, until I had a full tried-and-true Cuban menu, and (some of) my sanity back.

By 2019, La Bakería Cubana kept me constantly busy. I didn't date or go out much, bent on improving my culinary skills. Frankly, coconut candy and guava cheesecakes sounded more appetizing than any guy I had yet met. I was becoming what my friend Candela—a capable dog groomer and Tarot reader, all wrapped up in one quirky entrepreneur—called *una ermitaña*. She was right. I had turned into a hermit who lived to cook and eat.

"Unless you change, the universe will send something to shake you out of your funk," she said.

It did.

IN SEPTEMBER 2019, A tropical-storm warning had been issued for Miami-Dade County. Hurricane season was in full swing, which always made me nervous. My hands trembled a little as I took a two-layered chocolate cake out of the oven. A couple had ordered it whole to celebrate their fiftieth wedding anniversary with their kids and grandkids. The kitchen was still filled with the fragrance of cocoa and caramelized sugar when Lila, the waitress, rushed back. The family was so pleased with the cake that they insisted on congratulating me personally.

"They are Cubans like you," Lila said.

The rain pounded the roof. I wanted to go home before it got worse but couldn't very well say no to our customers.

"It was the yummiest chocolate cake I've had in years," the matriarch pronounced when I came to the table. "*¡El mejor!*"

There were no crumbs left. Everybody was smiling. It felt like a small, sweet victory over "the funk."

"I'm delighted you all enjoyed it," I said.

In a corner, a woman sat alone. Her blond hair was chin-length. Long bangs covered her forehead, making it difficult to see her face. My heart lurched. I walked away from the Cubans and approached the woman. Her table had been cleared, and she was scrolling through her phone.

"May I—help you?" I stuttered.

She kept her face down. "I'm just waiting for the check, thanks."

I stood there until she looked up with a mix of curiosity and annoyance. She was in her early forties. Too young. I mumbled an excuse, left the room and broke into tears upon reaching the safe harbor of the kitchen.

It wasn't my mother. Of course it wasn't. How many times had I been disappointed? Why did I keep looking for her? I wished to let her go but couldn't. Her absence had been a constant and painful presence in my life. Though I was thirty-one years old, it still hurt.

MY PARENTS HAD MET during a military parade in the mid-eighties. My father, Joaquín Montero, was a lieutenant in the Cuban Army. My mother, whose real name I didn't know, was a young American who had managed to visit Havana despite the travel restrictions of the time. They fell in love, got married and lived together in a house that Dad had received as a reward for his services to the government. The house was Villa Santa Marta, an Art Deco home located in Miramar, Havana's poshest district.

When I was two years old, my mother vanished. Back to her country, people presumed, but no one knew for sure. She didn't say goodbye and never wrote or contacted me. A few months later, my dad was deployed to Angola. Since there were no other relatives who could take care of me, his mother, Mamina, moved from La Coloma, a small Pinar del Río town, to Havana and settled in our house.

It was supposed to be a temporary arrangement, but when Dad died in combat, Mamina was stuck with me. She never put it in such words, bless her heart, but that's the reality of the matter. In her late fifties and having lost both her children—her daughter, my namesake Mercedes, to cancer and her son to a war six thousand miles away—she wasn't likely thrilled with the idea of raising another kid. But to her credit, she did it anyway. She gave me all the love and care I needed, and more. She answered all my questions, from the birds and the bees, which she called *cochinerías*, to the best way to make black beans—always add cumin, garlic and a bit of sugar—and how to walk properly through life: head up, shoulders down and looking people in the eye. But there was a topic we avoided: my runaway mother.

Yet, as a child, I thought of her often, dreaming up sudden, unexpected encounters. One day I'd be outside playing with my rag doll Saralí and a beautiful lady would open the gate, walk under the Villa Santa Marta wrought-iron sign and hug me with tears in her eyes. She had been sick for years. Or imprisoned, like the heroines in the telenovelas Mamina liked to watch, and had just miraculously escaped.

Though we didn't go to any church, I devised secret ceremonies: rudimentary attempts to make deals with whoever wielded power over people and events. Would my mother come back if I counted to one thousand without stopping? Did all my homework a week in advance? Helped Mamina clean the house? My offers weren't taken up. Then I turned to our neighbors. But by the time I was able to start snooping on my own, there were few left who had met my parents. Only Dolores, a schoolteacher, remembered them and was happy to share her memories with me. The little I knew about my mother (she was tall, with her blond hair cut to a square bob, and she spoke with an accent) I owed to Dolores, who talked fondly of her. "Your mom loved you, *mijita*," she used to say. "She didn't go anywhere without you."

"Until she dropped me like a hot potato," I countered.

"Ah, Merceditas, don't say that! She could have gone home to bring back dollars, or a car, or food."

"Why didn't she return?"

"It's hard for Americans to come here. But someday she may show up out of the blue. Have faith and behave well!"

Dolores was outspoken, funny and somewhat mischievous, like the kids she taught. I loved visiting her and listening to her stories, but Mamina didn't like for me to "go around pestering people." Though she never forbade me to drop by Dolores's house, she also made it clear that she didn't approve of it. It was nothing personal—she had the same attitude toward other neighbors. As I got older, my visits grew less and less frequent, though we always greeted each other and chatted when we met in the street.

In the late nineties, tourism was revived in Cuba. New hotels were built and old ones restored. Canadians, Europeans and even Americans were welcomed with open arms. But my mother didn't come back. She never walked under the wrought-iron Villa Santa Marta sign that had already started to lose letters.

I once ventured to visit the local police station. They didn't take me seriously at first—I was in high school—but I persisted long enough to find out that there had been an official investigation of my mother's disappearance. The case had been closed in 1991.

"State Security handled it," said the police officer who reluctantly agreed to talk to me. "They wouldn't give us all the details, but the conclusion seems to be that she left Cuba."

I gave up, accepting what Mamina's silence had implied all those years: my mother didn't care for me. Dolores had been wrong. There was no happy ending, just a lonely girl sobbing and holding a rag doll.

MAMINA AND I LIVED together in the Art Deco house until I met Nolan Spivey, an American professor who used to take his students for summer courses at the University of Havana. We got married and settled in Gainesville, Florida, in 2008. Once there, hopes of finding my mom were revived. After all, we were now in the same country. At Starbucks and Publix, I would stare at middle-aged women, often to the point of making them uncomfortable. Was one of them my mother? Did she ever look for me? But if she did (a big fat "if") how could she possibly know that Mercedes Montero, the daughter she had left in Cuba, was the same person whose driver's license read Mercy Spivey?

Speaking of names, hers was Tania Rojas. At least, that's what Mamina and Dolores claimed. There were no legal documents that could attest to it, not even my parents' marriage certificate, though Dolores assured me it existed—she had signed it as a witness. But even she admitted that "Tania Rojas" was probably a fake identity created by the Cuban government. To track my mother down in the United States, I needed a real name and a place of birth, and I had neither. I only knew for sure that she had last been seen in Havana, with me in a stroller, walking around the neighborhood.

Nothing could be done to find a person who, apparently, didn't want to be found. I tried to forget her for good and more or less succeeded . . . until my husband's death. Once I realized I was alone, truly on my own for the first time, the urge to locate my mother returned with a vengeance.

I stared at strangers' faces at restaurants, parks and grocery stores. I made embarrassing attempts at conversation with women who I imagined resembled my mother—not that I had a clear idea what she actually looked like, except for the blond hair and the blue eyes I had inherited from her. I even hired a detective that specialized in finding missing people. He posted ads like *Tania Rojas, your daughter Mercedes is looking for you* in several newspapers and websites, but nothing came out of them. Still, hope springs eternal. *La esperanza es lo último que se pierde*, Mamina used to say.

I kept hoping and waiting, even if my *esperanza* was crushed every single time.

# CHAPTER THREE

*February 15th, 1986*

*I'm so thankful to be here, learning from these proud, warm, cheerful people how to be a better human being! I'm honing my Spanish too. Oh, man, Cuban Spanish is like music. Think of drums and guitars and even castanets. But people talk so fast that I miss half of what they say. Particularly the jokes. Joaquín sometimes looks sad when I don't laugh at his, but I don't get them! People also drop the final consonants, slur words together and sound totally different from Mexicans and Salvadorians. I thought that comotauté was a weird Cuban greeting until Joaquín said it just meant ¿Cómo está usted?—the polite form for "How are you?"*

BEFORE SEALING THE ENVELOPE, Sarah added a note addressed to her parents for Rob to mail from Tijuana. In his last letter, he had mentioned that they were out of their minds about her absence and had reported her as a missing person to the police. Luckily, they didn't know she had traveled to Cuba, as she wasn't on speaking terms with them when she left San Diego. They kept trying to control her, forgetting she was an adult! Now, she was making her own decisions, building a brand-new life. *That* would show them. Still, she wrote a few lines about being "in a place where she felt like she belonged" and they shouldn't worry about her. Even if she knew that they would.

Sarah had made dinner early: rice and chicken and a tomato, avocado and cucumber salad. Joaquín didn't care for vegetables, but she didn't understand how one could live on a tropical island and not eat veggies and fruits. She had walked all the way to a farmer's market where prices were higher than in the *puesto* (the neighborhood store where they sold potatoes and sometimes withered lettuce heads) but was also much better supplied.

She had bought tomatoes, cucumbers, malangas, green peppers, a huge avocado and a whole chicken. There was also pork, which she didn't particularly like. She had spent three hundred pesos, all the money Joaquín had left in his armoire. She thought, though a little too late, that she should have asked if it was supposed to last for a week, fifteen days or, God forbid, the entire month.

She still had dollars—around seven hundred she had brought from San Diego—but there was no place to spend them. Joaquín had made it clear that she didn't need to worry about money. He would take care of her financially and in any other way. Later on, she would look for a job or go to college. What would Rob say if she started attending the University of Havana? Oh, he would be so jealous! But she would have to request her high school transcripts, or maybe that requirement could be waived for her . . .

In any case, she needed to get settled first. She had to improve her Spanish and find out some basic facts, like how much Joaquín made and how she was expected to spend it. There were so many things they hadn't discussed yet! The fact that he was so much older (eighteen years her senior, though she had led him to believe that they were just thirteen years apart) had something to do with it. At times she was . . . not exactly intimidated by him, but a bit hesitant in his presence. He seemed to know so much more than she did and was always so confident while she still felt lost and out of place. Well, *poco a poco*. They would continue getting to know each other, a little at a time. In any case, supper was ready, and now there was still food for two more days.

After taking a cold shower (the boiler didn't work), Sarah continued exploring the house. This time, she spent a whole hour in the library. The room was presided over by the portrait of a fiery-eyed lady in a black pillbox hat. She looked like the woman with the pearl necklace whose picture was over the piano. Only here she seemed sterner, almost threatening, as if she didn't like to have people around. Sarah shuddered, then laughed. Her imagination was getting the best of her.

She was still puzzled by the number of paintings in every room, all quite professional. Her favorite was the portrait of a young girl that hung in one of the second-floor bedrooms. The background was their backyard. She asked Joaquín if these people were relatives of his, but he had answered no, in a tone that didn't invite more inquiries. Perhaps he thought she was too nosy.

No, that was silly! Joaquín was happy to share everything he knew about Cuba, Havana and Miramar with her. The lady in the portrait was making her nervous with her intense stare.

"*¡Qué guanajería!*" she said aloud.

*Guanajería* meant literally the actions of a turkey—a *guanajo*—but it also referred to something foolish in Cuban slang. The word made her happy and she enjoyed saying it. She already knew some Spanish, having picked it up in Tijuana and during a brief stay in El Salvador. Now she attempted to speak it to herself, to practice. It made her feel less self-conscious than when she was in the company of those adorable but loud Cubans who spoke not only with their mouths but their hands, eyes and other body parts as well.

She avoided looking at the painting as she browsed the bookshelves where Madame Blavatsky's works sat next to theosophy books. There was a leather-bound manuscript entitled *Diario de una hechicera*. A sorceress's diary, huh? She couldn't decipher the small letters typed on absurdly thin pages.

More interesting was the other bookshelf that featured a *Reader's Digest* collection, in English, from 1950 to 1955. Spanish-language magazines like *Bohemia* and *Vanidades* were from the same era. Sarah had bought a new one called *Mujeres* outside the farmers' market. It looked like *Woman's World* with a socialist twist. She had found a recipe she planned to make on Sunday—*churros*, fried pastries rolled in cinnamon and sugar that could be served with coffee or, even better, hot chocolate. Well, she would ask Joaquín where cocoa powder was sold because she hadn't seen any yet.

Sarah sneezed. The library needed a deep cleaning. Like many other rooms in the house, it had been closed for too long. She suspected that there were mice and rats, judging by the droppings around the big pedestal desk and the bookshelves. She would have to find paper towels, a duster, a spray and wipe solution and . . .

The sound of footsteps downstairs made her jump. She ran down the marble staircase, being more careful this time.

"Joaquín!"

A tall man with angular features, almond eyes and a big smile had just come into the living room. He was wearing the olive-green uniform of the Revolutionary Armed Forces, which, in Sarah's opinion, fit him amazingly well. The fact that she had fallen for a military guy still surprised her. Her father, with whom she had argued for years about everything under the sun, from politics to fashion, had been in the Navy, and she thought that was why he was so pig-headed. But she loved him and was closer to him than to her mother.

"*¡Mi amor!*"

Joaquín handed her a bouquet of white lilies, *mariposas*, which by now Sarah knew were the Cuban national flower. They hugged each other and kissed so passionately that a few *mariposas* were crushed in the process.

"They smell amazing!" Sarah said, pressing the bouquet against her face. "Thanks!"

"And here's this too." He offered her a small package wrapped in fancy tissue paper.

She tore it open and discovered a perfume bottle with the cap shaped like a dome. When she opened it, the scent of bergamot blended with the *mariposa* fragrance. She tried to decipher the name, written in Cyrillic characters.

"It's called Red Moscow," Joaquín said.

"It's lovely! But you didn't need to—"

"Don't you know what day is today?"

She did. She had thought of it early in the morning, but he hadn't mentioned it. She assumed Cubans didn't celebrate Valentine's Day because that would imply a religious reference to Saint Valentine. Joaquín had told her that religion was considered an "ideological deviation." It made sense to her. The opiate of the masses and all that.

"*El Día de los Enamorados*," he said.

A day for lovers. Sarah liked that. She was *enamorada*, no question about it. And so was he. No, wait, he was *enamorado*—she still, sometimes, got her endings mixed up. They laughed, embraced again and hurried to the second floor. The *mariposa* bouquet and the Red Moscow bottle were left on top of the piano, between the blue vase and the silver-framed portrait.

A truck drove at high speed in front of the house. The piano shook slightly, and the ghost of a melody came from under the closed lid. The vase and the portrait stayed put, but the perfume bottle fell to the floor and shattered. A potent aroma filled the room and snuck upstairs, passed by the master bedroom and reached the library, where the lady in the painting wore an expression of disgust.

# CHAPTER FOUR

My grandmother Mamina was still living in Villa Santa Marta. The house, built in the early twentieth century, had seven bedrooms that needed plastering and painting, an overgrown jungle-esque backyard and nightmarish plumbing. My grandma refused to hire help and did all the cooking and cleaning herself, but it was taking a toll on her.

Though I had invited her to move in with me, she hadn't agreed, not even to a visit. She disliked planes, big cities and the United States. We had variations of the same conversation many times:

"I'm *not* going in a country where they throw old people in nursing homes!"

"That's not true! And do you really think I'd put you in a nursing home?"

"That's what Yankees do, and when in Rome . . ."

It had broken her heart when I jilted my Cuban boyfriend, Lorenzo, to marry Nolan, a decision that ended in disaster for all of us. I often wondered how Mamina's distrust of "Yankees" had played out in her relationship with her daughter-in-law.

Mamina had only one close friend, Catalina, who lived nearby, but she was getting on in age too. When I had tried to find someone to stay with my grandma at least a few hours a day, like a home aide, Mamina refused firmly. "I want no strangers nosing around the house! What if they steal something?"

To make things worse, her mind had started to drift. Sometimes, in the middle of our weekly phone calls, she halted and struggled to remember what we were talking about. Those long, silent gaps tugged at my heart. She would confuse places and names. I knew it was normal for her age—she had turned eighty-five—but how long could she be able to keep her independence? Fortunately, or unfortunately, she didn't seem aware of her mental slips. Her biggest fear was having a *zirimba*. I didn't know if a *zirimba* was a stroke or a heart attack, but it surely sounded like something to avoid.

Mamina had mentioned in passing that she might return to La Coloma, a sleepy village that I barely remembered. She had started visiting her hometown after I left the country. Before, she didn't use to go, at least not with me. Her niece Sonrisa still lived there, on the family's farm. But I hadn't seen her or her kids in years and didn't know them well enough to entrust Mamina to their care.

It would have been easy to find a modern apartment in El Vedado, the downtown of Havana, close to shops, hotels and the seawall, or a smaller house in Miramar, but Mamina had a love-hate relationship with our home. "Villa Diabla Marta is going to kill me," she repeated, looking exasperated, and then refused to leave. Satiadeva, a private taxi driver who often ran errands for her, had attempted to fix the ceiling and installed a new toilet, but I kept waiting for the other shoe to drop. And it did, at the most inopportune time.

MY HOUSE IN MIAMI had an open floor plan and stained-glass windows with geometric patterns. I had bought it after my husband's death and lived there alone. Like a hermit, as

Candela had said. Not surprisingly for a cook, the kitchen was my favorite place. It wasn't as big as Villa Santa Marta's but had a breakfast nook and a door that led to the backyard. Adding to the palm trees that were originally there, I had planted an avocado tree (still too young to bear fruit, unfortunately), a collection of geraniums that grew freely around the back porch and an herb garden—menta, marjoram, basil, sage, oregano and more—of which I was quite proud.

One day, while the tropical storm was still around, I was sheltering my plants when my phone rang. The call came from Cuba's code 53, but I didn't recognize the number.

"Merceditas? This is Catalina."

I stood frozen, with my fingers tightly wrapped around the phone.

"What happened?"

"Mamina's spending the night in the Hospital de Emergencias. She fell halfway down the stairs."

My stomach dropped down. The Villa Santa Marta staircase was treacherous. It had eighteen slippery marble steps I had descended on my butt more than once.

"It was a hairline fracture and the doctor just put her arm in a sling, but she was very disoriented," Catalina went on. "She didn't recognize me when I came over and found her on the floor."

"How's she doing now?"

"Better. But you should come."

"I will." A wave of fear rolled through my chest. "Now, why is she at Hospital de Emergencias? It's not her designated hospital."

"That driver, Satia-what's-his-name, knows a doctor there, Doctora Morales, and she's been taking care of Mamina for a while."

"Ah, good."

I made a mental note to bring a present for Doctora Morales.

I called Mamina as soon as she was released from the hospital. She was in good spirits and downplayed the accident.

"Catalina made a big fuss about nothing," she said. "It didn't even hurt! I just slipped because it was so dark."

"Why didn't you turn on the light, *por Dios*?"

"Because the stair sconces don't work anymore."

What else didn't work there? What else might go wrong? I couldn't stay away, happily cooking and baking for other people, while my grandmother was alone and in risk of another fall—or something worse.

"I'll get there on Monday, *oíste*? Call Catalina if you need anything."

She didn't answer. Her breathing was uneven.

"Mamina?"

"Does the school bus run on Mondays now?" she asked.

"What bus? I'm taking a plane!"

"A plane?" She sounded disconcerted. "There's no airport in La Coloma."

"I'm arriving in Havana."

"But you *are* in Havana, Mercedes."

She had never called me Mercedes, using instead the more affectionate form Merceditas.

"No, *you* are in Havana," I said slowly. "I'm in Miami."

"The Makarenkos moved to Miami? That can't be!"

My aunt, Mercedes, whom I was named after, had been studying at the Makarenko Pedagogical School when she passed away. We hadn't talked about her in years. I let it go, not sure of how to set Mamina straight.

The next time we talked, on Sunday night, she called me Merceditas and was as sharp as usual. But the incident, the latest in a series of mild and apparently harmless lapses, left me with a sense of impending doom.

# CHAPTER FIVE

*March 8th, 1986*

*I have my first Cuban friend! Her name is Dolores, and she looks like Jennifer Beals. She lives next door and is an elementary school teacher. Joaquín introduced us because he said that I looked lonely. Like, dude, what do you expect? See, today, even though it's a Saturday, he's on duty until 11 P.M. What kinda deal is that? I'm so bored that I even started watching a soap opera. It's a Cuban telenovela, though! It will help me practice my Spanish.*

GROWING UP IN PACIFIC Beach, Sarah used to hate soap operas. Passionately. When her mother watched *Days of Our Lives*, Sarah was quick to point out that the Bradys and the Hortons were not believable and the plotline was intended to dumb people down. Recalling those incidents, she thought that she had been a mouthy brat.

Now, she was following *Sol de Batey*, not only because she was bored, as she had just written to Rob, but because Dolores and Joaquín claimed that she looked like the protagonist. They were flattering her, she argued. The actress, Susana Pérez, was drop-dead gorgeous. Susana played Charito, a sweet but naïve sugar-plantation heiress. There were two parallel love stories set in colonial times, one between plantation owners and the other between slaves.

ONCE THE LETTER WAS finished, Sarah began to get antsy. She wasn't looking forward to spending the day alone in a house that, despite its many remarkable features, didn't feel like home yet. Dust seemed to pile up on the floor and furniture faster than in San Diego, and the sheer size of the place made it hard to keep it tidy. She was getting tired of *la escoba*, the old broom she had found in the garage, but kept cleaning so Joaquín didn't think she was a lazy American. That morning, Dolores's unexpected visit gave her the perfect excuse to forget housework.

"Let's go to an *actividad de mi cuadra alegre y bonita*!" she said.

"What's that?" Sarah asked. All the syllables had merged together in Dolores's mouth, and she hadn't understood a thing.

"You'll see! Come with me!"

It turned out to be a street-cleaning event where neighbors got together to make the block look "cheerful and beautiful." They picked up trash, swept the sidewalks and planted flowers in public areas. The event (or "activity," as Dolores called it) was sponsored by the local Committee for the Defense of the Revolution, CDR for short, of which Dolores was the president. Most neighbors belonged to it, but, as she explained to Sarah, that was on a volunteer basis, just like the communal cleaning.

"So you all are working for free?" Sarah asked.

"Sure!" Dolores flipped her curly hair and smiled. "Other weekends we paint park benches or carry out vaccination campaigns. There's always something to do."

Sarah was thrilled. That was community work at its best! Once the "activity" was over, Dolores invited her to lunch at her house. The main dish was Cuban tamales, which weren't made with dried hominy, like their Mexican cousins, but ground fresh corn just scraped from the cobs. Inside were pieces of pork, onions, garlic and tomatoes.

"This is delicious!" Sarah said, stuffing her face happily.

"Eat more, *chica*!"

Cubans often addressed each other as *chico* and *chica*, a quirk that Sarah found amusing. Did people really call each other little boy and little girl? Less amusing was the fact that she didn't have a proper name yet, as she would rather not use her real one. To smooth the awkwardness, Joaquín had implied she couldn't reveal her identity because of "secret political reasons." That was stretching the truth, to put it mildly, and Sarah wasn't sure Dolores believed it, but her neighbor had been discreet. Not so much about Sarah's appearance, though.

"You need to gain some weight," Dolores had said bluntly. "Unless Joaquín prefers you skinny," she added with a smile.

Skinny? Maybe for Caribbean standards. Sarah had noticed the curves that Cuban women showed off proudly. Big behinds seemed to be more appreciated than in California. She scarfed down another tamale.

After lunch, Dolores's husband, Pepe, left for a baseball game without offering to clean up the kitchen. Dolores didn't seem to mind, and shrugged when Sarah asked why he had gone alone.

"The stadium's full of rowdy guys," she said, wrinkling her nose. "Baseball is just for men."

Upon hearing that, Sarah, who had been a Padres fan since childhood, was tempted to argue. But Dolores was talking about Cuban customs, so she kept her opinions to herself. More important was to find out the proper etiquette for social functions. The following weekend, Sarah and Joaquín would be attending a party at his boss's house, and she wasn't sure what to wear. She had seen the short and tight attires women wore on the street but assumed there were different dress codes for different *actividades*. Dolores was happy to instruct her.

"If you go to an activity at a colonel's house, for instance, or you're hanging out with Joaquín's comrades and their wives, don't wear anything low-cut. Modesty, *chica*, modesty is the best in such cases because that's how *militares* are. Very proper and stuck-up. And don't even think of wearing spandex pants, though they're the rage now and I wish I could buy me a pair!"

Sarah assured her new friend that she didn't even own anything made of the aforementioned fabric. Truth was, she had never seen so many people wear spandex clothing outside the gym.

Dolores also advised her on the best times to go to the grocery store—either early in the morning or after seven o'clock at night.

"Working women like me are issued a pass called *plan jaba* that gives us shopping priority," she said smugly. "We can buy before everyone else."

"Oh, that's so neat."

Then Dolores remembered she had to run an errand. She wore a necklace with round red wood beads and started putting on makeup. The foundation was too light, the eyeshadow too pale and the lipstick didn't suit her tanned complexion.

"It's not my favorite," she admitted with a resigned sigh. "But that was the only one available at the store, and I had to use my coupon because the ration card was about to expire."

"You mean makeup is rationed?"

"Yes, so every woman can get some." She waved the topic away. "Want to come with me?"

"Where?"

"To Centro Habana."

Sarah agreed to tag along. Like, what else did she have to do?

They waited half an hour for a bus. The first two didn't stop, and the frustrated passengers-to-be shook their fists at the vanishing vehicle, cursed and called the driver a *cabrón*. Their behavior shocked Sarah, but Dolores informed her that, had they been inside the bus, they would have heard much worse terms.

"Imagine the poor people who were planning to get off here and now have to walk back eight or ten blocks!"

"Don't they protest?"

"Ah, yes! I bet they all shit on the driver three times over!"

Sarah presumed her friend meant that figuratively.

"Will the driver lose his job if they complain to the authorities?" she asked.

"Lose his job? No, *chica*, no! This is socialism. Nobody's fired here. At least, not for something like that."

The next bus stopped almost in front of them and wasn't too crowded. Bus fare was five Cuban cents, and passengers were expected to put coins in a slot, but if they failed to do so, nobody threw them out. Socialism, indeed, Sarah thought approvingly.

On the way to Centro Habana, she got to see more of Miramar. With its tree-lined avenues and ample sidewalks, it looked like a cross between La Jolla and Kensington. An affluent area, home to government agencies and embassies. Dolores pointed them out.

"Canada, here. Isn't it a beautiful building? Belgium, over there. Look at the façade!"

They all had security guards outside.

The bus got increasingly crowded, so much that the last passengers to board stayed at the door, hanging on for dear life. Dolores and Sarah had to push and elbow people to get out at the Astral Movie Theater stop.

"Uf! That was an adventure!" a very sweaty Sarah remarked.

"Adventure?" Dolores laughed. "That's normal life. You'll get used to it."

They passed by a building with tinted windows on Infanta Avenue.

"What's inside?" Sarah asked. That was the first time she had seen tinted windows in Havana.

"A *diplotienda.*"

Dolores didn't elaborate. Sarah assumed it was a shop for diplomats and followed her friend, who walked fast.

The errand consisted of picking up a *reverbero*—a Primus camp stove built in the thirties.

"It works with kerosene," Dolores said. "Handy to have around when the gas doesn't come."

"Where does it come in from?" Sarah asked, thinking she had misunderstood.

"I don't know, *chica*! The plant where they produce it, I guess."

In Cuba, things "came" to the place where they were sold, Dolores explained patiently. Basic food supplies came to the grocery store, vegetables to the *puesto* and bread to the *panadería*. It was quite simple, wasn't it?

By the time they got back to Miramar, Sarah felt like she had known Dolores forever. She even started calling her Lo because Dolores sounded, in her opinion, rather old-fashioned, like Dolores del Río. Lo accepted her moniker graciously and kept calling Sarah *chica* for lack of a better name.

# CHAPTER SIX

Two days later, at three o'clock, I boarded a Miami-Havana flight. Candela went with me. Born to Cuban parents in Hialeah, my friend had never been to the island. Her family, former land barons, had fled in 1960 after their bank accounts were seized and their properties confiscated. Candela had kept mum about the trip so as not to offend them.

"My grandparents never forgot their home," she said. "Same for Mom, though she was only a child when they left. They're still living in the old Cuba and don't want me to see the new. They'd rather remember everything as it used to be."

Memories die hard. Villa Santa Marta was still referred to as "the witch's house" because of a woman who had lived (and apparently died) there way back, before my father got the property. That annoyed Mamina, who had been asked more than once if she was related to the *bruja*.

When the plane took off, Candela dug a Tarot deck out of her backpack and spread the cards across the tray table.

"Are you going to read the cards *now*?" I asked, mortified.

Her eyes sparkled as bright as the five silver chains with charms she wore around her neck.

"*¡Claro!* I need to know what expects me in Havana. Do you want a reading too? This is the Andrew McGregor deck. It's inspired by the *orishas* and very good. I got it at a *botánica* on Calle Ocho."

"Nah. I don't believe in that stuff."

It wasn't exactly the truth. Some of my friend's predictions had turned out to be accurate, but in the most twisted way conceivable.

"To unlock the past, present and future," she whispered. "So mote it be."

"Mote *un carajo.*"

It was embarrassing. Or maybe not. Like, who cared? A blond guy sitting across the aisle was dressed in white from head to toe. The *Miami Herald* had recently run an article about Americans who traveled to Cuba to "make *santo*" or being initiated in Santería, often by bogus priests who charged them several thousand dollars. The unscrupulous *babalawos* convinced them that money could turn regular folks into "sons of Changó" or "daughters of Oshún." Behind him, a Cuban couple discussed the *quinceañera* party they were going to throw for a niece.

"Did you bring enough toilet paper, *vieja*?" the man asked.

"Yes, *viejo*!" the woman yelled. Next, she announced to him and everybody else, "Forty-four jumbo rolls from Publix!"

"Eh, keep an eye on them," a guy advised. "These Customs people, they steal anything they can get their hands on."

More than half the passengers aboard the small plane were Cubans, and most voiced their opinions about toilet paper, Customs officers and *quinceañeras.* I pulled a magazine from the seat in front of me. There was an article about "senior moments," the temporary loss of memory experienced by older people. Though not usually a reader, I devoured it.

The plane flew over the Florida Keys. We'd arrive in less than an hour. I longed to hug Mamina, reassuring her, and myself, that she was going to be fine. Then we would have a conversation. A long-overdue one.

"Fate's waiting for me in Havana!" Candela stated grandly, pointing to the Tarot spread. "See, I got Oshún, the *orisha* of love. She'll send a handsome Cuban guy my way."

I thought of my poor husband. Maybe I should have stayed with "a handsome Cuban guy." I would still be in Cuba, but Nolan would be alive . . .

Candela retrieved the cards, shuffled again and asked, "Are you sure your grandma doesn't mind me staying in the house?"

"Ah, not at all."

She *had* minded it at first, but I convinced her that my friend would be a quiet and amenable guest. It wasn't like she had anything against Candela personally. Mamina didn't like to have people over, much less for an extended time.

"I need to ask her some difficult questions before she forgets everything," I whispered.

"About what?"

"My—my mom."

"What is it?" Candela leaned toward me. "Why are you mumbling, girl?"

It wasn't the first time I had unintentionally lowered my voice when the topic came up.

"My mother," I said louder.

Candela's eyes lit up. She squeezed my arm.

"At last, Merceditas! I don't understand why you've waited this long."

"We had an unspoken agreement not to mention her."

I had learned early on to keep my mouth shut. Once, when I was in kindergarten, an older girl informed me with a gleeful smile that my mom was a Yankee. Some kids laughed; others looked shocked. That evening I had asked Mamina if that was true, though I didn't have the faintest idea of what "Yankee" meant. My grandma scowled.

"Who the heck told you that?"

"A third-grade girl," I said, holding Saralí, the rag doll I kept until my teens, when it became more rag than doll.

"She's a gossiper and a crap-stirrer."

"But what's a Yankee?" I insisted. "And where's my mom?"

In the two and a half years we had been living together, Mamina had always answered all my questions patiently. Not then.

"I don't have time to talk!" she snapped. "Go to your room and don't bother me with nonsense!"

She had never lacked time before. I hugged Saralí and scurried away to cry. Perhaps my mother *was* a Yankee, whatever that meant. There was nobody else to ask in the family, seeing that the family, at least in Havana, was only the two of us. Soon enough, however, I figured out that Yankee meant American. A *bad* American, the kind you wouldn't like to be associated with. In school, we heard about *el imperialismo yanqui*, the evil empire from the north. The place where my mother had come from—and likely returned to.

Later on, I struggled to remember what had happened after she left. If one day I woke up and she wasn't around, I must have asked some questions. But I couldn't recall what I was told, if anything at all. The school incident was the first memory I had of any inquiries, and its aftermath discouraged me from bringing up the issue again.

"That's ridiculous," Candela said. "Your mom may still be alive. You have the right to find out."

"I'm scared."

"What's the worst thing that can happen?"

I paused to think.

"That Mamina gets mad at me. No, wait, that would be the *less* bad thing. The absolute worst would be that I find my mother and she doesn't want to have anything to do with me."

"What if it's the other way around? What if she is delighted to reconnect with you?"

I doubted it.

The shifting blue greens of the Caribbean shimmered below, but a gray cloud appeared seemingly out of nowhere and cast a shadow over the waters. The plane wobbled. There came an announcement about turbulence.

"The storm's still hanging in there," Candela said. "This isn't a good time of the year to travel, much less in this puddle jumper."

"Well, your *orishas* will protect us. Surely they can handle a little wind."

"Don't make fun of them!"

A card had slipped to the floor while she was shuffling. I picked it up. It showed a yellow woman (the whole figure, not just the dress or the hair) holding a saucer, and a man in green. The man reminded me of a soldier because the color was the same as military uniforms in Cuba.

Candela elbowed me. "We can still do a reading."

"I'd pass on it," I said firmly.

A gust hit the plane, and it began swaying again. The window turned opaque, blurred by a sudden downpour. Someone prayed loudly to *la virgen de la Caridad*.

We flew over the José Martí International Airport for around twenty minutes, waiting for the weather to improve, and finally landed in a torrential rain. There was no covered ramp, or any kind of ramp, at Terminal Three, which was reserved for small aircrafts. Passengers made a run for the building.

"*¡Le zumba el mango!*" the jumbo rolls lady huffed, dragging a huge suitcase behind.

"What does she mean by the mango buzzes?" Candela asked. "And how can a mango buzz anyway?"

"It means 'I can't believe this crap,'" I answered. "Sometimes what buzzes is the *merequetén*, not the mango. And don't ask me what *merequetén* means because I have no idea."

"I love these expressions! I'm going to dust off my Cuban Spanish on this trip."

Candela and I cleared customs without incident and retrieved our luggage. Hers was only a backpack, while I had a duffel bag and two big suitcases with things one couldn't find in Cuba, including a new Bialetti coffeemaker for Mamina, her favorite lotion, Heno de Pravia, and a tablet for Doctora Morales's son. According to my grandma, she had hinted that the kid needed one.

We walked outside into Havana's humid, dense air, cleaned by the recent rain.

"It smells different," Candela said, "though we're only ninety miles away from Miami. Less pollution, maybe?"

"Maybe."

Satiadeva was waiting for us. I had met him during the fateful visit to Havana that resulted in Nolan's death. He had been our chauffer then, and later kept in touch with Mamina, driving her around and running errands for her. His *almendrón* was a well-preserved 1958 Chevy Impala, red and white. I was not sure if Candela swooned over him or the car, but either way, she looked smitten. The Chevy, bright and shiny under the rain, welcomed us with a waft of sandalwood.

"*¡Qué bonito!*" Candela exclaimed. "I *love* sandalwood."

Her collection of charms (silver elephants from India, Mayan and Egyptian pyramids and a Celtic cross) jingled as she settled on the passenger's seat. I shared the back seat with our luggage.

"So do I," Satiadeva answered.

She smoothed her blue broomstick skirt. He adjusted his Orioles cap and scratched his chin.

"How's Mamina?" I asked.

"Much better. She wanted to come, but I convinced her to

wait at home with Catalina, who is cooking for the party. They invited me too," he added, "though I didn't want to intrude."

"Come on, Satia! You are family now, and you know it."

Candela beamed. Satiadeva smiled shyly. They looked like they belonged together. He was tall and handsome while she was short, dark-haired and plump, the curvaceous Cubanita I had often wished I were.

# CHAPTER SEVEN

*April 1st, 1986*

*I am so sorry my parents keep harassing you. I was afraid of it, and so thankful to know you've kept mum. The good news is that they're still fixated on El Salvador. I don't worry about the San Diego Police Department because they likely have hundreds of more pressing cases in their hands to bother with mine, but the idea of a PI tracking me down is a bit frightening. You haven't mentioned anything about our trip to Compañeros de Cuba, right?*

SHE KNEW THAT WAS coming. Despite the notes she had included in her letters to Rob—notes that he had mailed dutifully from Tijuana, Rosarito and other areas of Baja California—her parents had started to panic. She had been gone for over four months now. They were probably wondering where she was and whom she was with.

In his last letter, Rob reported that "Commander Nelson" had shown up at his Berkeley apartment demanding to know where she was and threatening to beat the living crap out of him. The Nelsons had already traveled to San Salvador hoping to find their daughter there. The family she had lived with before said that they had no idea where she was. Now her parents had hired a private eye. Damn!

Rob had told few people about their trip to Cuba because it was, technically, against the law. He had even kept it from some of his Compañeros de Cuba friends. Not that Sarah's parents had met any of them, but the PI could sniff out the group and start asking questions . . .

Well, not much she could do about it now. In the worst possible scenario, if they found out she was in Cuba, too bad. They couldn't extradite her.

To get her mind off the disagreeable topic, Sarah went out in search of a seamstress that Lo had recommended. The backpack she had brought contained only a few T-shirts, shorts and a faded pair of jeans as she hadn't planned on staying in Cuba forever. And now that she had gained some weight, she couldn't even wear those items. To buy clothes in the stores she would need a *libreta de productos industriales*, but she didn't have an ID card yet, much less a ration card.

The situation bothered her, though she had never been vain. At home, she didn't own fancy clothes or jewelry, except for the locket with her grandmother's picture. But she longed to spice up her wardrobe with some accessories like the colorful necklaces Lo wore and a few formal pieces, maybe a couple of dresses and a long skirt for social functions with Joaquín's comrades. There was an ancient Singer sewing machine in one of the bedrooms. She attempted to use it, but the oil-smelling contraption didn't work. It might even have been lacking a part or two. She had no way to know.

"Talk to Fredesbinda," Lo said, writing down an address for her. "She lives in Pocitos Street, near that place where we picked up the *reverbero*."

"Why don't we go together?"

"It would have to be over the weekend, and her apartment

is crowded then because that's when everyone is off. You'd have a better chance to talk to her on a weekday. I already told her about you."

Ah, Lo was so kind! Sarah was grateful to have met someone who could offer her guidance in quite personal matters, like clothes . . . and menstrual care. Her friend had informed her that there were no tampons in Havana—in fact, she had never heard of them, much less of period underwear. Cuban women used only sanitary pads, called *íntimas*, and they were sold in pharmacies at reasonable prices. A box of six cost seven pesos. Lo had given Sarah her first package of *íntimas*, which she truly appreciated.

IT WAS A TUESDAY afternoon when Sarah took the Centro Habana–bound bus. It passed by the embassy row and under a tunnel that connected Miramar with Línea Street in El Vedado. The route followed the seawall for a while, and Sarah looked longingly at the shimmery waves.

Though Villa Santa Marta wasn't far from the ocean (Miramar meant *look at the sea*), nobody seemed to pay any attention to it. She had tried to explain the challenges and joys of surfing to Joaquín, but he hadn't even understood the concept. "Why in the world would anyone want to stand *on* the water instead of swimming?" he had asked, laughing. He had never seen a surfboard! Same with Lo, who claimed she was afraid of sharks.

"Haven't you heard Farah María's song?" she asked and started moving her hips. "*Yo no me baño en el Malecón porque en el agua hay un tiburón.*"

Bullshit, Sarah thought, though she wasn't about to swear in Spanish. Besides, *mierda de toro* didn't sound right. There had to be a better Cuban curse word. But to the point. When was the last time a shark had been seen around El Malecón? The seawall that ran alongside El Vedado, Habana Vieja and Centro

Habana was surrounded by shallow waters where big fish were unlikely to make an appearance.

The bus left behind Miramar and turned toward Zapata Street. They passed by the cemetery. She had a glimpse of classy white mausoleums with statues of angels that shone under the sun. Sarah looked away. Every year Rob tried to get her to visit the Tijuana cemetery for Día de Los Muertos, but she had never had any interest in La Catrina, La Calaca or whatever Death was called in Spanish. There would be time, much later, to get acquainted with all that.

She got off at the Veterinary Clinic bus stop and crossed Salvador Allende Avenue, finding herself outside a fenced botanical garden. According to Lo's detailed instructions, the place must be La Quinta de Los Molinos. From the street she saw thriving shrubs and trees and heard the loud chirping of dozens of birds. A giant yellow butterfly flew in front of her. Ah, she would have to come back with Joaquín!

There was no traffic light in the intersection of Salvador Allende Avenue and San Francisco Street. Sarah waited until no buses or cars were coming and ran for her life. She finally found Pocitos, a narrow and crowded street. Most building doors were open. In the balconies, sheets, clothes and underwear billowed in the wind. People came out of a veggie store with bags full of big red tomatoes and potatoes still covered in dirt.

Fredesbinda's apartment was in a two-story building. There was a grocery store on the ground floor and a small queue outside. Maybe some goodies had "come" to the bodega too.

Sarah took the stairs to the second floor. The apartment doors wrapped around a tall circular concrete wall. A guy was emptying what looked like a chamber pot down the wall—wouldn't that be the bodega courtyard? Sarah approached him shyly.

"Excuse me, *compañero*," she said in her best Spanish. "Can you tell me where Fredesbinda lives?"

With a fast movement, the guy hid the chamber pot behind his back.

"The seamstress? Ah, yes. She lives right here. And you are . . . ?" He gave her the once-over.

"A client," Sarah said, flustered. She didn't know how to say "prospective customer" in Spanish.

"Come with me."

He led her to an apartment and knocked on the door himself. A middle-aged woman opened.

"This foreigner was asking for you, Fredes," the guy said.

He referred to her as *extranjera*, which sounded strange. His voice had an edge to it, Sarah thought. Or perhaps he was just in a hurry. Cubans talked too fast for her to get all the nuances.

Fredesbinda blinked nervously.

"Ah, the comrade must be Dolorcita's friend." She spoke as if Sarah wasn't there. "Dolorcita's the president of a CDR in Miramar," she added, still addressing the guy.

He left. Fredesbinda let Sarah in.

"Juan belongs to the Surveillance Committee," she said, almost apologetically. "He's always nosing in everybody's business."

Sarah stepped into a small living room. In a corner stood a Singer sewing machine as old as the one in Villa Santa Marta but better preserved. A black vinyl sofa was covered by vibrant pieces of printed fabric that gave off a pungent smell. Still, Sarah wanted to touch them. So much blue, green and yellow! The front and the back of a blue blouse, still unattached, occupied a rocking chair. Fredesbinda picked them up so Sarah could sit down.

"Dolorcitas says you're an American," she examined her with genuine interest. "Do you live in Miami?"

"No, I've never been there."

Fredesbinda seemed disappointed but got down to business.

"*Bueno, chica,* I know the kind of dress that would look good on you. Long and flowery, eh? And fresh, because summer's coming. We just have to choose a fabric."

One with sunflowers on a blue background had already caught Sarah's eye.

"That one will be perfect."

Fredesbinda smiled.

"That's what I thought. Hope we have enough. *Caray,* you're tall! Now tell me about you. So you're Joaquín's girlfriend, eh? Are you guys going to get married soon?"

Sarah began to answer all these questions, thinking that a PI would have an easy job in Cuba, where that guy Juan wasn't the only one who nosed in other people's business. She didn't mind it, though. After all, she had nothing to hide from these *compañeros.* And that was part of what made Cubans so charming—their friendliness and childlike interest in everyone's lives.

# CHAPTER EIGHT

Satiadeva turned on Fourth Street and stopped in front of Villa Santa Marta. Someone—probably him—had fixed the wrought-iron letters over the arched entryway. Before, it had been impossible to make out the name, which accentuated the general atmosphere of neglect and decay.

The house had always had a malevolent aura. It could have been the porthole window above the main entrance, like an evil eye glaring at those who approached, or the dirty gray stucco that had peeled off in many areas, or the ungroomed lawn with weeds as tall as a ten-year-old child. But Candela didn't notice, too busy admiring the architecture.

"Look at these curved walls! And the stained glass in the window looks straight out of a fairy tale. *¡Mágico!* Is it original?"

"Uh, I guess. It's been there forever."

Mamina opened the door as if she had been waiting behind it.

"Merceditas! I'm so happy you're back! I was afraid—"

We hugged each other tightly. She looked thinner, older and fragile. Her usually straight back was hunched, and her eyes were sunken and dull. Her left arm rested in a sling.

Nena, her rescued mutt, started barking and jumping out

until Candela knelt down and petted her. "Aw, you're adorable!"

The pooch licked her face.

"This is Candela, my best friend," I said.

Mamina stuck out her right hand, but Candela stood up and kissed her on the cheek.

"So nice to meet you, *Abuela*! *Mucho gusto.*"

"Same, *mija.*"

"What a beautiful home you have!"

Mamina didn't answer and shifted her weight from one foot to the other. Candela shot me a puzzled look. Catalina came out and saved the moment by inviting everyone in. If my grandma seemed to have aged in a few months, Catalina, on the other hand, was healthier and bigger than ever. She was a mountain of a woman—over six feet of laughter and loudness, still sprightly and strong at seventy-five.

The inside of Villa Santa Marta was in no better shape than the outside. In the cavernous living room, yellowish *Granma* newspapers lay scattered on the coffee table. The upright piano and brown leather couch were covered in cobwebs. The many paintings, big and small, that hung from the walls were so dusty that it was hard to tell what they portrayed. The room was dark because the ceiling lamp—a big pendant fixture with heavy tubing—hadn't worked in years. It was too high for any of us to reach, and when something went wrong with the wiring, Mamina shrugged it off and stopped using it. Satiadeva had offered to bring in an electrician, but my grandma kept postponing the visit with different excuses. A brass table lamp with fat cherubs on the base provided the only source of light.

Darkness was just one of the many issues with the living room. The window glass was broken. Luckily, it had double panels and only the inside part was cracked; the stained glass that Candela had labeled "magical" had been preserved intact. Once or twice, after marrying Nolan and having access to dollars, I had attempted to have the inside panel replaced but couldn't find any that size.

A vague smell of mold floated in the air. The place was a disaster. How had I dared to bring Candela there? And why didn't I think of hiring somebody to help clean the house in advance? It was embarrassing, for both Mamina and me.

"I'm sorry it's such a mess," I muttered.

"¿*Qué* mess?" Candela said. "It's lovely!"

Satiadeva cleared his throat.

"Most urgent thing is to take care of the leaks," he said. "I've patched them up, but it's just a Band-Aid."

He had taken upon himself the care of Mamina and the house. Though a hardworking, resourceful guy, he was losing the battle. The building needed constant work, even under the best conditions. It was now under the worst.

"Where are the leaks?"

"In the master bedroom."

At least they weren't in Mamina's room, or mine.

"It doesn't look good, Merceditas. You need to bring over someone to fix the ceiling as soon as possible."

That had been a point of contention for years. Mamina didn't like strangers. It was a miracle that she had warmed up to Satiadeva. But she refused to meet with a stonemason and get an estimate of the repair costs. We had argued about it during my previous visits. This time I was determined not to leave until the restoration work was on its way—and all the light bulbs were replaced.

Candela was still oohing and ahhing over ornaments and pieces of furniture as if she were in a museum. (In a way, the house looked like a museum, trapped in a time bubble from the fifties or earlier.) Mamina showed her the guest room and we left her gaping at a full-length mirror with lights all around it. The fact that none of them worked didn't bother her.

I went upstairs to my former bedroom. The cherrywood set included a canopy bed—though the canopy had disappeared many years ago—a marble-top dresser, an armoire and a nightstand. The walls were painted light blue, but the color had faded to gray. On a wall hung the oil portrait of a nine- or ten-year-old girl in what looked like our backyard. She had an oval face, piercing black eyes and brown hair. I had named her Martita, after the house. When I was a child, I'd ask her silently to watch over me at night.

Mamina laughed and said I was a scaredy cat, a *miedosa*, but the fact was that we lived in an angry house. I was always getting my fingers caught on doors and tripping over chairs and thresholds. I thought I was just clumsy, but that didn't happen in Miami or Gainesville. It could be that my American houses were less cluttered, but Mamina had had similar experiences. I had never liked the place I called home.

AN HOUR LATER, SHOWERED and rested, I went back downstairs. The master bedroom was closed and closed it stayed. I wasn't about to deal with a big wet mess at that time.

The dining room was formal and stiff, with solid oak pieces that made the space feel cramped despite its considerable size. The chairs were carved, upholstered with brown leather. Next to the dining table were a buffet, a hutch and a china cabinet where Mamina stored the elegant dinnerware we never used. Catalina had set the table with it, perhaps wanting to impress the party. A chandelier with a two-foot bronze ring swayed over us. It had fifteen lights, of which only six worked.

"If you ever want to sell that lamp, *Abuela*, let me know," Candela said. "I'll give you whatever you want for it."

A childish wave of jealousy washed over me. Why did she call Mamina "grandma"? She was my *abuela*, not hers!

"Oh, I can't," Mamina answered. "Nothing here is mine."

She had always said so. Once, during the hardest days of the special period, a well-dressed man came over and asked if we wanted to "get rid of old stuff," adding that he would pay in dollars. Mamina showed him the door. She didn't feel like she owned the house, or anything in it.

"Dinner's ready!" Catalina announced. "*Picadillo a la habanera*, black beans and white rice."

If you follow the traditional recipe, *picadillo a la habanera* is made up of ground beef cooked with tomato sauce, green olives, onions, garlic and raisins, and seasoned with salt and pepper. For some reason, Catalina had added chopped hard-boiled eggs. A weird and unnecessary twist, in my opinion, but she seemed quite proud of the result. Maybe it was *picadillo a la Pinareña*. Like Mamina, Catalina was from Pinar del Río.

Food was served on the monogrammed dishes that had an embossed golden *M* in the middle. Everybody praised the *picadillo*, though the ground beef was too salty and the rice dry. Mamina was a much better cook. And she didn't put eggs where they didn't belong!

Catalina had brought a bottle of Havana Club Siete Años, but I stayed away from it—after Nolan's death, I realized that I had a drinking problem. Better sober than sorry, I thought. Mamina had never touched alcohol, and Satiadeva said that rum altered his aura. Candela's aura, however, didn't seem to have a problem with it.

While everybody chewed and chatted, and Nena begged for treats, I ate without much appetite and watched my grandma. She kept to herself, which was not unusual, but looked weary and down with the sling restraining her movements.

A tapping on the living room window made me jump.

"It's the rain," Mamina said. She was, apparently, watching me as well.

Just in case, I went to check it out. Back in the living room, I looked out the window and saw a car parked behind Satia's Chevy. The motor was running. It worried me because *almendrones* were frequent targets. Thieves would take tires and rims, leaving the vehicle standing on cinder blocks they carried for that purpose. *Cabrones.*

I opened the door and flecks of rain hit me in the face. I stepped out, shivering. Immediately, the car backed up and sped away, its taillights looking like bright ribbons under the rain. There was no need to alarm Satia or Mamina. The driver could have just been waiting for the rain to pass. I returned to the dining room.

"This trip is the first step I've taken to reconnect with my Cuban roots," Candela was saying. "But I'm going to need help because everything feels both foreign and familiar at the same time."

"I'll be happy to assist you," Satiadeva replied.

Catalina and Mamina exchanged a knowing glance.

The chitchat died down soon. Dinner was over. I insisted Mamina go to her room because she looked exhausted. Satiadeva and Catalina left. Candela said she would help me clean the table, but she spent most of the time checking out the silverware and glancing at the chandelier.

"There's a presence here," she said suddenly, pointing to the ceiling. "And it isn't a happy one."

I could have mentioned the *bruja* but didn't want to encourage her.

"Don't you feel it, Merceditas?" she insisted.

Before I could answer, one of the remaining chandelier light bulbs flickered and then went out completely.

"*¡Coño!*" we yelled at the same time and ran to the kitchen.

# CHAPTER NINE

*April 15th, 1986*

*"Year of the 30th Anniversary of the Granma Landing"*

*When I go out on my own, guys ogle and catcall in the most obnoxious manner. Some come-on lines are cute, like si cocinas como caminas, me como hasta la raspita (if you cook like you walk, I'll scrape the pot clean). Others are rude and disrespectful. Lo said I should be flattered. Really? I'm afraid Cuban women missed the memo on feminism, dude.*

THE ROUND CEILING LAMP bathed the library in a soft amber glow. Sarah sat behind the pedestal desk. Though the portrait of that woman in a black pillbox hat still spooked her, having her own office was a new and satisfying experience. Her bedroom in her parents' Pacific Beach cottage had barely had enough space for her clothes and surfboards.

It was close to 7 P.M. Joaquín would be late because he had a meeting. Again. She didn't remember her father having to attend so many meetings at the Naval Base. But obviously, the Cuban Army worked differently.

Supper was ready. It was Russian Spam, lightly breaded, per Lo's instructions, and fried in lard. Chicken-fried Spam was an odd dish, but Joaquín seemed to like it. That was the second time Sarah had made it. It was served with rice, like almost everything, and a side of *tostones* (fried green plantains). The Cuban diet had made her gain five pounds already, but her husband hadn't complained, and Lo insisted she needed to put more meat on her bones.

Now she had time to write a letter to Rob as she'd rather do it when Joaquín wasn't around. She found an old pencil and a piece of paper inside a drawer, wrote the date and added *"Year of the 30th Anniversary of the Granma Landing"* on the next line. How fascinating! Cuban years had their own names, always written surrounded by quotation marks. They helped remind people of revolutionary places and events.

> *Joaquín knows about our correspondence, which makes him a bit nervous. He says that letters from the United States are opened on a regular basis by State Security. I don't think they would do that to someone living in his house, given his total commitment to the revolution. But to some of his hardcore comrades, he's literally sleeping with the enemy. Anyway, in the unlikely case they open your letters, "they" (whoever they are) will find out that we have nothing to hide. We are compañeros too!*

Sarah stopped and reread the paragraph. Something wasn't right. She bit the pencil's eraser. But what was wrong, exactly? She considered herself a revolutionary. A *compañera*, as she had just written. After all, she had once belonged to a Marxist cell—a group of eight high school friends who met in a beautiful house in Point Loma to discuss *The Communist Manifesto*, which had been an easy read, and the three-volume *Das Kapital*, which had not. (The house belonged to a boy's parents who had made a fortune in the oil business in Hobbs, New

Mexico, who seemed perplexed by their offspring's political choices.) Sarah had tried hard to understand the concepts. She still remembered some quotes like "freedom of education shall be enjoyed under the conditions fixed by law and under the supreme control of the state."

She wondered if the state in Cuba had "supreme control." It looked like it, seeing that the government decided everything, from workers' wages to the amount of beans, milk and makeup that came to the designated stores. In principle, she agreed with the egalitarian reasoning behind the ration-card system. Everybody had the right to buy some basic products (like six pounds of rice and a few ounces of meat or chicken monthly) so no one would go hungry. That made sense to her. But if the food-ration card was relatively easy to understand, the distribution of clothes and household items was more difficult. The day before, when Joaquín showed her his *libreta de productos industriales*, she had stared at the cryptic tear-off coupons, not knowing what they stood for or how to use them.

"Ask Dolores to explain it," Joaquín had said, after his own explanations were of little use. "Women are better at this sort of thing."

Dutifully, Sarah had knocked on her new friend's door. Lo's house was a smaller, square one-story building, but the garden was well taken care of, with healthy roses and a bougainvillea that crept up the front wall. In the living room there was a carved rocking chair that Sarah had loved since day one. Its back and forth swaying soothed and comforted her.

Lo brought out her own *libreta*. It was printed on pinkish paper; Joaquín's, on the other hand, was blue.

"It's very easy, *chica*," she said. "See, here's coupon H7. I can use it to buy a pair of shoes. Now, if I don't want shoes, or there are none for sale, the same coupon allows me to get a bottle of wood polish."

Sarah laughed out loud, thinking she was starting to get the Cuban sense of humor. To her surprise, Lo remained serious.

"What's so funny?" she demanded.

Dang, it wasn't a joke. Sarah apologized profusely.

"Can you just get the shoes and pass on the wood polish?" she asked.

"Well, yes. You have to choose which one you want. Now, you can only shop when it's your group's time to buy. Mine was last week, by the way. I still had a perfume coupon left, but there were no perfumes. This week, there are dozens of Soviet and Bulgarian scents in the store, but I have to wait until my turn comes again."

"When will that be?"

"In two months."

Sarah nodded and rubbed a hand over her face, pondering her next question.

"When you use coupons, do you need to pay as well?"

"Yes, but nothing's expensive. Red Moscow costs forty pesos. On the black market, though, it's over a hundred. Kremena, my favorite Bulgarian perfume, is only twenty at the stores and eighty on the black market. It's very nice. You should try it!"

Sarah did a quick mental calculation. Now she knew that Joaquín's monthly salary was around three hundred pesos—and that day at the farmers' market she had spent a lot more than she should have. A hundred pesos bought a decent amount of food at the government stores, but the black market was another story. She was still trying to figure it out. Since they were on the subject of purchases, Lo revealed that she had been waiting for the right time to buy a Soviet electric fan, but they hadn't "come" to the Miramar stores in years.

"My only hope is to get one assigned in the Merits and Demerits Assembly at the school," she said. "But there's a lot of competition, and I honestly doubt—"

She leaned forward and dropped her voice to a whisper.

"There are some teachers who would slander their own mothers so they can get enough merits, or pile enough demerits on others just to get the damn fan!"

"How does the merit system work?"

"You get points for doing volunteer work and night watches. You get demerits for *not* doing them."

That struck Sarah as more Orwellian than Marxist, but she didn't dare mention it. Lo wouldn't know Orwell. His name might be forbidden here. Reason for a demerit. She moved on to a safer topic.

"Can someone ship you a fan from another country?" Sarah asked. "A friend of mine who lives in the United States could . . ."

"That's not possible," Lo replied. "Because of the blockade."

"What if he ships it from Tijuana?"

"He may try," Lo said, sounding unconvinced. "But I doubt it. I've never heard of anything being sent from capitalist countries. Supposing the fan got here, the postal service clerks will probably steal it."

"What? Aren't they afraid of a demerit, or even more serious consequences?"

"There won't be any, unless they're caught in the act."

She had left Lo's house more confused than she had been before coming in.

Sarah turned her attention to the letter in front of her. She longed to share all that with Rob but was afraid of sounding overly critical of the system, or as if she were making fun of these people's scarcities and hardships. And in case the letters were actually read . . . She ended up writing a social commentary on the *piropos*, the one-line catcalls that drove her crazy when she ventured outside alone. She added another note addressed to her parents, hoping it would placate them.

*I am doing fine*, she wrote, *and will go back home someday. I'm not in danger, I promise. Please, trust me.*

Suddenly, the light flickered and the amber glow vanished. Darkness filled the room. Sarah yelped.

Ashamed of her reaction, she opened the window and let the last rays of the sun in. But she didn't feel like staying in the library. She walked out to the hall, where the lights were still on. After some hesitation, she went downstairs and ran to the backyard.

# CHAPTER TEN

Villa Santa Marta had a French country-style kitchen with off-white cabinets and olive granite countertops. Big and airy, it was the only welcoming place in that monstrosity of a house. Mamina kept a TV set in the breakfast nook to watch her favorite telenovelas while cooking. The television faced an ancient cuckoo clock.

Candela and I pretended that the incident with the chandelier hadn't scared us. We laughed at our "nervousness" and started to wash the dishes. By hand, because Mamina refused to have a dishwasher installed.

"I love your *abuela*, Merceditas," Candela gushed. "What a sweetheart! And this is a mansion, girl."

"If you say so."

"Does that clock chime?"

She got closer to examine the pendulum, weights and permanently open-beaked bird.

"I've never heard it make a peep."

"Notice how beautifully carved that stag's head on top is. I'd say it was made in the thirties, though it may be older. A treasure!"

My husband had liked the clock so much that he suggested buying it from Mamina. I said no, failing to understand the charm of what seemed to me like junk.

"Everything's so—authentic!" Candela went on. "When you talked about your run-down house, I never pictured Victorian furniture and a Black Forest clock."

"The house *is* run-down."

"Nothing that can't be fixed. After things change—and you know they will change—the land alone will be worth a fortune. Ah, it must have been so nice to grow up in a villa like this, with history and character, instead of a cookie-cutter house in Hialeah!"

"It must have been nicer to grow up in a place where there was always food available, with both your parents," I said dryly.

Candela hugged me.

"I'm sorry! The grass is always greener on the other side, isn't it?"

"Greener *un carajo*. How come you know so much about Victorian this and that?"

"I used to manage an antique store before opening my dog-grooming business."

Once the dining room was somewhat tidied, Candela tried to take a picture of the chandelier.

"*Ay*, the battery's dead." She threw her phone on the table. "And I forgot to bring a charger!"

"I only brought mine, but Satia will know where to find one."

She smiled.

"Great! We'll call him in the morning. But in the meantime, could you shoot a pic of me with your phone?"

That was just the beginning. Candela, fueled by the Havana Club shots, kept asking me to take photos of her posing around our knickknacks as if we were in a Jurassic Park of trinkets. I obliged, hiding my annoyance. She also had *me* pose for some shots. In the silliest one, I sat in front of the piano with my hands awkwardly touching the keys. I had never learned to play. The piano was a nuisance whose main purpose had become to collect dirt and get in the way when Mamina swept the floor. Candela examined the blue vase that sat on top of it.

"It looks like Mu— Wait, it is signed. Yes, it's Murano glass!" she exclaimed.

You would have thought that it was covered in gold instead of dirt. I had had enough. It was time to bring up the *bruja* and see if that made Candela shut up.

"Be careful about the energy of this stuff. The neighbors say the house was built by a witch," I whispered, looking appropriately concerned. "Some say she's buried here."

Candela's eyes widened and she returned the vase to its place.

"Did your grandma meet her?"

"No, the witch died way before Mamina or even my dad moved in. But her spirit is supposed to be hanging around. You watch!"

"That was the presence I felt!" My friend got serious. "She made the light bulb go off. Let me inspect the energy patterns."

She bent over the piano, took a deep breath and closed her eyes while I tapped my foot, weary and impatient.

FINALLY, CANDELA GOT TIRED of sniffing out energy patterns, whatever that meant, and retreated to her room. Relieved, I went up the circular staircase that connected the foyer to the second floor. It *did* have an elegant feel, I had to admit, even after Satia had replaced the wall sconces with regular, naked light bulbs. They weren't precisely Art Deco nor did they match the marble steps, but at least they did the job. Mamina's bedroom was the first one in a long, dimly lit hall. I knocked on the door.

"Come on in."

Her room was a sparse, rustic space that had nothing to do with the rest of the house. When Mamina moved in, she had the bedroom set removed so she could attach two wooden posts to the walls and hang a hammock from them. An unpainted pine table, a trunk she had brought from La Coloma and a rocking chair completed the furnishings. The only new item was a faux shag fur dog bed that I had bought for Nena. The pooch, already curled up there, gave me a cursory tail wag.

Mamina was lying in the hammock, covered up to her shoulders by a light quilt. Her skin was pale brown and she had high cheekbones. She insisted that our family descended from the original inhabitants of Cuba, the Taínos.

"How's your arm?" I asked.

She smiled with chapped lips.

"It doesn't hurt anymore."

"Happy to hear that." I kissed her forehead. "Well, sleep tight. I just came to say good night."

She clasped my hands. Hers was cold.

"Stay a little longer. I've missed you, *niña*. You are my best medicine, you know? Let's talk for a while."

Oh, well, it wasn't like we had nothing to talk about. But it might be too soon to bring up my mother, I feared.

"Does your friend like it here?" Mamina asked.

"Sure! She took pictures of the piano, the cuckoo clock, the chandelier . . . Americans go crazy about that stuff."

"She kept saying 'vintage, vintage'!"

We laughed and shook our heads. Mamina sounded livelier than an hour earlier, which gave me courage. Afraid of chickening out as it had happened so many times before, I took the plunge:

"I'd like to ask you something about—Tania."

A little jolt passed through her face.

"Did you girls meet at school?"

I winced. Had she purposely ignored my last statement? But perhaps she hadn't heard me, given my tendency to mumble when talking of my mother.

"I haven't been to school in ages, Mamina," I answered cautiously.

"How did you meet, then?"

"We met in Gainesville," I said, since she seemed to be talking about Candela. "She's the cousin of La Bakería Cubana's owner."

"What bakería? Isn't she studying to be a schoolteacher, like you?"

*Here we go again*, I thought, frustrated and scared for her. The article had claimed that "senior moments" were common and pretty harmless. And yet—

"I always wanted to teach kids but only got to the fourth grade," Mamina said slowly. "That's why I'm so grateful that my children are able to study. Joaquín's already a lieutenant and you will get far too, *niña*, if you apply yourself. Be a good student. Mind your manners. Work hard."

Her gaze was unfocused. I had the feeling of being unseen by her. Nena stood up and put her nose on the hammock. Candela had once said that dogs sensed when something was wrong with their owners.

"Mamina, Joaquín, my dad, is—" I couldn't bring myself to finish the sentence.

It was unnerving and sad. I picked up the sling from the floor, caressed Mamina's thinning hair and waited until she asked, "How long are you going to be here?"

I didn't dare to mention Tania again.

"As long as you want me."

Mamina smiled. The familiar spark had returned to her eyes and she said, "You're an angel, Merceditas."

"Kick butted out of heaven."

That was an old joke between us that always made her laugh. She giggled and closed her eyes. I waited several minutes, but she fell asleep fast. Perhaps she had taken pain pills. I turned off the light and tiptoed out of the room.

# CHAPTER ELEVEN

*April 28th, 1986*

*I'm turning into a useful, productive Cuban citizen, even if I don't have an ID card and can't get a job yet—or a coveted plan jaba pass. But I'm not sitting idle at home! Yesterday, the CDR assigned me a task: visiting ten neighbors to remind them of the Workers' Day celebration. Lo went with me—I don't know if to offer support or make sure I didn't do anything improper.*

*There are only five houses on our block and they all look nice, even if the façades could use some paint. Our neighbors are either working-class people who, like Joaquín and Lo, got their homes as a reward for services rendered to the revolution, or the original "bourgeois" residents—gusanos, Lo calls them. I just met the Barbeitos, an older couple that falls into the latter category.*

AT LAST, SARAH THOUGHT, she was making progress in the social-relationships department. She had always considered herself outgoing and friendly, but felt pretty isolated in Miramar. She knew all the reasons, and agreed with Lo and Joaquín that it took time to adapt, but still missed being around other people. Lo worked all day and, upon returning home, had to cook and take care of that useless Pepe on top of her many CDR activities, so there was little time for anything else.

The Barbeitos, despite their *gusano* reputation, came to fill that void. Benjamín Barbeito was a retired doctor. His wife, Elena, used to be the secretary in their private clinic that had been nationalized in the sixties. Like most people, they seemed puzzled by Sarah's presence in Cuba but acted warm and welcoming the day she rang their doorbell to invite them to the May First celebration.

"Here's Joaquín's *compañera*," Lo said. "She's helping me spread the word about our activities."

She left it at that, and it felt awkward. The Barbeitos surely had to wonder why Sarah hadn't been introduced by name. Then Lo spotted another neighbor across the street and ran to talk to her.

"You aren't from around here, are you?" Elena asked Sarah.

"No," she answered, and added with the embarrassment that her admission always caused, "I'm from the United States."

The happiness on the old woman's face surprised her pleasantly. The Barbeitos asked Sarah to come in. Like Villa Santa Marta, their house was elegant, with expensive furniture and décor. A Tiffany lamp sat on top of a lacquered cabin. French doors opened to the bedrooms. There were two tall bronzes of dancers in the living room that wouldn't have been out of place at an art gallery and a fireplace that had no practical use, but added a touch of luxury.

Doctor Barbeito closed the door, Elena made a pot of tea and they started chatting with Sarah in English. Theirs was a little rusted but felt like music to her ears after so many months of Spanish immersion.

"You remind me of my old American friends," Elena said, patting her hand. "I hope you visit us frequently."

They didn't get to talk much because Lo came to pick her up and continue their rounds. The Barbeitos didn't commit to going to the May First activity, but Sarah left their house in good spirits. She was also determined to find out about her legal status because the identity limbo was getting ridiculous. She could invent a name for herself—Carolina, like her Salvadorean best friend, or Frida or Lupe . . . But what if they gave her a totally different one? The only people who knew her real name were Joaquín and the Immigration officers who handled her case.

The social-relationships campaign went on. That very week, Sarah and Joaquín hosted a dinner for one of Joaquín's colleagues, a young lieutenant named Cecilia who had been awarded a trip to the Soviet Union. The trips were all-paid, all-inclusive vacations assigned by a council of colleagues (a Merits and Demerits Assembly?) to exceptionally hardworking people. In certain cases, a family member was allowed to go as well. Sarah hoped that Joaquín—who was likely a *trabajador vanguardia* himself, judging by the many extra hours he spent at the unit—would get one too someday.

Captain Alberto Salgado also attended the dinner. He could have been Cecilia's romantic partner. Or maybe not. It was hard for Sarah to tell because they addressed each other formally as *compañero* and *compañera*, but she noticed some hanky-panky under the table despite so much *compañerismo*. A Russian guy whose name and rank she didn't get came too. He didn't say much, but smiled a lot and ate with gusto.

The Russian guy wore chinos and a red plaid Western-style shirt that made him look like a Slavic cowboy. Joaquín and Alberto wore khaki pants and ironed guayaberas. Sarah had chosen the dress with the sunflower prints that Fredesbinda had made for her. Cecilia wore green polyester pants and a white ruffled blouse. Her side buns reminded Sarah of Princess Leia's, but she knew better than to bring it up. Just a few days before, Lo had informed her of Cuba's official position about *Star Wars*.

"¿*La Guerra de las Galaxias?* That's capitalist propaganda, *chica*!"

Uh, what? It had never occurred to Sarah. Was the Galactic Empire supposed to be communist? The Republic? Lo couldn't tell, as she hadn't watched the movies. But she stuck to her guns.

The dinner turned out nicely. Even Villa Santa Marta behaved. There were no weird accidents, and the lights stayed on. Sarah displayed proudly the porcelain dishes with gold trims and floral designs, and the silverware—real silver, which she had spent several hours polishing—with the letter *M* embossed. She had also cleaned the portrait frames with a mix of baking soda and lemon, and all of them sparkled, particularly the one on top of the piano.

The menu was simple but tasty: shredded meat cooked in a flavorful sauce with onions, bell peppers and garlic, the ubiquitous white rice and a tomato and avocado salad that only Sarah ate. Cecilia brought a flan, and the silent Russian contributed a bottle of vodka.

Sarah played the out-of-tune piano to entertain their guests—early that day, she had rehearsed "La Bayamesa" by ear. She asked Joaquín to use her Minolta to take pictures of the party and herself in front of the piano. She planned to send the film to Rob and have it developed in San Diego because there was no place to do so in Cuba. It was taking a risk, yes. But even if her parents were to see the pictures (she hoped they didn't) they wouldn't associate that opulent ambiance with Havana. And let's face it, she wanted to brag a bit, even if just to Rob, about her new life. She would have liked for her friends in San Diego to know all about it, actually. They'd have been so happy for her!

Weeks passed. She and Joaquín were still floating in a honeymoon bubble. They talked for hours, with her asking so many questions about Cuba as he could answer. They took long walks together. Miramar had long avenues with ample sidewalks and quiet parks that made the neighborhood a walker's paradise. They would go hand in hand as Sarah admired the ornate façades and old manor houses that reminded her of Gaeta, Italy, where her father had been stationed when she was seven years old.

"What does your family say about you staying here?" Joaquín asked once, out of the blue, as they passed by the clock tower at Fifth Avenue. "Don't they want to come and visit us?"

The structure was a striking sight, with four balconies wrapped around the seventy-two-foot tower. Sarah pretended to admire it while she considered what to say. She had always danced around the topic.

"They may," she said. It wasn't a lie. They might, if only to try to drag her back home. "But it will be hard because of politics. You know how things are."

That was rather vague but he seemed satisfied.

"I'm so thankful that you have chosen to stay here with me," he said and kissed her tenderly.

The clock struck seven. It sounded like the Big Ben, Sarah thought. It was getting dark and they returned to Villa Santa Marta, her heart soaring with happiness. Maybe someday she would tell her parents everything and they would actually come and enjoy the city where she had found true love.

# CHAPTER TWELVE

The gentle rustle of the rain woke me up. It was seven-thirty in the morning. I got up and looked out the window. The backyard hedges had been trimmed—likely Satia's doing since Mamina wouldn't allow anyone else to help her around the house. The mango trees, green and bright under the light rain, looked healthy. The stone fountain needed to be cleaned and repaired, but Candela would have something nice to say about the statue of a thoughtful-looking woman that decorated it.

Tucked in at the end of the backyard was a smaller building called the servants' quarters, though we never had any servants. I didn't remember ever being inside, only a failed attempt to peek in when I was six or seven years old. I had been walking around when a blooming rosebush caught my attention—mostly because nothing else grew next to the plain, square structure that looked so different from the rest of the property. The flowers were an unusual deep purple and shot a pungent aroma into the evening. I went around the rosebush and found myself facing the door. When I was about to open it, Mamina called me from the kitchen and ordered me to stay in the house . . .

Suddenly, I remembered the leaks and headed for the master bedroom. Villa Santa Marta had survived six hurricanes during my lifetime and many more before, but was bound to run out of luck—and plaster or cement or whatever kept ceiling and walls together.

I stepped into what had been my parents' bedroom and caught a whiff of wet socks. The room was furnished with a solid walnut king-size bed, two matching nightstands, a triple-door armoire and a mirrored dresser. A porcelain tray, a vase, a trinket box and a powder jar were scattered on top. I held the vase and cleaned it with my hand. It was light, delicate—and old. Candela would love it.

The mirror was blanketed with dust and dead bugs. I stared at it longingly. My mother had likely put on makeup and combed her hair in front of the now opaque mirror while I played by her side . . . But I had little time for nostalgic memories. The distinctive, musty smell of closed-off spaces pervaded the room. The leaks were in a corner, covered with damp tarp. Fearing there was mold in the cracks, I covered my nose and hurried downstairs.

There was a landline phone with a rotary dial in the living room, under the cherub lamp. Candela hadn't seen it, or she would have made comments about the "ancient artifact" that Mamina insisted on using. I called Satiadeva.

"I've been trying to get a stonemason to look at those leaks," he said, "but Mamina doesn't want to."

"Well, *I* do. You have someone in mind?"

"My friend Ferradaz knows all there is to know about remodeling old houses. The whole crew is great."

For whatever reason I imagined Ferradaz as a tough-looking guy who would listen to reggaeton and wear a baseball cap backward. But who cared? As long as he fixed the place.

"Are they reasonable?"

"Very. And a hundred dollars goes far here."

"Bring them over."

In the kitchen, Candela and Mamina were busy making breakfast. Candela had brought oatmeal from Miami and served it sprinkled with cinnamon and topped with slices of mangoes from our backyard. Mamina prepared *café con leche*. Instead of the fine china from the night before, she took out ordinary made-in-Cuba dishes and cups. Candela asked why.

"I don't like to use other people's things," Mamina answered with a shrug.

Candela looked intrigued but didn't press the point. We ate in the breakfast nook, under the wooden stare of the silent cuckoo.

Later I informed Mamina that "Ferradaz and his crew" were coming to take care of the leaks. She sighed, obviously not happy, but didn't protest. She knew, better than anybody else, that Villa Santa Marta needed work, more so with a tropical storm approaching Havana.

"*Que sea lo que Dios quiera*," she said and shrugged.

Which sounded odd because she wasn't the type to talk about God, for good or for bad.

SATIADEVA ARRIVED AN HOUR later. Three people came with him: a tall skinny guy in his fifties, a shorter, younger man who *did* wear a baseball cap backward, and a thirty-something woman in a denim suit. Her long brown hair was in a pony-tail, tied with a yellow band. I assumed that she was someone's girlfriend.

"This is Ferradaz, a graduate from the School of Architecture and Urban Planning," Satiadeva said. "These are her guys, Santos and Suárez."

Ferradaz shook my hand with confidence. Her nails were painted red.

I ushered everybody in, covering my surprise. After a brief introduction, they went around the house while Mamina and I walked behind. My grandma's lips were tight, and she watched the crew with a suspicious eye.

The dining room, the guest bedroom and a bathroom occupied the right wing of the first floor, with the kitchen located at the end. I didn't think this section was in too bad a shape, but Ferradaz took notice of the many cracks that crisscrossed the walls and the areas where plaster had peeled off. I was so used to seeing them that they barely registered anymore.

The left wing comprised the living room and two smaller rooms where Mamina stored discarded furniture like a bed and a dresser that used to be in her room, a ladder, old paintbrushes and stuff that broke down but she insisted on keeping anyway. There were chairs with missing legs, an Admiral TV set that had never worked, as far as I remembered, and a smaller portable Panasonic that Mamina and I watched every night until it broke down in the early 2000s.

A pungent odor hit my nostrils. I hadn't set foot there in years and was horrified by the bulges and bubbles that had grown on the walls like tumors. A chipped door led to the two-car garage, home to rusty tools and auto parts. The floor was sagging.

"There's structural damage here," Ferradaz said matter-of-factly.

Mamina shot me an angry look, as if it was my fault that the house had gone to pieces.

The master bedroom, a bathroom, my room, Mamina's and a library occupied the second floor. In the library, Ferradaz discovered a rotten beam and another leak. I put a mason jar under it, hoping that the five thousand dollars I had brought were enough to cover materials and repairs.

When the inspection was over, we all converged in the living room to hear the verdict. As we did, I wondered if that manicured, ponytailed Ferradaz was to be trusted, then berated myself for my sexist doubts.

"This house is uninhabitable," she stated, fixing Mamina

with her small, beady gray eyes. "It is structurally unsound and a health hazard."

Her words came as a shock. I knew Villa Santa Marta had problems, but I didn't expect that. Neither did Mamina.

"Are you sure it's that bad, young lady?" she asked dismissively.

"Yes, *señora*. There's mold everywhere. And if the storm gets here, the ceiling may collapse."

"It doesn't look like it."

Ferradaz stood up.

"See the cracks?" She traced her fingers over the living room wall. "And this?" She walked to the door and pointed to a two-inch gap around the frame. "The foundation has shifted. When was the last time you had repairs done, *señora*?"

Mamina frowned. "Never."

"And how long have you lived here?"

"Since 1990. Or 1991. I don't remember now."

Ferradaz raised her eyebrows.

"That's almost thirty years, and the place was built in the thirties or forties. No wonder it's so damaged." She took a long, careful breath and concluded, "You all should move out as soon as possible."

"Well, we can't do that!" Mamina protested. "Where am I going to go?"

"With me?" I suggested.

"No way!"

I bristled. "I'm not going to let the house fall on your head! This is ridiculous!"

"Could we compromise?" Mamina asked between clenched teeth. "Can you fix some things, young lady, while I decide what to do next?"

Ferradaz nodded. "If you want to, yes. I'd start by propping up the main areas with jack studs and containing the leaks."

There was a pause. Santos, the younger guy, who had been examining the broken glass panel, said with a chuckle, "Looks like a pissed-off housewife threw a dish at it."

Was my mother the pissed-off housewife? I swatted the thought away.

"Do you want to fix this window?" he asked.

"What's the point?" Mamina answered, sounding like a petulant child. "Since everything's so bad and the place's 'uninhabitable—'"

I cut her off: "If you insist on living here for any length of time, the house has to be livable. So yes, let's take care of the window."

Ferradaz made some quick measurements. "We'll have to get three regular glass panels and glue them together. They don't make such big pieces anymore."

"Will it be possible to fix that too?" I gestured toward the pendant lamp. "And the stair sconces?"

"Sure," answered the older guy. "I'm an electrician. What's wrong with this lamp?"

Mamina shrugged. "It just stopped working."

"Do you have a ladder?"

Satiadeva stood up. "I'll fetch it."

I followed him to one of the storage rooms.

"Is she for real?" I whispered.

"Yes! Do you want recommendations? I can arrange that."

"Why does she go by her last name?"

"So people take her seriously."

"Where do you know her from?"

He grabbed one end of the ladder. "The crew is part of our metaphysical group."

"Metaphysical, huh? Candela's into that too."

He blushed.

"Is she? *Oye*, that's great."

"Do you think that Ferradaz's right about the house? Is it as awful as she says? I mean, it *looks* bad, but—"

"I've been worried about it since the first storm warning came. Yes, Merceditas, it *is* very bad."

I helped Satiadeva carry the ladder to the living room. Candela was settled on the couch with Nena on her lap.

"Cavachon," she said.

"Excuse me?" Mamina gave her a distrustful look.

"That's what Nena is, *Abuela*, a cross between a Cavalier King Charles spaniel and a bichon frise."

"It sounds like a curse word. If someone comes to me and says, 'Hey, you have a Cavachon,' my first thought is that I'm being insulted."

"I'd never insult a sweet grandma like you," Candela purred.

Brown-noser.

# CHAPTER THIRTEEN

*May 5th, 1986*

*The International Workers Day event was magnificent. Thousands congregated around a colossal statue of José Martí at Revolution Square. José Martí is a national hero, a founding father of sorts. Many public spaces are named after him, including the airport, a library, a theater, a park and several schools. The square was decorated with posters of Fidel and Che Guevara. People waved Cuban flags and carried cardboard signs with lemas, revolutionary slogans that they also chanted. Such heartfelt enthusiasm! Here are some lemas:*

*Morir por la patria es vivir. Dying for the homeland is living. A verse from the Cuban national anthem.*

*Los hombres mueren, el Partido es inmortal. Men die, the (Communist) Party is immortal.*

*Nacimos para vencer y no para ser vencidos. We were born to win and not to be defeated.*

*Patria o muerte. Homeland or death. That's how all Fidel's speeches end, and people respond Venceremos.*

SARAH HAD BEEN LOOKING forward to the May Day parade. It felt like a dream to be at Revolution Square, surrounded by so many people who breathed the socialist ideals she used to admire from afar. Now she was in the thick of it!

She went with Joaquín, Lo, Pepe and other members of their CDR. A special vehicle was available to take Miramar neighbors to the Plaza de la Revolución. They had been told to be at a designated spot by nine-thirty, and when the group arrived, a clean, large bus was already waiting for them.

"That's how it is when activities are under El Caballo's direct control," Lo said. "Everything runs smoothly!"

By the time they got to the square, hundreds of people were already gathered there. It felt odd that they weren't demanding higher wages or protesting this or that, which was Sarah's idea of an International Workers' Day march. They were simply showing their commitment to the revolution, and she liked the celebratory mood. She was composing in her mind a new letter to Rob. Too bad she couldn't find any new film for her Minolta camera because there were great photo ops all around them. The children in their school uniforms! The *milicianos*! And all those Cuban flags!

She felt happy to be there with a man who was a living embodiment of their shared ideals. In San Diego, she had met too many self-proclaimed Marxists who ended up becoming bankers, lawyers or accountants. Gah. Joaquín was different. Like Che Guevara, he had fought for the revolution—or for *some* revolution, in Africa. Like Che, he was a hottie too. How had she gotten so lucky?

The highlight of the day happened when El Caballo stood on a raised platform to deliver his trademark three-hour speech. The name Playa Girón kept coming up. It was obviously a battle, but it took Sarah a while to realize he was referring to the Bay of Pigs, whose anniversary had been recently commemorated. He also talked at length about a certain *Proceso de Rectificación de Errores y Tendencias Negativas*. Sarah didn't understand exactly what mistakes had to be corrected and which negatives trends had been denounced. It seemed to have something to do with revitalizing the economy, though.

Fidel didn't talk as fast as most of his fellow Cubans, and he repeated the same concepts more than once. That helped Sarah to get the idea if she had missed it the first or second times. He was, in her opinion, a remarkable speaker, but after standing for several hours in a compact mass of sweaty *compañeros*, she got hungry and thirsty and made Joaquín take her to a nearby cafeteria.

"You're such a spoiled *burguesita*!" he complained, just partially in jest.

But he went along. Sarah suspected he was starving too. Only cheese sandwiches and syrupy soft drinks had "come" to the cafeteria. Later, Sarah found out that some groups had brought their own food and drinks. Something to remember next year.

There was a mix-up with the buses at the end of the long day. When they got to the designated spot, theirs had already departed. Regular buses didn't run since it was a holiday, so they all started walking along Calzada de Ayestarán. A good Samaritan gave them a lift (*botella*, they called it, as in a bottle) from Hospital de Emergencias until Parque Central. There, they caught a small school bus that took them to Miramar. Sarah was exhausted when they finally made it home. She dropped herself on the couch and let Joaquín take care of dinner. He made a couple of omelets and reheated some rice. She didn't write a thing that evening, and they went to bed early.

It took a few days for her to sit at the kitchen table (she avoided the library now) and pen an enthusiastic description of the May Day parade when Joaquín was at work. Then she smiled to herself and added with a hand that shook just a bit:

*I will write again with more interesting news. Yes, there will be amazing news soon! But I don't want to get ahead of myself.*

*Love,*
*SL*

# CHAPTER FOURTEEN

Ferradaz and I discussed materials and prices, Santos got on the ladder and Suárez began to fiddle with the electric switch. Mamina left the living room grumbling under her breath. I apologized to Ferradaz.

"It's okay," she said politely. "Older people hate to have their privacy invaded."

It escaped me why Mamina was being so unreasonable. She surely realized how dangerous it was to stay in a leaky and moldy house!

Satiadeva volunteered to take Candela on a discovery trip of the city.

"Havana under the rain," she whispered, giggling. "Imagine that!"

It must be nice, I thought, to have a partner and laugh and play with him. That option had been taken from me, at least in the near future. But I felt happy for Candela.

"Have fun!"

When they were gone, I joined Mamina upstairs. She had already settled in the hammock. Her face turned hard when she saw me.

"Why are you doing this now?" she asked.

"Because I don't want the house to fall on your stubborn *cabeza*," I answered lightly, then kissed her on the head.

"I've only wanted the best for you, all my life," she said, rather out of the blue.

"And I want the best for you too. That's why I'm doing 'this.' I need you to be safe."

Mamina suppressed a sniffle. Funny, because she had never been the dramatic type.

"No need to get all Gina Cabrera on me," I said, referring to a telenovela actress we both liked.

"I wish. Ah, Gina's the best!"

My strategy to diffuse the situation with humor worked. After a few exchanges like that, the tension dissipated. Putting the repairs issue aside for a while, we talked about Candela and Satiadeva. Mamina agreed that they looked good together.

"Hope all the racket doesn't make that girl uncomfortable," Mamina said. "She's nice, but . . ."

She trailed off, her face all scrunched up. I tensed, fearing another "senior moment," but she just rolled her eyes and said, "Foreigners aren't used to the way we do things here. This morning, we had no water and she kept turning on the faucet as if she could will it to come."

"Don't worry. This is like a big adventure for her."

"An adventure, huh?" She smiled and moved on to another topic. "*Niña*, did you bring the tablet for Doctora Morales's son?"

"I did."

"Thanks! He's a bright kid, and she has been so helpful and caring."

Mamina was relaxing a bit. I hesitated to bring up my mother again, but there was never going to be a perfect time for my inquiries. I put the rocking chair closer to the hammock, sat down and took Mamina's right hand in mine. Her skin felt papery and thin.

"I'd like to ask you something, but please, don't take it the wrong way."

"As long as you don't try to convince me to move to Miami, we'll be fine."

The idea had occurred to me, though I had no illusions.

"It is"—I gulped—"about my mother."

I couldn't say "mom." It sounded too affectionate. Mamina jerked her head up, and I held my breath.

"Ah, *mijita* . . . what do you want to know?"

I exhaled. "Everything."

"I can't tell you much. We didn't see each other often."

"We can start with her name. Was it really Tania Rojas?"

Mamina gave me a half shrug. "That's what Joaquín called her."

"Where was she from? Did she ever mention a city or a state?"

"She might have, but I didn't always understand what she said. She had a heavy accent."

"What do you think happened to her? Where did she go?"

Mamina turned away from me.

"Back to her country, I'm sure," she said after a coughing fit that sounded forced. "She wasn't used to standing in line for hours or putting up with blackouts and shortages. Just like your friend. Americans are different. Spoiled, if you ask me."

"But why did she leave me here?"

Mamina didn't answer but gestured for me to join her on the hammock. I obliged and put my arm around her birdlike frame.

"Let's make this clear: I am just curious about her. Nothing to do with us. *You* are my real mother."

"Thank you, *mijita*. And you are the only kid I have left."

I waited a few seconds and whispered, "Didn't she have any maternal instincts? She must have been a cold-hearted bitch!"

Mamina got an odd look on her face. I felt the tension in her body.

"That was never my impression," she said in a low, measured tone. "She took good care of you. Last time I saw her, she had gone all the way to La Coloma to buy chickens. She wanted to make soup for you."

"Weren't there chickens in Havana?"

"Apparently not. You were sick, and she was so worried . . ."

Something warm and tender swept through my chest.

"The Padilla girl had an old hen and agreed to sell it. But your mom left in tears after a disagreement with her. She got the hen, though."

I tried to imagine "Tania" carrying a contraband old hen under her arm.

"*La* Padilla was always catty and rude," Mamina said with a sigh. "Not at all like your—"

She bit her lips and didn't finish the sentence.

"Like whom?" I asked. "My mother?"

"Yes, yes."

"What was the disagreement about?"

"Oh, I don't remember."

The Padilla girl had probably overcharged Tania, or at least tried to. Americans, foreigners in general and even Cubans who lived abroad, like me, were often perceived as "rich" and taken advantage of.

Mamina started coughing again, this time for real. I brought her a glass of water that was on the table. She drank fast. Her wrinkles had grown deeper.

"Do you want to rest?"

"No, no. I'm fine." She reached for my hand once more. "Even before the argument with *la* Padilla, I could tell that Tania was pissed. Up to then she was always saying 'long life to Fidel' and '*Viva la revolución*,' but that day she talked like a counterrevolutionary. She complained about the government and lack of food."

I listened avidly, adding touches to my mental sketch of "Tania."

"My guess is that she went back again to bring more canned food, baby clothes and—" Mamina started saying.

I jumped up.

"Went back again *where*?"

"The United States."

My mouth hung open.

"You mean she had been back before? When?"

"Late eighty-seven. I came to take care of you because Joaquín had to work. But she wasn't gone more than a week. She said she had missed you too much!"

I swallowed hard and struggled to reconcile that new, caring image of my mother with the cold, selfish one I had held for years.

"Why wouldn't she come back the second time?"

Mamina cleared her throat.

"She could have died abroad."

The conversation had taken a turn that I hadn't anticipated. It was, in fact, infuriating. After so many years of silence, letting me think my mother had deserted me, Mamina was now excusing her. Death was the ultimate justification. Or was it? I felt my eyes narrowing and my face tightening, but managed to ask hoarsely, "How old was she?"

"Twenty-something. But some die young. Your father—"

"But Dad was in a war! He died in combat."

"In combat?"

It sounded like a question.

"He was deployed to Angola, wasn't he?" I asked.

"Yes. I never saw his body."

"I know."

My father was buried in Africa, Mamina had told me, though she didn't talk much about him either.

"My daughter died young too," she muttered.

"She had cancer! Was my mother sick?"

"Well—she could have been."

Mamina sounded distraught, but the heat of rage that I tried in vain to suppress rose to my head, sharpening my tongue.

"Why didn't you ever talk about her?" I demanded. "Even Dolores said that Tania loved me, and I didn't believe her!"

"What else did Dolores say?" Mamina asked.

"Not much." *Because you never approved of my visits to her,* I thought. I trailed my hand over the bed and found the sling. "You didn't say she had gone back to the United States and returned either." I willed my voice to sound casual, but in the end, a wave of anger overcame me. "Why did you hide all this from me, Mamina?"

She patted my hand. "*Niña,* calm down, please. When I moved here, you were too young to have a conversation about . . . anything. Then Joaquín died. You had already lost both parents and you weren't even four years old! I thought it wiser to wait until you were older."

"But we didn't talk about it when I was older."

"You never asked."

I had asked! Or not? Not often enough? Not loudly enough?

Mamina shifted in the hammock and closed her eyes.

"I'm going to check on the crew," I said and left, still mad, not even waiting for an answer.

*You could have told me about the chicken, if nothing else!*

DOWNSTAIRS, SANTOS HAD UNHOOKED the lamp from the bronze chain and removed the chain from the ceiling. The blue pendant glass, separated from the holder, stood on the coffee table. It was bigger than it seemed from afar, around thirty inches wide and fifteen tall, all covered in a thick coat of dirt.

"It needs to be rewired," Santos said. "And a new light bulb. That's all. This lamp is a work of art. So is the plafond." He pointed to a round piece of the ceiling where the chain had been affixed.

I must have seen the ornate fixture a hundred times without paying attention to the gold trimming or the pink flowers and blue leaves carved into it. They were remarkable, indeed.

"First Candela, crazy about the Art Deco stuff, and now you guys with the lamp," I mused. "Since you all keep telling me how pretty this place is, I'm starting to see it."

"You were too close to notice," Santos said. "Sometimes a little distance is all it takes to shed a new light on the subject."

# CHAPTER FIFTEEN

*June 16th, 1986*

*Lo prometido es deuda. I had promised "amazing news," and here it is. Two days ago, I had an ultrasound done. It confirmed what I already knew: I am two months pregnant! My OB-GYN, a lovely lady from Holguín (an eastern province), put me on a monthly checkout schedule after asking a million questions. I'm not sure if the legal age of consent here is sixteen, eighteen or twenty so I bumped mine a little, just in case. She believed me. It's good to be a big-boned girl.*

THE PREGNANCY HAD BEEN sort of accidentally on purpose. Though Sarah had known Joaquín for only a few months, she was convinced that they belonged together. She couldn't imagine loving anyone else. Their relationship had been so solid since day one!

Once she was sure, she couldn't wait to tell him. She made supper—ground beef that had just come to the *carnicería*, fried plantains and white rice—and set the table with the beautiful china they had used for the party. She found two silver candelabras and put candles in them. Lo had advised her to reserve them in case of blackouts, which still happened occasionally, but Sarah decided to display them. The occasion merited it.

She kept the news until they were done with dessert—cheese and coconut flan—then took Joaquín's hands in hers and whispered, "I think you'd make a fantastic dad."

"I don't really like chil—" he started to say absentmindedly but noticed her smile. "You mean you are . . . ?"

He looked so serious, almost angry, that it scared her, but she managed to reply, "Yes, *mi amor.*"

"But we haven't even discussed it!"

"I know. It just happened."

There wasn't much to discuss, was it? After Joaquín recovered from the shock, he hugged her and relaxed a bit. The next day, still in bed, he kissed her and said he would love to have a baby boy. Sarah would have preferred a *compañerita*, but a boy who looked just like his dad would be a great addition to the family as well.

What would her parents say of her pregnancy? Likely nothing good. Her mother in particular was a tough nut to crack, though Sarah admitted that she was at least partly to blame for their frequent arguments. They had totally different personalities and couldn't help but clash.

Her mother was too uptight, she thought, with her penchant for bake sales and polka-dotted dresses. While some of her friends' moms happily went to Madonna concerts and encouraged their children to become "fully actualized," hers attended the Church of Christ and imposed strict curfews on her. On the other hand, her father, for his stern exterior, was a lot more agreeable. The truth was that Sarah had him wrapped around her little finger, as her mother often complained. Now Sarah could hear her mother asking (using that *mom's voice* that always made her bristle): *Didn't we raise you better than that?*

A way to sweeten the pill (because of course she would tell them, sooner or later) was getting married. Even if marriage was a "bourgeois" institution, like some of her most liberal friends believed. She didn't care. A proper wedding was a must. Joaquín hadn't mentioned it (as he should have!) so she started to work on it. The idea of having revolutionary nuptials was too exciting. They would invite El Caballo, and he might show up!

She already knew where the ceremony was likely to take place. One afternoon she had gone with Lo to Old Havana. Lo had been told that flashlights had "come" to a store located at a shopping mall called La Manzana de Gómez. It was her turn to buy, and she had the right coupon for it. Sarah eagerly agreed to go with her.

They took a bus from Miramar to Paseo del Prado. On their way to La Manzana, they passed in front of an ornate white building. Sarah peeked in and saw a long marble staircase and a crystal chandelier twice as big as Villa Santa Marta's. A couple had come out and was walking toward an old red Ford with blue-and-yellow balloons attached. The bride wore a white chiffon dress with a long train. The groom, a black suit and tie. A crowd followed, throwing something at them. Passersby stopped to watch and cheer.

"This is El Palacio de Los Matrimonios," Lo said, noticing Sarah's interest. "The place to get hitched in Havana."

She winked, and Sarah winked back.

"What are people tossing at them?"

"Rice. For good fortune."

Sarah envisioned herself and Joaquín leaving the Palacio enveloped in a cloud of roses and rice. (She added the roses for romantic reasons.) Her heart started beating happily. Lo pinched her arm.

"I will stand by you on your wedding day," she promised.

"You think that Joaquín will . . . ?" Sarah asked, blushing.

"I don't have any doubts," Lo said firmly. "He adores you!"

They went on walking. The people, the large and colorful revolutionary posters attached to lampposts, even the bronze lions that flanked Paseo del Prado seemed to smile at Sarah, and everything, in turn, made her want to smile. She loved Old Havana, her friend and her Cuban life.

La Manzana de Gómez turned out to be a four-story building that occupied an entire block—blocks were also called *manzanas*, Lo explained, so it actually meant "Gómez's block." It had been built in the early 1900s by José Gómez Mena, a wealthy Cuban businessman whose name still appeared engraved on the granite floor. On the ground floor were a pharmacy called La Central, a shoe store and many other shops.

"I'm going to try to find aspirins," Lo said when they got to La Central. "This isn't the pharmacy assigned to us, but I know someone here."

While Lo talked to her friend, Sarah stood in front of a huge fish tank that had been set up so it could be seen from inside and outside the pharmacy. Orange goldfish swam leisurely among green algae and swaying plants. A brown pleco with white spots came from the bottom of the tank and stuck to the glass, seemingly watching Sarah with its huge bright eyes. She thought of the waves slapping on Pacific Beach shores . . .

"I got the aspirins!" Lo took her by the arm, making her jump. "Now let's go get the flashlights."

They walked around the shopping arcade. Two inner diagonal streets crossed the building. The shop they were looking for was inside, and Sarah stopped often to glance at the other establishments. There was a toy store named La Concha de Venus but it was closed. Well, she would come back another day.

Lo led her to a small store with mostly empty shelves. A clerk was reading the newspaper *Granma*, his feet propped up on a chair.

"Sorry, comrades, I sold all the flashlights this morning," he announced as soon as they came in.

"When will you get more?" Sarah asked.

The clerk gave her a surprised look. Had her accent shocked him? she wondered. Or her question?

"One never knows, comrade," he answered with a shrug.

Lo didn't seem too disappointed.

"It's just a temporary inconvenience," she said. "Soon, we will have flashlights available all over the country, I promise! That's why we're building socialism."

Sarah tried to keep a serious countenance. Sometimes Lo sounded as if she had a direct line to El Caballo.

"Now let's get something to eat at Salón H. You will like it."

Salón H was a cafeteria located in one of the inner streets. After waiting outside for ten minutes—there were fifteen people in line—they were ushered in and shown a table. The marble top had the letter *H* etched in the center. A mirror covered one of the walls. Sarah was pleased with her reflection. She looked dewy and radiant, wearing another of Fredesbinda's creations—a spaghetti-strap white-and-pink dress.

"You're so pretty, *chica*," Lo said, elbowing her.

Sarah, who had never considered herself particularly beautiful, nodded and accepted the compliment. Cuba had changed her, and in more than one way.

It took a while for a waitress in a black-and-white uniform to come to their table. She recited the menu, which consisted of cheese sandwiches, mortadella sandwiches and a soft drink called *materva*.

"Two of everything for each of us," said Lo.

"We can only serve one sandwich per person," the waitress answered bluntly.

Sarah ordered cheese and Lo, mortadella. They were small, more like mini sandwiches, but yummy. The *materva* drink had a nice sweetish flavor.

"When I was little, my mom would bring me to La Manzana for my birthday," Lo said wistfully. "The place was always

bustling. At La Concha de Venus, she once bought me a porcelain doll. And the sandwiches they sold here! Ham and cheese,
with pickles. Hamburgers too. And mango smoothies! Ah, I
still miss them."

That was the first time Sarah had heard talk about prerevo-
lutionary times with a rosy tint of nostalgia.

# CHAPTER SIXTEEN

While Suárez changed the tarp in the master bedroom, I went to the library and replaced the mason jar, which was filled to the brim, with a metal bucket. The beam was visibly rotted, and the leak had left a zigzagging yellow stain across the wall. Fortunately, the furniture was away from it.

A low and wide bookcase contained only magazines: *Selecciones del Reader's Digest*, *Bohemia*, *Mujeres* and *Sputnik*. Above, a framed painting of a stern-looking woman with fiery eyes hung from the wall. She wore a round black hat with no brim. I had no idea who she was, but it wasn't hard to imagine her as the witch neighbors talked about. I had asked Mamina, but she knew nothing about the people portrayed in the many paintings that adorned Villa Santa Marta.

"They were all here when I moved in, and I had no one to ask," she told me once. "Those ugly paintings were the least of my worries then!"

A miniature brass Eiffel Tower and a heart-shaped glass ashtray sat on a pedestal desk. They were dusty and speckled with dead flies. The desk used to be in the middle of the room, but Mamina had pushed it to a corner so she could sweep the floor faster. I pulled open the top drawer and a rancid smell rose from inside, mingling with the musty odor that the walls and the beam gave off. The drawer was empty.

Having helped Mamina clean the room many times, I knew it well and wasn't looking for anything in particular. Our conversation still swirled around in my mind. *She took good care of you. You were sick and she was so worried . . .*

Why had she waited so long to tell me all that? But then, it could have been my fault. As a child, I had refrained from mentioning my mother, afraid to hurt Mamina's feelings and believing that *she* was the one who didn't want to talk about it. The "Yankee" incident didn't help either. No wonder Mamina thought I didn't care! No wonder she avoided the unpleasant topic. A simple woman with little formal education, my grandma had handled a difficult situation the best she could. She had taken care of me, raised me as her own daughter and given up a lot for my sake. It was unfair to blame her after so many years. And yet, I couldn't help but feel she had withheld some facts about my mother that she could have easily shared with me, no matter if I asked or not . . .

There was another bookcase, taller and narrower. It held grubby, heavy volumes that looked like they hadn't been opened, much less dusted, in a long time. I glanced distractedly at the titles. One struck me as odd: *Diario de una hechicera*, written in golden letters over a purple background, with *María Estela Sotolongo* in smaller letters below. I took it out, thinking that Candela would get a kick out of a sorceress's diary as she fancied herself a sorceress of sorts.

The other books in the row collapsed. A cloud of dust mites and spiderwebs rose up, making me sneeze. The *diario* was a thick manuscript with leather binding and typed pages. Vintage, for sure. I set it aside and started to put the books back in their place. *The Secret Doctrine; Theosophy: An Introduction to the Supersensible Knowledge of the World and the Destination of Man; The Book of Thoth.* Uf. I couldn't believe that anybody had read such dull-sounding titles.

A folded piece of paper slipped from *The Secret Doctrine* and fluttered to the floor. I picked it up. It was a marriage certificate, dated October 11, 1986, between Joaquín Montero Santurce and Tania Rojas Pérez. Holding the document with shaky hands, I stared at my mother's signature. It was a scribble. Her date of birth was 1962; place of birth, Havana, Cuba; occupation, housewife. Dolores's name appeared at the bottom as one of the witnesses.

Goose bumps rippled across my skin. Who had left the marriage certificate inside *The Secret Doctrine*? Mamina? This wasn't the kind of book she would have read. My father? Or my mother herself? My thoughts moved like quicksilver on a mirror. There might be something else around, like pictures of her and clues to her origin or whereabouts!

I took all the books out of the shelves, examined them one by one and did the same with the magazines. An hour later I was covered in cobwebs but empty-handed. Still, I had already found a treasure and was grateful for it. But I couldn't, for the life of me, figure out how the marriage certificate had ended up in that unlikely place.

INSTEAD OF ASKING MAMINA outright, I decided to surprise—or rather ambush—her. The tactic made me feel somewhat ashamed, but though I didn't want to admit it, not even to myself, I wasn't sure I believed everything she had told me anymore. Her favorite saying was *en boca cerrada no entran moscas.* Flies never had much of a chance to get inside her mouth, considering how closely shut she had kept it!

Ferradaz and her crew promised to return the next day and work on the leaks.

"But this is just a temporary measure," she said. "Seriously, you should get your grandma out of here before it gets worse."

As if it were so easy!

"Could the house be saved?" I asked.

"It could, but I wouldn't attempt to do it with my small crew. I'd have to put together another, and you may need to bring some construction materials from Miami. Besides, the place has to be empty. No people, no furniture, nothing."

AFTER THE COAST WAS clear, Mamina came out of her room. I followed her to the kitchen.

"¡*Mira!*" I said, opening the envelope and displaying its content in front of her.

She gave me a blank stare.

"What is it, *niña*? I can't tell without my eyeglasses."

"My parents' marriage certificate."

She seemed genuinely surprised.

"Where was it?"

"In the library. Did you know . . . ?"

She shook her head no, opened the refrigerator and took out a jar with mango jam.

"Do you think my dad hid it there?" I insisted. "Or *she* did?"

She dropped a generous spoonful of jam into a dish.

"I have no clue, Merceditas." She paused and looked around. "Where did your friend put the crackers? Ah, here they are! They go well with the jam."

"I also found a manuscript about witchcraft up there," I said. "The *bruja* stories may be true after all."

"Maybe that woman was a witch, maybe she wasn't." Mamina added a few crackers to the dish and placed it on the table with more force than necessary. "What do I know? I never met any of these people, and I don't like to gossip!"

After munching on jam and crackers, Mamina went back to

her room. I made myself a sandwich and decided to pay a visit to Dolores. She had been closer to my mother than anyone I knew.

Dolores lived next door—actually, the two houses were separated by enormous front yards. She was considered the old-timer of our block, the only one who had been there since the eighties. There was a steady exodus through the nineties, during the special period, and all the neighbors who had once met my parents had left Miramar or even the country.

Whenever I asked about Tania, Dolores always answered my questions and did her best to describe the woman who had been friends with her for around three years. I remembered that Mamina had discouraged me from visiting our neighbor, claiming I was just "pestering" her. Now I wondered if there might have been another reason to keep us apart.

# CHAPTER SEVENTEEN

*July 24th, 1986*

*So many exciting things are happening! Building facades have been repainted and potholes filled during the last three weeks. The reason is the carnavales. Which aren't carnivals, but a revolutionary all-encompassing holiday. The original carnavales used to take place in February, but the date was changed to July 26th to honor the attack on the Moncada Garrison that sparked the revolution. Fidel rolled Christmas and Mardi Gras into one big fat summer fête timed out to overlap with the end of the sugarcane harvest.*

*¡Viva el 26 de julio!*

HAVANA MIGHT'VE BEEN GETTING a makeover but one thing remained unchanged: waiting lines. *La cola del pan, la cola de las papas, la cola del café.* People stood for hours to buy their monthly rations of bread, potatoes, coffee and everything else.

It was precisely in a *cola*—the coffee queue—where Sarah had a strange encounter. She was waiting outside the grocery store among many other neighbors. It was around 4 P.M., not the best time for people like her, who had no *plan jaba*.

But coffee had just "come," and Dolores had advised her to get it as soon as possible because there wasn't always enough for everyone.

"It's not like you lose your right to buy it," she said. "But you'd have to wait until next month."

That would be a problem, as Joaquín loved his morning coffee. Sarah was patiently standing behind an old guy when someone bumped into her. She turned around and saw a woman almost as tall as her, with short hair and a defiant expression.

"Excuse me," Sarah said, thinking it could have been her fault. After all, the *cola* spilled onto the sidewalk, bothering passersby.

The woman said nothing and remained there for a while. When she finally left, Sarah heard her mutter something that sounded like *hija de puta*. A couple of neighbors, who had been watching, shook their heads. It puzzled Sarah—had she offended the woman by being in the wrong place?—but the *cola* got moving and she soon forgot the incident.

ON JULY 22ND JOAQUÍN was assigned a booth to enjoy the *carnavales*. The booths were built alongside the seawall, and their occupants had a good view of the ornamented floats that paraded up and down Malecón Avenue every night, from July 17th to the 27th.

The floats reminded Sarah of the Pasadena Rose Parade, only with sexier dancers and much louder music. They belonged to government entities like the Ministry of Transportation and the Ministry of Agriculture, mass organizations like the Federation of Cuban Women and some workplaces. Music played non-stop with popular bands perched on high wooden platforms. People threw multicolored paper streamers called *serpentinas* to the floats and each other.

LO HAD TOLD SARAH that *carnavales* used to be presided over by a queen and her princesses, but Cuba being a communist country, royalty had given way to astronomy. There had been an *estrella* and her *luceros* for a few years.

"Like the big star and the small stars, see? But the competition was fierce, with aspiring 'stars' pulling each other's hair and catfighting in the most indecent manner. Now there is no hierarchy, just pretty young women who dance and throw confetti and *serpentinas* from the floats."

The girls were indeed pretty. And they all danced so well! Cubans had an innate sense of rhythm, a way of moving the hips and the pelvis that would have put Elvis to shame.

Sarah and Joaquín shared the booth with another officer and his family. Fireworks boomed over the Morro Castle. Food trucks parked nearby sold ham croquettes and cheese sandwiches. There was also Pío Pío fried chicken, which came in small cardboard boxes and tasted just like Kentucky Fried Chicken. Other trucks advertised Matusalén and Paticruzado rum at two pesos a shot. Beer was even cheaper. Everything was highly organized, and *colas* were small. El Caballo had likely applied his magic touch to the event.

The floats were followed by troupes of dancers. Sarah's favorite was Los Guaracheros de Regla, from a little town across the Havana Bay. Then came the *muñecones*, Disneyland-esque figures, though more creepy than childlike, which threw hard candy toward the booths.

Sarah and Joaquín left relatively early, around midnight. When they walked to the bus stop, discarded *serpentinas*, bound into bundles, were carried by the breeze all over the streets.

"This was fabulous," Sarah said, hugging Joaquín.

He beamed.

"I'm so happy you enjoyed the evening."

They had gotten the booth for just one night. The next day

was too hot, and Sarah felt slightly dizzy. They watched the parade on TV, a black-and-white Admiral that Joaquín kept in the master bedroom. He said that he hoped to receive a Russian Electron soon.

Around seven thirty, Sarah went downstairs to make dinner. While crossing the living room, she looked out the big picture window. There was no particular reason; it was almost instinctual. Outside the wrought-iron fence stood the same woman who had pushed her in the grocery store queue a few days back.

# CHAPTER EIGHTEEN

Dolores was outside, pruning her roses. Divorced since 2004, she had taken early retirement and become a private tutor to help supplement her small teacher pension, preparing students for the University of Havana entrance exams. She exchanged her ration-card cigarettes for rice and beans—and the allotted rum bottles for sugar and eggs to make *merenguitos* that she later sold on the sly. An enterprising lady, and the neighborhood expert in black market techniques.

"Merceditas, what a surprise!" she exclaimed. "Are you sneaking up on me? I didn't know that you were coming, *chica*!"

Her hair had grayed in a chic sort of way, and her attitude was, as usual, a happy mix of motherly and mischievous.

"This was a last-minute trip."

"Glad you're back!"

She cleaned her hands, put the pruning shears away and hugged me.

"I heard Mamina fell down the stairs. Why didn't she call me? Doesn't she know that *no hay mejor hermano que el vecino más cercano?*"

Dolores had been keeping an eye on Mamina since I left, but my grandma didn't appreciate her concern. In fact, it bothered her. She never bought into the notion that one's closest neighbor was like a beloved sibling.

"You know how she is."

She nodded.

"Let's go inside. It's going to rain again. *Carajo* with this weather!"

Though not as fancy as Villa Santa Marta, Dolores's house had some "vintage" touches, like a gilded-framed mirror and a carved rocking chair, my favorite since I was a child dropping by unannounced. She seemed happy to see me, but her eyes kept darting from my face to the street.

"Are you busy?" I asked. "I can come back later."

"No, *mija*. I'm waiting for a woman who wants me to tutor her son. But they live in Alamar. I doubt she'll come today."

A thunder rippled through the sky and heavy drops of rain began to fall.

First we talked about the approaching storm. Dolores was concerned about her house. It was newer and in better shape than Villa Santa Marta but needed repairs too.

"I'm afraid to have that roof inspected," she admitted. "But I'm going to have to."

I gave her Ferradaz's number, then inhaled deeply and cracked my knuckles.

"What's up, Merceditas?" Dolores asked. "You didn't come here to talk about construction work, did you?"

Ah, how well she knew me! I related my conversation with Mamina and concluded, "You also said Tania was a good mother. Now, I'm not convinced but—"

Dolores's eyes grew sad.

"It's easy to judge. Not that I blame you. You have reasons to resent the way she left. But she might have had her own reasons. Life's complicated."

No one would argue that.

"I'd like to find her, but I don't know where to start. What do you know about her family?"

A dark blue car passed in front of the house and slowed down a bit, then kept going.

"Not much. She never mentioned them."

"What about childhood friends and classmates?"

"Once, when my brother traveled to Mexico, Tania gave him a letter to mail from there," Dolores said. "It was addressed to a guy. I asked her if he was a former boyfriend, and she laughed and said no, just a buddy."

"What if it *was* a boyfriend?"

"I doubt it. She and Joaquín were smitten with each other."

My parents had been together a little over three years. Married people didn't stay "smitten" for a long time, in my experience. The train of thought reminded me of the marriage certificate.

"Why hide it?" Dolores asked, puzzled, after I told her about my finding.

"And in the library of all places! Weird, isn't it?"

She tilted her head to the side.

"I don't see the point . . . Maybe Mamina shoved the envelope inside a book while cleaning, not knowing what it was?"

It was possible, and neither here nor there. I tried to think of questions it had never occurred to me to ask.

"What did my mother do before she came to Cuba?"

"She went to school, I assume, because she was too young to have had a career."

"Not so young. She was born in 1962, so she was twenty-four when she left the United States."

"Nonsense! Tania couldn't have been older than twenty. She had a childish air about her. She was big and tall, and that fooled people. But not me."

"Why would she lie about her age?"

She gave an almost imperceptible shrug.

"Well, what did she do *here*?"

"She took care of the house, which is a full-time job. One day she asked me, 'Where can I find a vacuum cleaner, Lo?' Imagine, a vacuum cleaner in Havana!"

"She called you Lo?"

"Yes. Didn't I ever tell you?"

"Not that I remember."

A soft breeze brought the scent of roses with it inside. Americans like to shorten names. What had my mother called me? Mercy, like my husband used to do? Merceditas? Mer?

"Now that we are on the subject, what about her real name?"

"I was tempted to ask, but didn't want to sound intrusive. Now I wish I had. Sometimes she looked so vulnerable, so lost—"

A thorn pricked me between my ribs. But the eternal question came back.

"Why didn't she take me with her if she loved me as much as you and Mamina say?"

"That wasn't easy, Merceditas. She would have had to get your father's permission, and he wouldn't have given it. Being so young and inexperienced, she might have been afraid to confront him."

"Was he much older?"

"Ten years, or more. Like I said, she was *very* young."

The older soldier and the college student. The image was off-putting—and familiar in a warped sort of way. I was younger than Nolan and had deferred to him often, letting him make most household decisions, even when I didn't agree. After all, we were in *his* country. He was supposed to know better. But I would have never relinquished a child to him!

"Did she have any enemies, Dolores? People who could have accused her of being a counterrevolutionary or"—the very thought was sickening—"harmed her?"

Dolores brushed a strand of hair from her face.

"Tania didn't interact enough with people to make enemies. She spent a lot of time alone and had few acquaintances."

"Do you remember any?"

"There was an old couple, the Barbeitos. She visited them often. But they left the country many years ago."

Dolores paused. Her expression was hard to read. Was she smiling or grimacing?

"And a woman called Valentina," she added. "Tania went out with her a lot because Valentina had a car and drove her around. She was Russian."

"What was she doing in Cuba?" I asked, intrigued.

"I don't know. There were many Russians here; we called them 'our Soviet comrades.'" Dolores sighed. "She probably left too. Most did after the Eastern bloc collapsed."

"Were you friends with her too?"

"Not really. Valentina didn't like me. I was a different person then. Well, we all were."

Her lips quivered a little. Maybe it pained her to recall a time when she was young, still married and probably happier than now.

"Did I ever see her? And the old couple?"

"Yes, many times. The Barbeitos babysat you. They used to live in Catalina's house."

Ah, if I could access the secret vault where my childhood memories were stored! But it was locked, impervious to my efforts to open it.

The rain had stopped, but the sky was still cloudy and gray. The car I had seen before passed by, slowly, almost too slowly, and stopped in front of my house. I got up to take a better look at it.

"Wait, I just remembered an incident with Berta, Joaquín's ex!" Dolores said. "She came over and made a scene once. It scared me because she used to carry a gun."

I sat down again.

"Could she . . . ?"

"No, no! Joaquín had broken up with her way before he met Tania. Berta was just the jealous type. Anyway, she got over it. She married another guy and had a daughter with him. I haven't seen her in a long time, but she lives nearby."

"Where?"

The blue car was still in front of Villa Santa Marta, as if waiting for someone. It looked new, or at least newer than most vehicles that ran in Havana.

"On Third Street, in the Cubo Amarillo."

"Ah, yes."

The building, shaped as a cube and with a bright yellow façade, stuck out among all the other houses.

"Mamina told me that my mother once traveled back to the United States," I said after a while. "Did you know that?"

Dolores raised her eyebrows.

"Ah, I always suspected it! She didn't tell me, but once disappeared for a few days and came back with clothes, food and stuff for the house, like a microwave and a small color TV. She said something about having to attend some political meetings. Bah! As if I didn't know that she wasn't into such things!"

*What* had she been into? Not politics. Not work either, since she hadn't had a job. What did she care about? I still found it hard to believe that she spent all her time looking after me or going out with her Russian friend.

"Do you think that Mamina knows more than she lets on?" I asked, in a sharp tone that surprised even myself. "She didn't like it when I came to your house, way back. Sometimes I wonder . . ."

Dolores kept quiet for a few seconds.

"Mamina can't know much about Tania," she said at last. "She lived in La Coloma then and seldom came to visit. As for not wanting you to come over, she has always been very private. She just . . . well, she doesn't seem to like people. But I doubt she would lie to you or withhold anything of importance."

A lock of her hair fell into her eyes. Dolores, "Lo," wouldn't lie to me either, would she? Like Mamina, she was an honest person. I clung to that certainty.

"You will find your mom, Merceditas." Dolores gave me an encouraging smile. "Don't lose hope."

I thanked her and left soon afterward. The blue car was still in front of Villa Santa Marta. It reminded me of the one that had been in the same spot the night before. I wanted to see who was inside. Plus it wouldn't be a bad idea to pass by the yellow cube and talk to that Berta.

# CHAPTER NINETEEN

*August 11th, 1986*

*My new name is Tania Rojas Pérez. Being officially a Cuban citizen will allow me to have a regular life and do many more things. (Like, ahem, getting married. I'm still working on it.) We had a ceremony to celebrate my socialist baptism at the Communist Party headquarters in Centro Habana, with a proud Joaquín by my side, his commander, Lo and some other comrades. It was fantastic!*

WHAT SARAH DIDN'T MENTION, because it embarrassed her so much, was how she had almost ruined the ceremony by asking if her first name had anything to do with Patty Hearst. Somehow, she had thought that was funny. All she got were blank stares.

"Sorry." She started stuttering. "I just . . . well, it's like . . . the Symbionese Liberation Army . . ."

"Is that an African guerrilla group?" Joaquín's boss asked.

The absurdity of the question made Sarah feel even more self-conscious. Was it possible that these fervent communists had never heard of the ultra-revolutionary organization?

"You are named after Tania La Guerrillera, an Argentine-German *compañera* who fought alongside Che Guevara," Lo instructed her.

Sarah resolved to find out more about her namesake, but it baffled her how little Cubans knew about American current events, including the ERA and the civil rights movement in general. Wasn't it all connected? When she told the *compañeros* about the UFW and César Chávez, they looked at her with distrust.

"Social activism in the entrails of the monster?" Joaquín's boss said, incredulous. "That can't be!"

She thought of bringing up her activities with the Sanctuary movement but in the end decided not to. The less she talked about her former life, the better. She did bring up the meetings to discuss *The Communist Manifesto*. Nobody seemed impressed.

"I am also friends with members of Compañeros de Cuba, an anti-embargo group," she added, as a last resort.

"Anti-blockade, comrade."

To their credit, they were more aware of what was going on in El Salvador. El Caballo and the higher-ups were probably well informed, Sarah concluded, but common people had too much on their plates to care. After all, she couldn't blame them. What did *she* know about Cuba a year ago?

During the event she met a *compañera* who was traveling to the "entrails of the monster" to attend a cultural activity. She agreed to mail a letter to Rob from New York. By then, some of Sarah's letters had gotten lost. The Cuban postal system was notoriously slow, even for national correspondence, so she jumped at the chance to bypass it.

A FEW DAYS AFTER the naming ceremony, Sarah was in the kitchen making the usual pot of rice for dinner. She had finished cleaning the countertops and sweeping the living room floor. There was always something to do in the house, and she often lost track of time. The cuckoo clock was cute but quite unreliable. It read three fifteen, but it was a quarter to four. Sarah made sure the rice had enough water left and lowered the heat before going upstairs.

She took a shower, put on makeup and spritzed Red Moscow over her hair. Standing in front of the dresser mirror, she looked distractedly at the porcelain tray and all the silver ornaments that she had cleaned recently with lemon and bicarbonate. It made her laugh when Joaquín called her *burguesita*. His surroundings were nothing if not "bourgeois!"

She had finally figured out that the house had been given to him with furniture and everything. Lo, who had moved to Miramar after Joaquín, didn't know the previous owners, but the Barbeitos must have met them. Sarah made a mental note to ask Elena what the *M* engraved in the china was supposed to mean, and who had used those delicate dresser pieces before she did.

She opened the first drawer and took out her American passport and her new Cuban ID card. Though the two photos had been taken within the last eight months, they appeared to portray different women. The American passport obviously belonged to a girl—wide-eyed, fresh-faced and a little startled. The Cuban ID card had been issued to a more responsible, serious-looking person. Her hair was shorter and she carried an edge. Or she had tried to look like she carried an edge. Truth is, she had made a big effort to look older. The frown helped. So did the tight lips—an expression copied from her mother when she was in a bad mood.

Her mother . . . Her dad. Oh, she missed them. Now she was happy that she had kept writing them those short notes. Rob mailed them from different places (sometimes Tijuana, sometimes San Francisco, so they wouldn't suspect where she really was). They knew she was doing fine, and it made her feel better about the whole thing.

She would go back to see them. After her child was born, because she wanted to have a Cuban baby, and so did Joaquín. Not that they had ever discussed *that* either. She had committed to living here, with him, like a Cuban, so the baby's nationality was taken for granted. But she longed to return home for a visit, no matter how much she loved Joaquín.

A noise came from the living room. She took a last look at herself—the shiny hair, the pink lips—and left the master bedroom in a hurry. The door closed itself after her with a loud bang. When she got to the first floor, there was nobody there. Joaquín usually arrived at five-fifteen if he borrowed a jeep from the unit. If not, it would take him until six or six-thirty, depending on the buses.

Sarah walked around the first floor, wondering where the noise had come from. Weird sounds and even weirder odors came from closed rooms at odd times. The library often smelled like ammonia, or something musky and earthy. Joaquín had promised to inspect the whole building over the weekend but didn't appear concerned.

"It's an old house," he had said, shrugging.

Sarah knew about old houses. Her grandmother Pauline had lived in a Victorian home built in the early twenties. But, except for some crackling and popping from the hardwood floors, it had been a quiet, pleasant place. Granted, it had been well kept, while Villa Santa Marta . . .

Something squeaked behind the piano. A mouse. Or worse, a rat. The piano hadn't been moved in years, and Sarah didn't dare to attempt it by herself, especially not in her condition. She opened the door and waited for Joaquín outside.

The excuse she gave herself was that the fresh air would do her good. In truth, she was ashamed of being afraid. Because honestly . . . afraid of what? Miramar was likely the safest neighborhood in the city, with so many embassies and uniformed armed guards all over. And she didn't believe in ghosts, did she?

# CHAPTER TWENTY

The blue car was a Kia. The trunk had a sticker with the Havanautos logo. Havanautos, a government-run rental car company, charged dollars and catered to foreigners. There was a woman behind the wheel. I couldn't see her face, but her hair was shoulder-length and dark brown. The woman held up a camera with a telescopic lens and was snapping pictures of Villa Santa Marta.

"Hey!" I yelled. "*¿Qué carajos* you think you're doing?"

Startled, she dropped the camera on her lap and drove away. Dolores, who had seen the whole scene from her garden, joined me.

"That car's been here before," she said.

The lines around her mouth were tight.

"When?"

"A week ago. I saw it circling the block and thought it was someone looking for a *casa particular*."

"Are you sure it's the same car?"

"If not, it was awfully similar. It was blue and had a Havanautos sticker, I remember that much."

Dolores paid attention to details that most people dismissed or simply didn't notice.

"And the driver?" I asked.

"A woman. Middle-aged or so. Probably a tourist."

"Yeah, that's what I thought."

We said our goodbyes again, and Dolores went back to her house. My throat closed, though there wasn't any logical reason to be nervous. It was not the first time that strangers had taken photos, with or without permission, of Villa Santa Marta. The house was frequently featured in American magazines as an example of Havana's early Art Deco. Other residences, like Cubo Amarillo, were also mentioned as architectural oddities or something of that sort. Most neighbors didn't mind the attention, but Mamina was known to yell at the onlookers when they got too close for comfort.

The woman in the blue car might have worked for an architecture magazine or just had an interest in old houses. But she didn't need to run away. After all, taking pictures wasn't illegal. And if she was the same person I had seen before, why had she been there *at night?*

I kept walking. A couple of houses that, like Villa Santa Marta, needed a paint job, plastering and more, had Cuban flags outside. A *SOCIALISMO O MUERTE* banner had been conspicuously glued on the grocery store window. The patriotic display surprised me until I remembered that the next day was a CDR's anniversary. In the early nineties, people would get together for the celebration. Even Mamina, despite her usual reserve, helped make *caldosa* and mingled with our neighbors. But the parties had stopped several years before I left Cuba. Few people belonged to the CDR, and even fewer had time, energy or enthusiasm for revolutionary shindigs.

I ALMOST DIDN'T RECOGNIZE the building. The façade had been repainted in tasteful earth tones and a room had been added on the roof, so it wasn't cubic anymore. The door had a brass handle that looked new. I rang the bell, and a young man opened it right away.

"Good afternoon!" he said in English, smiling widely. "Welcome, *señora*."

"Thanks," I answered, confused. How did he know me? I certainly didn't know him.

"My name is Yunelsys," he said. "Nice to meet you. Please, come in!"

The living room was fairly nice. There were two oversize stuffed chairs around a glass table, a red leather couch and an air-conditioning unit.

"Well, lady, let me show you around," he went on, still in English. "We have—"

"I'm Cuban, like you," I replied in Spanish.

He grimaced, disappointed.

"Sorry, I thought . . . But do you need a place to stay?"

It dawned on me that the former yellow cube had been turned into a *casa particular*, a private accommodation for foreigners. That was the fate of many old Miramar homes. Before meeting Nolan, I had considered taking that route.

"No. I'm Mercedes, Mamina's granddaughter."

His eyes lit up again.

"You're married to an American?"

"I used to be."

He blew out a loud breath.

"*Bueno, chica*, what do you want?"

"I'd like to talk to Berta."

He frowned.

"About what?"

Having gone there on an impulse, I didn't know how to broach the subject. More so with a guy too young to have met my mother or even heard of her.

"It's just something I'm curious about. Ancient history."

"My grandma's sleeping now, and I'd rather not disturb her. She is . . ." He pointed a finger to his head and moved it in a circular motion. "A little bit . . . you know?"

I sighed, thinking of Mamina.

"She had a stroke a year ago. When she's fine, she loves to talk. More so about the past—that's what she likes best. But she may as easily start babbling."

"I understand."

"Come back tomorrow and we'll see how she's doing."

"Okay."

Before I turned around to leave, Yunelsys added quickly, "If you know of foreigners looking for a place to stay, please tell them about me. I have a penthouse and three bedrooms, each with a private bathroom, hot water and color TV. Breakfast included, only fifteen dollars a night!"

"I'll keep it in mind."

On the way home, my eyes scanned the road. Another blue car had stopped on Fourth Street. But when I ran to take a closer look, it was just an old Lada. I was becoming paranoid.

# CHAPTER TWENTY-ONE

*September 27th, 1986*

*Another big celebration is coming up. Cubans have all sorts of them, most related to revolutionary events. September 28th marks the 26th anniversary of the Committees for the Defense of the Revolution. All the neighbors (except for the Barbeitos) are registered CDR members and will likely be at the party. It's a special occasion and Lo has already gotten ingredients to make a dish called caldosa, a communal stew with pork and vegetables that's cooked publicly over a big fire.*

SARAH WAS IN LO'S kitchen, earnestly cutting up potatoes, squash and plantains for the *caldosa*. The party started the evening before the actual date, like a communist Christmas Eve. Outside, Pepe and another guy were building a wooden platform where Lo would stand to deliver a speech that she had just finished writing.

Sarah was still marveling at the amount of food supplies they had gotten. Ten pounds of pork, six chickens and even a big chorizo sausage, the kind she had never seen in the Cuban stores!

"We'll get beer and rum too," Lo said. "If we are lucky, they may send a band. Sometimes, people sing. Improv style, you know."

"After they have had too much beer and rum?"

"That helps!"

When they went out to set the tables in Lo's garden, there were flags everywhere. Neighbors were also displaying posters and plaques with revolutionary slogans. Sarah had tried to hang up one that read FIDEL, ÉSTA ES TU CASA on the front door but couldn't glue or even nail it. The wood was so hard that the hammer bounced back. Villa Santa Marta didn't welcome El Caballo.

The *caldosa* was yummy. Sarah got a good juicy chicken leg with plantains, carrots and potatoes. She didn't drink alcohol but noted that, as Lo had said, beer and Paticruzado rum ran freely. Despite the festive mood, nobody was dressed up for the occasion. Three women wore nearly identical blouses (white with red or blue polka dots) because this was the only fabric that had "come" to the local store. They laughed it off, and Sarah thought that the idea was to discourage individualism. As for the music, there was no band or rum-fueled local talent. Someone brought out a tape recorder and people danced to "Another One Bites the Dust" and other Queen songs, which sounded somewhat out of place.

Sarah got to meet a few more neighbors. Not too many, as there were only five homes on their block—technically, it was over one block because all the houses had a lot of acreage. She attracted attention, and people were shy around her. But not a five-year-old girl in her school uniform—she had performed in a short play about the CDRs.

The girl got close to Sarah and tried to touch the locket that hung from a thin silver chain.

"How pretty! And you're a pretty lady too."

"Thank you, sweetie."

"Are you from the Soviet Union?"

Before Sarah could answer, Joaquín came to her rescue and said that she had come "from a cold and distant place" and was happy to be among Cubans. The truth might have been too shocking for the little girl, he said later.

A few minutes before midnight, Lo stood up and delivered her speech. It was about the history of the CDRs in Miramar and ended with the customary "*Patria o Muerte.*" Sarah joined the enthusiastic chorus that replied:

"*¡Venceremos!*"

All the neighbors stayed until 2 A.M., talking, eating and having revolutionary fun.

*SOL DE BATEY* WAS over. It had a happy ending, with Charito and her lover reunited. There was a new series, a Brazilian telenovela, but Sarah didn't follow it. Though she didn't say it aloud, she was getting tired of Cuban television. If one were to believe it, the United States—the entire western world, for that matter—was a dangerous place to live. Accidents and crimes that happened in the Eastern bloc or Cuba itself were never mentioned. Even the Chernobyl disaster had been barely acknowledged in the *noticiero*, the eight o'clock news that everybody watched. But they were still talking about the Challenger explosion.

There were few radio stations; a very unusual one called Radio Reloj announced the time every minute. Sarah favored musical programs like Hogar del Tango and Nocturno. It was hard for her to understand how the DJs determined which foreign groups and singers were allowed and which were, as Joaquín would put it, "a threat to the revolution." Obviously, Queen had gotten the seal of approval. The Beatles had been forbidden for years, and their songs were seldom played on the radio or in public events. On the other hand, Michael

Jackson was kosher. So was Madonna. Then poor Elvis, whom El Caballo had accused once of corrupting the Cuban youth, was still banned.

"I don't get it," Sarah confided to Lo. "Who actually decides what people can hear?"

Lo shrugged.

"It's complicated. See, Pastor Felipe, a Nocturno DJ, takes risks. He played 'Help' once. People thought he was going to be outed, but nothing happened. He's still there."

"What's the problem with 'Help'?"

They sat in silence for a few seconds. Sarah feared she had asked the wrong question but didn't know what she should apologize for.

"Well, there is a strong anti-American feeling in Cuba," Lo said at last. "No offense intended."

Sarah wasn't offended. She was nonplussed.

"But the Beatles aren't Americans!"

"They sing in the language of the enemy."

"Same with Queen. What's the difference?"

Lo eyed her warily.

"I don't know, *chica*. We don't go around discussing these matters here."

"People should have the freedom—"

This time, Lo looked horrified.

"Don't talk *gusanerías*, please!"

Sarah dropped it, not wanting to upset her friend, and a little scared herself.

She tried to focus on the positive. All in all, people seemed happy here, as the May Day parade, *carnavales* and CDR parties proved. There wasn't total censorship. A popular TV program, *Escriba y Lea*, was led by a panel of college professors who discussed historical events and famous figures. In *Tanda del Domingo*, a local movie critic analyzed well-known foreign films before the showing. Of less quality were the *Películas del Sábado*, back-to-back American flicks played on Saturday nights. Many were violent low-budget films Sarah had never heard of.

She tried to tell Joaquín and Lo that life in "Yankeeland" had little to do with the extreme cases they heard about in the news and saw in the movies, but they acted as if they didn't believe her.

"If these things don't happen, why are people allowed to make movies about them?" Joaquín asked.

Allowed? As Sarah pondered how to refer to freedom of expression without alarming him, he went on, "I understand that plots are not based on true events, but you couldn't make a movie about a guy shooting ten people with an AKM in Havana. That would be impossible in real life!"

Sarah sighed. Ah, these military types! One couldn't reason with them. No point in arguing. They simply had to work through their differences, like her own parents had done. Thankfully, she and Joaquín had a lot of things in common— more than one would expect, considering their vastly different backgrounds.

They both believed that communism was the remedy for all, or at least most social ills. (Well, she didn't know for sure what communism was, but Joaquín was teaching her. And Cuba, with its warm climate, awesome beaches and welcoming people, was a better place to find out than, let's say, China or even faraway Russia.) They were both athletic types and loved to walk. They clicked in bed; he was good in the sack, like Rob would say, and that was not to be taken for granted. Her previous boyfriend had been quite meh in that department. Last but not least, there was a baby on the way. Everything would turn out just right.

Now, when they went out for walks, Joaquín always made

sure to carry a bottle of water for her. He took her by her arm, so concerned when her face got red and she started to sweat.

"Take a sip. You aren't used to this weather."

He even got food for her on the black market, which was very much against his socialist principles. Sometimes he came home with a whole chicken, ground beef, a pound of steaks . . . Once, he showed up with a big red lobster he had bought from a clandestine fisherman in Jaimanitas.

"Because you need to eat for you and the baby," he said earnestly.

He would make a great husband, and a wonderful dad.

"You're lucky because not all Cuban guys are like him," Lo had commented, which made Sarah wonder about Pepe. But her friend, who was quite talkative otherwise, wouldn't share much about her own marriage.

When her husband surprised her with a bouquet of *mariposas* or just when she noticed him watching her adoringly across the dinner table, Sarah felt grateful. She was quite lucky, yes.

# CHAPTER TWENTY-TWO

Mamina was still in her room when I returned home. I went directly to the backyard, my refuge and thinking place since childhood.

There was a mango on the ground, red and juicy, just blown by the wind. I bit into it and the sticky sweet juice filled my mouth, distracting me, at least momentarily, from the worries about Berta, the woman in the blue car and the house itself. It was sprinkling again. The earthy fragrance of the moist soil enveloped me.

*You will find your mom, Merceditas. Don't lose hope.*

My aimless walking brought me to the servants' quarters. The rosebush was still there. It was a striking sight, but those purple flowers, as I remembered, were mean. Once, on Teachers' Appreciation Day, I wanted to bring a bouquet to Nancy, a third-grade teacher who had a soft spot for me, the only motherless girl in her classroom. Reluctantly, Mamina went outside and came back with a deep gash in her right hand. She threw three long-stemmed purple roses on the kitchen table. I hurried to put them in water, but by the next morning they had lost all their petals.

A friend of mine who used to live nearby (she was now in Miami) had once told me that purple roses grew only on graves, and their uncommon hue came from the deceased person's blood. She suggested that the *bruja* could be buried nearby. Even as a child I didn't believe her. Mamina and my teachers had taught me to despise superstition, but I stayed away from the rosebush, just in case. Now it had gotten so big that it blocked the entrance. It looked like a wild variety, with thorns the size of my pinkie.

We had skipped that part of the house during Ferradaz's visit. I decided to come into the servants' quarters and make the place presentable before asking her to look at it. The door had swollen with the rain and gotten stuck. It gave in after a strong push and opened with a cracking sound, like in a bad horror movie. The doorframe was coming apart, and I looked around anxiously, prepared to find more leaks and a number of things that would have to be fixed and cleaned.

To my surprise, there was nothing that needed fixing.

There was nothing. Period. Just a bare room that gave off the scent of abandonment. I dropped what was left of the mango and took a few tentative steps inside.

The floor was covered in dust, so much that I couldn't make out the tile color. My muddy shoes left angry tracks as I walked to a bathroom. The door was ajar, revealing a yellowish toilet and a cracked bathtub. There was a second room, smaller and equally unfurnished. Perplexed, I inspected the place to the extent that such a bland and empty area could be inspected.

I didn't linger. The "energy patters," as Candela would have said, were stale and stifling. On my way out, I squeezed by the rosebush and a thorn pricked the back of my left hand.

"*¡Ay!*"

When I tried to close the door, it collapsed. A piece of wood hit me on the arm. Others fell loudly to the ground. The rosebush, however, remained defiantly unscathed.

"*¡Alabao, mija!*" Mamina cried out from the kitchen. "What are you doing there?"

She had taken the sling off her arm and was standing at the threshold.

"What got into you?" she demanded. "Why did you break that door?"

"I didn't. It was rotten and came apart on its own."

She mumbled something unintelligible.

"Ferradaz was right," I said after a short pause. "The house is falling down."

"That's not part of the house."

"Well, it's on the property."

Mamina turned her attention to the stove.

"Let's see how this thingamajig behaves."

Water was boiling in the new Bialetti. Mamina took out two porcelain demitasses.

"Can you explain—" I started.

"I already told you all I know about your mom!"

I wasn't sure I believed *that*. Her hands shook as she retrieved the coffeepot from the stove.

"No, it's about the servants' quarters."

"I haven't been there in a long time," she said defensively.

"Why not?"

She served the coffee, added a spoonful of sugar to each demitasse and offered me one.

"What for? There's nothing there."

"I saw that. Was there ever any furniture in those rooms?"

We both sat at the table. She brought the cup to her lips and took a careful sip.

"Not too bad, Merceditas, but I prefer my own method."

Was she trying to change the topic? *No, señora.*

"Has it always been empty?"

A flicker of indecision crossed Mamina's face.

"Uh, no. There was a bed once. And a table, some chairs."

"Where are they?"

"I gave them to Sonrisa and her husband when they added another room to the farmhouse."

"When was that?"

"It was . . ."

Mamina stopped. To remember? Or to concoct a story?

"A couple of years after I moved in," she went on, taking another sip of coffee. "You know I've never liked to sell anything from here . . ."

Yes, I knew what she meant. Some nights, I thought that "Martita" stared at me reprovingly, like I was an intruder. That was *her* bedroom. The upright piano and the chandelier that had so much impressed Candela and Nolan weren't really ours. Or were they?

"But since the stuff there had belonged to the help and wasn't very valuable, I figured that nobody was going to claim it," Mamina concluded.

We didn't talk for a few seconds. I searched for a sign that she was telling a lie, but her expression was placid and sincere. A little remote, though she might just be lost in thought.

"You don't need to worry: the owners left, and everything was given to my dad," I told her at last, as I had told myself many times before. "The house was legally his. And now it's yours."

"It could be, but I don't like this place. Too showy, too stuck-up. I am a *guajira* at heart. For me, there's nothing like the countryside, the open skies and the smell of tobacco in the air. The crow of the roosters in the early morning. You used to love it, remember?"

I laughed.

"*Roosters*, Mamina? How could I have loved them? We never had any chickens here!"

"You were such a nervous kid," she went on without

listening to my comments. "It killed my soul to send you to Havana, where so many bad things happen. Those folks—they aren't like us. They have no respect for themselves, their elders or their *dead.*"

The demitasse slipped from her hand and coffee spilled on the table. Mamina didn't notice. She stood up and massaged her bruised arm.

"Joaquín got to be too much like them. It was the city that changed him. Havana is *una mierda!*"

Mamina seldom cursed. Not knowing what to say, I took a napkin and started to wipe the table.

"Do you want me to make more coffee?" I asked.

Mamina glanced at the Bialetti.

"That thing's shit too," she spat.

Without another word, she turned on the television, grabbed a chair and placed it in such a way that I was left facing her back. She started watching an old Argentinean movie and totally ignored me. It was baffling, but, above all, it hurt. I was losing her, like I had lost my parents and Nolan before. Different losses, same old wound.

Not wanting to upset her even more, I went upstairs quietly. My first stop was the master bedroom. The leaks were contained for the time being, but everything was still dirty—embarrassingly so.

I brought wet rags and old newspapers from the kitchen, where Mamina still sat transfixed, watching Carlos Gardel in *El día que me quieras.*

"Are you okay?" I whispered.

She didn't react.

Back in my parents' bedroom, I dusted and wiped the dresser, the mirror and the vanity set. The porcelain tray had the letters *L & C* in green, and stamped below, the words *Haviland and Limoges* in black ink among tiny rose petals and butterflies.

It looked vintage—and cute. There were no storage spaces for rent in Havana, but if we ended up having to vacate the house, Mamina could sell all this. I smiled, thinking we would give Candela first dibs.

There was also a small square glass bottle labeled Kremena—a younger kind of vintage, probably from the eighties. I opened it and had a sniff. The scent was slightly metallic but not unpleasant. It reminded me of L'Air Du Temps. Had my mother bought the perfume or gotten it as a gift? I put it back on the dresser, but the smell lingered in my nostrils.

When I looked at the now sparkling mirror, a medium-height woman whose blue eyes and short blond hair contrasted with her light olive skin looked back at me. I imagined her paler, taller and a few years younger. The realization that I was older than my mother had been when she disappeared weighed heavily on my shoulders. Even if we were to meet now, we would never catch up. The floral Kremena notes suddenly smelled like desperation.

*You will find your mom, Merceditas. Don't lose hope.*

I opened the armoire though I knew it was almost empty. Four years ago, during one of my visits, Mamina had asked for my help to organize it. Together we had gone through my father's belongings and gotten rid of most. She kept one of his uniforms and his Makarov pistol, inside the holster, which we placed in the middle section of the armoire. It was still there. I took it out, handling it with extreme care though I assumed it wasn't loaded. Its weight surprised me because it was relatively small and didn't look heavy. The Makarov shouldn't even have been in our possession. There was a rigorous weapon-control policy in Cuba, but no one ever came to retrieve it. An oversight, probably, since Dad had died in Angola.

There was also a manila envelope with documents I had read before—military records and a medal my father had received during his first time in Angola, from 1982 to 1984. Nothing from his second tour, though. And that was it. No pictures of my parents together, much less my mother alone. Mamina kept an album with some of my early birthday pictures, when my mother should have been with me, but "Tania" wasn't in any of them. Dad had probably gotten rid of everything that reminded him of her.

I attempted to guess, for the umpteenth time, what could have happened. Did someone force my mother to go away? Had Dad returned to Angola because he had wanted to die? He had been killed soon . . . How soon, exactly? Where was his death certificate? I would have to ask Mamina. Another topic she would rather avoid, but I had kept unpleasant questions to myself long enough.

HAVING CLEANED THE MASTER bedroom, I took a shower and rested for a while. It was about seven o'clock when Mamina came in.

"Are you sleeping, *niña*?" she asked, apparently recovered from her earlier fit.

"Not at all." I smiled and patted the bed. "Sit here, like you did when I was a little girl."

She sat next to me. But the calm demeanor that had soothed my childhood fears was noticeably absent. Perched on the edge of the bed, Mamina was uneasy, edgy and, like the previous night, avoided looking me in the eye. She was hiding something, or at least there was something she didn't want to mention but thought she *should*. And she knew I had picked up on it.

"Do you know a woman named Berta?" I asked finally. "Dad's former girlfriend?"

She stared down at the bed. Her face was unreadable.

"She lives in what used to be Cubo Amarillo. You must have met her at some time or other."

"I don't know many neighbors."

That was true. And not just about neighbors. Dolores was right: Mamina didn't seem to like most people. At school functions, she'd stay apart from the other parents and seldom talked to the teachers. It must have been uncomfortable to be the oldest person in the room, and perhaps the least educated. But she had been there. For me.

"Tell me about Dad, then," I whispered.

Mamina opened her mouth. A plaintive, meowing sound came out.

"Is it too hard for you to talk about him?" I asked softly.

"No. Well, a—a little," she stammered.

It was uncommon for her to be overly emotional. Even now, her face was tense but not particularly sad. I forced myself to go ahead.

"Where is his death certificate? I've never seen it."

Her jaw clenched.

"Why are you so concerned with death certificates, marriage certificates and legal stuff *now*?" Her tone got sharper as she spoke. "Is that why you came back this time?"

"I came to see you." I kept my voice low and conciliatory. "The marriage certificate was a surprise; I wasn't looking for it. As for the death . . ."

"Stop talking about death, will you? You're calling her!"

"Who?"

*"La Pelona."*

The Cuban version of the Grim Reaper is a bald woman with skeleton arms. She wears a long purple robe. Sometimes she's depicted with a wreath of yellow roses around her head to hide the lack of hair. Could she be around? Was *La Pelona* the presence that Candela had felt? I shuddered despite myself but went ahead.

"Come on, Mamina. I know you don't believe in ghosts.

Where is the death certificate?" The image of a Cuban flag draped over a coffin flashed in my mind. "Wasn't he given a posthumous award since he was killed in action?"

"I can't stand this anymore!" She stood up and glared at me. "You're going to give me a *zirimba*, Merceditas!"

Mamina left the room faster than you would expect from an eighty-five-year-old lady. Her bedroom door slammed shut. When I recovered enough to go after her, she had already locked it.

Sadness and confusion bubbled up through my chest. I didn't think she was about to have a stroke, but the outbursts were out of character for her. When I was little, my classmates lived in fear of *la chancleta*, the wooden sandal that often landed on their butts, but Mamina never lost her temper with me. It helped that I was a quiet kid, more so after realizing she was my only relative. (In my heart, I must have feared that if I misbehaved, she would disappear *too*.) But on the few occasions when I'd disobeyed her, she had been gentle and forgiving. Now it felt as if she was becoming someone else.

# CHAPTER TWENTY-THREE

*October 12th, 1986*

*Felicidades to us! Joaquín and I tied the knot. It wasn't hard to convince him. He wanted our relation to be official as much as I did. I had asked him to invite Fidel, but he laughed and said that if El Caballo were to attend all the officers' weddings that he's invited to, he wouldn't have time to do anything else. I'm a bit disappointed!*

THE CEREMONY WAS QUITE different from what Sarah had expected. First, not even one of Joaquín's relatives attended. His mother had agreed to come, but her daughter, Mercedes, had been admitted to the hospital the day before.

"My sister has cancer," Joaquín said somberly, "and I don't think she's going to make it."

"*¡Pobrecita!*"

Sarah had yet to meet her in-laws. They all lived in another province and hadn't shown any interest (or perhaps didn't have the means) to travel to Havana. She had been looking forward to seeing them at the wedding.

Then, she had assumed they would get married at El Palacio de Los Matrimonios. The very name, Palace of Weddings, sounded so romantic! She had loved the white building, the car

outside with the balloons attached, the rice tossing . . . But Joaquín had other plans. On the Big Day, they went to an office
downtown, a *notaría*, in a borrowed jeep. Lo and a friend of
Joaquín's signed as witnesses, but there were no formal brides-
maids or groomsmen. Afterward, they all drove to a small park
located near the University of Havana. Five more couples were
there to participate in a public collective wedding. They gathered around an obelisk.

"The ashes of Julio Antonio Mella, a revolutionary leader
from the thirties, are inside," Lo whispered. "It's such a special
place!"

Sarah would have preferred a location with a happier vibe,
but it was too late now. Well, the Alma Mater statue on the
university steps as a background would make for an interesting
wedding picture. Rob would appreciate it. More so now that
he had started college and found his soulmate too, another
Berkeley student named Vincent. Oh, what a pity they couldn't
have come to her wedding either!

The grooms wore crisp uniforms and the brides, white satin
gowns accentuated by mariposa bouquets. Fredesbinda had
added an extender to Sarah's dress at the last minute. (The dress
had been rented at a shop called La Casa de las Novias.) Sarah
was showing a little, but not embarrassingly so. In any case, it
didn't bother her, at least not as much as the fact that she stuck
out like a sore thumb, too white and blond, taller than all the
women present and even some men.

The couples left their bouquets at the base of the obelisk.
The ceremony proceeded with military marches played by a
brass band and came to a close with a long patriotic speech
delivered by a colonel. Sarah couldn't help but notice that he
did his best to imitate El Caballo's emphatic style.

"We will defend this soil, this flag, this country with our
own blood if needed! *¡Patria o Muerte!*"

*"¡Venceremos!"*

Sarah rolled her eyes. Revolutionary slogans were okay at a CDR event, but at a wedding? Please. While the speech elongated into infinity, she kept thinking of Pauline and how much she would have enjoyed being there despite the agitprop. Would she have traveled to Havana? Sarah believed she would, when she was in good health. Pauline had been adventurous, and Sarah was proud to have inherited her drive. In moments like that, she missed her grandma terribly. She missed her parents too and thought she was cheating them out of an important occasion they would have loved to be part of. Though . . . would they? They didn't have Pauline's open-mindedness.

Finally, with the speech and the marches over, the now married couples went to a house in El Vedado and had a real party.

"Could you help us pass *cajitas* around?" the hostess asked Sarah.

The *cajitas* were little carboard boxes that contained a slice of meringue cake, two croquettes and cold elbow salad. To drink, they had Havana Club, Viña 95, beer and a concoction called *crema de vie*. Sarah took a sip. It tasted like eggnog with rum. She stayed in the kitchen helping Lo and the other *compañeras* while the men joked and talked in the living room.

"There's too much machismo here," another bride pointed out.

Recalling Pepe, and Joaquín's own lack of enthusiasm to help around the house, Sarah wholeheartedly agreed.

"But there have been many official campaigns against it," Lo hurried to say.

Maybe that was part of the *Proceso de Rectificación de Errores y Tendencias Negativas* that El Caballo had talked about.

Newlyweds were given access to vacation resorts at discounted prices, like a wedding gift from the revolution. Joaquín and Sarah spent four days at the sought-after Hotel Internacional de Varadero in Matanzas.

The building was worn out but still classy, with a fifties atmosphere. It was a few steps from a splendid beach with white sands and glassy waters. The Varadero waves were sapphire and green, and crashed on the shore with a gentler rhythm than on Pacific Beach. Yet again, nobody was surfing. When Sarah approached a hotel employee and asked about a surfboard, the man shook his head furiously.

"No, *compañera*, no!" His voice sounded tainted with fear. "We don't have that. These activities are forbidden here!"

"But, dude!"

She said it in English, without thinking. The employee gave her a blank look.

"Let's go, *mi amor*!"

Joaquín called her from the hotel entrance, already changed into his swim trunks. Sarah joined him, but even as they frolicked in the deep Varadero blues, she couldn't stop thinking of all those wasted waves.

IT WAS IN VARADERO where Sarah experienced a wave of love so strong that made her forget about surfing. Joaquín's hands in her hair, his eyes taking her in so lovingly, the tenderness of his touch . . .

"I've waited all my life for you, *mi amor*."

She felt the same. He was the one. She had had to cross an entire continent and the Caribbean Sea to find him, but here they were. Together and forever. Nothing else mattered. *That* was love.

# CHAPTER TWENTY-FOUR

Candela returned around 9 P.M. with pinkened cheeks and bright eyes. She had hit it off with Satiadeva. He was unveiling for her the hidden face of city, the Havana that didn't appear in touristy websites or on the news. He had skipped Varadero Beach for Playita de 16, a rocky stretch of coastline in our very own Miramar, where hippies used to congregate and now some people went to meditate and receive "the healing energies of the ocean," as Candela put it. He wouldn't offer her a mojito at El Floridita Bar, famously favored by Hemingway, but invited her to sit under the Paseo del Prado bronze lions and iron lamplights. While there, he had shown her El Palacio de los Matrimonios, but Candela was disappointed to find it empty and with a lonely vibe.

"Such an amazing building! Why don't people use it?"

"When I was young, most couples got married there," I said, "but these days they'd rather have parties at home, or in big renovated residences whose owners rent them for the occasion. They have more . . . cachet."

"What a pity."

They had strolled down the Paseo del Prado granite walkway all the way from El Malecón seawall to Parque Central. Once there, they had admired the baroque Gran Teatro de La Habana, home to the Cuban National Ballet and Opera.

"And then we passed by a ginormous hotel called Manzana Kempinski," Candela reported. "It's near Parque Central too. A luxury hotel, owned by a Swiss company. Do you know it?"

"When I left, the place was called La Manzana de Gómez. There were only a few stores with little selection on the ground floor, and the rest of the building was closed off."

She flung her arms up.

"It's crazy, Merceditas, the kind of shops that they have there. L'Occitane en Provence, *chica*, and Armani and Mont Blanc! How many Cubans can pay four thousand dollars for a gold watch? How many tourists are coming to Havana to spend that kind of money either?"

I snorted. I always found it funny when foreigners tried to make sense of Cuba. As if Cuba made any sense!

"Not many," I said. "But that's the way things are here. So, where else did you go?"

A wide grin spread across her face.

"He also took me to an Instituto meeting. It was lovely. Ferradaz and her crew were there too, and many other people. They study astral travel, meditate and do energy work."

"I didn't know there was an institute dedicated to such things in Havana."

"That's just the name they gave to their group. Instituto de Ciencias Ocultas de La Habana."

"Occult sciences, girl? And where's that esoteric spot located?"

"Eh—they meet at Satia's house, in a place called La Víbora. Everybody sits on the floor and there's a jasmine plant outside the window that smells amazing. Ah, the vibrations are so high and clean!"

It was past dinnertime and I hadn't prepared a thing yet, but Candela had brought a big container with paella and two bowls of creamy rice pudding for dessert.

"It's from a *paladar* called La Casa del Arroz that makes all sorts of rice-based dishes," she said. "You have to go and get ideas from them."

The shrimp was luscious, the mussels opened and the rice, a vibrant yellow hue. Stripes of roasted red and green pepper topped it with an intricate pattern. The aroma was mouthwatering. My stomach growled.

"This is perfect!"

I started to set the kitchen table but stopped halfway, thinking that I should call Mamina. Should I? Had my questions been out of line? Was she still mad at me or becoming senile? A rush of sorrow overcame me. Candela put an arm around my shoulders.

"What's going on, Merceditas?"

I told her about the last episodes, but forgot to mention the marriage certificate. It had lost significance in view of Mamina's sudden and scary decline.

"She said 'shit.' That's so unlike her. Later she began talking about *La Pelona*. I'm afraid her mind has—"

Candela sighed. Her maternal grandmother had Alzheimer's.

"When did you first notice it in your *abuela*?" I asked.

"When she started repeating the same stories over and over. She gradually stopped speaking English too, though she was fluent, and reverted to Spanish. It was as if she had gone back forty years."

"That's happening to Mamina! She has referred to my dad as if he were alive more than once. She didn't talk about him before."

"She didn't, eh? Same as with your mom?"

"Same. Well, she isn't talkative as a rule."

Candela's eyebrows raised in a mischievous way. "Would she allow me to read the cards for her?"

I laughed. "Mamina isn't into that. She's worse than I am!"

"I'd like to try anyway."

"Will the cards help me find my mother?"

This time it was Candela who laughed.

"No, *chica*. That's not how it works. But they can give you pointers. Most importantly, you can get a lot of information about people by the way they react to what the cards show."

It wouldn't hurt. I shrugged. She glanced over her shoulder.

"Where's *Abuela*?"

"Upstairs."

Candela walked out to the backyard. I followed her. The light was off in Mamina's room.

"She's gone to sleep," I said. "Without eating!"

"Were you talking about your mom when Mamina started acting—strange?" Candela asked.

"The first time we weren't. The second, I had just brushed the subject. The third time, I had asked about those rooms"—I pointed to the servants' quarters—"when she began to go away. And the last time, she got all upset when I mentioned my dad's death certificate."

"What if all this is somehow related?"

She had a point. Why hadn't I thought of it myself? I kicked a small rock and heard it hit a mango tree. I felt like kicking myself too for not having suspected . . .

"You mean she's pretending to be crazy to avoid my questions?"

Her bracelets jingled.

"That's a possibility. Another is that she wants to tell you something she has avoided for a long time, but her mind, her *unconscious* mind, is playing tricks on her."

"Like a secret?"

"Not necessarily a dramatic secret, but something she has kept from you all these years."

There was a noise in the kitchen. Mamina was inspecting the food containers. She must have been going downstairs when Candela and I went outside.

"Paella!" she squealed. "Who made this?"

"I brought it, *Abuela*," Candela said, hurrying inside. "Please, have a seat. I'll serve you."

"You're a darling. And where's Merceditas? Isn't she going to eat too?"

"Sure!" I said as cheerfully as I could, coming inside the kitchen with a fake smile plastered on my face.

Mamina acted as if nothing had happened. She ate more than usual and even praised the paella. I watched her and caught her looking back at me with a concerned expression.

When dinner was over, Candela asked casually, "Have you ever had a Tarot reading, *Abuela*?"

"What's a Tarot?"

"A card reading," I said. "*Tirar las cartas*."

"My grandma taught me how to do it," Candela said with a charming expression. "She was very sweet, like you."

To my surprise, Mamina agreed to hear what *las cartas* had to say. Candela brought her Santería-inspired deck, spread it over the kitchen table and asked, "Are we ready?"

Mamina nodded enthusiastically.

The backs of the cards were red, black and white. Inside, the figures had bright colors. Men and women were depicted with big and intense eyes. When Candela explained that the deck was based on *patakis*, old African stories and Santería deities, I feared Mamina would balk because she had never been religious, but it didn't appear to bother her. Maybe I didn't know my grandma as well as I thought.

"Shuffle and pick three cards with your left hand," Candela instructed her.

Mamina obeyed.

"Now lay them on the table and turn over the first one to your right."

The card showed a tall woman dressed in white, her hand over a man's shoulder. A disproportionately big chicken hovered in the background.

"That's the empress," Candela said. "A nurturing presence, like a godmother."

"A godmother, huh?" Mamina glanced at me again before looking back at the card. "Is it good?"

"Well, I'd say yes. It also tells us that an elder may need help and care."

Mamina nodded. "I could use some help around here."

"Turn over the next card."

It didn't look auspicious: a man behind three long orange bars. Only half of his face was visible. There was a tiny horse nearby, as small as the chicken had been big.

"Ten of wands," said Candela, shaking her head. "Do you feel stuck, *Abuela*? Somehow trapped?"

Mamina didn't answer.

"Could it mean," Candela suggested in an innocent tone, "that you have something to release?"

Mamina put a hand on her chin.

"I'm not sure about the release part," she said. "But this house *does* feel like a trap at times."

"That's why I've suggested you move to a smaller place," I said. "A modern apartment in El Vedado would—"

"I don't like El Vedado! Or Havana! I just want—"

"Come and live with me in Miami, then," I offered eagerly.

Candela shot me a *shut up* look.

"You can discuss that later. Now, what else does the card say to you, *Abuela*? The iron bars . . . could this be a cell? A prison?"

Mamina started fidgeting.

"I know nothing about cells or prisons."

A brief pause followed.

"Let's go on," Candela said when the silence became oppressive. "Turn over the last card, please."

The third card was the same I had picked from the floor of the plane: the yellow woman and the man in green who looked like a soldier. This time, I noticed that there was a chain around the guy's head. He looked determined. Strong. The woman was holding a tray. Mamina's face darkened.

"The hierophant," Candela said.

"Hiero-what?"

"It represents a family, *Abuela*. Traditions. A conventional marriage, perhaps. The painting is based on the story of Oshún and Orula, a couple that had a big fight about their divination tools."

Mamina held the card close to her eyes.

"What happened at the end?"

"Orula won. Actually, he allowed Oshún, his wife, to use the cowrie shells to divine, but then he created a new tool that she wasn't allowed to touch. He was a *cabrón*. So—let's see how this can be applied to your situation."

Mamina stood up.

"I don't think it does. Not at all. My husband died many years ago, and he wasn't a *cabrón*."

"Could it refer to someone else in the family?" I ventured.

Mamina ignored my question.

"I'm getting tired, girls. It's late for me. And these things— they aren't real, *verdad*? Only for entertainment."

On that note she left. When the sound of her shoes tapping the marble steps stopped, Candela and I looked at each other.

"There was a disagreement between your parents," Candela said, "and she knows what it was about."

"She's not telling, though."

"She will. But you have to let her. Just a moment ago, she

was going to say something about what she wanted, and you cut her off."

"I'm sorry."

"Let her decide when and what to share. Be patient."

My fingers traced the outline of the third card, then moved over the soldier and the woman.

"I've been patient all my life, you know?"

She patted my hand.

"I bet this isn't a joyride for her either, but she'll come around."

"If you say so."

# CHAPTER TWENTY-FIVE

*November 16th, 1986*

*Lo invited me to visit her second-grade class. The kids were so cute in their white-and-red uniforms! They wear red berets too, and a number of badges. They are studying José Martí's works. Many already knew his poems by heart. The school used to be a house, and there's an inner courtyard filled with plants. Very nice, though the classroom walls were chipped and the windows needed new blinds. But all in all, it was a nice, welcoming place.*

*The Cuban pledge of allegiance consists of a class leader saying, "Pioneros por el comunismo" to which the others respond, "Seremos como el Che." As in "Pioneers for communism, we'll be like Che." Not sure what "pioneers" means in this context but didn't want to ask. We kept the exchanges short, and the kids weren't told I was American. Lo didn't want to explain the presence of a "Yankee" at the school and only said that I was there as an internationalist worker.*

THE SECRECY ABOUT HER nationality puzzled Sarah, to say the least. Couldn't she be an example of the "good Americans," since there were many of them? Look at Rob and all those Compañeros de Cuba members! They weren't monsters, certainly, nor did they live in the entrails of one.

But she had more urgent concerns. As her pregnancy advanced, Sarah feared she was starting to resemble a balloon. Joaquín assured her that she was more beautiful than ever, but what was he going to say, right? Even her face had gotten bigger and rounder. The clothes that Fredesbinda had made for her didn't fit anymore, and she couldn't find maternity dresses in the stores. Though she had at last been issued a *libreta de productos industriales*, she hadn't learned the quirks of the ration-card system yet and had missed her turn to shop twice.

Fredesbinda would come to her rescue, as she had done before. Besides the maternity dresses, she could make a few onesies and rompers. She might even have pink fabric. But what if the baby turned out to be a boy? Well, there would have to be two items of everything, one pink, one blue. And in several other colors! Sarah giggled as she put together a list.

Going to Centro Habana still felt like an adventure to her. She wore the sunflower dress, though it was a tad tight. Behind her ears, she dabbed a few drops of Kremena, a Bulgarian perfume that had been Lo's wedding gift. Finding a taxi on Fifth Avenue got the day started just right. She knocked on the seamstress's door feeling excited and hopeful. A man she hadn't yet met opened.

"*Hola*," she started. "Is Fredes—"

"Fredesbinda left," the man said curtly.

Sarah peeked in. The sewing machine was still in the same corner.

"When will she be back?" she asked.

He examined her curiously.

"Never, lady," he said at last. "She's in Miami now."

THAT PUT A DAMPER on Sarah's enthusiasm. Where was she going to find a layette set? She resorted to Lo, who got red in the face when she heard about Fredesbinda's departure.

"What?" she cried out. "I would have never thought she was a *gusana*! Dirty worm!"

Sarah winced. So what if Fredesbinda wanted to leave Cuba? She had left her own country! For a moment Lo reminded Sarah of her mother, rigid and critical of everyone who didn't think like her. She went home, more upset about Lo's reaction than she wanted to admit.

ONLY TWO SHOPS IN Havana sold diapers, pacifiers, blankets and other baby must-haves. A *libreta de productos industriales* especially designed for newborns was required to shop there, but Sarah hadn't been issued one yet. The process usually took a long time, more so in her case. She was fretting about it when Lo came over with a big plastic bag.

"Here are some clothes for you and the baby, *chica*!"

Sarah hugged her. Maybe she had judged her friend too harshly.

"*¡Gracias!* How much . . . ?"

"Don't mention it! I collected them among my students' moms. They were all so happy to help."

Lo had to hurry back home and make dinner, so she wasn't around when Sarah opened the bag. The diapers were stained and the booties, wrinkled and yellowish. The maternity dresses smelled as if they had been stored for too long. Sarah washed everything and let them dry on a clothesline in the backyard. The sun took care of most of the dark spots, for which she was grateful.

A few days later Joaquín bought a crib from a friend whose son had outgrown it. It was sturdy, though a little chipped off.

"Once repainted, it will be fine," he said.

But they still needed a mattress, sheets, pillows, a bassinet, more outfits . . . The list grew long and daunting. Sarah told Elena about her predicament. She didn't want to give Lo the impression that she was asking for more things.

"Sweetheart, you'll have to nose around for all that on the black market," Elena said. "That's what everybody does."

"I'd rather not . . ."

"That's the way things are here, like it or not."

Joaquín didn't agree with black market practices either. But that night, over dinner, he admitted that if he couldn't find a stroller, he would resort to a local wheeler dealer who would know where to get one.

"It's all the fault of the Yankee blockade!" he said, pounding the table with his fist.

Sarah studied the dish in front of her—a cheese omelet and white rice—and fought the urge to reply that a blockade would mean the Seventh Fleet surrounding the island, not commercial restrictions. That was why Compañeros de Cuba was an anti-embargo group instead of an anti-blockade group! But she was too tired to argue. And yes, the embargo, blockade or whatever it was ought to be lifted. She was getting fed up with so many shortages and the endless lines.

Then there was Villa Santa Marta to contend with. Rob had gushed over the photos, but if you actually lived in it and had to keep it clean . . . Tidying the living room alone took her over three hours, mostly because she lacked the proper supplies. The bathroom tiles were coated with grime. The toilet and the sink had water stains. As for the stairs, those marble steps were slippery and treacherous, as she had found out after a couple of near falls. Even the kitchen, though better maintained than the rest of the house, had issues—one of the stove burners didn't work and the oven was temperamental.

One area she hadn't yet checked was the small building in

the backyard. Joaquín had told her there was nothing of value there.

"That's where the house help used to live, and they just had leftover furniture."

Sarah believed him. Something about that square, lonely structure repelled her, though she didn't know exactly what. But one afternoon she was in the backyard and decided to take a look. "The house help" might have left a stroller around, or something usable. She passed by the mango trees and the stone fountain. With some trepidation, she approached the building and opened the door.

Joaquín had been right. The furniture was nothing to write home about. A crude pine table, four chairs and a tattered wicker sofa filled the main room. The paint was a dark blue that made it look smaller than it was, and stuffy. A bedroom contained a bed with only a mattress, a dresser that appeared to have once been elegant but was now missing a drawer and a wall mirror that had seen better days. A closed door probably led to a bathroom, but Sarah didn't care to look inside. A vague rotten smell made her feel faintly sick.

She left soon, wishing that she had "help" herself. Houses like Villa Santa Marta were never intended to be taken care of by one person. If properties were truly distributed according to people's needs, that mansion should go to a family of ten. The most logical thing would be selling it and buying a more manageable home, but Sarah still didn't know if Joaquín owned the house or the state did. Lo suggested they do a *permuta*.

"It's a house swap," she explained. "Sometimes people get money under the table if they move from a big place like yours to, let's say, a two-bedroom apartment in Centro Habana. It's not legal but everybody does it."

Things were so complicated! Sarah had a hard time

understanding what was legal and what was not. At any rate, the baby would give her a good excuse to lobby for a one-story home. In the meantime, she was extra careful with the stairs and spent as much time as possible on the first floor.

# CHAPTER TWENTY-SIX

In the morning, the Radio Reloj weather broadcast reported that the tropical storm was moving away from Havana. It was still windy, but the rain had stopped.

Mamina stayed in bed longer than usual and asked me to handle Ferradaz and her crew. I rubbed Icy Hot into her arm when she complained that it hurt. We made small talk, but I didn't bring up my parents again. Candela was probably right. I had gone from not mentioning Tania at all to asking a million questions about her, and that was stressing Mamina. Time to back off—for a while.

Candela was in the kitchen, peeling off a mango and looking pensive.

"I was just thinking of my folks' old home," she told me. "If it looked anything like this."

"Haven't you seen pictures?"

"My grandma smuggled out an album, but I don't know what happened to it. Hope it's still around. The only photo I remember is of a big clay pot in the front of the house. The pot was as tall as my grandfather!"

"That sounds like a *tinajón*. People stored rain water and grains in them. Was the house in Camagüey?"

She sucked in her bottom lip.

"Could be. That's another province, right?"

"Camagüey used to be a province. Now it's a municipality, and there's a city of the same name."

"I'll ask Satiadeva to take me there."

"You'd like it. It's prettier than Havana, and the people are nicer."

I had been in Camagüey twice, and thought that had I stayed in Cuba, I'd have chosen to live in that beautiful colonial city built on the shore of the San Pedro River.

Leaving Candela in charge of breakfast, I returned to Berta's house. Yunelsys was waiting for me and said that his grandmother had awakened early and was having "a decent morning." He had already found new clients—a Canadian woman and her daughter who had rented two rooms.

"They paid for five days in advance," he told me with a big smile, "and didn't even bargain, like so many cheap foreigners do. I haven't had anyone for two weeks, so I'd say that you brought me good luck!"

I suppressed a laugh. First Mamina and the Tarot reading, and now this kid. Since when were Cubans so superstitious?

"Are they here now?"

"No, no. They went to pick up their luggage at a crappy hotel where they were paying three times more. Someone told them that a *casa particular* was the way to go."

As we walked through a black-and-white checkered tile hall, he insisted on showing me the house. The master bedroom had a king-size bed, an old-fashioned armoire and a hurricane lamp on a nightstand. The other rooms had queen beds and more contemporary décor. The dining room was furnished with a cheap set of table and chairs made to look "vintage" and a plastic chandelier that only got points for trying.

"If you want, I can take you to the penthouse," he offered.

"Maybe later."

Behind the kitchen was a smaller hall with a cement floor and, at the end, a closed door. This area must have been their servants' quarters—more modest than ours but still far enough from the main part of the house.

"I keep grandma out of the way when we are expecting guests," Yunelsys said. "It pisses her off, but what am I supposed to do?"

"What pisses her off? The guests?"

"The whole *casa particular* business. I tell her, *vieja, ¿con qué se compran los frijoles?* We need money for rice and beans."

He opened the door without knocking, and we entered a windowless room. An enlarged framed photo of a woman in full uniform, with gun and helmet, occupied half a wall. Despite being a bit faded, it was an imposing sight and dominated the space. There was something in the picture that reminded me of the *bruja* at home. The women were not physically similar because the *miliciana* was younger and had lighter hair. But both looked like people who believed that they had all the answers, right or wrong.

"Grandma, this lady's here to see you," Yunelsys said loudly.

A withered woman, more aged than old, sat on a rocking chair with a bedpan under it. "Don't you yell at me, *coño!*" she answered in a surprisingly deep voice. "I'm not deaf!"

An unmade bed was in a corner. The place was depressing. But Berta's short hair was neatly combed and she wore a clean flowery muumuu and red plastic sandals.

"Nice to meet you, *señora*," I said.

"*¡Compañera!*" she barked. "There are no *señoras* left in this country!"

Funny she had said that. When I was a child people still called each other *compañera* and *compañero*, but the term had become less and less common except for official situations, like talking to a custom or police officer.

"I'm sorry, *compañera* Berta," I said mildly.

"And who're you, anyway?"

The doorbell rang. Yunelsys bolted out of the room. Berta swatted at the air though there were no flies around and looked at me quizzically.

"I'm Mamina's granddaughter," I said.

"Mamina?"

She smiled in a distracted, I-don't-know-what-you're-saying kind of way.

"Joaquín's daughter."

Her smile disappeared.

"You are the Yankee?"

I stiffened. Was that a very good or a very bad start?

"That would have been my mom. Did you know her?"

Berta glared at me.

"Yes, many years ago. She's gone, isn't she?"

"She is."

"Joaquín fell hard for her," she said and leaned forward. "But he was mine first. We met when he had just been promoted to lieutenant and I was heading the first battalion of *milicianas* in Miramar. Look!"

A gnarled finger pointed to the photo. I realized that the woman in uniform was Berta herself.

"We did volunteer work every Saturday. Nobody does that anymore. If you don't pay them, they don't get off their *culos*. My own grandson, all he wants is money." She folded her thin arms and frowned. "We were a different breed. I took part in the literacy campaign when I was a teenager. We taught people for free. *Somos las brigadas Conrado Benítez, somos la vanguardia de la revolución . . .*"

Her words came out garbled as she went on singing about the literacy brigades, the forefront of the revolution. No one talked about them anymore, and I didn't even remember who Conrado Benítez had been—a revolutionary hero?

"You know the Literacy Campaign anthem, don't you?" Berta asked, cutting the song short.

"Ah—yes. You must be proud of yourself, Berta."

"Fidel is proud of me too. He gave me a medal with his own hands. It's here somewhere, unless that *comemierda* boy has thrown it away."

"But you were saying that my mother, the American . . ."

"Ah, yes! They're invading us." Her voice turned hoarse. "They are here, even in this house. I have seen them. Somebody has to tell Fidel. If he only knew that we are opening our doors to them and letting them take over! But he's kept in the dark. He's old—we're old." She paused and looked at me with a far-off expression. "What does Joaquín think about that? He didn't like Yankees. Didn't use to."

"My father is dead, *seño—compañera.*"

"Yes, I forgot." She closed her eyes. "Was it Angola? Ethiopia?"

"Angola."

She rocked back and forth.

"We need help!" she yelled suddenly, opening her eyes big. Her pupils were dilated. "The Yankees are coming! My grandkid, that good-for-nothing who neither studies nor works, says I am crazy. But I'm not! I hear them at night, yipping in their horrible language. I *smell* them! Someone please tell Fidel! Call him!"

Her arms jerked back and forth as if they had a mind of their own. The sight anguished me. What if Mamina ever got like that?

Yunelsys rushed in, bringing a pill and a glass of water. He made Berta drink some water and swallow the pill.

"Call Fidel, call Fidel!" she wailed.

"Grandma, Fidel's dead," Yunelsys said. "I've told you many times."

Her eyes gleamed with new tears.

"Joaquín's dead, Fidel's dead—we are all dead!"

Yunelsys gave me a slight shrug and pointed to the door.


WE MET AGAIN IN the living room.

"My parents left for Spain a year ago, but I was of military age and had to stay," he said. "They send me some money, and I get by renting off grandma's house."

"It must be hard for her,"

"It's hard for everyone." He rolled his eyes. "We need dollars. With her pension, she can barely buy food for a week."

"Have you ever heard her say anything about Tania? An American?"

"Honestly, lady, I turn her off. No disrespect, but when she starts talking about how good things used to be when Fidel was alive, I feel like strangling her. Instead, I just cancel the noise."

He must have left Berta's door open because I heard her singing from her room, "*Somos las brigadas Conrado Benítez, somos la vanguardia de la revolución . . .*"

# CHAPTER TWENTY-SEVEN

*December 18th, 1986*

*Glad to know that you and Vincent are spending Christmas in San Diego. Your parents, unlike mine, are so liberal! I used to think that the whole Christmas business was phony-baloney, throwing together people who didn't care for each other the rest of the year. But I miss it now. I miss my family, the Christmas tree (Dad always got a Fraser fir, remember?) and, silly as it sounds, the gifts. And I miss the food too! Turkey isn't sold in the carnicería—the store where chicken, fish and occasionally red meat "come to," different from the puesto and the bodega. Wait, there's also the panadería, where they sell only bread. Not a bakery, though. That would be a dulcería, where sweet treats and cakes are sold. Are you confused yet? I wonder why they don't bring everything to one place, like a supermarket, to save time and avoid so many waiting lines.*

SARAH DIDN'T HAVE TO wonder for a long time. Doctor Barbeito's wife was happy to enlighten her.

"*This man* does it on purpose, my dear!"

"You mean Fidel?"

"Yes! Who else? He keeps people busy with queues and

scarcities so they don't think about the political situation and attempt to overthrow him."

"Is that so?"

"Of course! Who has time to think about politics when all the pots and the pans are empty?"

Sarah didn't agree. Yes, *colas* were a pain in the neck, and the distribution of goods could be more organized, but most Cubans she had met appear to support the revolution despite such inconveniences.

"They control everything!" Elena went on angrily. "From what we read to the clothes we can or can't wear. Did you know that wearing blue jeans is considered a kind of ideological diversionism? As for food, I guess that apples are 'deviated' too because I haven't seen one in years!"

Sarah listened politely. By then she knew that the Barbeitos wanted to leave the country.

"These two aren't trustworthy," Lo had told her in a reproachful voice. "You shouldn't be visiting them so often."

Joaquín was of the same opinion. But Sarah enjoyed the old couple's company. She liked to speak English for a change. The majority of the neighbors worked during the day or weren't interested in talking to her. She still felt very much like an outsider, a "Yankee," despite her efforts to make friends and become part of the CDR community.

That year, the Barbeitos put up a Christmas tree and showed it to Sarah with conspiratorial smiles. It was small and old, decorated with satin balls, glass ornaments and aged tinsel garlands.

"Oh, it's so cute!" Sarah cooed over the porcelain Nativity scene. "Where did you get it?"

"In Chicago," Elena answered, with a nostalgic face. "Many years ago, when you weren't born yet."

"When you weren't born yet" was a phrase that Sarah's

grandmother had used often. Elena, like Pauline, loved to tell stories and had a penchant for the occult. That was another reason why Sarah enjoyed visiting the Barbeitos. They made her feel—home. They would offer her tea and delicacies like butter cookies and scones that Elena made herself, with ingredients bought, like the tea, on the black market.

It was during a conversation over tea and finger sandwiches that Elena revealed the identity of Villa Santa Marta's former owners.

"The house was built by a witch named María Estela Sotolongo, who, by the way, is buried on the property," she whispered, looking around as if the spirit of the aforementioned *bruja* hovered above them.

"Come on!" her husband replied. "That isn't true. I remember when the funeral carriage came to take her body to the cemetery."

"But the casket was empty, people said."

Since they were at it, Sarah brought up a few incidents that defied logical explanation. She didn't mention being pushed down the stairs because that sounded too far out, but there were other issues.

"Our lights flicker for no reason at all. And some rooms smell . . ." She struggled to find the right word. "Odd, really. And they are empty."

"You see?" Elena turned to her husband. Her eyes shimmered like the Christmas lights. "That's the *bruja*'s work. She cast a circle of protection around the house!"

Sarah assumed the "protection" was being used against Joaquín and her, the intruders. Doctor Barbeito laughed.

"We have the same problem here. The wiring is just old. As for the smell, all these houses need a good deep cleaning."

"Which is impossible because *this man* makes sure we never get all the proper supplies at the same time."

Every time they criticized El Caballo in her presence, Sarah felt uncomfortable and somewhat guilty. She didn't believe Castro was personally responsible for the lack of resources (that was probably caused by the embargo/blockade) but admitted, in her heart, that the situation could be improved. In any case, she'd rather steer the conversation away from politics.

"I've always suspected that our home is haunted, Elena. Did you say you met the previous owner?"

"Oh, we were good friends! Not so much with the witch, but her son and—"

"The alleged witch," her husband corrected her.

"Are you a lawyer now? *¡Bruja bien!* Like I was saying, we were closer to her son and daughter-in-law, a very nice couple. He was a painter—"

"Ah, that explains the many portraits there! Are they all his?"

"I don't think so. María Estela had built an impressive collection when she lived abroad"—Elena arched an eyebrow—"in the United States. Anyway, when we moved here, they were the first neighbors we met. Ours were the only two houses on the block. Anselmo and his wife were such sweethearts! We baptized their daughter, Aurelia."

Sarah listened eagerly.

"Why is an *M* engraved on the china?"

"That must have been for María Estela."

At least now she knew something. Sarah took a sip of her tea and asked casually, "Did Anselmo and his family leave Cuba?"

The Barbeitos looked at each other. A frown formed on the man's usually affable expression.

"They all did," he said hastily. "We haven't heard from them in—forever."

"Would you like to try some cider?" Elena asked, almost too fast. "A woman came by selling some bottles. The real thing, from Spain!"

The fact that they didn't want to talk about the circumstances of their neighbors' leaving wasn't lost on Sarah. Maybe, despite their kindness, they didn't think she was "trustworthy" either.

The bell rang. It was Carmita, a woman who came to clean the Barbeitos' house once a week. Joaquín wanted Sarah to rest as much as possible and not to worry about housework, but wouldn't think of hiring anybody, and she didn't want to bring it up. She was tempted to ask Carmita to go to Villa Santa Marta and do some contraband cleaning for her. In the end, though, she didn't dare to. She said goodbye and walked to the door.

"*Feliz Navidad*, my dear," said Elena, giving her a hug.

When Sarah left her neighbors' house, the spirit of Christmas, which was conspicuously absent from the Cuban streets, followed her.

# CHAPTER TWENTY-EIGHT

The Conrado Benítez Brigade's anthem rang in my ears all the way home. Mamina was still in bed. Ferradaz and her crew had arrived and started working on the roof.

Candela and I had breakfast together. I told her about Berta over *café con leche*, but she shrugged it off.

"Merceditas, your mom was an oddity here. An American. Good-looking too, it seems. She lived in a beautiful house. It's not surprising that other women were jealous of her. That doesn't mean they were out to harm her. That poor lady sounds more pitiful than dangerous."

Later I mentioned the marriage certificate and took Candela to the library, which she found impressive and, naturally, vintage, like everything else. But it was the sorceress's diary that made her gasp.

"*¡Chica!*" she said, holding the volume with reverence. "This is a treasure! Now, let's see if María Estela Sotolongo wants to send us a message. Bibliomancy, you know?"

"What's that?"

"A form of divination that uses books."

"That's not a real book but a bunch of typed pages."

"So what?"

Candela whispered something and opened a random page. To her disappointment, she could hardly read it.

"*Ay*, the font is too small, and the paper so thin! I'll need a magnifying glass. May I keep the diary until we leave?"

"Sure."

She hugged me impulsively.

"The book might hold answers for us."

"Right."

I knew Candela well enough not to argue. Instead, I gently steered her away from bibliomancy and toward more important topics, like the marriage certificate. She didn't buy Mamina's story.

"You mean she's lived here all these years and never saw it?"

"I didn't see it either. The library was always closed."

"Still—she's very sweet, but this, her 'memory problems'"— Candela made air quotes—"and her reaction to the cards . . . *Esto está oscuro y huele a queso.*"

I smelled a rat too. A big fat one.

"What can I do?"

"Not much," she admitted. "Just wait."

SATIADEVA CAME AND PICKED up Candela to continue with her Havana immersion program. I kept cleaning and straightening the rooms by myself since Mamina showed no intention of leaving her bed.

Ferradaz had been asking about the availability and cost of materials. They were not as expensive as I had feared, but it would take several days before she could collect everything and put together a bigger crew.

"Now, remember that we won't be able to start until the house is empty," she said. "Sorry to be such a stickler about it, but I can't risk having an accident here. And it's obvious that your grandma doesn't want to deal with us."

"I'll take care of it," I answered.

My plan was asking Catalina to take Mamina in while Villa Santa Marta was repaired. I couldn't imagine either of them refusing to hold a series of uninterrupted gossip sessions. Like Mamina, Catalina lived alone. Her house had once been furnished with old-fashioned pieces, likely left behind by the old couple that my mother befriended. Unlike Mamina, Catalina had no qualms about selling her "vintage" ornaments.

Ferradaz checked the servants' quarters and, to my great relief, declared them "not too awful."

"That area is in much better shape than the main house," she said, "so let's make sure that water and dirt don't get inside. I have a door that will fit. Secondhand but still functional. Fifty-five dollars because you are already a client, and we can install it tomorrow."

"That's a deal."

By noon, Santos and Suárez reported that they were done with the leaks. They would come back the next day with the new door.

I escorted the crew outside and went back to the kitchen in time to take the frying pan out of Mamina's hand. She was still wearing her nightgown and looked sleepy and tired.

"*Niña*, I was just going to make myself an omelet!"

"You don't have to make yourself anything." I poured lard on the pan. "Not while I am here."

"I am not used to having anybody cooking for me."

"Then get used to it."

I ignored her protests, made two omelets and reheated the paella leftovers. When I brought the dishes to the kitchen table, she showed me a leather-bound album.

"It was in my trunk," she said in an almost apologetic tone.

I had seen the album before but started leafing through it again as we ate. The first pictures showed a baby in a sturdy crib, a baby playing with a rattle, a one-year-old in Coney Island Park . . . And then a birthday party. Two candles in a meringue cake.

A piñata shaped like a number two. Plates full of salad and croquettes. Dolores, young and pretty, holding a little girl's hand as she attempted to stick a finger in the cake, grinning playfully.

"Was my mother in Cuba at this point?" I asked.

"Yes. Your birthday is in January, and she didn't leave until late in the year."

"When exactly was that?"

"November." She stopped and thought it over. "No, it was December. Close to the holidays."

Tania might have taken the picture herself! What was she thinking? Was she already planning to flee?

"I made the dress you're wearing here," Mamina said.

"You did!"

It was blue, like the pair of hair bows that kept the girl's bangs to one side.

"Were you at the party?" I asked.

"No. I couldn't travel that day. But I sent the dress and some other gifts with—a friend."

Next came a Polaroid. The same girl, a bit older, stood near the piano, holding a rag doll. Her eyes were serious and her expression worried, unlike the carefree grin of the previous shot. She had been too young to understand adult conversations but could have sensed trouble or witnessed an argument.

*A couple that had a big fight—*

There weren't photos of other birthday celebrations because there hadn't been any, except for my *quinceañera*. Though she didn't like to have people over and loud music gave her headaches, Mamina didn't have the heart to deny me that kitschy rite of passage. A whole album was devoted to my fifteen-year-old party, where I wore a pink frilly dress that made me look like a two-legged piñata.

I stated the obvious, closing the album. "My mother isn't in any of these pictures."

"I was looking for the newspaper *Granma* write-up," Mamina said. "I thought it was here."

"What write-up?"

"The one with Fidel."

I tensed, remembering Berta.

"Fidel Castro?"

"*Granma* ran a story about his visit to the unit where Joaquín used to work," she said reverently. "Tania appeared in the picture because she had been Fidel's interpreter and was standing next to him. After our conversation, it occurred to me that you might want to see it."

My heart started beating quickly.

"I do! Where is it?"

"Joaquín sent me a copy, but it got lost after I moved to Havana. But you can probably find it in the archives somewhere."

A trace of hope hung in the air.

"When was the story published?"

"Late 1985 or early 1986. Tania had just moved in with Joaquín. They weren't married yet."

Lunch was over. I called Catalina and asked her to come and stay with Mamina. I didn't want to leave her alone, but I needed to see that article. The possibility of having a glimpse of my mother's face had shaken me to the core. I felt a rush of blood pounding in my ears and my hands trembled as I dialed Catalina's number.

Once the two old ladies were settled in the kitchen, I called a government taxi. Satia had agreed to reserve the *almendrón* for me, but he was with Candela and she would have insisted on joining us. If I found Tania's picture, that would be a precious moment I wasn't about to share with anyone, not even my best friend.

THE NATIONAL LIBRARY WAS a behemoth of a building located on the east side of Revolution Square. On the north side, a marble statue depicted a worried-looking José Martí.

I had bad associations with the library, where my relationship with my deranged boyfriend Lorenzo had started, but I couldn't let old history get in the way of what looked like a promising lead. *Pal carajo*, Lorenzo.

In the granite-accented lobby, I showed my American passport and gave an embellished version of my quest to the uniformed receptionist. I would repeat the same version to the librarian, a middle-aged woman who came over to assist "the foreign visitor." Using an affected American accent, I explained that my mother had been in Cuba between 1985 and 1986 because she was a staunch admirer of the revolution and had acted as an interpreter for El Comandante during his visit to an army unit. *Why* she had been in the unit I didn't say because I couldn't think of anything believable.

"We were told that a photo of the visit was published in *Granma*, and I'd like to share that historical document with our family," I concluded.

The librarian smiled encouragingly.

"I'm sure we can arrange that."

She led me to a small office and turned on a boxy computer. The digitalized *Granma* archives popped up.

"The fact that Fidel was in the picture will make the search easier because the stories about him were always given front page," she said. "Here's everything we have for 1985 and 1986. Do you know the month?"

"My mom doesn't remember. Imagine, that was so long ago!"

"Oh, yes. How sweet of you to come looking for the article! Is your mother in Cuba as well?"

"No, she couldn't make it."

"How come she didn't keep a copy of the paper?"

That's the problem with embellishing facts—a little lie inevitably leads to bigger and more convoluted ones.

"We didn't know about it until someone told us."

The librarian started clicking through headlines:

*25th anniversary of official relations between Cuba and the Democratic People's Republic of Korea*

*Contributions to expand the outreach of Cuban cinema at the New Latin American Film Festival*

*Carlos Rafael Rodríguez welcomes Ion Ceaușescu*

*Cuban architects received prestigious international award in Bulgaria*

*Jorge Risquet meets with parliamentarians from Guinea-Bissau*

*Homage to Máximo Gómez on the 81th anniversary of his death*

*Frei Betto will attend the Latin American and Caribbean Meeting of Popular Education*

*Intellectuals recognize socialism as an essential door to the future*

*Fidel inaugurates Revolutionary Army Forces unit in Cienfuegos*

"What about this?" she asked.

There were no women in the picture that accompanied the story nor did it mention any foreign visitors. My dad had never worked in Cienfuegos, as far as I knew.

"No, it was in Havana."

*La Plata Highway finished in Granma Province*

*Puerto Rico's Juan Ríus Rivera Brigade visits Havana*

*Fidel meets with envoy from President Mugabe*

An hour went by, and we hadn't found anything. A shadow of a doubt crept over me. Mamina could have been wrong about the paper—there were two more: *Trabajadores* and *Juventud Rebelde*. Or the date. Or—everything. What if there was no article at all? I was getting discouraged, but then the librarian pointed to a grainy black-and-white photo of Castro in his customary fatigues next to a man in a suit. Between the two stood a woman almost as tall as Fidel—she towered over the other guy. I strained my eyes. Though it was impossible to make out many details, there was something familiar about her.

"Is that your mom?" the librarian asked.

To my surprise, I started to sob. *Calm down*, I said to myself, mortified. *You don't know if that's really her!* The tears kept pouring, though. The librarian put an arm around me.

"This is a piece of history!"

I focused on the headline: *Delegation from the Workers Party of Barbados tours army facility.*

"Is it possible to enlarge it?"

When she did, I saw that the woman's hair was light, straight and chin-length. She had a strong, determined jaw.

"You do look alike," the librarian stated.

I started bawling again.

"There, there. I will print a few copies."

She left to retrieve them because the printer was in another room. I finished reading the article. It was about some Barbadian diplomats stopping briefly at an army unit where Fidel Castro had met them.

The date was January 28th, 1986.

# CHAPTER TWENTY-NINE

*January 12th, 1987*

*You're the tío of an adorable six-pound baby girl! My appointment at Maternidad Obrera was scheduled for early February, but contractions started on January the 8th, in the morning, after Joaquín had left. I panicked and called Doctor Barbeito, who came over and delivered the baby in my own bed. I won't get into the gory details, but it hurt like the devil. Though I forgot the pain as soon as I saw my niña. We don't know whom she will resemble in the end, but one thing is for sure—she has my eyes!*

AFTER IT ALL WAS said and done, Sarah was relieved that Joaquín hadn't been home while she gave birth. The poor guy had been so stressed out lately! When she experienced some minor bleeding a few weeks before, he had gotten so scared she'd lose the baby that he wanted to consult a *babalawo*.

"What's that?" Sarah asked.

"A Santería practitioner. They know. They can help even when doctors can't."

She thought that he was kidding.

"But Santería . . . Isn't it some kind of voodoo?"

"Yes and no. This is a special case."

In the end, she had refused. The jeep wasn't available and she was afraid of taking a crowded bus to Guanabacoa, the city where the "practitioner" lived. She felt more comfortable dealing with Barbeito, who had done a great job. Even Joaquín had gone to their neighbors' house for the first time and thanked the doctor personally.

Sarah had expected the baby to bring a wave of bliss into their lives, but that wasn't exactly the case. Joaquín was still nervous, and they started having arguments. Nothing of importance, though. They agreed that having a daughter was the most wonderful thing that had ever happened to them. They adored her! But Joaquín didn't know a thing about babies. Neither did Sarah, having grown up a single child, but she was the mother. So *she* should know better, she maintained.

The silliest spat had been about the girl's name.

"I've been thinking of Natasha," Joaquín said. "Or Katiuska. Something along these lines."

Sarah vetoed Natasha because it reminded her of Natasha Fatale. It was hard to explain why since Joaquín had never heard of *Rocky and Bullwinkle*. Even if she had been able to convey the message, he would have said that Fearless Leader was intended to mock El Caballo or Stalin or some well-known communist leader. Another *Star Wars* situation. Katiuska wasn't too bad, but Sarah wanted a name that meant something to her.

"What about Pauline, like my grandmother?"

"Uh, no. We don't want anything in English."

"We?" Sarah, who was rocking the baby, must have stopped too suddenly because the girl's big blue eyes opened in alarm.

"I mean, it's better to give her a Spanish name," Joaquín backpedaled. "Easier for people here to pronounce."

"What about Paulina?"

"That's very old-fashioned."

"I don't think so!"

"You don't know enough about Spanish names."

They were still at it when Mamina came in. She had stayed at Villa Santa Marta for a week to help Sarah (whom she called by her new name, Tania) and make sure that the baby was taken care of. At first Sarah wasn't too happy with the arrangement, particularly when she realized that her mother-in-law was uneasy around her, which in turn made her self-conscious. Mamina often asked her to repeat what she had just said and spoke as little as possible. One day she had been making *arroz con pollo* when Sarah came into the kitchen and attempted to fry a chicken thigh in lard, just like Mamina was doing. Mamina had taken the piece of chicken away from her.

"*¡No, váyase!*" she said firmly. "I can do it myself. You rest."

Sarah left with her feelings hurt. But soon they became, if not friends, at least comfortable with each other's company. The still unnamed girl was the tie that bound them.

The day of the name argument, Mamina had been, as usual, in the kitchen, making supper for all. She brought a cup of lentil soup and handed it to Sarah. She insisted that lactating women should eat plenty of lentils to increase milk production. Sarah thought that was an old wives' tale but thanked her and tasted the soup. It had tiny pieces of bacon that lent it a smoky flavor.

"*Muchas gracias*," she said.

Instead of leaving them alone, as she usually did, Mamina stayed in the living room for a few minutes. She cleared her throat and finally asked, "Wouldn't you like to call the girl Mercedes? Like her aunt?"

Mamina's daughter had died a few months before, in La Coloma. Joaquín had gone alone to the funeral because the trip, that involved taking two buses and a train, would have been too hard and long for Sarah. She still felt bad about it, but the jeep hadn't been available that week either.

"That's a great idea!" Joaquín said. "My sister would have loved it. What do you think, *mi amor*?"

Sarah went along. She wished she had had the chance to meet her sister-in-law, or more members of Joaquín's family. But she still found the name odd. Mercedes, like a car? Later, Elena explained that Nuestra Señora de las Mercedes was an advocation of the Virgin Mary.

"It's really a pretty name, very popular here."

"Ah. Okay."

Other issues followed. Despite eating two servings of lentils every day, Sarah didn't have a lot of milk, and Mercedes wrinkled her nose at the powdery formula that the pediatrician had recommended. Sarah didn't like the look or smell of it either, but there was nothing else.

ROB'S LETTERS KEPT GETTING lost. In one dated January 28th he mentioned that a friend was traveling to Havana soon, but Sarah had no idea who it would be. She hoped it wasn't anybody who knew her parents. Ah, how she wished they could talk on the phone! But that was horribly expensive, and she feared that State Security might find out.

Truth was, she felt a little paranoid those days. Mamina had explained that freaking out about minor issues (*problemitas*, she called them) was natural for new moms—a protective instinct that kicked in after the baby came. And maybe Mother Nature had something to do with her worries, but there were other reasons as well.

One day, around three o'clock, a woman in uniform had knocked on the door. Sarah thought they had met somewhere and assumed that the newcomer was a colleague of Joaquín's.

"Good afternoon, *compañera*," she said. "Are you looking for my husband? He's still at work."

The woman launched into a tirade. Soon she was yelling.

Drops of her spit landed on Sarah's face. She understood the expressions *hija de puta* and Yankee *cabrona*, but not much else. She focused on the woman's body language, the hands that slapped the air. There was a gun in her hip holster. Not that she gave any indication she was going to use it. But still.

Sarah thought of Mercedes and felt a rush of adrenaline. She would have strangled the woman had she made a move to come inside the house.

"You took my man away from me! You stole him! *¡Me cago en tu madre!*" were her parting words.

It wasn't until much later that Sarah recognized the intruder as the same person who had bumped into her at the grocery store queue.

# CHAPTER THIRTY

I left the National Library with three photocopies of the *Granma* page after thanking the librarian profusely.

"Tell your mom to come by someday!" she said.

How I wished I could do so! There was a bicitaxi outside. The driver was a young man who sported a Miami Marlins cap.

"Need a ride, lady?" he said in English. Obviously, I was still channeling my inner American.

"Miramar?"

"Yes!"

A portable radio had been attached to the vehicle handle, and I was treated to a reggaeton concert on the way home. The lyrics, about a cat that finds a bunch of mice and skinny rats dancing in its territory, were downright nonsensical. The chorus kept repeating the nonword *bajanda*.

"That's Chocolate MC," the bicitaxi driver informed me officiously. "You must have seen him on TV many times, eh?"

"Sorry, but I've never heard of him."

"Don't you live in La Yuma? He's super famous there!"

During the bumpy ride, I took out one of the pages and examined it again. There was a clear resemblance between that tall blonde and me. I touched my own hair, which was a few inches longer than hers, and traced the contour of my face.

Her posture was straight and she looked at ease—I wouldn't have appeared so self-confident in the same situation, so close to Fidel Castro!

I added years and wrinkles to the woman's blurred face and envisioned our meeting. Would it be emotional? Awkward? Painful? Could a long-lost mother-daughter bond be restored? I let many scenarios run through my mind (in some, we had slid backward in time and I was still a little girl) until it occurred to me that without a real name, I wasn't any closer to finding her than before.

Or was I? If she had a Facebook account, or any social media presence, facial recognition technologies could help me track her down. It might be difficult but not impossible. I wouldn't give up now that a tangible image of "Tania" had finally come to my hands.

I thought of the card with the bars. This was, perhaps, Mamina's way to "release" what she knew about my mother. The *orisha* deck had helped, and I was grateful to Candela. But the fact that Mamina had waited so many years to tell me about this write-up still hurt. I could have started looking for Tania much sooner had I known!

As the driver pedaled through the Havana streets, the resentment I felt toward my mother for having abandoned me began to melt. I saw myself again in our backyard under a mango tree, at the ashen hour. "Tania" approached me quietly, her feet not quite touching the gravel path. A smell of roses engulfed me . . . The voice of reason interrupted my reverie. *Wait until you find out for sure. It may not be her after all.* But my heart said it was. Everything matched Mamina's story: the date, her presence at the military unit and our similar looks.

I caressed the page and realized I wasn't angry at Tania anymore for having dropped me "like a hot potato." If we had met at that moment, I wouldn't have reproached her for anything.

I wouldn't have asked questions, even. My old and low-simmering rage was gone. I had *released* my mother and was finally ready to meet her.

WHEN WE TURNED THE corner, the same blue rental Kia that I had seen the day before, and perhaps the night of my arrival, was parked outside Villa Santa Marta. I had only a glimpse of a tall woman opening the door and getting in. And, just like it had done the previous times, the car sped away.

"Can you follow it?" I asked the Chocolate MC fan.

"Eh, I have legs, not wheels!"

By then, the Kia had already vanished. I jumped off the bicitaxi before it came to a full stop.

"Hey, lady! You forgot to pay me!"

I grabbed a ten-dollar bill from my purse and threw it at him.

"No change?"

"Keep it."

"*¡Bajanda!*"

Panting, I ran to the house and tried to open the door. It had been locked. I knocked several times. It was Catalina who finally let me in.

"Sorry, Pulgosa was barking and we didn't hear you."

She disliked dogs and called Nena unflattering names. *Pulgosa* was a favorite, though Mamina swore that the pooch didn't have fleas.

"Who was in that blue car?" I asked.

"That woman," Catalina answered after a pause. "Mamina wouldn't talk to her, but she keeps coming back."

My pulse quickened.

"Have you seen her?"

"No. Mamina is the one who's been dealing with her. Or *not* dealing with her."

"What does 'that woman' want?" I asked.

Catalina pursed her lips, seemingly focused on the dust that covered the floor.

"What do I know?" she retorted.

*More than you want to tell me*, I thought.

"Where's Mamina?"

"In the kitchen. I'm going to sweep the mess that the construction guys left here. If not, she'll try to do it herself."

"Thank you."

I hurried to the kitchen clutching the photocopied pages against my chest. Mamina was slumped on a chair, still wearing her nightgown. She didn't look up when I came in.

"Who was here?" I asked point-blank.

She gave me a sideway glance before shrugging.

"What's going on?" I insisted. "Who's the woman in the blue car? Have you talked to her?"

"Just a couple of words." Mamina drummed her fingers on the kitchen table. "She's one of those people who . . ."

She stopped talking and waved her hand, a gesture that confused me.

"Which people, Mamina?" I asked, impatient. "Please, tell me what's going on."

I sat across from her. The album was still in the same spot where I had left it. I placed the photocopies next to it. Mamina's eyes were glassy, as if she were, again, unseeing me. She couldn't be pretending—I knew her well enough to be sure of that—but her attitude confused me.

"They're coming back," she said. Her breathing was labored. "I always knew they would. That's why I've never wanted . . ."

She fell silent again. Her blank expression reminded me, for one painful moment, of Berta when she talked of Americans "taking over." The air was thick, and I felt myself suffocated. I let a slice of seconds pass before asking, "Are you having memory problems, Mamina?"

It was a loaded question, more than I had intended to make it.

"What do you expect, my dear? I'm old. And very tired." She gripped the table and stood up with a visible effort as her chair scrapped across the floor. "Please, tell Catalina to come back tomorrow. I'm going back to bed."

I felt like physically restraining her so she couldn't get away.

"Wait! I found the article you told me about at the National Library—"

Mamina stiffened.

"Good," was all she said.

"Do you want to see it? You can tell me for sure if she—"

She waved a hand in the air.

"Not now, *mijita*. It's been a hard day. I don't need more excitement."

*Excitement?* I wanted to cry out. It was my mother we were talking about! My long-lost mom! But a glance at Mamina's shriveled face made me bite my tongue. Yes, she was old. And she certainly looked beat.

She plodded toward the stairs. I followed her, took her arm and helped her reach her room. When I went back to the living room, Catalina had already left.

I placed a photocopy of the *Granma* article on the kitchen counter. My mother (because that had to be my mother!) kept me company as time passed sluggishly, as if the cuckoo clock's hands had been glued. The day's events danced in my mind. Berta, Tania, the woman in the blue car . . . They were all connected, and maybe in a good way, but I was afraid of putting a jinx on it by daring to give a concrete form to my vague hope. I went outside and walked up and down the backyard. A strong smell of roses filled the air.

# CHAPTER THIRTY-ONE

*March 16th, 1987*

*Thank you, thank you for all the pretty things! The booties are so cute! Mercedes looks like a princess in her new pink dress, and the disposable diapers, unheard of in Cuba, are a godsend. Dorothy was a sweetheart. She took me out to lunch at the hotel where she stayed, in El Vedado. That was a treat as well. It has been so long since I didn't have to wait in line at a restaurant! Now, when are you coming back?*

THE TWENTY-FIVE-STORY HABANA LIBRE Hotel, a former Hilton, was located in El Vedado, about five blocks from El Malecón, in the intersection of two busy streets, L and Twenty-Third. Pushing the stroller that Joaquín had finally bought from the wheeler dealer, with Mercedes in it, Sarah walked inside through the automatic doors. A cool blast of air-conditioning provided a welcome respite from the outside heat.

She stood in the lobby admiring the plush sofas and sweeping central staircase. Potted palms next to marble-top tables and red leather armchairs created inviting spots to sit and relax. Water cascaded in a lighted fountain producing a soothing murmur while soft instrumental music played on the overhead speakers.

There were three Cuban men standing in a corner. An unsmiling clerk at the reception desk kept an eye on them. An older couple sitting on a sofa talked in hushed tones in a language Sarah couldn't identify. No one else was around. She wondered why there weren't more people in this beautiful, welcoming hotel. Well, maybe everyone else was working. She approached the clerk.

"Could you call Dorothy Parson's room?" she asked. "She's waiting for me."

"Who are you?" the clerk asked in return, watching her intently.

"A friend. She . . . she just called me," Sarah stuttered, shifting under the guy's scrutinizing gaze.

"What's your name?"

Sarah hesitated. Better to play it safe.

"Tania Rojas."

The clerk's eyebrows raised.

"Do you have an ID?"

"No. I'm sorry." She hadn't even thought of it when she left the house. Was she supposed to carry her Cuban *carnet de identidad* at all times, like a driver's license?

"Take a seat while I locate her," the clerk said after a long, uncomfortable pause.

Sarah made sure Mercedes was comfortable before sinking into an armchair. She was a little winded. Joaquín had been working that day. Afraid of getting on a bus with baby and stroller in tow, she had taken her chances waiting for a taxi by the clock tower. She got lucky—a black-and-yellow government-operated car stopped in front of her. The driver dropped them off in front of the University of Havana because Twenty-Third Street was out of his route. She still had to walk several blocks to the hotel but was utterly grateful for the ride that had cost only twelve pesos.

Ten minutes later a well-dressed woman came out of an elevator carrying a big plastic bag.

"Are you Rob's friend?" she asked, and added before Sarah could answer, "I'm Dorothy. What a thrill it is to meet you and your baby, brave girl!"

Dorothy hugged Sarah as if she had known her forever. Mercedes made happy gurgling sounds as the old lady cooed over her.

Half an hour later, they were at the Sierra Maestra restaurant on the last floor. The hostess greeted Dorothy by name and glanced dubiously at Sarah before escorting them to a table. It was by a window that offered a spectacular view of the city: El Vedado's skyline and the ocean in the distance.

"Havana is quite the place, isn't it?" Dorothy said. "It looks like it's stuck in the fifties. In a good way, though! No conspicuous consumption here."

No, no one would accuse Cubans of conspicuous consumption, Sarah agreed. They shared a memorable lunch of chicken-fried steak, the ubiquitous white rice and avocado salad. "The food was delicious," Sarah said. "I'll have to bring my husband. He's going to love it!"

Dorothy looked uneasy.

"Only hotel guests are allowed to eat here," she whispered. "You snuck in because the hostess didn't think to stop someone who looks—like you do."

"Oh. That's odd."

Dorothy was petite, with short and nicely cut bluish hair. Like Rob, she was part of a Cuban support group, but hailed from Vancouver, far away enough that he felt confident sending the package with her.

"I also brought a donation for the Cuban people on behalf

of our group," she said over the dessert, a creamy *flan al cara-melo*. "It's four hundred Canadian dollars. Do you know of a good place to leave it?"

"An elementary school?" Sarah suggested, thinking of Dolores's classroom.

"Schools are taken care of by the government. We had in mind a more community-oriented project."

Sarah gained time by wiping Mercedes's mouth. She was embarrassed not to know about any of such projects. Perhaps an organization that did volunteer work?

"A friend of mine can help," she said. "She's the president of the Committee for the Defense of the Revolution on my block. She will know."

"Great! Please, call me at the hotel when you find out." Dorothy took Sarah's hand over the table and gave it a gentle squeeze. "Ah, if I had your age, I would stay on this amazing island! I wouldn't miss my country at all."

"Well, I do miss home a little," Sarah admitted. "My parents, surfing, going shopping with my friends . . . But I have so much more here. No regrets!"

Still, it would have been nice if she could have brought Joaquín to the Sierra Maestra restaurant. She didn't remember the last time they had eaten steak at home.

THAT EVENING, WHEN SARAH told Lo about the donation, her friend got nervous and, strangely, upset.

"Canadian dollars?" she asked, pressing her lips together. "Money from a capitalist country? Uh, no. I don't think so. We all could get in trouble."

"Why? This lady belongs to an anti-embargo organization!"

Still, Lo wouldn't hear of it.

"If State Security finds out, we all will become suspects. And who knows? She may be an undercover agent."

"That's ridiculous," Sarah chuckled, thinking of the very proper, blue-haired lady she had met that afternoon.

"To you, maybe," Lo said in a strained voice, "because you aren't from here. In any case, don't get me involved. I don't trust her."

Joaquín was of the same opinion. Though he didn't accuse Dorothy of working for the enemy, he ordered Sarah, kindly but firmly, "Tell that woman thanks but no thanks."

AFTER DOROTHY LEFT, SARAH caught herself thinking of her parents more often. One afternoon she sat to write a letter to Rob but started a different one.

> *Dear Papa,*
> *You have a granddaughter and she got your (and my) eyes.*
> *She's cute and better behaved than I ever*

She stopped and crumpled the page. She couldn't make such an announcement by mail. It wasn't fair. And her parents would be so mad! Or wouldn't they? It wasn't like she had had a child out of wedlock, but it would have made no difference to them, seeing that she was married under another name. And to a Cuban *militar*. Though that wasn't necessarily bad. Sarah hoped that her father would eventually accept someone with a background similar to his, once he looked past the ideological differences. And her mother would certainly fall in love with Mercedes. They both would. But it was going to take a lot of explaining.

# CHAPTER THIRTY-TWO

Candela came back around six-thirty. She had that foolish, happy glow that people get when they're falling in love. Before she started yakking about Satiadeva, I took her to the kitchen and filled her in on what had happened.

"*¡Santo cielo!* Let me look at the picture right now!"

I handed her a copy of the article. She studied the photo and scrutinized my face.

"You two look very much alike, Merceditas."

We stared at each other.

"You *will* find her," Candela whispered. "This is a good sign."

The unbearably tight feeling in my chest unfurled, even if just a little. Until I remembered Mamina's odd reaction to the mysterious visitor in the blue car.

"Now, this woman who keeps coming." I swallowed. "She has to be a tourist. Regular Cubans don't rent cars from Havanautos."

Candela clasped her hands together. "Remember those ads that the detective posted?"

"That was over a year ago. And he never got a response!"

"Which doesn't mean she didn't see the ads."

I crossed my arms, feeling suddenly as if the temperature had dropped ten degrees.

"You mean that—could be her?" I whispered, my head pointing toward the photocopy. "The woman in the car?"

Candela nodded. A chill rippled across my flesh. I had thought of it, yes. Vague, unformed thoughts I hadn't dared to acknowledge.

"It doesn't make sense." I groaned. "Why would she be looking for me *here* and not in Miami?"

"The ads didn't include your address. She wouldn't know where to find you there, and she might not have wanted to contact the detective. But you two lived here together."

My legs wobbled.

"You're imagining things. That just can't be."

"Maybe hunger is making me think strange thoughts," she conceded. "I haven't eaten a thing in hours."

"Didn't Satia take you to any *paladar* today?"

"No. We just—uh, meditated. And then he had to drive a longtime client to Varadero. I tried to talk him out of it, but he had already committed. He's a very conscientious guy."

"That, he is. By the way, I'm starving too."

"Why don't we go to La Casa del Arroz? My treat. It's a delightful place, and you will find the food inspiring."

LA CASA DEL ARROZ was a small bungalow set in a garden of luscious hydrangea and jasmine plants. The path to the door was lined by herbs housed in clay pots. It smelled like saffron, cumin, fried onions and roasted garlic. A tall woman with auburn hair greeted us warmly.

"Candela, welcome back! And thanks for bringing company!"

"Hi, Rosita! This is my friend Mercedes. She's a chef and will appreciate your cuisine."

"Oh, cool! Do you have a *paladar* too?"

"Candela's flattering me. I work at a restaurant. But I am not a chef, only a self-taught cook."

Inside, the décor was "vintage" with a touch of rustic. A tower of books rested on a credenza that had a lacquered top. Faded paintings depicted assortments of apples, grapes and oranges—Candela told me they were called *bodegones*. A philodendron sat in a porcelain container surrounded by aloe vera plants in apothecary jars.

"So many beautiful things!" Candela said. "So much to explore! I could live in Havana for a month and not miss home at all."

"Until you try to buy fresh fruit and find out there's none," I replied. "Then you eat what's in the *bodegones* or go hungry."

"Oh, shut up! You're spoiling it for me."

Rosita came to our table. I noticed that she wore a white-and-purple Santería necklace.

"We're lovers of the grain at La Casa del Arroz," she informed me. "All our dishes are rice-based or served over rice. I suggest a rice soup with cilantro, basil, cumin and coconut to start."

"It's so yummy," Candela said. "We had it yesterday."

The rice soup was creamy and yet light, with a hint of ginger. Similar to a Thai soup, but the cumin gave it a Cuban twist.

The main dish, which Candela and I shared, was a big plate of fried rice with vegetables: regular onions, green onions, garlic, tiny carrots and bean sprouts. It came with wheat flour fritters in a sweet and sour sauce. I ordered another ration to go, for Mamina.

"Full belly, happy heart," Candela said, pointing to a sign over the credenza that read *Barriga llena, corazón contento.*

I didn't think there was any space left for dessert in my *barriga*, but when Rosita mentioned the house specialty, rice with mango, Candela said that I *had* to try it. It was a bowl of sticky, sweetish rice with generous mango slices on top.

"There's a strong Thai influence here," she said.

I nodded, chewing enthusiastically. "This would be a

fantastic addition to La Bakería, but we'll have to change the name."

"Why?" she asked.

"Do you know what an *arroz con mango* is, Candela?"

"Duh, what we just ate."

"It's also an old expression meaning that there's a big mess. Or something weird."

She nodded pensively.

"I'd say that all this business with your mother and the woman in the blue car is an *arroz con mango*, then."

"It is."


BACK AT HOME, MAMINA was locked in her room. I didn't disturb her. Bedtime came, and I refused to let Candela's foolish ideas influence me. Okay, I had already had the same foolish ideas without her input, but was determined to keep them at bay. If my mother was in fact looking for me, she wouldn't have left in such a hurry when I approached the car the day before. And the driver didn't look like her. Or did she? I hadn't seen her face clearly enough to tell.

*Stop it.*

Instead, I chose to rack my brain about places where Mamina could stay, supposing she didn't agree to live with Catalina. Thinking it over, I had realized that both old ladies were fussy and particular and wouldn't enjoy each other's company constantly. They got together almost every day, but their visits were short. Satia's home in La Víbora was out of the question too. I couldn't imagine Mamina living with a guy, no matter how much she liked him, or sharing space with an "institute of occult sciences."

Then there was La Coloma, Mamina's former home. The idea of shipping her off to the countryside still made me feel guilty, but in truth, I had nothing against the place. The few times we had visited, when I was a little girl, Mamina's niece, Sonrisa had always welcomed us. Her daughter Yulisa, who was around my age, looked up to me in a charming way because I was *la prima de La Habana*. The boy, Yoel, was younger, skinny as a rail and so shy that he used to sneak out of the house the minute we arrived, then peeked from behind the trees. The problem was that I hadn't seen them in ages. I couldn't even remember the last time Mamina had taken me to the farm.

Slowly, a memory surfaced. Yulisa and I, around seven years old, had been alone in the kitchen, away from the adults.

"So you are now, like, Mamina's daughter?" she had asked.

"Yep."

"But you have no dad."

I had agreed. No dad.

"We don't have any either. Well, he's around but doesn't live with us anymore. He's got himself a new girlfriend, and she's going to have a baby with him. That's bad, but still better than—"

Mamina had rushed in and scolded us. At the moment, I thought she had found Yulisa's reference to the other woman inappropriate—*cochinerías* we kids weren't supposed to talk about. Now I wondered if what had set her off was the talk about our fathers.

*That* was the last time she had taken me to the farm.

# CHAPTER THIRTY-THREE

*April 27th, 1987*

*How different my life would be had I stayed home! I'd be taking notes in a Berkeley classroom or discussing Max Weber with you. Instead, I just had my daughter baptized. In a Catholic church. Today, a total stranger called Canario became my compadre and Mamina isn't just my mother-in-law but my comadre as well. Aren't they weird, the twists and turns of fate?*

SARAH'S PARENTS ATTENDED THE Church of Christ. Her grandmother Pauline was more into New Agey stuff. She had taken Sarah to seances in an old Del Mar mansion that was said to be haunted. They both were regulars at the San Diego Psychic Fair that gathered thousands of visitors every August at Balboa Park. But Sarah, after becoming a member of the Point Loma Marxist study group, had resolved to stay away from religion and any kind of supernatural beliefs. The way Cubans, who lived in an ostensibly atheist country, treated such matters intrigued her. Santería was a discreet presence in many people's lives. Some would wear colorful beaded necklaces under their clothes, which Dolores had explained meant they were devotees of a particular *orisha*, or Afro-Cuban saint.

"Red and white beads are for Shangó, the *orisha* of thunder," she said. "White and blue for Yemayá, who reigns over the ocean."

"Do you believe in that?" Sarah asked, surprised at her friend's earnest expression.

"Me? Oh, no! I'm a Marxist-Leninist. But I still respect it. Because one never knows, does one?"

Sarah suppressed a laugh. She still remembered Joaquín's insistence on seeing that *babalawo* when he feared she would have a miscarriage. Like some voodoo guy with no medical background was going to prevent it, right? And then, on a Monday morning, Mamina showed up unexpectedly in a battered and dusty Buick sedan. The driver was a pleasant middle-aged guy she introduced as "Canario."

"What a surprise!" Sarah greeted her mother-in-law the Cuban way: an air kiss on the cheek and a light hug. "I didn't know you were coming. I would have made something special for lunch."

"No need to bother, *mija*," Mamina said, speaking slowly and louder than usual, as she always did when addressing Sarah. "I'm going back home in a couple of hours."

"Well, let me call Joaquín right away"

"No, no! I just came to baptize the girl."

"She's too young for that," Sarah responded quickly.

All the baptisms she had seen were by bodily immersion. No way she was going to allow anyone to put Mercedes under water!

"What do you mean, too young? She's already three months old. The priest said that's old enough."

The priest? Sarah didn't know Mamina was Catholic. Well, at least *that* kind of baptism didn't involve anything dangerous.

"If you insist," Sarah said and shrugged. "But it'll have to be on a weekend because Joaquín—"

"*Mija*, this is between you and me. My son doesn't believe in anything."

"Oh, he does—"

Mamina started getting agitated. "Baptizing a child is ideological deviation. We *can't* tell him! He will get mad, and this son of my mine has a temper!"

Sarah thought that Joaquín was a rather mild-mannered guy, not prone to outbursts of anger, at least around her.

"So how are we going to do it?" she asked.

"We take the girl to the Sagrado Corazón de Jesús Parish. No one else has to know."

"Where's that parish?"

"In Centro Habana. Far enough from Miramar that we won't risk running into a neighbor. I already talked to Father Miyares. He's waiting for us. Now let's go get Mercedes!"

Sneaking behind her husband's back to perform a clandestine baptism didn't feel right, but it seemed so important to Mamina that Sarah ended up agreeing. It wouldn't hurt, and she welcomed the chance to get out of the house. She would tell Joaquín later since he likely wouldn't mind anyway.

The Sagrado Corazón de Jesús Parish looked more like a cathedral than a regular church. Neo-gothic in style with an impressively high bell tower topped by a huge bronze cross, it was located on a busy street called Reina. Across from it was a five-story building with the name *Yumurí* written in bright letters over the main door.

"That's a good place to buy clothes and stuff *por la libre*," Mamina said.

"*Por la libre?*" Sarah repeated. "You mean *gratis*? For free?"

"No, just without coupons."

Sarah committed the street to memory. She had finally learned to anticipate her turn to buy, but the few dresses she had found in the stores were unflattering and poorly made. With Fredesbinda gone, she didn't know where else to turn.

A life-size statue of Jesus with his arms spread open stood at the church portico. Inside, the light filtered by stained glasses lent a magical vibe to the space. There was a marble baptismal font near the altar. It was big, but not dangerously deep.

The three of them took seats in the back rows—the driver, for whatever reason, had followed Mamina and Sarah into the church. A nice guy indeed, he also offered to carry a bag with extra diapers and a milk bottle.

Mamina's precautions and the "ideological deviation" tag had made Sarah think that the Catholic church was underground in Cuba. But there were around twenty people—most white-haired, like the Compañeros de Cuba folks—and they all seemed at ease. A standing Westinghouse fan created the illusion of a breeze in the central nave, where Mass was celebrated.

Sarah didn't know the proper responses to the priest in Spanish—or English, for that matter. Mamina wasn't all that familiar with them herself. They waited to see what other people did, when they knelt and when they sat, and followed their lead.

When the collection basket was passed, Mamina put a ten-peso bill inside. A sermon, mercifully short, was delivered by Father Miyares, a tall guy with piercing green eyes. There was no music despite the presence of a regular-sized piano. All in all, Sarah found the Catholic mass more palatable than the services her mother used to drag her to in Pacific Beach.

The baptism as such took place afterward. Father Miyares didn't bring Mercedes to the baptismal font, but met with Sarah, Mamina and Canario on the altar steps. The ceremony was performed while Mamina and Canario held the girl.

The rapid-fire set of questions and answers between Canario, Mamina and the priest happened too quick for Sarah to follow.

"As godparents, you must be able and ready to help Mercedes on the road of Christian life," Father Miyares said, addressing the pair.

It was then when Sarah found out that Mamina was going to be Mercedes's godmother. The godfather turned out to be the Buick driver. Talk about a fast move! Had she been asked, Sarah would have suggested the Barbeitos—after all, Mamina was already the girl's grandmother. But it was too late to change the arrangements. She only had the chance to add one more name to the list.

Mercedes behaved well until the priest put salt in her mouth. She made faces and tried to spit it out, but Mamina soothed her, patting her softly on the back, and the ceremony went on.

"Mercedes Paulina Montero Rojas, I baptize you in the name of the Father and of the Son and of the Holy Spirit," said Father Miyares. "Amen."

A long name for such a tiny person, but Sarah felt elated when it was written in the baptismal record book with the priest's ornate calligraphy. It had been worth the trip.

# CHAPTER THIRTY-FOUR

When I got up the next morning, around eight-thirty, a plan was fully formed in my mind. It had come up in bits and pieces throughout the night. Carrying it out would require stealth and a few omissions, if not outright lies, but that wouldn't be a problem. I was already getting used to them. (After all, I had had a good mentor, though I had not realized it at the time.) I felt as if my head had been turned upside down and I was now looking at the world from an angle that made all the familiar people and things look distorted and a little scary.

Downstairs, the smell of freshly brewed coffee wafted in from the kitchen. Mamina had skewed the Bialetti in favor of her old, trusted method, the *teta*—a cloth strainer on a wire frame. She was wearing a blue dress with black Skechers and looked much better than the day before. The sling was off, and her left arm moved normally as she walked around.

"Good morning, *niña*."

A photocopy of the *Granma* article that I had left accidentally on purpose on the counter, where she couldn't miss it, was lying on the table.

"Hi."

She served me a cup of coffee and sat down.

"Don't tell me that *café carretero* isn't better than that Bia-whatever-you-call it."

Indeed, it tasted different. Stronger but not as bitter.

"Yours is the best."

She smiled and pointed with her chin to the photocopied page. "I read it. Yes, that's Tania. Sorry about yesterday, but I was worn out."

"Are you sure it's her?"

"Absolutely."

The confirmation made my heart soar. I knew it had to be her! Now I just had to find "Tania." My mother, who might very well be looking for me. I hugged Mamina, my past hurt now forgotten.

"Thanks for letting me know about the article."

She sighed.

"*Mija*, I'd have told you before if I had thought you cared."

A loud chirping noise resounded in the kitchen. The cuckoo had come out and was chiming away. I listened, astonished, while the bird struck nine.

"How in the world . . . ?"

"Your friend fixed it early this morning. She said it only needed cleaning and balancing."

"Where is she?"

Mamina served a big glass of *café con leche* for herself and leaned back comfortably in her chair.

"Out with Sato. They just went to the *diplotienda* to buy food."

When I was little, going to a *diplotienda* was a big deal. They were mostly open to diplomats and foreigners. Now anyone could buy there . . . if they had dollars.

"Such a pretty couple, eh?" Mamina went on. "Love's in the air!"

We winked at each other. I finished my coffee and asked in a casual way, "Who's living in La Coloma now?"

"Sonrisa . . ." She trailed off. "And Yoel. He helps her with the farm and is also a veterinarian."

"How interesting! Is there a veterinary clinic in La Coloma?"

"Yes." Mamina added more sugar to the *café con leche* and stirred it nervously.

"What about Yulisa?"

"She got married and moved to Holguín."

Our eyes met for a second, then she averted hers. She took a breath and blew it out.

"Do you want to go visit the farm while I'm here?" I asked, still in nonchalant mode. I knew what the answer was going to be, but played dumb.

Mamina squinted.

"What do you mean?"

"Visit as in taking a car"—I smiled and pantomimed driving—"and hitting the road."

"No, *mija*, no! I was there only a month ago. And there's nothing to do in La Coloma. That's *el culo del mundo.*"

"I thought you'd like it."

She took her time to answer, and when she did, there was an uncharacteristic indecision in her voice.

"Well—I do. To me, the town is home. But you'll be bored out of your mind."

"Is that why you stopped taking me there?"

If Mamina sensed that there was a second intention behind my words, she didn't let it show.

"Yes. And because it was so hard to make the trip back then."

"Not anymore?"

"Now Sato takes me."

"I see."

I walked around the kitchen and wiped the counters. Mamina was always fastidious about keeping them super clean. It was also time to change the subject, so she wouldn't suspect—

"Ferradaz wants the house emptied for the repairs." Seeing Mamina's horrified expression, I hurried to clarify, "That's not going to happen tomorrow, but we need to start planning ahead. Would you like to stay with Catalina?"

Mamina had gone pale.

"No! I'm not going anywhere, I told you!" She exhaled and composed herself, adding in a softer tone. "Catalina doesn't like Nena. She thinks the girl has fleas."

I tossed the coffee grounds in the trash and washed the cloth strainer.

"I'll send a special collar that keeps fleas away."

"But she doesn't have any!"

Nena came in wagging her tail. Mamina put the fried rice I had brought the previous night in a bowl and placed it before the pooch. Nena licked her chops and got at it.

CANDELA AND SATIADEVA CAME back with steaks, chicken, several cans of condensed milk and five pounds of rice because my friend wanted to try her hand at *arroz con mango*. While Mamina stored the bounty in the refrigerator, I told Satia that I had to look at construction materials to get a better idea of the prices, then visit an old friend.

"I'm going to need your *almendrón* all day," I said loudly, making sure Mamina heard us. "Hope you don't have any other commitments."

"Merceditas, you'll always come first."

"I can stay with *abuela*," Candela offered, but it was clear that she would rather not.

"Oh, you can come too. My friend has an old house . . . everything's super vintage! You won't mind it, Mamina, will you?"

"*¡Claro que no!*" Mamina huffed. "I don't need company all day long. Goodness, I've spent the last ten years alone, and I'm no worse for the wear."

Ferradaz and the guys arrived. Mamina started to complain about having to deal with them, but they had brought the new door for the servants' quarters and it didn't make sense to waste a whole day just because I wasn't going to be around. Grudgingly, Mamina agreed to let the crew work, but warned me that she would be in her bedroom or out to see what groceries had come to the bodega.

"No problem at all," I said. "Ah, if that woman in the blue car comes by again, ask her for a phone number. *I'd* like to know what she wants."

"I'm not opening the door to anyone," Mamina said firmly.

"Why not?"

"Because I don't like strangers here when I'm by myself."

"You won't be by yourself," I reminded her. "In fact, let Ferradaz talk to her."

Ferradaz promised to take care of the issue.

"I will make sure to get a name and a number," she said confidently. "Don't worry. Because of my job, I'm used to handling all sorts of folks."

That settled, I was heading for the door when Santos called out from the backyard.

"*Señoras*, could you come here a second?"

Mamina didn't move.

"*You* talk to him," she grumbled, "and tell them not to pester me when you're gone, or I'll kick everybody out!"

Santos was poking around the rosebush. Though they had taken off the doorframe and what was left of the old door, the plant had survived. In fact, the flowers looked bigger and brighter than ever.

"The roses will have to go for us to install the new door," he said. "It's a pity because they are so beautiful."

"No big deal. But be careful with the thorns. They're nasty."

He caressed a petal.

"I hate killing anything. We are all sentient beings. I can transplant it, if that's fine with you."

It was ten-thirty. We had to get going if we were to be back before dark.

"I don't care one way or the other," I said. "Just leave Mamina out of it. She doesn't want to be disturbed."

"Okay, *señora.*"

FINALLY, CANDELA, SATIA AND I got in the *almendrón.* It smelled of sandalwood and freshly cleaned leather.

"Which store do you want to see first?" he asked. "The Fifth Avenue *diplotienda*? That's where Ferradaz buys most of the stuff when she can't find it on the black market."

"We aren't going to look for materials," I announced. "We're going to La Coloma."

Satia stared at me goggle-eyed.

"Without Mamina?" he asked.

"Without Mamina," I answered. "You've taken her before, so you must know the way."

# CHAPTER THIRTY-FIVE

*May 15th, 1987*

*Your letter was a breath of fresh air. I was feeling a bit down. Nothing is wrong, don't worry. Just the stress of life in a place where—let's just say things don't always work as expected. I am happy here, no question about that! But I wish we had access to more food and new household appliances. I'd like to go back briefly, see everyone and bring some supplies home.*

MAY FIRST HAD COME and gone. The Barbeitos offered to babysit, but Sarah didn't feel comfortable being away from Mercedes half a day. Sleep deprived and stressed out, she wasn't in the mood to listen to El Caballo pontificate for hours either. Joaquín was tired too so they skipped the "activity" and used the holiday to get some rest.

A few days later, an envelope addressed to Tania Rojas arrived at Villa Santa Marta with a Cuban stamp. Rob had sent it with a friend who was visiting Havana. He knew some of his letters were getting lost. Probably some of hers as well.

Oh, well, at least they had kept in contact. Besides, Sarah didn't have anything uplifting to share, except for Mercedes's milestones. The girl was starting to crawl ahead of schedule, according to her pediatrician. She also had a growing repertoire of sounds—no words yet, even if Joaquín insisted she was attempting to say "papa." But she didn't eat much and never slept more than four hours straight through the night.

However, Sarah managed to make a Saturday afternoon free. Joaquín, though scared he wouldn't know how to handle Mercedes, had agreed to stay with the girl. Sarah wanted to check out Yumurí, where clothes and some electronics were sold *por la libre*, as Mamina had said. Which turned out to be just partially true. A small Soviet color TV was on display, but only people who had accrued enough merits in their workplace could buy one. They also needed to place the order several months in advance, way before the devices "came" to the store.

On the second floor, where the women's department was located, Sarah bought a yellow dress made in Bulgaria and a silky white blouse, spending over two hundred pesos on them. There was no children's department, but a clerk told her that sometimes toys would "come" to the store.

"What kind of toys?" Sarah asked, hopeful. "Anything for little girls?"

"Yes. We get dolls, teacup sets, stuffed animals . . . we just never know when," the clerk concluded with a shrug.

On the third floor Sarah found an elegant blue shirt, the last one on the rack. Unfortunately, it was a size too small. But Joaquín assured her that he really appreciated the thought.

A WEEK LATER, AFTER waking up at 4 A.M. to feed Mercedes (which Joaquín never did because he had to work early in the morning), Sarah went back to sleep and had an unusually vivid dream. She was driving her mother's Datsun down Garnet Avenue, listening to "Girls Just Want to Have Fun," her hair blowing in the Pacific breeze. Then she came to a stoplight and remembered Mercedes. Where was the girl? Had she lost her daughter? But she didn't have children! Or did she?

She woke up with a throbbing headache. For a few anguishing seconds, she didn't know where she was. Still in her parents' home, dreaming she had moved to Havana? Or in Havana, dreaming that she was in Pacific Beach?

When the fog of the dream cleared up, she recalled Mercedes's appointment at the Pediatric Hospital and the two buses they needed to take in order to get there. Talk about starting the day on the wrong foot! The last time they went, Joaquín had borrowed the jeep from his unit, but he didn't like to because the gas and the vehicle belonged "to the state." Something Sarah understood, but she wished "the state" allowed people to get their own cars. Lo had told her that new Soviet Ladas and Moskvitchs were assigned to doctors who had served abroad, but it wasn't legal for Cubans to buy or sell any vehicle.

"Why?"

Lo shrugged.

"That's the way it is, *chica*. Selling a vehicle would be too . . . I don't know, commercialistic. In any case, they can do a change of ownership with no money involved." Lo grinned. "Supposedly."

Like a *permuta* was "an exchange of houses," even if there was (and there usually was) an exchange of money as well. What a way to complicate things!

THE PEDIATRICIAN SEEMED HAPPY with Mercedes's overall progress, but recommended a syrupy B-12 concoction to improve her appetite. The girl refused to eat *compotas*, the baby food distributed through the ration card. Frankly, Sarah would have refused too. The *compotas* came from Russia and tasted bitter, like made from sour apples. She pureed carrots and sweet potatoes the old-fashioned way, with a strainer and a spatula, because food processors were hard to find, even on the black market.

Mamina came to the rescue with bags of guavas, bananas and oranges. She was patient and managed to feed Mercedes everything, even the awful *compotas*. But she was anxious to return to La Coloma.

"I miss home," she told Sarah with a long face.

Sarah bit her tongue so as not to answer *Me too*. She also missed the supermarkets where she could pick and choose and compare prices. She didn't care what Joaquín said, wanting better food and gadgets that made life easier wasn't wrong or bourgeois. The ration-card system and those "designated days" to shop made everything harder than it should. She had to agree with the Barbeitos on that one.

Mamina tried to teach her how to cook Joaquín's favorite dishes, like *tasajo* with a light gravy called *mojo* and mashed plantains. But cooking bored Sarah out of her mind. So did sweeping floors, dusting and the whole housekeeping business. Damn, she didn't even do these things at home!

She thought about getting a job, any job, just to be out and meet new people—and get away from Villa Santa Marta.

"But you don't want to work in a factory or a bodega," Joaquín argued. "That would mean long hours standing and dealing with people. You aren't used to that."

"What about some secretarial work? Like in your unit?"

"Your Spanish isn't good enough to be a translator or do any official paperwork. And we'd have to send Mercedes to a *círculo infantil*, a state daycare center. Not a good idea, at least for now."

He was right. Maybe after Mercedes started eating better and on her own . . .

When it was too hot to go out, Sarah took the baby and a book to bed and read. Her collection of magazines had grown with glossy copies of *Sputnik*, a socialist incarnation of the *Reader's Digest* full of stories about the land of the Soviets.

Her favorite was still *Mujeres*, particularly a section called "*Mil Ideas*" where she once found a recipe for scrambled eggs with caviar. How was that for decadence? She assumed that caviar came from Russia, though she had yet to see it in the local stores.

If the weather cooperated, which happened less and less as the summer advanced, she would put Mercedes in the stroller. Sarah wished they could have playdates with neighborhood kids, which would also give her the opportunity to meet other parents, but it just so happened that most people on their block were childless, like Lo and the Barbeitos. Some of Joaquín's colleagues had children, but they lived too far from Miramar.

There was an amusement park called, oddly, Coney Island, that they had visited once, when Joaquín had the jeep. Though Mercedes was too little for the roller coaster and most rides, they all had enjoyed the fun house mirrors, frozen yogurt and cheerful atmosphere of the place. Unfortunately, it wasn't close enough for Sarah to venture there alone with the girl. Having no other options, they just walked around the neighborhood. People sometimes stopped her and commented on how pretty the baby looked.

"You have to get her an *azabache*," Lo said seriously, when Sarah told her of the compliments.

"A what?"

"An onyx charm to ward off the evil eye. I'll find one for you. Please, don't take her out again until she's wearing it!"

"Won't the charm be considered ideological deviation?" Sarah asked, only half joking.

"Who cares?" Lo replied. "One has to be flexible. And people don't need to know about it. Keep it hidden under her clothes."

The next day she presented Sarah with a bib pin brooch with the *azabache* and a smaller red stone.

"That's coral," she explained. "They work better together.

Now don't forget to have Mercedes wear them when you guys go out. People can harm babies, even without intending too. One has to be careful with such things, *chica*!"

Sarah tried not to giggle. "Okay, thanks."

They resumed their outings, with Mercedes now properly protected. Sarah settled into a happy routine. She loved her daughter, Joaquín and the life they had built together but continued to feel the pull from home, which grew stronger by the day. She didn't believe anymore that she belonged to just one place, as she had once foolishly written to her parents. She was a Pacific Beach surfer girl as much as a young Miramar mom. There had to be a way to merge both.

# CHAPTER THIRTY-SIX

As the *almendrón* drove away from Villa Santa Marta, Candela kept glancing at me, silently asking for an explanation.

"I want to find out more about Tania from my dad's relatives, and why Mamina kept me away from them," I said when we reached Fifth Avenue. "It occurred to me last night that there might be a reason for it."

Once Candela realized what I was up to, she got on board immediately, enthused about seeing the countryside.

"Oh, *¡el campo cubano!*" she said with a longing sigh. "That must be totally different from Homestead! Too bad it's in the opposite direction from Camagüey!"

Satia, who was quite loyal to Mamina, didn't look pleased with the arrangement, but I told him that we were dealing with a disagreeable family matter and it was best for my grandma's peace of mind to stay out of it.

EXCEPT FOR THAT SNIPPET from my childhood, my memories of La Coloma were fuzzy. By the time I married Nolan and left Cuba with him, I had lost contact with Sonrisa and my cousins. In my mind, they lived in the ass end of the world—*el culo del mundo*, as Mamina herself had said. They didn't, really. I had driven from Miami to Fort Myers and back (roughly the same distance between Havana and La Coloma) in a day without thinking much of it. Yes, the fact that I had a car helped. Mamina was right when she talked about the difficulties of travel in Cuba during the nineties, but people managed to visit the countryside by train or bus. It wasn't as hard as she made it look.

We entered Pinar del Río and rode quietly for half an hour. Candela was amazed at how smoothly the old Chevy ran.

"Does it have the original engine?" she asked.

"It does," Satia answered. "Meticulously maintained."

"How do you do it?"

"With ingenuity and a little magic, *mi amor*."

*Mi amor?* I grinned. Candela blushed.

A big sign pointed the way to the Soroa Orchid Garden, a nature preserve surrounded by round-topped boulder-like hills called *mogotes*.

"I love orchids!" Candela said.

"We'll go together before you leave."

"Will we have time?"

"If not, you're coming back, aren't you?"

"You bet! And we also have to visit Camagüey."

While they chatted, I silently evoked the image of my mother, whose picture I carried in my purse like a talisman. But I was also working on a strategic plan. If I were to demand straight answers from Sonrisa, she'd likely become defensive and tight-lipped, more so if Mamina had sworn her to secrecy. Instead, we would pretend that it was an impromptu visit and try to get her and Yoel talking.

I finally explained everything to Satia, who was baffled by the situation. He then revealed that Mamina went to La Coloma at least once a month—more often than she had led me to believe—and sometimes stayed for a couple of days.

"She loves the place," he said. "They all take care of her, and she has her own room with a hammock and everything." He paused and shook his head. "But this story about your mom . . . I hope you find her, Merceditas. I had no idea. By the way Mamina talks, I got the impression that both your parents were dead."

"Mamina's good at giving people the wrong impression when she wants to."

After we got to La Coloma, Satiadeva left behind the main street, flanked by huge *flamboyanes*, and turned onto a dirt road. A small house was nestled in at the end, flanked by two coconut trees. Rows of what I assumed were tobacco plants, with pale pink flowers and bright green leaves, stretched out before us. The breeze made them sway gently.

"What a pretty place!" Candela said.

Satia parked the *almendrón*, and we all came out. The house seemed as if it had been recently painted (an off-white color) and had a metal roof. There was a newer-looking front porch, yellow and red.

A woman in her fifties, with short grayish hair, saw us through the window. I felt suddenly shy and nervous. But she opened the door and smiled—and a big toothy smile it was.

"Merceditas!" she cooed. "How tall you've gotten!"

To my surprise, she hugged and kissed me.

"Are you Sonrisa?" I asked, though I didn't need to. She looked like a younger Mamina.

"Sure, *mijita*. Don't you remember me? Ah, well, you haven't been here in . . . in a long time. We . . ." She cut herself off.

"But you recognized me," I said, trying to gloss over the awkwardness of the moment.

"I've seen pictures of you. Where's Mamina?"

My fabricated answer was ready.

"She didn't know we were coming. We came to Pinar del Río because my friend Candela wanted to see the Orchid

Garden. Then we decided to pay you a visit since Satia said it wasn't too far."

"That's great! Well, come on in, *mija*. And Satia and your friend too. *¡Mi casa es su casa!*"

That was a greeting you didn't hear in the city anymore.

In the square living room, five wicker chairs had been placed in a circle. There was a black-and-white Electron TV set. A Singer sewing machine sat under a window. A vase of hydrangeas stood on top of an unpainted dining table. The flowers' sweet scent curled around my nose, competing with the smell of smoke that came from a wood burning stove in the backyard. The kitchen, to the right, was mostly occupied by a big ancient Frigidaire painted green. The motor hummed. Candela surveyed everything. This was another kind of museum, not precisely Art Deco, but museum anyway. Noticing her interest, Sonrisa offered to give us a tour of the house.

"My Yoel put on a new roof and built two new rooms," she said proudly. "One's for Mamina and the other for guests. Not that we have many, but if you'd like to spend the night here, as my aunt does, you're very welcome."

The rooms had cement floors and were furnished with hammocks and pine tables. Candela looked at me with a panicked expression. As much as she wanted to get in touch with her Cuban roots, the accommodations were too rustic for her taste.

"Thanks, but we can't," I said. "I don't want to worry Mamina."

"You can call her from Yoel's phone at the clinic."

"No, we'll be back before she starts wondering where we are. But I'll come again with more time."

"At least have something to eat. You must be hungry after such a long trip."

The trip hadn't been that long, but it would have been impolite to refuse. Sonrisa served us rice and chicken "from last night, but still good." Candela wasn't used to eating other people's leftovers but took it in stride. We put the chairs around the table and devoured the *arroz con pollo*, washing it down with fresh coconut water. As we ate, we fell into an easy conversation.

"I always ask Mamina about you," Sonrisa said, "and tell her to bring you here, but she says you come for just a few days."

That gave me the opening I was hoping for.

"I wish she had brought me more often before I left," I said. "You guys are the only family I have, besides her."

She cocked her head.

"Ah, yes, that would have been nice. But you know how hard transportation was."

"Yes, but—"

Before I could finish the sentence, Sonrisa added with real or fake enthusiasm, "Mamina says you have a restaurant! Does La Bakería have anything to do with cows? Did you bring any pictures?"

"Bakería is a play on words from 'baking.' And yes, I'll show you some pics that are on my phone. But first I'd like to know more about my dad, if you don't mind telling me."

The turn had been too fast and put Sonrisa on the alert. Her expression changed and resembled Mamina's when she said that *en boca cerrada no entran moscas*.

"Ah, my poor cousin Joaquín, may his soul be in heaven!" Sonrisa answered at last and crossed herself. "I didn't get to know him well. He enlisted in the army and moved to Havana when I was very young."

"What about my mom? Did you ever meet her?"

"Eh—your mom—I saw her only once." She ran her fingers over her hair. "Let me look at those pictures, girl!"

No, she wasn't going to be any help. At all.

A truck arrived in a cloud of dust and stopped in front of

the house. It was an old and rusty Ford, the kind that would have been taken to a demolition derby in Miami. The greenish paint was peeling. The bed was made of wood and secured with ropes.

"*¡Mijo!*" Sonrisa yelled. "Your cousin's here!"

A six-foot-tall guy with cropped hair unfurled himself from the truck and walked to the house.

"My cousin?" he repeated. "Which one?"

"Merceditas!"

He came over and shook my hand, looking slightly confused. I saw a glimpse of the shy guy he had once been.

"Why didn't Mamina tell me you were coming?" he asked.

I repeated my story. He accepted it and seemed happy to see me. With his high cheekbones and tanned skin, my cousin looked like a Native American. Mamina's claims that our family descended from the Taínos finally made sense.

"How have you been, *prima*?" he asked. "I wouldn't have recognized you if I saw you in the street."

"You've changed too, *primo*. Remember when you used to run away from me?"

"And you would call me a *güije*!"

We both laughed. Sonrisa started to make coffee using a *teta* like the one Mamina had. Satiadeva and Yoel went outside to examine the truck.

"What's a *güije*?" Candela whispered.

"A goblin with huge eyes who walks with his feet backward," I said.

"Your cousin's nothing like that!"

"He grew out of it."

In the front porch, the guys were talking cars, or rather trucks.

"*¡Bárbaro!*" Satia said.

"I just got it, man."

"I love Ford trucks! They're the best. If I could afford it, I'd exchange the *almendrón* for one in a heartbeat."

Candela crinkled her eyes and elbowed me. "They also like 'vintage' stuff here, don't they?"

# CHAPTER THIRTY-SEVEN

*June 18th, 1987*

*Mamina will stay here and take care of Mercedes while I'm away. Joaquín has reluctantly agreed to let me go but says that there's no way that a daughter of his is going to "Yankee-land." We'll see about that in a couple of years. For the time being, Mercedes is too young for such a long trip. I'll fly to Mexico City first, then to Tijuana and take the Greyhound to San Diego. I'm still concerned about the probation issue, but it's unlikely that Interpol is waiting for me at the border or watching my folks' house. I am not Patty Hearst.*

ONE DAY, CROSSING FOURTH Street, Sarah thought she had seen her father. It wasn't him, of course, but she couldn't stop reliving the moment, the fleeting happiness that she had felt. Homesickness was like a low-grade fever—barely noticeable on the outside, but simmering under her skin.

She began asking around about travel arrangements. The initial results were discouraging. The paperwork to leave the country could take months, if not years.

"We started the process in 1984," Elena told her, "and have no idea when we'll get the exit permit. But don't worry. Foreigners don't have to jump through as many hoops as we do."

Sarah, however, was now a Cuban, according to her ID card. She didn't have high hopes when Joaquín took her to a tall gray building that housed the Ministry of Immigration and Foreign Affairs. They had planned to come in together, but upon seeing the crowd that waited outside before the offices were even opened, he refused to stay.

"You can handle it," he said cheerfully. "Just tell them what your situation is. If they have questions, they can call me at work."

"Oh, I'm pretty sure I'll manage," she answered.

But she wasn't too confident. Some people found her story suspicious, or totally unbelievable. And the name change . . . She didn't look how Cubans thought a "Tania Rojas" would look. It would be hard to explain all that, and her Spanish failed her when she got nervous.

"Good luck. Everything will be fine."

Joaquín kissed her and left. Sarah had the impression that he didn't really expect her to get the permit. He was just being nice about it.

THE MINISTRY OF IMMIGRATION and Foreign Affairs was staffed by stern, armed men and women in uniform. A bulky guy directed Sarah to a section marked "foreigners." He didn't ask, simply gestured for her to follow him to an empty room. She was going to explain her situation, as Joaquín had advised, but the areas marked "nationals" were getting crowded fast. Cubans were separated into two groups: *salida permanente* and *salida temporal*. Those who were applying to leave the country permanently were taken to a small cubicle with no seats and given dirty looks by the employees.

Sarah sat on a hard bench. She had come prepared, with three hundred dollars and her American passport in case she had to pay for the exit permit as a foreigner, and four hundred pesos and her ID card in case they treated her as a Cuban. Another blonde was brought in by the same guard who had ushered her earlier. She wore an intricately embroidered blouse and a long blue skirt. Sarah admired the blouse discreetly and detected the fragrance of Red Moscow. The woman plopped down on the bench and said a long sentence in a language Sarah had never heard.

"Sorry, I don't . . . I only speak English and Spanish," she said.

"Ah!" The other blonde looked surprised, then asked the dreaded question. "Where are you from?"

"The United States."

Once the newcomer got over the shock (by now Sarah was used to it), she introduced herself as Valentina. She was from Moscow and, unlike the Russian guy who worked with Joaquín, quite a chatterbox.

"I'm married to a Cuban," she said. "You too?"

"Yes."

"What are you doing here? Trying to go back home?"

"For a short visit. Have you gone back before?"

"Over twenty times, if not more."

That was encouraging.

"Is it too hard?" Sarah asked shyly.

"Not at all." Valentina smiled. "But I already know everybody here!"

Their common language was Spanish, which neither of them spoke fluently, but they managed to communicate. When Sarah mentioned her fear of being denied the permit, Valentina snorted.

"Do you have dollars?" she asked point-blank.

"I do. But I am not sure if—"

"Give me fifty."

Though the request sounded strange, Sarah handed her

three twenties—she didn't have smaller bills. Valentina's name was called.

"Don't go anywhere or talk to anybody," she instructed Sarah. "Skip your turn."

Other foreigners had come into the room. An officer announced that those who didn't have appointments would be seen by a *compañero* in the order they had arrived. Sarah didn't claim her place in the queue. She just waited. Thankfully, she had brought an issue of *Mujeres* and entertained herself reading recipes. There was one for borscht soup.

Valentina came back with a wiry uniformed guy who led Sarah to an office.

"Your passport, please, *señora*?" he asked courteously.

"The . . . American one, right?"

"Yes."

The guy sat in front of a typewriter and filled out a form.

"You'll get your exit permit in a couple of weeks," he said afterward.

He smiled knowingly and shook her hand. Sarah was amazed . . . and a little scared.

VALENTINA WAITED OUTSIDE, LOOKING quite pleased with herself.

"I only gave him forty," she told Sarah. "The other twenty, I kept as a commission."

"Oh, that's—that's fine," Sarah stuttered. "Thanks for your help. It wouldn't have occurred to me—"

Valentina laughed and offered to take Sarah home. She had a car, a small brown Russian Lada.

"Unless you want to come with me to the *diplotienda* first," she said.

"Are you a diplomat?"

"No. Here in Cuba, I'm just a housewife. But *diplotiendas*

aren't only for diplomats. Any foreigner can go there. You have to pay with American dollars, though."

"I thought dollars were illegal."

"Yes, for Cubans they are."

"Why is that?" Sarah asked.

Valentina opened her arms in a helpless gesture.

"That's the way it is. Same in my country. The enemy's currency, you know?"

"But they don't mind if we use it."

"They don't. Let's go now!"

It wasn't one o'clock yet. Having some free time at her disposal—Elena had agreed to babysit Mercedes until four o'clock—Sarah squeezed herself into the Lada's passenger's seat. Valentina drove to a modern building with tinted windows on Fifth Avenue and 42nd Street.

A security guard stopped the women at the door.

"Identifications?"

Valentina showed him a red document with Cyrillic characters. Sarah took out her American passport, which was getting a lot of attention that day. The security guard inspected them and waved them in.

"What was that about?" Sarah asked.

"He was making sure we aren't Cubans."

"Why?"

"They aren't allowed in. Unless they come with one of us."

The segregation shocked Sarah as much as the bribery of the immigration officer.

"But . . . really. Why?"

"They don't want Cubans to be 'polluted' by consumerism," Valentina said with a little quirk of her lips. "I guess."

"But that's not fair!"

"Like I said, that's the way it is."

Sarah found a shopping cart—the first of its kind she had

seen in Cuba—and began perusing the shelves. The merchandise was scattered, but there was a bit of everything. Cans of condensed and evaporated milk sat next to orange and strawberry preserves. Ground-beef trays filled a freezer. Another freezer contained whole chickens, from Kansas of all places! There were tomatoes, cucumbers and lettuce, healthier-looking than those sold at the *puesto*, and more exotic finds like green apples at five dollars a pound. Sarah bought ten pounds to make *compotas* for Mercedes.

Clothes were expensive and low-quality. Lycra in all its permutations (blouses, pants, even dresses) reigned supreme. Shoes were plastic and smelled of glue. There was nothing for toddlers. Sarah got a cute leather pouch with the words *Viva Cuba* embossed. There were a few appliances too, but she had already spent all her money.

"I wish I had known about this place before," she said to Valentina as they left the *diplotienda* carrying several bags.

"There are more. But this one is the best."

Sarah lowered her voice. "I still don't understand how they can keep Cubans out. It seems so unfair, so—"

"There are solutions to every problem," Valentina said. "I bring some nationals in and charge them ten percent off whatever they spend. That's the usual rate. I always get more requests than I can take on without attracting attention, so if you're interested . . ."

"Isn't that against the law?"

Valentina chortled.

"Where have you been living, Jackie O, under a rock?" She opened the car with a clunky key. "I'll show you the ropes. Now hop in!"

She made Sarah laugh but also feel foolish, as if she had landed on the wrong planet. A *guanaja*, like Cubans say. But hey, she wasn't *that* naïve. As much as she loved Joaquín, she knew better than telling him about Valentina and what had transpired at the Ministry of Immigration and Foreign Affairs. Maybe it was an echo of an old "loose lips sink ships" poster that her father had glued to the wall at home, but she simply reported that her exit permit had been granted. Joaquín seemed surprised, which confirmed her suspicion—he had counted on it being denied.

# CHAPTER THIRTY-EIGHT

The house smelled of hydrangeas, *arroz con pollo* and coffee that Sonrisa was making using the old-fashioned *teta*. It was a warm, embracing fragrance, but I couldn't relax enough to enjoy it. If there was in fact a conspiracy to keep a family secret from me, I needed to talk to Yoel in private, before his mother had a chance to forewarn him. Supposing he wasn't already part of the conspiracy, that is.

"I'd like to stretch my legs," I said, faking a groan, when he and Satia stopped gushing over the old Ford.

"Same here." Candela rubbed her knees.

As I expected, Yoel offered to show us the farm.

"Visitors always like to see the drying barn," he said, "though the smell can be intense if you aren't used to it."

"I won't mind it."

Sonrisa looked as if she was going to say something, but didn't. Candela, Satia, Yoel and I went outside and walked around row upon row of tobacco plants as tall as my waist.

"I didn't know they could grow so much," I said.

"They do when someone speaks to them," Yoel answered.

Satiadeva and Candela nodded—they had found a kindred spirit in La Coloma! Then the conversation turned to the business side of the operation. Yoel explained that the government allowed farmers to keep and sell ten percent of their crops, most of it acquired by tourists in Viñales, but they still had to turn in the remaining ninety percent to the state.

"Why is that?" Candela asked.

Yoel scratched his head as if it hadn't occurred to him to ever ponder it.

"Well, because . . . that's what the government has established. That's the way it has always been. The state owns everything."

"I thought the revolution had given the land to the peasants."

"Well, we have the land, but the crops still belong to the state."

Candela was clearly baffled, like Nolan when I tried to explain to him how things worked—or didn't work—in Cuba. Most people did what they were told to do. We didn't question why *diplotiendas* sold their products in dollars but we were paid in pesos, for example. Or why we needed an "exit visa" to leave the country. Yes, some brave souls rebelled. But the dissidents tended to end up in jail.

"Anyway, that ten percent is the only real money we see because buyers pay us dollars," Yoel went on. "We don't use any chemicals and all cigars are rolled by hand. That makes a difference, and foreign connoisseurs appreciate it."

"How big is your farm?" Candela asked.

"Ten acres. But I don't do all the work myself. I can't, with my work at the clinic. Arturo Padilla takes care of my field during the weekdays, and we share the proceeds. It's an under-the-table arrangement, but nobody here is going to tattle on us."

"Mamina told me that a Padilla girl had a fight with my mother," I blurted. "I'm looking for her!"

He blinked.

"My mother, not the Padilla girl," I clarified. "She disappeared many years ago."

Yoel didn't answer. Wind ruffled his hair and it occurred to me, as I waited, that he was indeed a handsome guy. Candela and Satiadeva marched ahead of us arm in arm.

"It must have been hard for you," my cousin said at last, a twinge of pity shining in his dark, sincere eyes. "Are all gringos like that? They just up and leave their kids?"

"No, no. They are regular folks. I mean, there are some pretty awful ones out there, but in general, Americans are like us."

"I have never met one."

"You have now—Candela."

"She looks Cuban."

"Her parents are."

He seemed surprised but said nothing. I shaded my eyes from the sun. The *mogotes* were sketched in the distance. I inhaled the earthy smell of the grass and waited, not sure what else to say, or how to start . . .

"*You* look American," Yoel spoke finally. "Or Russian or from somewhere else." He stopped and slapped his forehead. "*¡Oye!* Old Canario Padilla told me once he had something that belonged to Joaquín's wife."

"What was it?"

"A brooch, I think. Some kind of jewelry. He's probably given it to Mamina, but since you're here, we may as well ask him."

It was strange, a piece of Tania's jewelry ending up in La Coloma. Unless she had lost it during her first or second trip . . .

"Where does he live?" I asked.

"Very close. *Al cantío de un gallo.* And he'll appreciate it. Poor Canario has been so lonely after he lost his wife a year ago."

My mother had walked down this same dirt road. I wondered how she had felt because I didn't find it easy. Small rocks and goatheads got inside my shoes. The sun made my eyes

hurt. But, at any rate, it seemed like I had made the right decision going to La Coloma. Encouraged, I proceeded with my
questioning.

"What did you hear about my mom?"

Yoel slowed down. We were near the drying barn—a long,
narrow structure with a thatched roof.

"Not much. Only that she left you and Joaquín, and that's
why he did . . . what he did."

A shiver bolted down my spine. I stiffened and my mouth
felt dry.

"What did he do?"

He came to a full stop.

"We weren't supposed to tell you"—he rubbed the back of
his neck—"but so much time has passed—"

"*What* weren't you supposed to tell me?"

"That he shot himself."

I stared at him. Yoel looked down and added, "Mamina said
he was depressed about your mom leaving him."

My mom. It all came back to her. I let the information sink
in and asked, weakly, "You mean he didn't die in Angola? That's
what I've heard all my life!"

"Well, yes, he died in Angola."

"But not in combat?"

"No. The war was over. He went there as an internationalist
worker, a civilian."

I didn't say anything else until we reached the drying barn.
Yoel opened the gate. I followed him inside a big rectangular
shed full of wooden poles where brown tobacco leaves were
hung to dry. The dense, potent aroma of fermentation made
my eyes water and did nothing to clear the confusion in my
head. I kept mulling over Yoel's words while Satia and Candela talked to him. Their voices came to me muffled, as if
from a distance.

"How long do the leaves stay here?"

"Fifty days or so."

"Then they are rolled into cigars?"

"Oh, not yet! It's a long process—"

I stepped out in the fresh air and inhaled deeply. Staring at the green expanse of tobacco plants, it dawned on me that I couldn't trust Mamina anymore.

The others came out. Satia and Candela said something about taking a stroll by themselves. Yoel stayed with me.

"Mamina and I talked about my dad two days ago," I told him. "She maintained that he had died in Cuito Cuanavale."

"No way. Cuito was the last battle of the Angola war, and it ended in March 1988. I know because my dad's brother fought there. Joaquín died in 1991."

My hands started shaking with fury.

"That's why I never saw the death certificate! Is he buried in Angola, or is that another fib?"

He put a hand on my arm, protectively.

"No, that is true. He shot himself shortly after he got there. They only sent back the bodies of soldiers, not—" He swallowed. "Sorry."

"Why would Mamina lie about my dad's suicide?" I asked, more to myself than Yoel.

"To spare you the pain?" His voice was softer. "Your mom had just vanished, then he goes and— How do you explain all that to a little girl?"

"That made sense *then*. But now?"

"Yeah, she should have told you at some point."

I felt winded.

"It was a family conspiracy, wasn't it? You all agreed not to talk about my mom? Or my dad's death?"

He nodded and gave my arm a gentle squeeze. I was about to burst into tears.

"Mom forbade us to mention your parents when Mamina brought you over. Then you guys stopped coming. She probably thought that we were going to spill the beans." He paused and frowned. "She never invited us to visit her in Havana until you left."

I broke into a run—not away from Yoel but my own thoughts. He caught up with me soon. We kept walking in silence among the rows of tobacco plants.

# CHAPTER THIRTY-NINE

*October 20th, 1987*

*I miss you so much, dude. And Mom, Dad, home, the waves
. . . but I couldn't be away from Mercedes any longer. She
was so happy to see her mommy again!*

*The rag doll you bought outside Berkeley Bowl? She loves
it. We've named her Saralí. Here are some pictures I just took
with the Polaroid. Lo's brother, who's traveling to Mexico,
will mail them.*

AS SARAH WAITED IN line (ah, *colas* . . . she hadn't missed
them!) at the José Martí International Airport, she tried to
estimate how much excess-weight tax she would have to pay.
Cubans who traveled back home usually brought an array of
suitcases and backpacks bursting at the seams, but even that
paled in comparison with the luggage she had taken to the
Tijuana airport.

"*Señorita*, are you moving to Cuba?" a surprised Mexican
customs officer had asked.

"I already live there," Sarah replied.

"Ah, I see."

There were clothes for her and Joaquín, who would dislike
the fact that they had come from "Yankeeland" but would

wear them since his wardrobe was painfully limited. Dresses, jumpers and shoes for Mercedes in different sizes. Gerber jars of all kinds. (An ungodly amount that filled two suitcases.) Disposable diapers. A new stroller. A food processor, a portable Panasonic TV set, a toaster, a small microwave oven. *Rolling Stone* and *Vogue* magazines. Hair curlers. Five Polaroid cameras. Films for her Minolta. A flashlight . . . She even brought gifts for Lo, Valentina and the Barbeitos. And six thousand dollars in cash. Pauline had left Sarah what was supposed to be a college fund, which she had barely touched before her Cuban adventure started. It was now put to good use.

The most difficult part had been to convince her parents that she was happy and safe in her new home—El Salvador, they assumed, and she hadn't disabused them. They hadn't yet gotten over her long absence, and rightfully so, she admitted.

At first, her mother had gone into hysterics. "Where have you been? We thought you were dead!" Which couldn't be because she knew Rob had been sending them her notes regularly. But that's the way she was, a drama queen. In any case, Sarah made it clear that she wasn't going to reveal anything about her current home or situation.

"We aren't even going to discuss that," she said firmly. (It turned out that she had a mom's voice as well.)

Her parents relented.

Then, one day, her mother had come into Sarah's old room when she was changing clothes. Though she had covered herself quickly, her mother asked, "Are you pregnant?"

"How ridiculous!" Sarah pretended to laugh.

"Have you been?"

"Oh, Mom." She looked away, nervously. "No, no!"

The questions had stopped, but she started bugging Sarah to call her probation officer. The mess that she had caused getting involved with the Sanctuary movement and smuggling those people across the border! Sarah doubted that anybody remembered her case. The INS had more pressing issues to attend to than silly little her.

Her father, who was the silent type, hadn't asked anything. He just said that, though he was hurt by the way she had left, he still loved her.

"I know that, Daddy."

One morning, as he read the *San Diego Union Tribune*—the paper looked so big and long compared to ten-page *Granma*!—Sarah realized how much her father reminded her of Joaquín. Same gestures, same square shoulders . . . Ah, she couldn't wait to introduce them to each other. They were going to get along fine.

But she wasn't ready to talk about Joaquín, Mercedes or her life in Cuba. A communist country, good grief! Her parents might even call the police and have her arrested so she couldn't go back. She avoided her old friends and spent most of the time home, shopping or surfing. But even her beloved waves seemed to have lost their shine because she would see Mercedes in every little girl playing in the sand.

She had only left San Diego to spend a day with Rob and meet Vincent. Wasn't it wonderful that her best friend had found true love as well? Rob had insisted on traipsing through markets and toy stores to buy gifts for Mercedes—a huge plush giraffe, a rag doll, a stuffed bunny . . . But the visit had left Sarah with an uneasy feeling. Though clearly elated to see her, Rob didn't say much—Vincent had done most of the talking. Rob looked thinner and had gotten tired sooner than he used to.

"Is there anything wrong?" she had asked.

"Nothing at all!" he said too quickly. "I had a cold a few weeks back, but I'm fine now."

Sarah had the impression that there was more to it than a cold, but didn't insist. Rob had been a sickly child and hated when people fussed over him. She hooked her hand with his arm and placed her head on his shoulder.

"I'm so glad to be here with you, dude."

He kissed her hair. They had always been affectionate toward each other, being only children and both a little lost. But Sarah sensed something had changed. She felt a shadow between them, the ghost of things unsaid. And Vincent, welcoming and warm as he was, had a worried expression . . . But she had just met him. That could have been his usual look.

"There's a Puerto Rican restaurant on this block where they make the best *arroz con habichuelas* in the world," Vincent said. "Let's go."

"In Cuba, we call them *arroz con frijoles*," Sarah said.

"We?" Rob laughed and patted her back. "*Compañera* Tania has turned into a real Cuban, hasn't she?"

Sarah laughed too but wasn't too sure about it. Vincent was right, though. The *arroz con habichuelas* was excellent, and so was the *pernil*, the tender, slow cooked roast pork that came with it.

SARAH CLEARED CUBAN CUSTOMS effortlessly because Valentina's method worked with a harsh-looking officer. Joaquín was pacing outside the gate. He ran to hug her, teared up and said he was afraid that she wouldn't return. (What kind of mother did he think she was, anyway?)

"*Mi amor*, I have little to offer." His voice trembled. "And you can have so much outside of Cuba!"

In a way he was right, but he also didn't get America, and not just politics. He believed that all "Yankees," when not busy shooting each other, lived in mansions with swimming pools and drove brand-new cars. That was despite Sarah telling him about her parents' two-bedroom cottage and their 1984 Volkswagen.

"I have all I need in Havana," she answered, and kissed him. "Where's Mercedes?"

"With Mom. I wanted to bring them, but the jeep is having transmission problems."

On the way home, Sarah did her best to summarize her trip but didn't mention how much cash she had brought. The amount would have seemed astronomical to Joaquín, who was stunned at the sight of the baby food and the many packages of disposable diapers.

"What do you need all that for?" he asked.

Men were so clueless!

SARAH HAD ONLY SPENT eight days in San Diego. Yet, short as her absence was, it took her over a week to get used to Havana again. Buildings looked smaller, streets dirtier and stores emptier. Villa Santa Marta felt more haunted than ever. Smelly too. The toilet in the second-floor bathroom had gotten clogged in her absence, and Joaquín hadn't noticed, or didn't care.

Well, nothing was perfect. All things considered, she had a good life there. And a beautiful daughter, who seemed to have doubled in size. Mamina laughed and assured her it was normal because kids grew so fast.

"If you don't see her for a month, you won't recognize her."

Sarah couldn't imagine being away from her little girl a whole month! Ah, she adored her. Her skin wasn't pasty white like Sarah's, but olive like Joaquín's, which made her big blue eyes more striking.

Next time (because there would be a next time!) it would be easier to travel, now that Sarah had the right contacts. She hoped to convince Joaquín to let her and Mercedes spend part of the year in San Diego. Ideally, the three of them, but given his job, that would have been next to impossible.

Yet that too could change soon. He was planning to apply

for a civilian job in a new military-owned tourism venture called Gaviota. Gaviota had ties with Canadian and Spanish businesses. There was a chance that Sarah could get a job with them as well. She certainly didn't want to be a housewife, much less a Cuban housewife, all her life.

SARAH HAD BROUGHT LO a makeup case with shadow and lipstick in the right colors for her complexion, but didn't reveal where she had gotten it. Joaquín had asked her not to tell anyone that she had gone back home. It wouldn't look good. He had explained to the neighbors that she was taking a week-long political workshop at the Communist Party School Ñico López. As for the brand-new clothes and appliances, she could say that her family had sent them. She went along with the story, but Lo didn't seem to believe a word of it.

To the Barbeitos, though, she told the truth. They listened and sighed.

"Ah, lucky you."

# CHAPTER FORTY

We reached another farmhouse. It was similar to Sonrisa's, but the outside blue paint was worn off and peeling in patches. Two banana trees with big and shiny leaves grew in front, providing shade and a nice touch of green. A horse was near the porch, not fenced in or tied, just standing there, munching on grass. The animal didn't appear to notice our presence, but I made sure to leave ample distance between us.

"Have you ever ridden a horse?" Yoel asked.

"No. They terrify me."

"If trained properly they are very gentle. Smart too. I'll take you later for a ride if you want to."

"Uf, no. But thanks."

"Good afternoon to Yoel and company," said a man's voice from inside the house. "Come on in!"

Canario Padilla was a big tall guy with white hair and a salt-and-pepper goatee. He was sitting on a three-legged stool, but stood up like a gentleman to shake our hands. His were rugged and capable, like Yoel's.

There were two bedrooms on each side of the living room, a kitchen at the end and a door that opened to a small yard. The walls were painted white. I smelled black beans with cumin, the way Mamina would make them.

Yoel made introductions and Canario's green eyes sparkled.

"So you're Joaquín's daughter?" He hugged me. "What a wonderful surprise! I always ask Mamina about you."

"She's never mentioned it."

"She hasn't?" he asked, looking stunned.

*Among many other things*, I thought, but just nodded.

He gestured for us to sit on a beige fabric sofa. I sank into it. A spring was loose, but there was no other place to sit.

"Don't you know I am your godfather, Merceditas?" Canario asked.

A sense of exhaustion passed over me.

"Are you? I didn't even know I was baptized."

"Is that so?" He gave me a quizzical expression. "Well, we didn't tell many people, but still—"

*But still.* I gritted my teeth. To avoid rolling my eyes, I looked around and saw a 2010 calendar hanging from the wall.

"Where was I baptized?" I asked. "Here?"

"No, at a church in Havana."

"Who is my godmother?"

"Your grandma."

Another deception. Or just an omission. But it was bad enough. Canario took a cigar out of his pocket and lit it up, still watching me fondly.

"When was that?" I asked.

"You were a tiny toad—two or three months at the most."

"Before my mother left?"

Canario took a fragrant puff.

"Ah, yes, way before. She was there. But Joaquín wasn't. We didn't tell him because he belonged to the Communist Party and wouldn't have approved."

He smoked placidly, unaware of the distress that his revelations had caused me. Not about the baptism as such, but the silence around it and the web of lies that Mamina had weaved around our family and my own past.

"Would you like some black beans, Mercedes?" Canario asked. "I just made them."

"That's very kind of you, but no, *gracias*."

"You told me you had something that belonged to Mercedita's mom," Yoel said. "What is it?"

Canario straightened.

"That's right, *mijo*," he said, and his eyes dropped. "I had forgotten. *Dios mío*, what a shame!"

He put the cigar away. Yoel prodded him.

"What's a shame, man?"

"The whole thing was my daughter Isela's fault," Canario said, frowning, "See, Mercedes, your mother came once from Havana. She wanted to buy . . . pork, I think."

"A chicken," I said.

"Yes, a chicken! Do you know what happened?"

"Mamina said she had a disagreement with a Padilla girl."

He nodded.

"That would be Isela. Tania had brought money, Cuban pesos and American dollars, but my daughter asked for a locket she was wearing."

I waited, crossing and uncrossing my fingers. A roar filled my head as I stared at a black-and-white framed photograph on the wall—Canario, fifty years younger, holding hands with a pretty girl.

"It's here somewhere." Canario stood up and continued talking as he entered a bedroom. "Isela refused to sell her our old hen unless she got the locket too. When I heard the story, months later, I was so mad at my daughter that I slapped her."

Silence filled the space for a few seconds.

"In the end, she got nothing for it," he went on from the bedroom. "When she took the locket and the chain to La Casa del Oro in Havana, the buyer rejected them because they didn't want alloys. She brought them back, and that's when I found out. Your mom had left by then and Mamina had moved to Havana so I kept it."

There was the sound of an armoire door opening. I felt dizzy. Yoel patted my arm.

"Calm down, *primita*."

"Can you believe Mamina never said I was baptized either?" I whispered.

He whistled.

Canario came back with a small package wrapped in a newspaper page.

"I'm happy to give it back to you," he said.

My hands shook as I took out a thin chain and a locket, both so tarnished that they were almost black. The chain was broken, but the locket looked intact. I opened it carefully and saw the faded picture of an old woman with gray hair in a bun. On the other side was the face of a smiling little girl.

"This means a lot," I muttered. "Thanks so much."

Canario gave me a sad smile.

"Don't mention it, *ahijada*. It was embarrassing. That's not how we do things around here. We are neighborly. And your mom wasn't a stranger but my own *comadre*. Mamina's daughter-in-law. Joaquín's wife!"

I pressed the locket against my chest, relishing the fact that my mother had worn it. She had had my picture with her all the time, just like I was carrying hers now.

"It's very nice of you to have kept it all these years," I managed to say. "I really appreciate it."

*And I appreciate even more that you didn't give it to Mamina*, I added silently. Aloud, I said, "What else can you tell me about my mom?"

"We saw each other only twice: the day of the baptism and

when Joaquín brought her here a few months later. We didn't have a chance to talk too much. Ah, the three of you made such a beautiful family." He paused for a second. "I'm sorry she left the way she did. But those were difficult times. Shortages everywhere. No food, no power, nothing . . . We used to have a restaurant here in La Coloma, El Fogón de Fefa, which was nationalized in the sixties. It worked on and off, and was finally closed down in eighty-nine."

"The special period was around the corner, wasn't it?"

"Yes, only we didn't know it." He cocked his head. "The Soviet Union was on its way out; the Berlin Wall had fallen . . . You have to consider all that."

The intrusion of Big History in my sad private story startled me.

"What does politics have to do with my mom?"

"I'm not saying it has anything to do with her. But there were tensions here: the Ochoa case, Fidel's fears that we would follow the eastern bloc."

"Do you think she could have been involved with"—I hesitated to say "the CIA" because it sounded too absurd—"counterrevolutionary groups?"

Canario denied it vigorously.

"Ah, no! I can't imagine Joaquín marrying a woman who didn't *love* the revolution. But if she was accused of working for the American government or something like that, she might have had to flee. Even if it wasn't true."

I listened respectfully to what sounded like one of my childhood fantasies. My mother, the international spy!

"That's just a thought," Canario concluded. "Here in *el culo del mundo*, we know nothing about what goes on in the world."

"What about my dad? Yoel just told me he committed suicide in Angola. I had no idea!"

I braced for the answer, but Canario shrugged.

"Mamina was always secretive about it. I suspect that's the reason why she didn't let any of us get to know you."

WHEN THE VISIT DREW to a close, I thanked Canario for the locket "and everything else."

"Do you mind if I take Caballero to ride back home?" Yoel asked. "*La prima* has never been on a horse."

"Sure, *mijo*. He needs the exercise. The saddle is by the door. Come back soon, my *ahijada*."

Canario hugged me and kissed my forehead, which made me feel like crying. That was something else Mamina had withheld from me: the affection of this compassionate man who might have cared enough to be a father figure.

We went outside. I watched as Yoel saddled Caballero. At close distance, the horse looked bigger and scarier.

"Don't be afraid, *prima*. He's really sweet."

Once I straddled the animal's solid body and wrapped my arms around the not-less-solid back of my *primo*, I felt strangely comforted. I had a godfather. My cousin was a nice, helpful guy. The locket, in my purse, had joined the copy of the *Granma* write-up. I was putting together pieces of my mother's life. There was hope after all, and despite everything.

WE MET SATIADEVA AND Candela at Sonrisa's house. Satia had been trying to check his messages, afraid to miss a client's call, but his cell phone didn't work there. Candela's and mine didn't either, but they just didn't work in Cuba.

"You can always call me at the veterinary clinic," Yoel said.

I stared out the door at the green, beautiful tobacco fields and breathed deeply. Life seemed simpler here, and Candela was obviously enthralled too. But we were only looking at the surface. There were secrets and ill will and all the nasty things we found everywhere else, made worse by poverty and hardship. What kind of people asked a desperate mother for a piece of jewelry in exchange for a crappy old hen?

There was no need to pretend anymore. When Sonrisa went to the kitchen, I followed her and demanded answers.

"Why did you all lie to me?"

She cleaned her hands, nervously, in a tattered dishcloth.

"My mom and Mamina agreed not to tell you about your dad's suicide." She paused and looked out the window toward the *mogotes*. "To protect you."

"That excuse is getting old, you know? She didn't say a word about Canario either. Did you know he was my godfather?"

She nodded. Her voice sounded drained when she finally spoke.

"My aunt has always been very reserved."

"That's a nice way to put it," I snapped.

"She's had a hard life, *mija*."

"Haven't we all?"

I rubbed the middle of my chest and left the kitchen. Candela and Satia were sitting on the porch. Yoel gave me a quiet hug that I couldn't return. I felt sad, angry and, above all, betrayed.

# CHAPTER FORTY-ONE

*December 22nd, 1987*

*You probably won't get this letter until late January, but still—¡Feliz Navidad! What are you guys doing? We will be spending a few days in La Coloma, the town where Joaquín grew up and his family lives. He knows how hard last Christmas was for me, so we are going to do something fun this time. I'm so excited!*

THE TREES THAT USED to shade the Miramar sidewalks had lost their leaves and it didn't get unbearably hot in the afternoons anymore, but those were the only signs that winter had arrived. Though the temperature kept above seventy degrees Fahrenheit, everybody seemed to be freezing. Sarah tried not to laugh when she saw Lo wearing a thick blue wool jacket and a matching beanie. Elena sported elegant scarves and cardigans that had been in style twenty years ago, and even Joaquín didn't leave the house without a trench coat.

"Wait until we get to La Coloma," he said. "It gets even cooler there! You should have brought more winter clothes!"

"I think I'll be fine," she assured him.

THEY STARTED PREPARING FOR the trip a week in advance. Joaquín borrowed the jeep again. He also brought home a sturdy army tent.

"Are we going to camp out in La Coloma?" Sarah asked, giggling.

"We have to. My mom's house is small."

It sounded like a great adventure. Sarah packed disposable diapers, Gerber jars and evaporated milk for a week.

"You don't need to take food," Joaquín said. "There's enough in Pinar del Río."

"Just in case."

The two-and-a-half-hour trip showed Sarah a different face of Cuba. She hadn't yet seen any mountains, and the rounded hills called *mogotes* were a revelation. They could even hike there! The jeep passed through Viñales. Red-roofed homes with big front porches and rocking chairs in them looked inviting.

"This is a beautiful town. And the houses aren't that small!"

"We haven't gotten to La Coloma yet."

The city gave way to the countryside. A sign pointed to an orchid garden.

"Can we visit?" Sarah asked.

"It isn't open to the public now. Soroa is being repaired as part of a national campaign to make tourist sites more appealing."

Once in La Coloma, they drove by lush green tobacco fields, took a dirt road and stopped in front of a (very small indeed) house surrounded by two palm trees. Mamina lived there with her sister Olimpia, her sister's daughter Sonrisa, Sonrisa's husband and their little girl, who was a few months younger than Mercedes.

"Come on in!" Mamina said warmly. "*¡Mi casa es su casa!*"

They hadn't yet sat down when Sonrisa brought a bottle of mango juice for Mercedes.

"Such pretty blue eyes! God bless her."

JOAQUÍN'S FAMILY OWNED A tobacco farm. Or perhaps "owned" wasn't the right word. The land belonged to a *cooperativa*, which *wasn't* a co-op, but a government-run operation that encompassed several neighboring farms. They harvested together and handed over the cured leaves to the state, but each family kept a tobacco stash that they sold—illegally, it seemed, though it was hard to tell.

They all made Sarah feel part of their tightknit clan and spoiled Mercedes rotten. Sonrisa called her *chiquitita* and prepared a portable cradle for her. But they were so, so poor! There was no running water on the farm. They got it from a well using a metal bucket because there was no electric pump either. The whole family squeezed together in a one-bedroom, one-bathroom, around-seven-hundred-square-foot house. And there used to be more people: Mamina's late husband and her daughter, Mercedes.

Mamina's sister, Olimpia, was a widow too. She was older than Mamina and looked sickly. Sarah felt they were imposing on her and tried to help out in the kitchen, but her inability to cook on a wood stove—the rustic kind she had only seen in movies about frontier life—or wash dishes with ash rendered her useless.

When they went out, Joaquín seemed half proud and half ashamed of her. Though most people already knew he had married a "Yankee," they still found it hard to believe. How could a communist like him have fallen in love with someone from the evil empire? There were a few awkward moments at first, but once relatives and neighbors got used to Sarah, they started to pepper her with questions that she didn't always know how to answer.

Mamina and Olimpia were curious about Mercedes's other set of grandparents. Sarah couldn't very well explain, much less in Spanish, that "the other set" didn't know they had a granddaughter. Well, her mother suspected it, but—she simply said that they lived "in a faraway city" and "maybe" would visit Cuba to meet the girl soon.

Other inquiries were even more difficult to field.

"Is Reagan planning to invade Cuba?" Sonrisa asked, her eyes round and scared.

"I don't think so," Sarah answered. "Why would he?'

"He invaded Grenada!"

Sarah was getting flustered.

"I really can't tell you—"

Thankfully, Sonrisa also wanted to know all about Michael Jackson, Cyndi Lauper, "We Are the World" and teased hair. Sarah promised to send her an issue of *Rolling Stone*. She was also asked to explain the difference between Republicans and Democrats. Older folks got it because *conservadores* and *liberales* had been the main parties in Cuba before Fidel, but those born in the sixties and later didn't understand the difference, or the very idea of having more than one party.

As usual, Sarah steered clear of politics, afraid of saying something offensive or counterrevolutionary, but other people didn't. Her *compadre* Canario told her (when they were alone and in a whisper) that nationalizing private farms had been a mistake.

"See, *comadre*, before, we didn't have land but there was food. Now the state has the land and we have nothing to eat."

Despite Canario's complaints, Joaquín had been right: there was more food there than in Havana. Farmers grew vegetables and fruits to supplement the bodega rations. They couldn't kill cows, even their own, without a special permit, but pigs and goats were fair game. In fact, a traditional holiday meal was roasted pork, just like Puerto Rican *pernil*, and they all enjoyed a whole animal, something that would have been impossible in Havana. The Montero family also had a chicken coop, and fresh eggs were always available.

Mercedes's baptism was still a secret because Sarah hadn't gotten around to telling Joaquín about it. She didn't want to cause trouble for Mamina, and it wasn't important. Anyway, nobody seemed surprised when Canario gave them a bag of malangas and three pounds of tiny, sweet bananas, excellent for making *compotas*.

One afternoon, after leaving Mercedes in Sonrisa's care, Joaquín took Sarah for a tour of the village.

"Let's have lunch at El Fogón de Fefa, where my grandma used to work as a cook before the revolution," he said. "I would come in on Sundays, and she snuck out a ham sandwich or some *croquetas* for me. Fefa pretended not to notice. She knew we had too many mouths at home, and not much food."

They walked from the farm to Calle Colón, the main and only paved street in town, passing by an old Catholic church with broken windows and a decapitated bell tower next to a newly painted elementary school named Ernesto Che Guevara. Signs of the times, Sarah thought.

The sidewalks, where they existed, were often uneven, with the cement cracked by the roots of huge leafy trees.

"These are *flamboyanes*," Joaquín said. "When they bloom, the red flowers look like little flames. And in the fall, it seems like a red carpet has been rolled all over the street."

"I'd love to see that."

"We will come back."

The smell of freshly baked bread greeted them from a

small shop named Panadería Pedroso. A milkman pushing a little cart full of milk bottles passed by their side.

"*Buen día*, Joaquinito and company," he said, tipping his hat.

"*Hola*, Onelio."

The sound of the milk bottles clinking filled the air. Sarah, who had always bought milk at supermarkets, felt a wave of nostalgia. An odd nostalgia, since it was for a time that she hadn't actually known.

"There's a bodega here, but it doesn't have refrigeration yet," Joaquín explained. "That's why Onelio still delivers to people's doorsteps."

Sarah smiled. She felt in a time warp, but in a good, back-to-nature sort of way.

El Fogón de Fefa was a one-room log cabin with an ancient cast iron stove, the *fogón* as such, located outside, in the open air. The aroma of chicken fried with onions and peppers made Sarah's stomach rumble. The tables were unpainted, and instead of chairs, there were three-legged stools. Baskets made of jute rope hung from the vigas. The baskets contained plants with tiny violet flowers. Some fell over Sarah's head as she came in.

"This is adorable!" she said, surveying the place. The flowers had a strong, heady scent, similar to carnations.

Joaquín's eyes lit up.

"When I retire, maybe we could move here," he said. "Would you like that?"

Any other time Sarah would have balked at the idea of living in a one-street town, but the pink mist of love clouded her mind.

"Yes! This is paradise!"

He planted a kiss on her hand.

"We'll be so happy, *mi amor*."

WHEN JOAQUÍN, SARAH AND Mercedes departed La Coloma, the jeep was full with half a roasted pig, three cans of lard and enough plantains, fresh eggs and guavas to hold them for a month. In return, Sarah left some Gerber food and disposable diapers for Sonrisa's daughter, Yulisa.

# CHAPTER FORTY-TWO

When we returned to Havana, puffing on the fumes from the *almendrón*'s exhaust, I kept replaying in my mind the conversations with Yoel and Canario and simmering with rage at Mamina's betrayals. Candela and Satia were surprised at my discoveries but accepted the excuse that I had been lied to "for my own good." I didn't.

Tears ran down my face as I opened the locket and stared sadly at the woman's picture. At first I had assumed that she was my maternal grandmother, but if Tania had been as young as Dolores said, then her mother would have been in her forties or early fifties then. This lady was much older. And there was my own photo, the laughing eyes, the confident smile—the expression of a girl who felt loved and secured.

Canario's theory about a political issue was intriguing. I had always believed that my mother supported the revolution. Otherwise, why would she have travelled to Cuba in the first place or stayed so many years? But my *padrino* had a point: Americans were often suspected of being "in cahoots with the CIA." Even my deceased husband, an avowed leftist, had been watched, albeit discreetly, when he brought his students to take summer courses at the University of Havana.

My mother, being young and naïve, might have said the

wrong thing or acted, without realizing it, in a suspicious manner. She could have been kicked out of the country. Labeled persona non grata. Forbidden to come back. Her letters, if she ever wrote to me, could have been intercepted by the secret police. I found some comfort in the idea of politics being the reason behind her disappearance. I had not been abandoned. She had been forced to leave me. That was encouraging, even if it didn't explain her lack of contact later.

After my head was cooler, it occurred to me there was another reason why Mamina had lied about my dad's suicide. As the daughter of a Cuban soldier who had died fighting in Angola, I often got special considerations at school. It made sense that she preferred to use that version for public consumption. But she should have told *me* the truth.

¡*Ay*, Mamina! No matter how I felt at that moment, it was my duty to take care of her like she had taken care of me. If the arrangement with Catalina didn't work, maybe she could move to La Coloma, since she had already been staying there for days at a time. I had been too angry to even think of it while we were visiting, but had no doubts that Sonrisa would welcome her. We could also try to sell Villa Santa Marta "as is." The money would allow Mamina to make some improvements to the farmhouse or build a new place for her nearby. At any rate, it was up to her, as the legal homeowner, to decide. Before, though, we needed to have a talk. Another one.

I closed my eyes and thought of La Bakería Cubana's kitchen, wishing I was there baking a double-layered chocolate cake.

THE RAIN STARTED WHEN we entered Havana and soon became a downpour. The *almendrón* wipers got stuck and the tires skidded. Candela's bracelets jingled in alarm. I stopped worrying about Mamina to focus on our immediate safety.

In a regular car, the rain wouldn't have mattered, but the old Chevy, though "meticulously maintained," made the ride dangerous.

The wind picked up. Satia's knuckles were white against the wheel as he tried to control the car.

"*Recurvó el ciclón*," he said.

"What does that mean?" Candela asked.

I didn't understand it either.

"The storm took a turn and came back," Satia answered. "Bad news. Mamina can't stay in Villa Santa Marta, and neither should you girls."

"We all can check into a hotel," I suggested. "The Nacional or the Capri."

"What about Nena?" Candela asked.

I grimaced. Cuban hotels weren't pet-friendly.

"Why don't you all come to my house instead?" Satia offered. "I'll make room for everyone. Including Nena."

He looked at Candela. She grinned and winked. The rain got heavier. I wished Satia kept his eyes on the road.

"Let's ask Mamina," I said wearily.

AS SOON AS WE got to Fourth Street, I knew something was wrong. Outside Villa Santa Marta were two police cars with their blue lights blinking on top. Despite the rain, several people had gathered around. A cop dressed in a yellow jacket tried to keep them away.

My first thought was that something had happened to Mamina. Satia stopped the car, and immediately I ran to the house. The cop blocked my way.

"You can't come in, comrade! This is a crime scene."

"I live here!"

"What's your name?"

"Mercedes Spivey."

My last name sounded more American and out of place than it had ever been.

"Espaivi?" he repeated, suspicion growing in his eyes.

"I don't actually live in this house anymore, but my grand-mother does. Is she okay?"

"Do you have an ID?"

Mamina came out and hurried to the curb with her hands stretched toward me.

"Thank God you're here, Merceditas! Ferradaz's guys found a skeleton!"

"They found what?"

"It's actually an *old* crime scene," the cop said, indicating with a gesture that I was allowed to follow Mamina inside.

Ferradaz, Santos, Suárez and a young cop were assembled in the living room, but Mamina dragged me past them. She was still clinging to me when we got to the kitchen. Three men in uniform, wearing rain jackets and gloves, hovered around the servants' quarters.

"It's there." Her eyes shone like pieces of dark broken glass.

The uprooted rosebush had been tossed aside. The building had no door. At the men's feet, a full skeleton laid out under the rain. I walked outside.

"Do you know if these remains belonged to a woman?" I asked.

The guys took no notice of me. I realized that I hadn't spoken. Words were trapped in my throat and threatened to smother me. I got closer. The skull's mouth was open as if ready to reveal a secret kept untold for years.

# CHAPTER FORTY-THREE

*February 12th, 1988*

*Remember when we used to sneak out of class and go to the movies? I don't do it too often anymore—going to the movies, not skipping school! Joaquín favors Russian war films that I can't stomach, and when American films (that are very, very popular despite what my dear husband says) are shown, there are always long lines.*

LO GOT TWO TICKETS to watch *Plaf, o demasiado miedo a la vida*, a Cuban comedy, and invited Sarah, who at first wasn't overly enthused. The Cuban movies she had seen were nothing to write home about, or at least nothing to write home anything *good* about. It was partly her fault, as she couldn't understand all the dialogue. People would be roaring with laughter, and she had no idea why.

But *Plaf* was showing in the Yara Theater, across from the ice cream parlor Coppelia, in El Vedado. Lo promised that no matter what, they would get ice cream afterward. Sarah, who had developed a taste for Copa Lolita—two scoops with a small round flan in the middle—agreed to go. She left Mercedes with the Barbeitos and boarded the Miramar-El Vedado bus with Lo. For once, it wasn't crowded.

Good luck was still on their side because they didn't have to wait in line at the Yara either. It was three o'clock, when most people were still working. Lo had taken the day off.

"I fell asleep during the CDR watch last night," she confided. "Clearly, I needed a break."

IN THE THEATER, THE air conditioner was working in full gear. There was an indefinable scent—not popcorn, unfortunately, but cigarette smell, dusty curtains and faint perfume—that brought Sarah childhood memories.

Contrary to what she had expected, she actually enjoyed the movie. She followed the story and got most of the jokes. The main character was Concha, a frazzled, distrustful lady that couldn't figure out who was throwing eggs at her house. The movie poked fun at popular superstitions (eggs were routinely used in Santería ceremonies) and people who were "too afraid of life."

A thorny topic because Sarah had already realized that most Cubans lived in fear, like poor Concha. They were loud and appeared cheerful, but underneath it all, they were afraid. Of the government, the secret police and each other.

"Be careful around Dolores," Elena had warned her. "Don't tell her anything that you don't want broadcast to State Security."

At first Sarah had attributed the comment to the old couple's political prejudices, but then Valentina echoed it.

"Who's that friend of yours? She is in charge of the CDR, huh? Don't ever mention our deals to her!"

As the president of the Committee for the Defense of the Revolution, Lo had a lot of power. A bad report from her could send people straight to jail. When Sarah found out, and no matter how much she still liked Lo, she started being more careful with what she said in front of her.

The CDR, which Sarah used to think was a neighborhood association, turned out to be a collective surveillance network. Its purpose was to be "the eyes and ears of the revolution." A night-watch patrol called *guardia cederista* operated every day from midnight to 6 A.M., and all the CDR members were expected to participate at least once a month. Sarah paid the monthly CDR fee but had never been invited to be part of a *guardia*.

"Is it because I am a 'Yankee'?" she asked Lo.

"*¡Ay, no, chica!* The problem is that—you aren't in the system yet."

But Lo had blushed and stammered. The true answer was likely *¡Ay, sí, chica!* Not that Sarah cared. After all, *guardias* appeared to be a waste of time. Miramar was a residential district with no military targets or factories, and all embassies had their own security guards. Were "they" afraid of people blowing up a bodega? Breaking into an empty *carnicería*? It looked like the main purpose of the *guardias* was to find out who was cheating on whom and with whom, and who was buying or selling on the black market. The Barbeitos confirmed it.

"Haven't you heard the saying *siempre hay un ojo que te ve*?" Doctor Barbeito asked.

"There's always an eye on you?" Sarah blinked nervously. "So Orwellian!"

"That's part of *this man*'s strategy," Elena said with a frown. "Keep people busy finding food, watching over their shoulders and parroting slogans."

Ah, if Joaquín were to hear such conversations he would have said that Sarah was on her way to become *gusana*. But she loved the revolution as much as she loved him. In fact, they were one and the same for her. The problem, she told herself, was that in 1959, Joaquín had been a kid living in a poor, remote area of the country. He had never been out of Cuba and had no idea how democracy worked.

She was so conflicted about her feelings that she had to get them off her chest. She finally did in a letter to Rob. After making fun of the *guardia cederista* and her snoopy neighbors, Sarah concluded:

> *Though I still believe that socialism is a fairer system than ours, it also has many drawbacks. I don't want to live here forever or raise my daughter in this environment. But I am not ready to give up! Hopefully we'll achieve a happy medium and spend half the year here and the other half in San Diego. Don't tell anybody, but I am dying for a cheeseburger with a double order of french fries. And a movie theater with a popcorn machine!*
>
> > *Your friend, ashamed of feeling like a capitalist piglet,*
> > *SL*

Before, Sarah wouldn't have dared to include that in a letter that State Security could have intercepted. But Valentina had a network of trusted Eastern European friends who traveled back and forth and carried correspondence.

"Is it easier to mail letters from Romania, Bulgaria and other communist countries?" Sarah asked.

"No, they do it from Gander, Newfoundland, when the plane stops to refuel," Valentina answered. "Sometimes they mail the letters. Other times, they ask the Canadians for political asylum and we never hear from them again."

# CHAPTER FORTY-FOUR

Villa Santa Marta had never been spookier than that evening, when Mamina, Ferradaz, her crew and I sat together in our now brightly lit living room. With us was Lieutenant Varelo, the clean-cut police officer who had answered a call from Ferradaz about their grim finding.

Santos and Suárez had discovered the skeleton under the rosebush in the process of transplanting it to a less inconvenient place. They had also unearthed something else described vaguely as "a little leather bag." Valero had already stashed it away in his briefcase—an old-fashioned black Samsonite—so I never had a chance to see it.

Satia and Candela retreated to the guest room. After signing some documents, Ferradaz and the guys were dismissed too. Sitting on a rocking chair under the pendant light, Mamina fingered the hem of her blouse. She looked a little more composed than at the time of my arrival, but was still worried and nervous. I was worried and nervous too. Though not sure ("I am no expert on bones," he admitted), Varelo said that the skeleton might have been buried for over twenty years, if not longer.

A conversation that had started before I got there went on. Valero addressed Mamina since she was the homeowner. He already knew that I lived permanently in Miami.

"So, comrade, did you ever suspect that there was anything out of the ordinary in your backyard?"

"Never," Mamina said, but her color faded.

"How long have you lived here?"

"Twenty-eight years."

The three men who were in the backyard walked by carrying a long box. I saw them leave and thought of Tania, the locket, the newspaper article and what Canario had told me . . .

"Who owned this house before?" Valerio's voice brought me back.

"My son," Mamina said.

"Where is he now?"

"He died in Angola."

"I am sorry. Who else lived here?"

"His daughter." She gestured at me. "When he passed away, I moved in to take care of her, who was a child then."

"Wasn't he married?"

She gave a casual wave of her hand. "His wife had left him."

As my family history unfolded during the brief questioning, Mamina avoided making any reference to the most crucial facts about my mother. She was leading Valero to believe that her daughter-in-law had just up and left, which wasn't exactly a lie but not the total truth either. She didn't mention Tania's unexplained disappearance nor that she was American.

"Now, before my son got it, Villa Santa Marta belonged to a bourgeois family," she went on calmly. "Counterrevolutionary elements who left during the Mariel boatlift."

"Do you know their names?"

She rubbed her chin.

"I'm trying to remember. Sotelongo? Gavilongo?"

"People called them the Sotolongos," I said.

Valero looked at me.

"Did you know them?" he asked.

"No. They left before I was born. I just happen to recall the name."

He took notes while I considered how to set things straight without making Mamina look silly, senile or worse. It escaped me why she wasn't bringing up the Sotolongos. Wouldn't it make more sense to?

"A woman in that family," Mamina plodded on, "was buried here, according to the neighbors."

A wave of relief passed over me. I had totally forgotten the *bruja*!

"I never believed such stories because they were so outlandish, but . . ."

Valero stopped writing. "When did she die?"

"In the fifties, I think."

Valero went over his notes, asked Mamina to repeat several details and confirmed what she had said before I arrived. (Nothing about Tania.)

"Those people," Mamina added suddenly, her eyes brighter and her voice stronger, "want to take their old home back, skeleton and everything. We have to stop them!"

"Don't worry, *compañera*," Valero answered in a soothing tone. "The revolution will never allow that to happen. Now, you should get some rest. I'm sure all this has been very disturbing for you."

He wrote down his phone number on a piece of paper and gave it to Mamina.

"If you happen to remember anything of importance, don't hesitate to give me a call," he added.

"I doubt it, *compañero*. I can't even remember what I did yesterday. That's the problem with getting old!"

Valero nodded sympathetically. Maybe Mamina reminded him of his own grandmother. He stood up.

"Well, I'm going to take a last look at the site, and then I'll be on my way."

I waited until he was out of sight to face Mamina, who looked frozen under the blue pendant light.

"Why didn't you tell him the truth about my mother?" I hissed.

Her eyes rounded with real or feigned surprise.

"What truth? And what does your mother have to do with the skeleton?"

Before I could come up with an answer, she asked defensively, "Where were you, anyway? I've been dealing with this by myself all day long!"

My purse felt heavier. Inside, my mother's picture and the locket . . .

"I was in La Coloma," I said.

Mamina startled.

"You were?"

"Yoel told me about my dad's suicide."

Mamina held a hand in front of her face as if to ward off an attack.

"I also met my godfather, Canario Padilla. He said that you were my godmother. Why did you hide all that from me?" I concluded, furious. "What are you trying to cover up, *carajo*?"

I had never cursed in front of her, much less at her.

She opened her mouth but didn't make a sound. Fear hung in the air between us for a second, then she fell down.

"Mamina!"

I struggled to lift her but couldn't. Her thin body slipped from my hands. Feeling guilty and horrified—had I caused her to faint, or something worse?—I yelled for help. Valero and Satia came running back and took her to the police car, placing her on the back seat. Then Satia went back to the house and retrieved a cushion.

"Let's go to the Hospital de Emergencias," he said as he put the cushion under Mamina's head.

"Why so far away?" Valero asked. "The Clínico Quirúrgico is closer."

"That's where all her medical records are, Lieutenant. The doctors know her and will know what to do."

"Fine. Let's go!"

I sat with Mamina and kept caressing her cold forehead and holding her hands. Satia and Candela followed us in the *almendrón*. It occurred to me to tell the detective everything Mamina had omitted, but I just couldn't. Not yet. Not with her body lying, seemingly lifeless, next to me on the back seat.

# CHAPTER FORTY-FIVE

*September 22nd, 1988*

*You wrote about a doctor's appointment at Scripps Hospital but didn't say what it was about. We're still having problems with missing letters. Bummer! What's going on, Rob? Let me know as soon as possible, okay?*

THE SEPTEMBER SKY WAS gray like a grainy picture from the fifties. Valentina parked on Parque Central. Around a hundred people were there, waiting at the bus stop.

"I have never seen the park so crowded," Sarah said.

"Buses only pass every two hours now," Valentina answered. "Gas is rationed. I mean, more rationed than ever. I just paid eighty dollars for ten gallons."

They crossed the street toward La Manzana de Gómez and waited half an hour to get into Salon H. Once they were seated, the waitress informed them that the only available drink was water. No mortadella that day, and the slices of cheese were thinner than before. The fly-spotted mirror showed Sarah a pale face with a troubled expression.

Valentina had picked her up early at Villa Santa Marta. A Bulgarian friend of hers was traveling in a week and would carry a letter to Rob. There had been months without news from him.

"It worries me," Sarah confided. "It's not like him to just stop communicating. He may be sick, but the letter where he says what's going on has been lost."

Valentina thought it over for a while.

"Is that husband of yours the jealous type?" she asked abruptly.

"Oh, I'm sure Joaquín wouldn't . . ." Sarah started to protest.

Valentina cut her off. "You can never be sure of anything here. That, and State Security is more active than ever."

"Why?"

"Things are changing in Europe. Do you know that we are withdrawing from Afghanistan?"

Sarah didn't ask where that was so as not to sound like a bumpkin. Somewhere in Asia? And what relationship could exist between the Soviet Union's foreign policy and the loss of her letters?

"My country is changing fast, and Fidel is afraid that Cuba will follow suit," Valentina explained. "State Security is keeping all foreigners under surveillance now. They don't want people here to find out about glasnost."

Glasnost, Afghanistan, surveillance . . . Sarah couldn't wrap her head around Valentina's discourse. She only wanted to know what health issues Rob had and why his letters weren't getting to Cuba. What if her own letters weren't reaching him either? She took another bite of the cheese sandwich.

"Something's going on with Rob," she whispered. "If all else fails, I'll have to go back home and find out for myself."

Later, when they crossed La Manzana's shopping arcade, Sarah noticed that the shelves in most of the stores were empty. La Concha de Venus was closed.

VALENTINA WAS STILL "SHOWING Sarah the ropes." They went together to the *diplotiendas* at least twice a month, though Joaquín didn't approve.

"I thought those stores were just for diplomats," he said.

Sarah doubted he was telling the truth. He had to know, didn't he?

"It isn't *just* for them," she replied. "Any foreigner can shop there, but Cubans can't. Does it bother you?"

He harrumphed.

"The revolution needs hard currency. If we, the masses, have to make sacrifices, so be it. Yes, you brought your own money"—he made a face as if dollars were poisonous—"but I'd prefer you don't go there so often. It's not fair to other *compañeros*."

That was too bad, Sarah thought. The heck with other *compañeros*. The Gerber food was gone, thanks to Mercedes's improved appetite. It was either the dollar shops or the black market, and, after a few disagreeable experiences, Sarah had started to distrust the quality of stuff sold underground.

When another CDR anniversary came around, she wasn't inclined to celebrate. More so after neighbors were ordered to provide the *caldosa* ingredients themselves, which didn't sit well with most. Even Lo was incensed.

"*¡Éramos pocos y parió mi abuela!*" she exclaimed.

"Did your grandma give birth?" Sarah asked. "Or is that one of these weird Cuban sayings?"

"It means things are hard enough as they are. And now we are asking people to donate pork or chicken. Where are they going to buy them?"

Food supplies were dwindling at the grocery store. Milk, that used to be sold without a coupon, was rationed. Red meat hadn't "come" to the *carnicería* in weeks, only tilapia. Queues were longer than ever, and shoppers more aggressive. Thank God for the *diplotiendas*, Sarah thought as she filled her shopping cart with ground beef, ham and cheese. There was no fresh milk there either, but at least condensed and evaporated cans were available, though limited to six cans per person.

Lo knew about the *diplotiendas*, but her attitude was less cavalier than Joaquín's.

"It sucks to be stopped at the door of a shop in my own country!"

That was the first *gusanería* Sarah had ever heard from her. She felt so bad that she went and bought a five-pound bag of chicken quarters as well as tomatoes, carrots and a cluster of ripe grapes.

Lo graciously accepted the chicken and the veggies to make a *caldosa* but said that grapes would arouse suspicions. Younger neighbors had probably never seen them.

"There aren't enough for everyone, so it wouldn't be fair to offer them," she declared, sinking her teeth into one. "Ah, they are yummy!"

The CDR celebration was rather subdued. The *caldosa* wasn't as substantial as people were used to. The neighbor who owned the tape recorder didn't attend, so they ended up listening to the radio. The only music that evening was of a political nature, like the Literacy Campaign anthem. Patriotic indeed, but not conducive to dancing. Everybody went home before midnight.

Sarah and Joaquín watched El Caballo's speech on TV. He didn't bring up the *Proceso de Rectificación de Errores*, using the time instead to explain why Cuba didn't participate in the Seoul Olympics even though the Soviet Union did.

"Is that why people are so displeased?" Sarah asked.

Joaquín assured her that no one was displeased.

"Don't pay attention to rumors," he said. "There's no reason to worry."

People *did* look worried, however. And annoyed. Was it because of the shortages? Sarah thought to ask Valentina, who seemed to know everything—like the reason why surfing wasn't allowed.

"Fidel's afraid of people surfing their way to Florida, Jackie O!"

SARAH KEPT THINKING ABOUT Valentina's comment. Her husband wasn't the jealous type. But his comrade and State Security might suspect her of working "for the enemy." She tried to shake the thought. The Cuban paranoia was catching up with her.

The first time she found apples at the *diplotienda*—they looked like Granny Smith, but smaller, harder—she remembered Elena's comment and bought a few for the Barbeitos. Her neighbor was delighted.

"Ah, I had almost forgotten what they taste like!" Elena said, kissing the fruit.

She had started to peel one when Carmita came in to do her weekly cleaning. Elena hurried to hide the apples in the refrigerator, covering them with a kitchen towel.

"Why are you doing that?" Sarah asked when Carmita was out of sight.

"I don't trust her."

And the woman had been working for them over ten years! Was it just old people's mistrust? Or the expected result of *"siempre hay un ojo que te ve"*? There's always an eye watching you. Cuban Big Brother. Uf.

Sarah still appreciated the free healthcare and education. But if it weren't for her money, the family would have been much worse off, particularly in the food department. *No es fácil,* Cubans said way too often. It was not easy indeed. She sometimes caught herself wanting to be home. In a supermarket, filling her basket with big red apples, pears and Hass avocados. Or a clothing store, buying a new pair of blue jeans. Of course, she still liked Cuba, but not as much as she had at first. The honeymoon was over, that was all.

Like between her and Joaquín. They still loved each other, no question about that, but seldom walked anymore. He was too busy at the unit and would stay for hours after his shift was supposed to end. They didn't talk too much, unless it was about Mercedes. But such was life, right?

# CHAPTER FORTY-SIX

Valero drove down Salvador Allende Avenue, turned onto Espada Street and stopped in front of the emergency care area. Though the hospital's name was Emergencias, it functioned like a regular medical center, and I'd have rather gone somewhere else. We were uncomfortably close to La Quinta de Los Molinos, where my husband Nolan had been killed, and not too far from the University of Havana, which I had attended for a few months with disastrous results. The entire Centro Habana district brought me bad memories. But that's where Doctora Morales worked, and I remembered too late I had left the tablet at home. Mamina had been so anxious to give it to her son!

Doctora Morales wasn't there, but another doctor who had taken care of Mamina before recognized her.

"¡*Ay*, Mamina! Did she fall again?" she asked while a nurse took my grandma's vitals.

"Something worse," I whispered.

Mamina was admitted immediately to the ICU. It was a stroke, the doctor said. A heart attack, the nurse argued. A *zirimba*, my grandma would have said. At any rate, her condition was serious. She hadn't regained consciousness. Last time I touched her hands, they were cold as ice.

And yet, I had to tell Valero. It felt like a betrayal, more so at that moment, but I had just discovered a new kind of loyalty in me: to my mother, or, God forbid, her memory. Mamina would have to understand. After the admission paperwork was completed, I took the detective aside and told him the whole story. He listened intently, standing in the disinfectant-smelling hospital hall.

"I thought it was my questioning that scared her," he said. "But clearly, your grandmother knows way more than she lets on."

"She does."

"There has to be information about your mother's de—I mean, situation." He stumbled over his words.

At close distance, the detective looked even younger. I had the impression that this was one of his first cases, and he wasn't too sure how to proceed.

"I was told that State Security handled it."

He nodded.

"It makes sense, since she was a foreigner. Well, good evening, *compañera*. I hope your grandma recovers soon, because I would like to talk to her again."

CANDELA, SATIA AND I spent the night in the hall, waiting for the nurses to come out and report. They were running several tests. Mamina's vitals had stabilized, but she was still unresponsive. At nine-thirty in the morning, Candela convinced me to leave. The rain had stopped, and Satia insisted we go before it got heavy again.

"We will call the hospital every hour," he said, "and I can drive you back here anytime. But you need to get some rest, Merceditas."

She was right. As we walked down the hospital hall, I caught my reflection in an office window and saw blue bruises under my eyes and the face of a much older, tired woman.

I blamed myself for Mamina's heart attack, *zirimba*, stroke or whatever it was. Compounding my guilt was the almost certainty that the skeleton belonged to my mother. Someone had killed her and buried her in our backyard. The idea that the remains belonged to María Estela Sotolongo was a distant, dim possibility. The *bruja* had died too long ago. Would the bones still be intact? Besides, I wasn't even sure she had been buried there. The story was likely an urban legend. My only hope was the woman in the blue car. I wished Candela were right and the mysterious visitor happened to be Tania, coming back for me . . .

The drive home was silent and somber.

THE STORM HAD ALREADY made its presence felt in Miramar. Power lines had been knocked down and broken tree limbs blocked the streets. At Villa Santa Marta, the stained glass window had been shattered on the outside too. There was water everywhere in the living room. Leaves and trash had come in. The cherub lamp was on the floor with the shade crinkled and the light bulb smashed. The Murano vase was on the floor, broken into tiny fragments of blue. Only the piano stood up, silent and dignified against the wall, a mute witness to the wreckage.

Nena, shaking and whining, welcomed us. Candela fed her and made breakfast for everybody. We ate in the kitchen. A pool of water had formed behind the backyard door and a dishrag was floating on it, but at least it wasn't a disaster zone like the living room.

The cuckoo clock chimed ten times.

"Thanks for bringing the bird back to life," I said.

"It was nothing!" Candela answered. "I love fixing old stuff. Oh, what fun I would have with a house like this!"

I wished I could offer her the property right then. Just take it off my hands. Rebuild it, repurpose it. Whatever. But I didn't because it wasn't mine.

Candela came closer, hugged me and whispered, "*Abuela* will be fine. We know nothing about the—findings. Remember, Merceditas, it's always darkest before the dawn."

Dawn *un carajo*, I was going to reply, but the phone rang. It amazed me that we still had service because it was usually interrupted when storms hit Havana. I answered.

"This is Lieutenant Valero."

My heart skipped a beat.

"Yes?"

"Comrade—I mean, *señora* Mercedes, do you go by any other name?" he asked.

I was expecting something more substantial.

"My maiden name was Mercedes Montero Rojas," I said wearily, "but in the United States I took my late husband's last name, Spivey, and shortened Mercedes to Mercy."

"Have you ever used a different name?"

"No."

He paused briefly.

"Do you know any Galina Ivanova? Olga Ivanova?"

"Growing up, I had several classmates called Olga," I said. "But none had the last name Ivanova. It sounds like Russian."

"Right. Did you have any Soviet friends?"

My neck muscles tensed.

"I didn't. But someone told me that my mother had a friend from the Soviet Union. Her name was Valentina."

"Do you know her last name?"

"No."

"Who told you about her?"

I hesitated, not wanting to get Dolores in trouble. Her many illicit dealings made her a target for the police. And she had already told me all she knew . . .

"I don't remember. Anyway, it seems like her friend left."

I immediately regretted having said that. Maybe Valentina could be located. What if she knew about something my mother? I was going to backtrack and relate my conversation with Dolores when Valero asked another question.

"Did you ever travel out of Cuba as a child?"

Someone knocked on the door. Candela signaled for me to go on talking and went to answer.

"Not that I remember."

Dolores's and Candela's voices came from the living room. I heard the words "Mamina," "hospital" and "*zirimba*." I would talk to Dolores again and then decide what to do.

"Well, that's all for now," Valero said. "Thanks."

"Have you found out anything about the remains, Lieutenant?" I asked eagerly. "Like the age and gender of the person who . . . ?"

"No, the forensic anthropologists are still working on it. It'll take them a while. This isn't like the *Law & Order* episodes that you watch in Miami."

My checks reddened.

"When they have an answer, please contact me first. My grandma's still unresponsive."

"I know. I went there before calling you."

Poor Mamina. Why hadn't I stayed with her? My legs got weak. If she got any worse, how would I live with myself?

Valero didn't have much to add. I hung up the phone and returned to the living room.

Dolores, in a raincoat and plastic boots, was talking to Candela. Humming quietly under his breath, Satia was trying to cover the broken window with a sheet of plywood left behind by Ferradaz's crew. Someone had swept the floor. The remains of the window glass and the Murano vase were gone.

"Merceditas, *mija*!" Dolores hugged me. "I'm so sorry! I

heard all the commotion yesterday, but the cops didn't let me in. How did it happen?"

I told her everything without sugarcoating Mamina's lies and omissions. Dolores acted surprised first, angry later.

"How could she have kept mum about that all these years? *¡Qué cabroncita!*"

"She didn't mention the suicide to you either, eh?"

"Never. I was under the impression that Joaquín had died in an accident. But she couldn't have pulled the Cuito story on me. Most people my age remember that the Angola war ended in the late eighties."

"She made an *arroz con mango*, tailoring her lies to suit her audience," I said with a sigh. "Anyway, Lieutenant Valero is going to look into my mother's case. A cop once told me that there had been an investigation. But I was a teenager then, and he didn't take me seriously, so—"

"Yes, they assigned a detective to the case. He talked to me several times because I was the CDR president."

"You were?"

The idea of Dolores—wheeler-dealer Dolores, always buying and selling stuff on the black market and whose tutoring business was under the table—being the president of the CDR was so strange that I smiled despite my troubles.

"I resigned not long after Tania disappeared," she said quietly. "She had made me realize that not all 'Yankees' were as bad and greedy as the official discourse wanted us to believe. I started to question things, ideas . . . Your mom wasn't aware of it, but she had a profound influence on me."

Tania's image was becoming clearer and sharper, as if a camera lens had been adjusted.

"Do you have any idea where to find that Russian friend she had?" I asked. "Her last name or address?"

"I think she lived in Alamar, like most Russians did then.

But I don't know anything else. Like I said, that woman didn't trust me. She was active in the underground market and feared that I would rat on her."

"Would you have done that?"

She looked down.

"Sadly, yes."

Dolores left soon, vanishing into the rain that enclosed the house like a glass curtain. I hadn't said much after her last statement. My entire body ached with disgust. It wasn't just Mamina. Everybody had dirty little secrets—shameful, unpleasant facts that they kept from their family and friends. What were my mother's secrets, supposing she was still alive? I shuddered and held on to the cold, mold-smelling wall to keep from falling.

Candela helped me sit on the wet couch and said firmly that I *had* to sleep.

"How can I with all that's going on? I'm too wired."

She offered me two pills. "Take this. You *will* sleep."

"What's that?"

"Alprazolam, five milligrams each."

"Isn't it too much?"

She pressed the pills into my hands. "You need them."

I waddled back to the kitchen, opened the refrigerator to get a glass of water and found it dark and funky. Blackouts were also common during storms, but that was an added inconvenience. I chewed the pill and a bitter taste filled my mouth.

"Now go to bed," Candela said. "I'll wake you up when we hear from the hospital."

I looked at the servants' quarters. Everything—the removed door, the uprooted rosebush, the building itself—gleamed under a soft, funereal drizzle.

The second floor smelled murky. I entered Mamina's bedroom and started sobbing. Nena followed me. Her bright dark eyes stared at me inquisitively.

"Grandma will be back soon," I said, but she wasn't convinced.

Neither was I.

I picked up a sweater for Mamina, a dress, a housecoat, her slippers and her ID card, which they had requested in the hospital. I also threw in a small pillow, the Heno de Pravia bottle and the tablet I had brought for her doctor.

Still weeping, I came into my room. Martita's face looked stern, almost forbearing. I shook my head, hoping the pills didn't cause hallucinations. In the duffel bag I had brought from Miami, Mamina's belongings joined my passport, phone, wallet and the purse with my mother's locket and picture. Then I took a quick bath and got in bed. Nena curled up by my side.

As soon as my head hit the pillow, I noticed that a leak had sprouted in a corner. The ceiling had swollen around it, forming a bump that looked like a plaster tit ready to fall down. While I considered what to do about this new problem, my mind fogged up and a deep sleep overcame me.

# CHAPTER FORTY-SEVEN

*January 3rd, 1989*

*I had a dream with you last night. We had gone together to see Grandma Pauline. We knocked on her door and there she was, looking ten years younger than I remember. The dream was so . . . so real! I am planning another trip, hopefully soon, and this time around we will hang out longer. I really miss you, Rob.*

SARAH WANTED TO ADD that she missed her parents too, and their home, and shopping malls and the freedom to come and go as she pleased. But she didn't. What she *really* wished to do was talk over the phone, but Joaquín had told her in no uncertain terms that she couldn't do that.

"Why don't you call your friend from my house?" Elena suggested.

"I'd love to," Sarah said. "But it may create problems for you."

And they had enough as it were. An *éramos pocos y parió mi abuela* case. Elena shrugged it off.

"Everybody knows we are *gusanos*, so calls from our number to the United States won't attract attention."

After some back and forth, Sarah took on her friend's offer.

She sat in her living room, facing the bronzes she had admired before—two detailed ballerinas on marble bases.

"Will you accept a collect call from Cuba," she heard the operator ask, "from a Tania Rojas?"

"Yes, yes!" Rob exclaimed. "What happened, Sarah Lee?"

"Oh, nothing." She tightened her fingers around the handset. "I just thought: Oh, my God, I can't believe we're actually talking!"

"How is my little niece?"

He was clearly happy, but his voice sounded weaker than Sarah remembered.

"Right here! Trying to grab the phone."

Elena did her best to keep Mercedes entertained. The girl, seeing her mother so excited, wanted to join her in the fun.

"Send me some pics soon." He stopped to cough.

"Are you okay, dude?"

"Yes, yes. It's my asthma acting up again. Nothing to worry about."

She remembered the day they had spent together. He had been sick then too. And that hospital visit . . . What was going on?

"Tell me about you," Rob said before she could ask. "How's Joaquín?"

"Working a lot, as usual. But what about you?"

"I am *fine!*"

The conversation didn't last over ten minutes. When it ended, Sarah was left with two certainties: both Rob's and her letters were vanishing along the way, and he wasn't doing well. She had known him since they were five years old and had been through enough asthma attacks with him to realize that was different. Her heart ached when she hung up the phone.

"How are your friends and family?" Elena asked.

"Everybody's doing well." Sarah made an effort to smile. "I really appreciate you letting me use the phone."

"Any time you want, my dear. Any time."

MERCEDES'S SECOND BIRTHDAY WAS happening a few days later. The first year they hadn't done a thing because Joaquín was busy at work and Sarah had her hands full with the girl, whose lack of appetite had put a damper on everything. But now Mercedes was eating properly and Sarah, more comfortable in her new mom role, actually knew enough people to invite.

"We are having a party," she announced to Joaquín.

"Okay," he answered quietly. He must have figured out that she was not going to budge.

Valentina drove Sarah to the Fifth Avenue *diplotienda*, but it turned out they didn't sell party supplies, or meringue cakes— which Lo had told her was a must-have for birthdays—or any kind of baked goods. She bought canned pineapple, chocolate kisses and big bottles of soft drinks.

That day, it surprised her to find more Cubans than ever inside the store. Even more surprising was the fact that they weren't accompanied by foreigners, as it had been the case up to then. They bought mostly food—ground-beef trays and whole chickens—as well as cheap jewelry, sunglasses and plastic watches. They all bore furtive expressions, and she also noticed some quiet conversations and suspicious glances among the store employees.

"Are Cubans allowed to shop here now?" Sarah asked Valentina, once they were out the store.

"They use fake passports to pass as Bulgarians, Romanians or Russians," her friend answered with a sly smile. "People bring blank passports from Eastern Europe and sell them here. The problem is that it only works for light-skinned Cubans."

Sarah mulled it over for a while.

"Then, conceivably, they could also board a plane pretending to be Russians, Bulgarians or whatever," she said. "And—leave!"

Valentina high-fived her.

A FEW DAYS LATER, Sarah stood in line several hours at a store located in La Manzana de Gómez shopping mall, in Old Havana, to buy party balloons. The first afternoon, she had no luck. The clerk was allowed to sell a limited amount per day, and Sarah didn't dare to bribe her in front of several dozen frazzled young mothers. Lo said that sometimes condoms were used instead of balloons.

"People paint them in bright colors, and nobody knows what they are."

"What? Arf!"

Undaunted, Sarah returned to the store and finally bought twenty balloons. Piñatas weren't available, but Lo promised to make one using school supplies. Sarah crossed it off her list and focused on the always elusive food. And all that effort was for a small, intimate celebration! She wondered how people managed to throw *quinceañeras*, and hoped that they could celebrate Mercedes's somewhere else. Like San Diego.

She still had to get the cake. Naturally, parents couldn't go to a bakery and just buy one. That would have been too easy—sometimes she had to agree with the Barbeitos. Three months before the birthday, parents were expected to place an order at La Antigua Chiquita, the only bakery that sold birthday cakes in Havana. "Why is it the only place when there are six or seven more bakeries in the city?" Sarah asked Dolores. She got the usual answer: "Because that's the way things are here." No use arguing or complaining. When she finally figured out the process, it was too late.

"Sorry, but we can't help you, *compañera*," the bakery

employee said, looking distractedly at the family ration card Sarah had brought. "We're way behind this month and the next one. You should remember for the girl's third birthday—"

They were alone at La Antigua Chiquita. Sarah smiled and took out her wallet. For ten dollars, the guy backdated her order and even added a *brazo gitano*, a guava-filled roll.

Sarah had made *croquetas*—cylinder-shaped fritters—for Joaquín and herself, but producing fifty or so at once was a daunting task. Fortunately, Lo and Elena came to her rescue. The three women got together the evening before the party in Villa Santa Marta's kitchen and, ideological differences forgotten, chatted and laughed while making one hundred chicken *croquetas* that would be fried in lard the following day, before guests began to arrive.

While they were at it, Sarah used the microwave to warm up a glass of milk for the *croquetas* dough. Lo stared at the device, open-mouthed, and touched the glass.

"It got hot so fast!" she said, amazed. "Where did you get this thing? In a *diplotienda*?"

"No," Sarah answered, uncomfortable. "My family—sent it."

"Ah."

Another party dish, elbow salad with red peppers and mayonnaise, was easy. Sarah bought Spanish olives at the dollar shop and tossed them in to give the salad a fancier touch. She also got dinner rolls and filled them with a mysterious spread known as *pasta de bocaditos* that Lo provided.

Though Mamina and the rest of the family were invited, they couldn't make it. But they sent Canario with a huge *arroz con leche* plate, a box of malanga and plantains and a handmade blue dress with matching hair bows for Mercedes.

The party took place on a Sunday. Lo, Pepe and two young couples from Joaquín's unit attended with their children, who were a little older than Mercedes. The Barbeitos did too. Despite

Joaquín's protests, Sarah insisted on inviting them. Elena wore a neatly pressed white linen dress and looked like a dream grandmother. Or godmother. Once again, Sarah regretted not having had the chance to choose her as a *comadre*.

Valentina and her husband, a handsome Black Cuban named Carlos, entertained the guests with tales about their adventures when they were both students at Lomonosov University in Moscow. It just so happened that Valentina was, like Carlos, an electrical engineer.

"Why don't you get a job in your field?" Sarah asked her.

"Cuban guys don't like women engineers," Valentina said with a shrug. "They claim my Spanish isn't good enough, but the real reason is they are afraid I know more than they do. Which is probably true!"

Later in the evening, while Carlos, Pepe and Joaquín talked politics and Sarah and Lo washed dishes, Valentina cozied up to the Barbeitos on the sofa and spent a long time chatting in whispers. The three of them left together, which Sarah found a little strange. But she was happy that all the people she cared about were getting along well.

# CHAPTER FORTY-EIGHT

It was the silence that woke me up. A sudden quietness, the absence of rain and wind, cut short the chemical sleep induced by Candela's pills. I opened my eyes and found Nena sitting on the bed, apparently as surprised as I was. Martita was still glaring at me from the wall. But before anxiety and remorse attacked again, three loud raps on the door broke the startling stillness of the house.

How popular had Villa Santa Marta turned recently! Mamina and I used to go on for months without a single visitor, and now—

I went downstairs. The living room was freezing. Satia had nailed the plywood to the window frame, but the outside air, cold and humid, still passed through the gaps. There was another, more urgent knock.

"Coming!"

A woman in her late forties, maybe early fifties, stood at the threshold. Her hair was brown and her eyes dark. She didn't look at all like Tania's picture, and yet there was something eerily familiar about her. The blue Kia was parked on the curb. A warm current that I didn't dare identify as hope ran though my veins.

"I apologize for showing up at this time," she said. Her

accent sounded like Candela's, Cuban but with a hint of foreignness. "I was the one taking pictures the other day, remember?"

I nodded.

"I'm sorry I didn't come out and explain why. You surprised me, and—well, I just got nervous."

"Why were you taking pictures?" I asked.

"Because this house . . ." She stopped and inclined her head. "I've been trying to talk to the old lady who lives here, but she refuses to deal with me, and I'm leaving tomorrow evening." She glanced inside and added, "Are you related to her?"

"She's my grandma," I said hoarsely, and a flash of recognition hit me. "And you . . . you are Martita!"

"No, my name's Aurelia," she said, looking confused. "Aurelia Sotolongo."

"I mean the girl in the painting."

Her face lit up.

"Do you still have it? My portrait? It used to be in a room upstairs. Not the master bedroom but mine."

"Yours?" It wasn't really a question, though it sounded like it. Of course my bedroom had been hers.

"I used to live here with my parents. We left in 1980." Her voice quivered. "You mind if I come in?"

We were both shivering.

It was an awkward moment. There was disappointment, yes, but not too much. In truth, I had never believed that Tania . . .

"Please do."

I closed the door behind her. Unlike so many people, I had no dirty little secrets. There was nothing to hide.

Aurelia Sotolongo walked in the middle of the mess that was our living room. She wore a gray suit and brown pumps with round toes, slightly muddy. I noticed all the details because I watched her, not knowing what to say or do. I couldn't exactly welcome her to her former house, much less invite her to sit down since the couch was so damp and dirty.

"Sorry," I muttered. "My grandma is old, and she's just had—"

I made myself stop. Why was I giving excuses to her? It wasn't her home anymore! Anyway, she didn't seem to have heard me. Her expression was guarded, almost neutral, but she was obviously trying to keep her emotions under control.

"Everything's the same and different." She looked around, taking the whole room in. "The lamps, the furniture . . ."

She approached the piano, opened it and let her hands rest on the keys.

"I learned to play"—her voice trailed—"with the Czerny method."

Candela, a sheet wrapped around her body, came out of the guest room with a questioning look. I waved her away. Despite the strangeness of the situation, Aurelia, with the same dark eyes and oval face from the painting, felt like an old friend who had unexpectedly arrived after many years of absence.

"Sorry, I didn't mean to . . ." she said, recovering and blinking as if to stop tears.

She was so close that notes of her perfume, Youth Dew, reached my nose, muting the overpowering smell of mildew. I recognized it because the scent was one of my favorites.

"It's okay," I said. "What exactly do you want?"

"Nothing. Oh, my goodness!" She stepped back. "Was that what the old lady thought? No, no! I didn't come to ask for anything. I live in Houston now and don't need . . . I returned to Havana for the first time in almost forty years because of a work-related matter, and decided to pass by and see the house one last time. Just that."

It started raining again. The plywood sheet shook as if it were made of paper.

"You can walk around," I said. "I don't mind."

Sadness flickered in her eyes.

"People say that when you come back to your first house everything looks smaller, but that's not the case. Villa Santa Marta looks as huge as ever. Even bigger."

My hands were balled into fists. I stretched my fingers and tried to sound casual.

"It'll have a hard time looking small, no matter how many years have passed since you saw it last. This is an elephant, if you don't mind me saying so."

Her lips parted with the shadow of a smile.

"Do you live here? I hope the house has made you and your family happy."

"Happy!"

The accumulated tension erupted. I started to laugh hysterically. Aurelia looked at me with understandable surprise but said nothing. She might have thought that Villa Santa Marta now belonged to a crazy tribe.

"Never mind," I said. "I've been going through a lot lately. My grandma is in the hospital, and I'm super stressed out."

"So sorry to hear that. I don't want to impose . . ."

I made an effort to compose myself.

"You aren't imposing. Where would you like to start? The kitchen?"

She hesitated.

"Actually, I'd like to see my room and the portrait you mentioned. It was my dad who painted it. And those too." She pointed to the many pictures that covered the wall.

"Ah."

As we went upstairs, it occurred to me that Aurelia might be able to help identify the remains. Her presence there, at that moment, seemed like a sign from the universe—at least Candela would say so. What if the skeleton belonged to the *bruja* after all? But there had to be a good way to bring it up. You just couldn't say to someone who's been abroad for almost four decades *and by the way, did you happen to bury someone in your backyard?* And she must have been a child back when . . .

She got to the second floor before I did. Her face was flushed.

"I used to run up and downstairs for the fun of it. Too much pent-up energy, my dad said." She turned to me. "But we've been talking all this time, you've been so gracious, and I don't even know your name!"

"Mercedes."

"Thank you so much for this, Mercedes."

We were at my bedroom door. It was open. She stepped in tentatively.

"Wow, the bed, the armoire . . . How have you managed to keep all the furniture?"

"There wasn't a lot to replace it with," I answered with a shrug.

Aurelia inspected the painting as I observed her. Her hands were a little shaky as she traced her fingers over Martita's hair.

"I looked so innocent," she whispered.

"Don't we always, as children?" I answered, thinking of my second birthday photo.

"Life was so simple then," she said dreamily. "The Mariel boatlift was unimaginable. Our neighbors were so nice to us. I felt safe here—"

Her fingers moved over the background of the painting.

"Would you like to take it with you?" I asked.

She smiled openly for the first time and resembled the girl in the painting even more.

"Are you sure?"

What difference would it made? Mamina wouldn't even notice, or care.

"Yes. If it were me, I'd like to have it."

"Oh, I do! I surely do. I don't have any keepsakes from those years." She took my hand and gave it a quick but warm shake. "Thank you, Mercedes. That's very generous of you."

"You're welcome. I used to talk to Martita before falling asleep. She . . . it . . . you always seemed so real."

She unhooked the painting carefully. "My dad was quite the artist."

"Did he paint the lady in the library too?" I asked.

"He painted many people," she answered. "But I'm not sure who you're talking about."

"Come see it," I said. That would be the perfect opening for my question about the backyard burial.

A gust blew the window open. The ornaments on the dresser flew around the room. Aurelia and I hurried to close the window. It took our combined efforts against the wind and the now intense rain to shut it again.

We walked back to the hall. She entered the library, more confident this time, and stopped in front of the *bruja*'s portrait.

"Ah, María Estela!" she exclaimed. "This painting used to scare the daylights out of me when I was little. I didn't even like to be here alone."

"She was an imposing-looking woman." My mouth was dry, and I cleared my throat before adding, "Your grandmother, right?"

Carefully, Aurelia placed the painting of herself on the desk and examined the *bruja*'s.

"Yes, but not by blood. María Estela never married. She adopted my dad when she was in her forties."

"Did you meet her?"

"No, she died before I was born. However, I grew up hearing about her and her powers. Greatly exaggerated stories"—she grinned—"but they did nothing to reassure me that the portrait was harmless."

It felt like the house was moving. Shaking off, like an animal. I put the blame on the alprazolam and my imagination, and spoke as calmly as I could.

"There're lots of books on witch . . . occultism here."

"People used to say she was a witch." Aurelia started to wipe the dust off María Estela's face. "My dad never contradicted them."

"Do you know if she was"—my voice cracked—"buried in the backyard?"

Aurelia gave me a side glance.

"Definitely not!" she said, then shrugged. "At school, kids used to tease me about it, though."

"Well, there was—" I began.

She cut me off.

"It's not true, Mercedes. Believe me. I asked my parents many times. They would have told me. María Estela is buried at the Havana Cemetery. I visited her grave—the family mausoleum—last Sunday."

The *bruja*'s eyes bore into me with a triumphant expression.

The building rattled. It wasn't my imagination. The bookcases swayed. There was a pounding sound, like a dangerously close thunder, and the ceiling cracked open. Pieces of the rotten beam swirled around us. Aurelia yelped and ran out of the library. I heard Candela's cries below.

"Merceditas, get out!" Satia yelled. "The house is falling down!"

I returned to my bedroom, grabbed the duffel bag and hurried downstairs. Satia was at the threshold, waiting for me.

"Run!"

Candela and Aurelia had already taken refuge on Dolores's front porch. I stumbled under the downpour and joined them. Satia followed me. As he knocked on the door and the rest of us hunkered down, I saw Villa Santa Marta shake like a concrete mammoth and flatten itself against the ground with a horrific crash.

# CHAPTER FORTY-NINE

*March 5th, 1989*

*We have "a situation" with food. There's a saying that the revolution has solved all the people's problems except for three—breakfast, lunch and dinner. It isn't a joke. The bodegas sell nothing but black beans, which I can't stand anymore, and a new, disgusting kind of rice teeming with weevils and worms. The weevils are so tough that they survive hot water!*

SARAH REREAD THE LETTER and signed her initials with a determined movement of her hand. Everything was true, and she wasn't going to change a comma. If she sounded like a *gusana*, so be it. She would be happy to explain to State Security why she had written that. There were some questions she would like to ask the secret police as well. The way it was, she would welcome the chance to have an exchange with them.

She was at the kitchen table, her favorite place to write or simply sit and think. Joaquín was at work, though it was a Sunday. She didn't mind. In fact, it was better not to hear his opinion about the *diplotiendas* just when she was getting ready to visit one. She took Mercedes to the Barbeitos' home.

"So sorry to keep inconveniencing you," she told Elena.

"You aren't inconveniencing anybody," her neighbor answered. "This baby is our only *rayito de sol* these days."

Sarah smiled. She liked the idea of her daughter being "a little sunray." Once, she had been called "sunshine," but didn't think that term described her anymore. Honestly, she felt dispirited, frazzled and sometimes so, so tired . . .

Valentina picked her up, as usual, and they drove to the Fifth Avenue shop. It was closed. The security guard was still there, smoking a cigarette and looking bored.

"When will it reopen?" Valentina asked him.

"Who knows, *compañera*? I haven't seen any new merchandise in weeks, so don't get your hopes up."

"No danger of that," Valentina muttered. "They're at an all-time low."

A disappointing tour of the Havana *diplotiendas* followed. Only the small store on Infanta Avenue was open, but there was no food other than Pomi tomato sauce. Though Sarah didn't need any, she bought ten cans. That was the extent of her grocery shopping that day.

*MUJERES* THE MAGAZINE DIDN'T FEATURE fancy caviar dishes anymore. In the most recent issue, the *Mil Ideas* author had come up with a recipe for poached eggs. Cooking oil had vanished. Even lard was hard to find. Red meat was scarce, and so were chickens. Rumors ran rampant about more rationing and shortages.

Mercedes wasn't gaining weight. She had, in fact, lost a couple of pounds. Sarah was beside herself.

"Why don't we go to La Coloma and buy chickens and pork from your relatives?" she asked Joaquín.

They had just finished dinner—rice and a one-egg omelet for each. She was still hungry. Mercedes had devoured a mix of plantains with *picadillo* (all the meat that was left in the house) and drank half a bottle of milk.

"I can't take the jeep now," Joaquín answered with a frown. "We don't have enough gas for personal use. Anyway, I don't think my folks are much better off than we are."

"But they have their own animals!"

He didn't answer. Sarah thought for a while, and her eyes lit.

"Valentina can drive us! I'm sure she knows where to find gas!"

Joaquín's frown deepened.

"I don't like her or her husband," he said. "I'd rather you stay away from them."

IT ALL BEGAN WHEN Valentina invited Sarah and Joaquín to dinner at their house, after the birthday party. Sarah was delighted. It was about time their guys became friends too. The four of them could go out and do couple things together! She didn't understand why Valentina hadn't suggested it before. Her friend still seemed a bit hesitant, but, really, what could go wrong?

Valentina and Carlos lived in Alamar, a large-scale housing complex to the east of Havana known as "the Soviet bloc" because so many Russians had been given homes there. The homes were mostly apartments in prefab buildings, all painted white on the outside, though some high-level military advisers lived in bungalows.

"I didn't get one because I'm just an engineer, and a woman to boot," Valentina had said, bitterly.

Going from Miramar to Alamar involved taking two buses: one from Miramar to Parque Central in Old Havana and the other from Parque Central to Alamar. The second bus went into a tunnel under the harbor and came out in Habana del Este. By car, the trip would have been around half an hour, but buses were scarce and slow. Joaquín and Sarah left Villa Santa Marta at 4 P.M. and got to Alamar after six, sweaty, sticky and with wrinkled clothes. Luckily, Lo had volunteered to babysit Mercedes.

"You don't want to get inside an Alamar-bound bus with the girl," she had said.

She was right.

In Valentina and Carlos's two-bedroom apartment, modular furniture—a bed that folded up into the wall and a desk that doubled as a dining table—coexisted with antique pieces like a green gondola sofa that occupied most of the living room.

"It was my mother's wedding present," Carlos said proudly. "Sit down, my friends. What would you like to drink?"

The visit had started well, with beer and vodka, and an *arroz con pollo* to share—Valentina had bought a chicken from the Bulgarian embassy cook. But as the evening progressed, the conversation turned to politics and the guys ended up arguing about the program of reforms started by Gorbachev.

"Fidel thinks the Soviet Union is going to take care of Cuba until the twenty-first century," Carlos said. "That's not going to happen."

"I don't think he has such expectations," Joaquín replied, annoyed. "And the Soviets aren't doing us any favors. It's a matter of international solidarity."

"Solidarity time's running out. The Russian economy is in shambles, and so is ours. There's too much *blah-blah-blah* and too little productivity. It can't go on forever. That's what perestroika is all about: changes for good."

"The so-called perestroika betrays the principles of Marxism-Leninism!"

"We can't eat principles, *carajo!*"

Tucked away in the kitchen, Sarah and Valentina listened to the men's angry voices.

"It seems to me that we also need some reforms here," Sarah whispered, "seeing that the *proceso de rectificación de errores* hasn't solved our three main problems: breakfast, lunch and dinner. Right?"

Valentina squeezed her arm.

"You're finally getting it, Jackie O, aren't you?"

TWO DAYS LATER, WHEN Sarah went to visit the Barbeitos, she noticed that the bronze sculptures weren't in their usual place in the living room.

"We gave them to your friend as payment," Elena confided. "She's helping us get out of here. But that's top secret! Don't tell anyone I told you!"

Sarah didn't know, and preferred not to know, if the Barbeitos were planning to use the fake-passport route. She kept quiet about it. She didn't even mention it to Valentina, much less to Joaquín.

# CHAPTER FIFTY

On the third day after the fall of Villa Santa Marta, I was still in shock. The changes had been so fast and drastic that everything around me had an air of unreality. I had gone from having my own room in a big, old and perhaps haunted house—but my house after all—to being a guest in Satiadeva's home, and Instituto de Ciencias Ocultas de La Habana's headquarters.

The living room was devoid of furniture because the Instituto members sat on cushions and pillows on the floor. The only decorations were on the walls: a chakra chart and a psychedelic watercolor of purple and blue triangles inside red circles, or the other way around. Satia informed me that it was called a mandala and consisted of "sacred geometry." Sacred or profane, looking at it for too long made me dizzy. I slept in a windowless room under a turquoise dreamcatcher. Satia and Candela shared the master suite.

Mamina was still in the hospital, though fortunately out of the ICU. She was now conscious, but very weak, and Doctora Morales recommended not to bring up any disturbing topics. I had seen her twice, briefly. She had recognized me, but had only spoken to ask about Nena, which broke my heart, or what was left of it.

After the worst of the storm passed, Satia, Candela and I returned to what once had been Villa Santa Marta and looked for Nena, but she didn't answer our calls. It was impossible to see under the collapsed walls and destroyed furniture. Dolores wasn't in her house, though it hadn't been as badly damaged as ours.

"She's staying with her brother for a few days," a neighbor who lived next to the bodega informed me. She was an older woman who had moved here while I was out of Cuba. "She was scared! So was I, but I have no other place to go."

"Have you seen Mamina's dog?" I asked her.

"No, but I know it. A fluffy white thing, right? Don't worry, *mija*. I'll keep an eye out for the dog."

I gave her Satia's number but didn't have high expectations. Everything had turned out so badly that I didn't allow myself the luxury of hope.

Still, I wasn't despairing about finding my mother. Aurelia had acknowledged the story of the witch's burial in her own backyard. Despite her insistence that it wasn't true, I was waiting on the forensic anthropologists' conclusion. Surely they could determine if the remains were thirty or sixty years old! I had also told Valero that Dolores knew Valentina, who had probably lived in Alamar. He might be able to follow the Russian connection. A long shot, but it was worth a try.

In the meantime, I stayed away from what Candela called "negative thoughts" and forbade myself from dwelling on the grim discovery, which might (just might) not have anything to do with Tania after all. Sometimes, however, a phrase came back to me—*a couple that had a big fight*—and the card with the yellow woman and the soldier flashed before my eyes . . .

Satia had saved Candela's backpack, and I still had my passport and wallet in the duffel bag. We canceled our return flights to Miami. At first I suggested Candela leave alone, since

I planned to stay until Mamina was out of the hospital, but she wouldn't hear of it. Aurelia had left, after giving me her phone number and address in Houston—not that I cared to have any contact with her afterward.

It was around four o'clock when I got a call from Valero. He had gone to the hospital to see Mamina, and the nurses had directed him to my current home.

"*Señora* Mercedes, I have some information I'd like to discuss, seeing that your grandmother is in no condition to do so."

"Is the information good or bad?" I asked, the phone pressed against my ear.

"Not the best kind, I'm afraid. But the story still has many holes."

I spent the three hours that passed until the cop arrived on the proverbial pins and needles. Candela and Satia made a ceremony that involved sandalwood and crystals, intended to bring me strength and peace of mind.

"Why don't you pray for something good to happen for a change?" I asked sharply.

"Well, if bad things have already occurred, prayers don't have retroactive effect," Satia said, bowing his head.

"And we don't actually pray," Candela added, and her voice broke.

I began to cry softly. She stroked my hair.

"Merceditas, wherever she is, your mom still loves you."

Wanting to believe her, I wiped my tears and prepared myself for whatever was ahead of me.

VALERO ARRIVED WITH HIS old Samsonite. We sat together in the living room, in two chairs that Satia had brought and set across from the spooky mandala. The cop placed the briefcase on his lap and took some papers out. As we made small talk (Mamina was doing better, but Doctora Morales still wanted to keep her in the hospital; yes, I would stay in Cuba as long as necessary) my left eye started to twitch. It had never happened before. Perhaps I needed more alprazolam.

"An investigation began immediately after your mother disappeared," Valero said finally. "Even before that, she was under surveillance, like all Americans who made Cuba their home. Some letters addressed to her were intercepted by State Security."

He handed me two photocopied pages: a handwritten letter in English and an envelope stamped on June 12th, 1986, addressed to Tania Rojas at Villa Santa Marta. The sender was Rob Laumer, from Camino del Mar, Berkeley, CA.

"*¡Gracias a Dios!*" I exclaimed, and quickly went over the letter.

*Berkeley, June 10th, 1986*

*Dear SL,*
*How is compañera Tania?*

*Our Compañeros friends ask about you quite often. If they only knew!*

*I wish I had spent more time there. Tell me about Cubans, their homes—and yours!—what they eat, what they think of their leaders—and ours.*

*College life is better than expected. But I miss you, more so because I know that you would be happy among so many liberal and like-minded people. Vincent and I are living together and loving every minute of it. Except when he claims I leave stuff all over the place. "I may not always know where you are, but I know where you have been." He's fastidious like that. You will adore him!*

*Bueno, querida, enjoy your tropical adventure, but remember that you belong in Berkeley!*

*—Rob*

"What's her real name?" I asked. "He calls her SL."

"I don't know." Valero shrugged and added, "Yet. It's somewhere in a State Security archive. It won't be impossible to find out, but it's going to take time. They are quite secretive and don't always like to cooperate with us."

Still, I had a starting point: a name and an address. Rob Laumer probably wouldn't be living there anymore, but I would track him down, and he could guide me to—

"Thank you." I felt like hugging Valero. "Thank you so much!"

"Ah, we aren't done yet. I just wanted to proceed in order." He had a grave expression that made me fear the worst. "When 'Tania' vanished, your father was the main suspect. This is often the case."

The fuzzy feelings vanished in an instant. My chest constricted.

"He was questioned, as well as your grandmother and several neighbors. Nobody admitted to knowing anything. Your father said that he had come home one day and his wife was gone. You were alone in the house, in a cradle. A few months later he volunteered to go to Angola again, where, as you know, he shot himself. A year after his death, your mother's case was closed because it had gone cold for lack of leads. But now—"

Realizing what was coming next, I doubled over in pain and felt myself sliding down to the floor. Candela, who had stayed nearby, came and held me.

"The remains found in the backyard belong to a woman who was killed by a gunshot wound to the head. The bullet was there too. It's nine millimeters, the kind used for Makarov guns. Your father had one."

I remember its weight, the way it felt heavy in my hand.

"So, as things are, and though we have no conclusive proof yet, the remains are likely to be your mother's. But we'll need

a blood sample from you for confirmation and positive identi-
fication of them."

I nodded, unable to speak. I had reached the end of my
quest, though the final answer would come from a few drops
of blood and some fragments of bone. Nothing else was left
from the bond that once tied me to my mother. After a silence,
Valero went on.

"Your deceased father is the main suspect."

"What if it was his former girlfriend?" I asked hoarsely,
clinging to an absurd hope. "She had a Makarov too!"

Valero shook his head.

"There were two passports inside a leather pouch that was
found near the remains."

He handed me two photocopied pages with Cyrillic characters. One had the photo of a woman with short blond hair,
blue eyes and the same slightly square face I had seen in the
*Granma* write up.

It was my mother. My mother, who hadn't ever left me, but
had been close, oh, so dreadfully close all the years I had lived
in Villa Santa Marta. While I was concocting stories about
imprisoned heroines or seething over her abandonment, she
was right there in the backyard. But maybe her spirit, like the
ghosts Candela believed in, had been around as well, protecting
me, comforting me from another dimension.

When I stopped crying, and after Satia brought a glass of
water, I noticed that the name under the picture was Olga Ivanova.

The other passport belonged to a blond little girl with
smiling eyes whose resemblance to the woman was obvious.
Everything fell into place like a poisoned puzzle.

"Why did he bury the passports with her?" I asked when
my voice was steady enough. "Wasn't it . . . incriminating evi-
dence?"

"Because he knew he wasn't coming back? Or he thought that if the body was discovered, the passports would explain why—"

The room, Valero and Candela started to dissolve. My eyes found the mandala. It didn't make me dizzy anymore; in fact, it beckoned me, having taken on a life of its own. Inside the web of triangles and circles were my mother and Mamina waving while Nena barked nearby, her little tail a happy powder puff. I reached out to them and got lost in the sacred geometry.

# CHAPTER FIFTY-ONE

*April 11th, 1989*

*I don't know when or if you will get this letter, but I just have to vent. I've had the worst day ever. Mercedes got sick. I wanted to make chicken soup for her, but there were no chickens in the diplotiendas or the peso stores. Joaquín suggested feeding her Russian compotas. Stupid!*

VALENTINA HAD DONE HER best to find a chicken. None of her contacts, not even the Bulgarian chef, could help. She managed to buy a five-pound eye of round that turned out too tough even after being boiled for four hours. Mercedes swallowed a bite and immediately threw it up.

"Red meat's too rich," Valentina said. "We have to get a chicken, dead or alive!"

"Let's go see my mother-in-law," Sarah replied, determinedly.

It was a weekday, around 10:30 A.M. Joaquín was at work.

"Wouldn't your husband want to go?" Valentina asked. "It's his family, after all."

Sarah shrugged.

"I don't care what he wants to do. We're going *now*."

"Easier to ask for forgiveness than permission, eh?"

"I don't need his permission to take care of my daughter!"

Valentina looked at her with a mix of surprise and respect. "*¡Estás de ampanga*, Jackie O*!*"

Sarah didn't know exactly what that meant—Valentina was better than her at Cuban slang—but it sounded good. The Barbeitos agreed to babysit Mercedes. They left before eleven o'clock.

VALENTINA HAD NEVER BEEN in Pinar del Río or heard of La Coloma. Sarah remembered that the town was around an hour and a half from the Orchid Garden, which, being a touristy spot, was easy to find. She carried an old envelope with Mamina's address that she had found in Joaquín's armoire.

The Orchid Garden was still closed to the public, but they met a guy who patrolled the place on a horse. Sarah showed him the envelope.

"Uf, that's in *casa del carajo*, ladies!" the man said, then proceeded to give them directions. "Merge onto the Autopista Este-Oeste and go on straight. You'll pass San Cristóbal, Los Palacios and Consolación del Sur before you see a sign pointing to La Coloma."

Valentina wrote the directions in Russian. Sarah admired her skill to translate mentally as the guy spoke.

"We're getting there, Jackie O!" Valentina said, and added in English, "Onward ho!"

Sarah laughed.

"Why do you always call me Jackie O?"

"Because your smile looks like hers."

Sarah had never felt so flattered. But this was the only good thing that happened that day.

THE LADA DROVE NOISILY down the highway, with a permanent pounding sound that Valentina said was a misaligned rod. She had bought several cans of gas in Havana. Surprisingly, a gas station outside the Orchid Garden was open and in business. She refilled the tank. They got to La Coloma at two o'clock and, after asking a couple of times, found the house.

Mamina came out, looking surprised.

"Tania!" she exclaimed, and peered inside the Lada. "Where are Joaquín and Mercedes?"

Valentina parked in a shady spot under a coconut tree.

Sarah got out of the car. She hugged Mamina and said hastily, "I need chickens."

"Chickens!" her mother-in-law repeated as if she had said "diamonds."

"Yes, for Mercedes. I have nothing to feed her. What kind of country is this where you can't even find a damn chicken to make soup for a sick child?"

Mamina seemed shocked at the outburst.

"*Ay, mijita,*" she said after an awkward pause. "I don't have any chickens left. We ate all of them. The hens weren't even laying anymore. But let's go see Canario."

Valentina left on her own to scout the territory. Sarah followed Mamina under the scorching sun, burrs sticking to her leather sandals, until they got to Canario's house. He wasn't around. His daughter, a young woman in tattered jeans and a faded T-shirt, met them at the threshold. Mamina explained their predicament.

"Sorry, but we only have an old hen left," Canario's daughter said. "Mom's saving it for an emergency."

"This is an emergency, Isela," Mamina replied. "My granddaughter is sick."

Isela didn't answer. Her attitude said, clearer than words, that Mercedes's sickness was none of her business.

"I will pay for it," Sarah said. "In pesos or dollars, whatever you want."

Isela grinned as if she had been expecting to hear that.

Mamina made a sound of protest that the younger women ignored. Isela turned around and made a gesture for Sarah to follow her.

The living room was furnished with three-legged stools, a wooden box that acted as a table, with a metal ashtray on top, and a beige sofa, newer than the other pieces. In a small yard, a chicken cackled loudly. Isela pointed with her chin at the bird.

"Forty dollars," she said matter-of-factly.

Sarah felt nauseated and, though not invited to do so, sat down on the sofa. She opened her purse and took two twenty-dollar bills. Mamina looked appalled but said nothing.

"You can go get it," Isela told Mamina, putting the money dismissively inside her jeans front pocket.

The air was hot and the atmosphere oppressive. Sarah unconsciously put a hand to her throat. Isela's eyes followed the movement.

"I want that too," she said.

"What?" Sarah asked. "What *else*?"

"That thing you're wearing. It's silver, isn't it?"

"No, I—" Sarah swallowed hard. "It's an alloy. It's not worth much. I can give you forty dollars more instead."

Isela's eyes shone with greed.

"Ha! And you said it's worth nothing? I want it!"

Mamina came back from the patio with the chicken still cackling furiously in her arms.

"That thing and the chain, or no deal," Isela said calmly.

Sarah unlocked the chain, threw it on the wooden box and bolted out.

MAMINA KILLED THE CHICKEN, wrapped it in old newspaper pages and added two sweet potatoes and three malangas that another neighbor agreed to sell after much pleading. Sarah thanked her and tried to remain composed, making a monumental effort to be polite to her mother-in-law and Olimpia, the only ones who were at home at that time.

Fortunately, Valentina picked her up in less than an hour. She had found two chickens (relatively fat and young) at ten dollars apiece, plus oranges, onions and two pounds of green beans.

They drove through Colón Street, with the Lada drawing a few curious glances from the townspeople. The *flamboyanes* had lost all their flowers, and Sarah knew, by then, that she would never see them in full bloom. She broke into tears as soon as they left the village behind.

"I didn't even think of taking out the pictures," she sobbed. "I can replace Mercedes's but not my grandma's. I felt so humiliated and taken advantage of! Why, Valentina? Why would that woman care about something that has only sentimental value? What's wrong with her?"

Valentina cracked a sad smile.

"She probably wants to sell the locket at La Casa del Oro, where people exchange jewelry for a new currency called *chavitos*. Then they use the *chavitos* to shop in stores that look like *diplotiendas* but allow Cubans in."

Sarah felt dizzy. Everything looked surreal, in a sick and dystopian sort of way.

WHEN SHE ARRIVED IN Villa Santa Marta carrying chickens and vegetables, Joaquín was on the phone. He was giving somebody her real name.

"Are you talking to State Security?" she asked.

He dropped the phone. "Where's Mercedes?"

"With the Barbeitos."

"And where *carajos* were you?"

"Looking for food, since you are unable to!"

They exchanged a few more bitter words, but didn't have the

fight that Sarah had anticipated and, frankly, wouldn't have minded at that moment, so angry she was.

"I thought that you—that you had left Cuba with Mercedes," Joaquín muttered.

"Are you crazy?"

They got the girl back from the Barbeitos and (kind of) patched things up. Sarah made chicken soup and pureed malangas, and Mercedes ate all of it. Joaquín didn't say anything about the escapade to La Coloma. The next morning, he was conciliatory, clearly wanting to put the incident behind. But Sarah's heart was heavy. Not just about the locket and her grandma's picture, but because she suspected "the situation" regarding breakfast, lunch and dinner was only going to get worse.

# CHAPTER FIFTY-TWO

Life was looking pretty grim on the fifth day after the fall of Villa Santa Marta. All I could think at first, after recovering from my own *zirimba*, was that the search for my mom was finally over. And yes, now I could call her "mom"! As for Joaquín Montero, I hadn't really known him. Mamina had turned him into a distant valiant figure, the war hero and not much else. Now that he wasn't even that, there was nothing left in his place. Except the Makarov.

The bell rang. There had been people coming and going—Instituto members and Satia's friends or family. I was lying on the bed with a cold washcloth over my forehead. Valero had left all the photocopied pages with Candela, who had been handling everything, calls from the hospital included. I didn't want to see anybody, even Mamina. Particularly Mamina. My own grandmother, who had to have suspected . . . No, I wasn't ready to deal with her yet. But when I heard a familiar barking, my spirits revived and I got up and rushed out.

In the living room, a very filthy Nena was going in circles and snapping at the cushions on the floor while Candela tried to get hold of her. Catalina was there, an empty leash still in her hand.

"Thank you for rescuing her!" I said, relieved, because *that* was another reason why I didn't want to face Mamina. "Where did you find her?"

"Around your house, sniffing out where it used to be." Catalina frowned. "That was a shock, *mijita*. A building that looked so solid! And how's Mamina doing? I keep calling the hospital, but they don't put her on the phone."

"She's a little better."

"What happened, anyway? Was it the storm that gave her a *zirimba*? Or something else? People said that the police were there earlier that day."

"Merceditas and I were out of Havana when all that was going on," Candela answered quickly. "We're waiting for Mamina to tell us. Would you like a cup of coffee, *señora*?"

"No, thanks. I have to go and see about the potatoes. They just came to the *puesto*, but I wanted to bring Pulgosa first since the neighbor from across the street said you all were so concerned about her."

"*Ay*, we were! And how's Dolores?"

"Okay, I guess. She's put her house up for sale and is planning to move to a newer place. Everybody on the block is terrified after Villa Santa Marta fell down. If that happened to a big solid mansion, what can the rest of us expect?"

"Well, the 'mansion' wasn't as solid as it looked," I said.

Satia took Catalina back to Miramar in the *almendrón*.

Candela gave Nena a bath. She was dirty but didn't appear to have suffered much. Her little eyes were as bright as ever, and her tail, though full of goatheads and dead leaves, never stopped wagging.

"Everything will start to get better," Candela said.

I was going to reply with a snarky remark, something like it was about time, but the phone rang. It was a landline, though more modern than the one in Villa Santa Marta. Before

Candela answered, I knew in my heart it was Mamina. I don't know how I knew it; I just did.

"*¡Abuela!*" Candela shrieked. She had an odd way of holding the receiver, as if she wasn't sure how to use it. "This is like a series of miracles . . . Oh, nothing. I'm delighted to hear your voice. Let me put Merceditas . . . What? No, no, she's right here!"

She handed me the phone.

"—doesn't want to talk to me, I'm sure," Mamina was saying. Her voice was fragile, clear but weak. "Just tell her . . ."

"Why do you think that I don't want to talk to you?" I asked.

Mamina breathed heavily for a few seconds.

"Valero came to see me," she said, "and told me that you guys had met."

"We did."

Another pause.

"They're releasing me from the hospital," she said. "I was wondering if Satia could take me home."

Was it possible that she hadn't heard about the house? Perhaps Valero hadn't told her much.

"Home isn't there anymore, Mamina," I said quietly. "The storm—"

"I know what the storm did." She sounded stronger now. "And everything else. When I said home, I meant La Coloma. If he can't, then Yoel will come for me. But he's not sure that his old truck can make it to Havana."

"Wait. You called Yoel first?"

"Well, I needed to know if Sonrisa was okay with me moving there."

I put my back against the wall where the chakra chart was and let myself slide to the floor. Candela pushed a cushion in my direction. Nena, still wet, nosed me.

"And she said yes," Mamina concluded, "so . . . I'm going home."

The pain I had tried to shove down for days leaked up. My eyes welled with tears.

"I will go with you."

She kept quiet for the space of a few breaths. I wanted to hug her and say I would take care of her as she had done for me all those years. I still loved her. I would bring her back to her true home, the one she had left to raise me.

"Are you sure?"

"Well, of course! Just give me an hour. I will be there with Satia as soon as he comes back."

"I'm sorry, Merceditas," she whispered. "Valero said—"

"We'll talk about it later. Please, wait for us."

I CLOSED MY EYES as we passed by La Quinta de Los Molinos. Satia parked on Espada Street, and we walked to the hospital. In the marble-accented lobby, wearing the same blue dress she had on five days earlier, Mamina looked stricken. She seemed to have shrunk and withered. I took her in my arms. My embrace, however, felt a little stiff.

"I never thought . . ." she muttered. "I had started to believe she was still alive. I'm so sorry."

I remained silent. She did look genuinely sorry. But about what?

Doctora Morales came out with a pack of medicines for Mamina. She was about my age, with a gentle smile and a professional demeanor.

"Keep watching your blood pressure, *Abuela*," she said. "And don't forget to take the pills."

I retrieved the tablet from my duffel bag and gave it to her.

"*¡Gracias, señora!*" She hugged me. "I'm sorry to have asked, but my son . . . I had no other way to . . ."

"I understand."

ONCE WE WERE OUT of the hospital, Mamina walked slowly and unsteadily, leaning on my arm.

"Would you like to stay in my house a few days, until you feel stronger?" Satia asked, opening the car's door for her. "There's space for all of us."

"No, *mijito*." Mamina shook her head with more energy than she appeared to have. "My niece is waiting in La Coloma. And I don't have it in me to settle in one place and then move again. Let's just—go."

We all got in the *almendrón*. Mamina sat in the passenger seat with Nena, who looked out the window and sniffed the air with her pink-speckled nose. Candela and I shared the back seat. I carried the duffel bag with the few belongings I had put there for Mamina. She didn't even ask about them. She acted as if she didn't mind the loss of her house and possessions—the few she had had, anyway. As for me, I didn't care much either. The loss of Villa Santa Marta paled in comparison with all the others: my mother, first, and the memory of my father the hero. Besides, I had never felt that the place really belonged to us. My real home was in Miami, where I couldn't wait to return.

The trip was quiet as none of us talked much. We passed the Soroa Orchid Garden, entered La Coloma, and took the dirt road that led to Sonrisa's house.

Sonrisa herself was outside, and so was Yoel, next to his battered Ford. As soon as Satia opened the door, Nena jumped out and ran behind the house, ignoring Mamina's anxious calls.

"*¡Prima!*"

Yoel's bear hug comforted me. He smelled like sun, tobacco and, faintly, aftershave.

"How are you holding up?" he asked with such concern that it warmed my heart.

Nena came back with her tongue hanging out and a satisfied expression. Mamina carried her inside, leaving all of us behind.

"Did Mamina tell you?" I asked.

"Yes. I thought it was so strange, after we had been talking . . ."

"It was strange," I agreed. "The whole thing."

"Well, come on in. And you too, guys," he said to Satia and Candela. "*Mi casa es su casa*, you know."

# CHAPTER FIFTY-THREE

*July 19th, 1989*

*Oh, not that awful thing! Couldn't it be a mistake? How is Vincent? He doesn't have it, right? Then it can't be! I want so much to be there with you! But then Mercedes . . . I feel trapped, Rob, and wish . . . I am not sure what to wish for anymore.*

IT WAS SUMMER AGAIN, stiflingly hot. Sarah was in bed with Mercedes, the electric fan she had brought from San Diego keeping the room temperature tolerable. Outside, it was nearing ninety-two degrees.

The phone rang. Sarah hurried downstairs.

"My friend who works at La Central says they're selling *íntimas* at the pharmacy," Dolores announced, breathless. "Please, go right away and buy four packages. We will share them."

Sarah looked out the picture window. There were around fifty people waiting in line in front of the bodega.

"Okay," she said with a loud sigh.

How could she refuse? *Íntimas* had been in short supply lately. She had resorted to cloths, cut-outs from sheets, which she later washed and boiled. Gross! Since *íntimas* had been available in most pharmacies without coupons when she visited San Diego, it hadn't occurred to her to bring some.

Valentina was out of Havana. She had gone to the Matanzas province, where farmers were selling pigs or exchanging them for foreign clothes. Sarah left Mercedes with Elena, as usual, and walked to the bus stop. Sweat drenched her clothes and clouded her eyes. It was like being inside a sauna. After waiting for ten minutes, she leaned against the nearest wall, feeling she was about to faint. A woman approached her.

"Are you okay, *mija*?" she asked.

"Yes, thanks," Sarah mumbled. "It's just too hot for me."

How come she had lived there almost three years and the heat hadn't bothered her that much? She was just tired.

"Sick and tired, that's what I am," she muttered.

A bus stopped ten feet away from the bus stop. She ran like everybody else, pushing and elbowing people to get inside.

THE *CARNAVALES* WERE ABOUT to start. They had been scaled down, with less floats and music and, more disturbingly, less food. There were no booths available either. It wasn't a good idea to go out at night now that unexpected blackouts darkened, all of a sudden, the already somber streets. The first blackout took Sarah by surprise, but it only lasted forty minutes. The next one stretched for over six hours, and a bottle of milk she had saved for Mercedes went sour.

One night, while Joaquín was still at the unit, at 7:30 P.M.—another meeting, as usual—Sarah dialed the operator and placed a call to Berkeley. She longed to hear Rob's voice, to find out how he was doing. At that point, she didn't care if "they" had the phone tapped.

DESPITE GORBACHEV'S VISIT TO Havana in April—which got little attention from the local press—most Russian supplies, from gas to magazines to preserves, were slowly vanishing from the island.

"Fidel's against our reform process," Valentina told Sarah as they walked out of another half-empty *diplotienda*. "He banned *Sputnik* because it was publishing too much perestroika news."

By then, Sarah had already decided that she didn't want Mercedes to grow up in Cuba. Perhaps becoming a mother had made her selfish, she reasoned, but she didn't care anymore about free medicine, education or social programs. She still hoped to convince Joaquín to let Mercedes spend time with her maternal grandparents in San Diego. How long that time would be, she didn't dare to anticipate. But her husband was a good man, and they would reach an agreement. And if that didn't happen, Valentina would help, as she had done with the Barbeitos. They were leaving that afternoon.

Sarah was dressing Mercedes to say goodbye to their neighbors when the portrait of the young girl in their backyard caught her attention. She had examined it often, admiring the vibrant colors and the sunlight that shone onto the girl's face. She had to be one of the Sotolongos. Sarah knew that Joaquín had gotten the house furnished, which made sense if those people had left the country. Naturally, they couldn't take the piano, much less those massive bedroom sets. Maybe they didn't care for the silverware either. But couldn't they have at least taken the portraits? Especially if the owner of the house had painted them, as Elena said. She decided to ask the Barbeitos. This would be her last chance to find out.

"AH, WE'RE GOING TO miss you!" Elena cooed, holding Mercedes. "You've brightened our lives, *bebé*!"

They were all teary-eyed in the Barbeitos' living room. The couple didn't offer too many details about the circumstances surrounding their departure, and Sarah didn't ask. But she wanted a way to locate them so they gave her the postal address of an old friend, a colleague of Doctor Barbeito's who lived in New York. They hadn't seen each other in almost thirty years, but the Barbeitos expected to reconnect with him upon their arrival.

"We'll meet again," Sarah said firmly, folding the piece of paper. "I will contact him when I get back home and get in touch with you again. I promise."

"I'm glad to hear that, sweetheart," Elena answered, "because you can't stay in this country forever."

Sarah nodded and swallowed hard, giving herself away. A few months before she would have argued, but now, she couldn't even say a word. Her fingers curled nervously over her lap.

When the conversation died down, and the sadness of the upcoming parting fogged the spirits, she leaned over and asked in a low voice, "What exactly happened with the Sotolongos?"

"Why do you want to know?" Elena asked. Her tone wasn't reproving, but Sarah felt her ears getting warm. Was she being too nosy again?

"Well, you have mentioned them often, and . . . I'm curious, since we're living in their house and all that."

The couple fell quiet.

"Well, what do you know about the Mariel boatlift, dear?" Elena said at last.

Sarah had seen on TV the boats arriving in Miami. Was Reagan president then? No, it was Carter. She wasn't sure. She had been a teenager. Later, *Scarface* had left her with the impression that all those Cubans were lowlife types, if not out-right criminals. When she said so, stumbling over her words, the Barbeitos looked outraged. She bit her lips. Ah, she should have known better than to trust Hollywood!

"That was what *this man* wanted people to think," Doctor Barbeito said. "But it's not true. Many decent families like the

Sotolongos left at that time. They had stayed in Cuba because they supported him at the beginning but became gradually disenchanted."

"So here's the Mariel story," Elena went on. "After a group of discontents asked for political asylum at the Peruvian embassy, and were followed by thousands, *this man* said that anybody who didn't like it here could get out of the country. He called them 'scum.' Some people claimed to be homosexuals in order to be allowed to go . . ."

What, being gay was considered unsuitable for a revolutionary? Oh, how disappointed Rob would be! Sarah listened quietly.

"When the CDR president found out that the Sotolongos were leaving, she organized an *acto de repudio*. The minute they came out of the house, neighbors started throwing eggs and stones at them. The same people who had known them forever! It was like a scene from the Middle Ages. A rock struck Aurelia, my goddaughter, in the face. She was thirteen years old."

"And Lo allowed it?" Sarah asked, afraid of the answer but unable to contain herself.

"She didn't live here yet. It was another woman."

It was a small relief.

"But those neighbors . . ." Sarah's head was swirling. "Why would they . . . ?"

"They were ordered to," Elena said.

"Some were more than happy to do as they had been told," Doctor Barbeito added. "Others didn't want to attract unwanted attention by staying away."

So 1984! A wave of anger overcame Sarah. Why hadn't Joaquín told her?

"Why didn't you guys leave too?" she asked shyly.

"Because we had no family in the United States to send for us."

WHEN SARAH WENT BACK home, she felt utterly ashamed to be living in Villa Santa Marta. She was also furious at *this man*, the system, her own naïveté and, above all, Joaquín. She couldn't wait to confront him. And she did, as soon as he stepped in.

He rolled his eyes dismissively.

"Where did you hear these counterrevolutionary lies? Just so you know, people, the masses, acted spontaneously during the Mariel time."

"*If* that was the case," Sarah said as calmly as she could, "then 'the masses' needed to be contained, by force if necessary. Why didn't the police protect those who were leaving? Freedom of travel is a human right!"

They were still in the living room. Mercedes, who had been playing in the backyard, came in and stood in the dining area, looking at her parents with big, scared eyes.

"Sarah Lee, don't come here talking about freedom!" Joaquín snapped. "You're a spoiled *burguesita* who doesn't understand life in Cuba! You have no right to criticize the revolution. No right at all!"

It was the first time he had called her by her real name in years.

"I do, because I live here!" she replied.

Joaquín grabbed the silver-framed portrait from the piano and threw it against a window. The glass panel exploded into a thousand glittery shards. Mercedes watched the whole thing from a corner, clutching a rag doll against her chest.

THE NEXT DAY, SARAH and Joaquín apologized to each other profusely. He took most of the blame.

"*Mi amor*, I shouldn't have reacted that way. I'm sorry. It won't happen again. I'm just under too much stress at work."

"Why?"

"Meetings. Disagreeable things."

"I shouldn't have been so upset either. After all, there are many injustices in my country too."

"There are injustices everywhere. But tell me"—he kissed her hand—"was it Valentina who put those *gusanerías* in your head?"

"No, no! The Barbeitos told me."

It was the truth, and now they were safely out of the country. But Joaquín didn't seem to believe her—not that she cared one way or the other. As for the "disagreeable things," she thought they were related to the execution of General Arnaldo Ochoa, who had been accused of drug smuggling and treason. The trial was broadcast live on television, but Joaquín refused to watch it or discuss the matter.

"Ochoa tried to bring perestroika here," Valentina told Sarah. "Fidel got pissed at him."

Sarah had given up trying to understand Cuba—and Cubans. That a decorated war hero had been sent to the firing squad was just one among the multiple pieces of this giant puzzle of an island. Perestroika or no perestroika, she wasn't going to wait for a civil war to break out. She would close her eyes and see her parents' house and hear the sound of the waves that had once rocked her to sleep. Soon they would rock Mercedes too. It was time to go home.

# CHAPTER FIFTY-FOUR

Mamina's new bedroom was half the size of her former room in Villa Santa Marta. There was only a small window with a faded flowery curtain. A thin, square red rug covered the cement floor. But a new hammock hung from the walls, and she had placed the Heno de Pravia bottle on a pine table. A raggedy gray loveseat that I didn't remember seeing during my first visit had been brought in.

After taking a bath, Mamina had changed into the house-coat and was now wearing her slippers. Her arm had healed, and her color had returned. She looked fine, as if we were just going to have a regular conversation. Her eyes, though, told another story. They were reddish and sunken, and, like the night of my arrival, avoided me. We shared the loveseat, which smelled vaguely like camphor.

"Mamina, how much did you know?"

She covered her face with her hands.

"Nothing! Look, it's bad enough for me to accept that my son could have done—what the cop said he did. And notice that there is no proof."

I was going to bring up the Makarov, which she had seen numerous times, but changed my mind and just waited.

"Had I ever suspected . . ." She uncovered her face, slowly.

"It's too awful. I still don't believe it! It could have been somebody else."

"Didn't Valero tell you about the passports?"

She nodded, deflated.

"She was going to leave with me, and he killed her. Do you really need to see a smoking gun?"

There was a pause. Long and heavy, like the cloud of silence that had covered my mother's memory all throughout my childhood.

"Please, no more lies, Mamina. Tell me everything. I have the right to know."

I made an effort to sound even, but was aware of the accusatory ring of my words. She sighed.

"When the police called me after Tania . . . disappeared, they made it sound like Joaquín was a suspect."

"What did he tell you?"

"Not much. But he was desperate. Crying all the time."

"*Why* was he crying?"

"I assumed, like everybody else, that he missed her. They were such a nice couple. I never saw them argue. I know nothing, my love. I am not lying to you. Why would I?"

*Oh, I don't know*, I wanted to reply. *Because you've been doing it my entire life?* But I kept quiet. I felt her pain and wished that we could drop it, never mention my parents again, go on as before. Mamina had given me a good life. She had loved me. But there were too many—skeletons in our past. I had to speak up.

"What about my dad's death? You said he had died in combat. That wasn't true!"

Her eyes swelled with tears.

"Other kids had lost parents in the Angola War. It occurred to me that it would be less painful if you thought he was a brave soldier."

"Why didn't you tell me later, when I was an adult?"

"I should have. Now I realize I should have. I almost told you a few days ago when we were talking about him."

*Almost doesn't cut it.* But I kept quiet. She was an old woman who had already endured too many hardships. Both her children had died quite young, and now she had to live with the certainty that her son had killed his wife. She might have been living with it for a long time. And if she did, how could she have come up and told me? As if reading my mind, she said, "I honestly thought I was protecting you."

"When they found the skeleton, you knew, didn't you?"

She slumped in the loveseat.

"Shortly before he left for Angola, I found Joaquín knelt down by the rosebush. He had just planted it."

A knot in my chest ached as I recalled the purple roses and their potent smell that used to wrap me up in the backyard.

"He had a gun in his hand," Mamina continued, "and was ready to . . . I took it away from him and began to suspect—"

She burst into tears. I hugged her as the ache spread through my body. Something inside me turned warm and liquid and finally melted away, except for a few tiny needles that kept pricking my heart.

A few minutes passed. Or it might have been an hour. Tears leaked out of my eyes though I tried to stop them. The red rug looked bloody. The Heno de Pravia bottle suddenly resembled a gun. The thought of having another *zirimba*, this time in front of Mamina, was unbearable. I reigned myself in.

"Are you going back to Miami now?" Mamina asked.

"I can stay if you want me to."

Not that *I* did. The anger, or some of it, was still there, but my heart ached with sorrow too. The two emotions, in a way, cancelled each other.

"Ah, no—you aren't used to this," she said. "And you have your job and things to do, right?"

"That's true. Marlene must be going crazy in La Bakería."

"Will you ever come back to La Coloma?"

I nearly jumped out.

"Mamina! What kind of question is that? *Claro que* I will be back! I will call you every week at Yoel's office too, until we find a cell phone that works here."

She stretched her right hand and caressed my hair softly, almost tentatively.

"I'm glad to hear that, *mijita*."

"What did you expect, Mamina? You still are—"

I didn't finish the sentence. She leaned against me. Slowly, we twined our fingers together.

WHEN I WALKED OUT of the room, Canario was on the porch, talking to Yoel. Caballero was nearby.

"My *ahijada*!" Canario said. "I didn't expect to see you so soon, and under such sad circumstances."

He gave me a hug. Sonrisa and Yoel joined the embrace. I took comfort in the fact that I had, at least, regained a family. A family that would always be there for Mamina and me.

# CHAPTER FIFTY-FIVE

*November 27th, 1989*

*Please, keep strong. Never, ever give up! Here, everything is on hold as the shockwaves from Europe are reaching Cuba. Joaquín has been irritable and tired. Though he assured me it had nothing to do with us, he didn't explain what was in the works. Which you probably heard of already, but in Havana, most people had no idea.*

ON NOVEMBER 10TH, VALENTINA picked up Sarah and Mercedes in the morning, and they spent most of the day in Alamar. Carlos made spaghetti—with cream cheese, which was the only kind of topping available. They all huddled around the radio, listening to Voice of America broadcasts. Alamar was so close to the ocean that some American stations bypassed the Cuban interference.

*"East Germany announced yesterday it was opening its borders to the rest of the world and that its citizens can now travel or emigrate anywhere, including through the Berlin Wall."*

Sarah gaped at the radio. Valentina jumped up and spun in a circle.

"They made it!" she cried out. "We're next!"

She added something in Russian. Carlos joined his wife on the floor.

"And then us!" he yelled.

*"Egon Krenz has called for free and democratic elections, the main demand of the opposition movement."*

Valentina and Carlos hugged each other. Sarah stayed put, not sure how to react to the news. She thought of her old "Marxist cell," Joaquín, the *diplotiendas* . . .

"This is the beginning of the end, Jackie O," Valentina said. "If Gorbachev didn't mind letting go of our next-door neighbor, why would he care about a faraway island that's costing us an arm and a leg?"

"Yes!" Carlos lifted up his fists. "Cuba's time is coming too!"

Sarah was still trying to wrap her mind around the fact that communism was on its way out. Despite all her recent discoveries, she was still ambivalent. But her friends looked so happy that she joined them, and they toasted (with vodka, naturally) to a better future for all.

VALENTINA DROPPED SARAH OFF two blocks from Villa Santa Marta and advised her not to talk to Joaquín about what she had just heard.

"Keep your American passport with you all the time," she added. "You may need it."

"Well, I'd like to travel again, but . . ."

"This isn't about traveling," Valentina replied. "If protests start here, you can go to the American embassy and ask them for protection. Fidel is not a Krenz. He won't go down without a fight."

But the United States had no embassy in Havana, only an Interest Section, whatever that was. Supposing they offered her asylum, what about Mercedes? Joaquín wouldn't allow the girl to leave the country, and Sarah wouldn't go anywhere without her. When she told Valentina as much, her friend patted her back.

"Where there's a will, there's a way, Jackie O. Let me know when you're ready, and I'll help you and the girl get out of this crap hole. But don't wait too long," she added with a wink, "because we are leaving pretty soon."

JOAQUÍN WAS ALREADY THERE when Sarah and Mercedes came back.

"Where were you two?" he asked, kissing the girl.

Sarah smiled sweetly.

"We went shopping in Yumurí. Lo told me to use the coupons before they expire in December."

"Ah, good. Did you find anything?"

"No."

Five days later, when most people in Cuba had gotten wind of what was going on in the world, she casually mentioned the Berlin Wall fall. They were watching the *noticiero*, which had yet to report anything of substance.

"Do you think that the changes in Eastern Europe will affect Cuba too?" she asked, feigning indifference.

Joaquín got livid.

"Changes *ni un carajo*! If counterrevolutionaries attempt to harm the revolution, Fidel has promised to take the tanks to the street!"

"Would he?"

"You bet!" He looked at her suspiciously. "But do you know about it? And what is it to you?"

She pretended to be interested in a report about the potato harvest in the Isle of Youth.

"Oh, nothing. I was just curious."

They didn't talk politics again that night. The next morning, as soon as Joaquín left, Sarah called Valentina.

# CHAPTER FIFTY-SIX

The plane took off. The José Martí International Airport became smaller until a big white cloud totally covered it. I exhaled a sigh of relief. I was done with Cuba, at least for a while. I had been living in a haze for over a week. Everything felt as if it had happened to someone else, from my affectionate but somewhat tense goodbye to Mamina to my last conversation with Yoel.

"I'll take care of Mamina," he said.

"I know that," I answered. "She already feels at home here. And so does Nena."

The pooch had taken to the farm like a champ, running all over the place and chasing lizards while Mamina yelled at her to go back to the house. It was comforting to think of them together. I had visited my *padrino* Canario again. No doubt I would come back and spend more time with the family. But before that happened, I would have to locate Rob Laumer and convince him to help me find my mom's folks, supposing that they were still alive.

To distract me, Candela disclosed that she and Satiadeva had clicked not only physically but also "vibrationally," and she wanted to return to Havana soon.

"At least one good thing came out of all this," I said.

"Ah, more than that! Yes, it's tough now, but at least you *know*. Your life will be easier from now on."

"I hope so," I said, believing just the opposite.

She dug through her backpack.

"You are not going to read the Tarot again, are you?" I bristled.

She grinned at me. "Not this time. Look what I brought." She took out the *Diario de una hechicera*.

"You saved it!" I exclaimed. "How——"

"Satia and I were reading it together when the house began to fall. I made a beeline for the street but first grabbed my backpack and put the manuscript inside."

María Estela would be pleased, I thought. Someone had cared enough about her precious writings to save them. I didn't, but that was a safer topic of conversation than my problems.

"What is it about, anyway?" I asked.

"Many things, among them the golden light," Candela said in a low, respectful voice. "And there's a whole section devoted to Madame Blavatsky."

"Madame who?"

"A famous mystic and cofounder of the Theosophical Society. María Estela met her in New York!"

*"Alabao."*

I stifled a yawn, but Candela didn't notice.

"Do you want to try a guided visualization, Merceditas? My favorite is about wrapping the body and soul up in a golden aura——"

This was getting too metaphysical for me.

"What if I just try to relax and sleep a bit?" I interrupted her.

The plane jumped in the air, and I felt a tug in my heart. An internal switch must have been turned on by the jerking motion because I started to sob. Candela put an arm around me.

"Have a good cry, *chica*," she said. "Every now and then, it's all we need to feel fine again."

I gave her a rueful grin.

"I am not sure I'll ever be fine."

"You will. But first, release the sadness you have been bottling in. See all you have gone through, all these painful discoveries? You have shed hardly a tear."

"I have, just not in front of you!" I protested.

"Not enough. Cry now, cry to your heart's content."

I bawled my eyes out for the remainder of the flight.

AS SOON AS WE cleared customs in Miami, I whipped out my smartphone and googled *Rob Laumer* and *Berkeley*. Among the first results was an obituary. *Berkeley—Robert Laumer, 22, passed away peacefully in his home on January 8, 1990. He is survived by his parents, Emma and Joe Laumer, and his partner, Vincent McCoy. Rob was born in San Diego, California, and graduated from Canyon Academy in 1985. He was attending the University of California Berkeley.*

"Just my luck," I said, dejected. "The only lead I have, and he's dead too."

"Who *else* is dead?" Candela asked.

"My mother's friend."

"You're kidding, Merceditas."

I showed her the phone.

"This is old news. January 1990!"

"What can I do now?"

"Google this Vincent guy, and let's hope he is alive."

I kept browsing while we waited for the airport parking shuttle. My hands were shaking so much that I couldn't even type on my phone keyboard. When we got to Candela's car, she took over.

"There are so many Vincent McCoys!" she said, clicking on a Facebook profile.

I glanced at a skateboarder's photo.

"Too young. If Vincent was Rob's partner in 1990, he must be around fifty years old."

"We'll follow every online thread until we find him."

"As long as the threads don't turn into a thick spidery web."

"Don't say that! Keep a positive attitude!"

Soon she got a more hopeful prospect.

"Here's a sociology professor at CUNY. PhD from New School University, BA from UC Berkeley 1991. That could very well be him."

AS SOON AS I opened the door, my house welcomed us with the scent of cleanness mixed with the faint aroma of spices and condiments. Cumin, cinnamon, saffron, anise . . . I dropped my duffel bag on the floor and inhaled the familiar, comforting smells. For the first time in my life, I felt truly home in a place.

Candela and I sat in the breakfast nook with my laptop, for which I usually didn't have much use. The heady fragrance of the geraniums that grew in the back porch added a happy note to the ambiance. My herb garden was thriving. I noticed, as if for the first time, the metal gleam of the stainless-steel appliances that I had collected over the years.

"*Mi casa,*" I whispered, grateful to be there.

Candela googled the professor. The CUNY website informed us that *Doctor McCoy's research concerns the intersections of culture, politics and social inequality.*

"Send him a short message asking if he had known Rob Laumer," Candela suggested. "Don't add anything else, or he may get spooked."

No, we certainly didn't want to *spook* him. I did as Candela said. She left. I took a shower, ordered food from a little Cuban restaurant in the corner and nibbled at an acceptable *arroz con pollo*. By six o'clock I was already in bed. I felt exhausted, as if I hadn't slept properly in a week.

Thinking of it, I hadn't.

THE NEXT MORNING, I woke up to a message from Doctor McCoy stating that he had indeed known Rob Laumer and closing with a question: *May I ask why you inquire?* I wrote back describing the search for my mother and how his name had popped up online when I looked for Rob. I left out the part about the backyard burial and simply wrote: *My mom's remains were recently found in Havana, and I'm looking for her family.*

I had started to make breakfast when a beep from the laptop announced a new message.

*From: vmccoy@gc.cuny.edu*
*To: mspivey@gmail.com*
*Dear Mercedes,*

*Your message came as a surprise, but I indeed remember how fondly Rob spoke of a friend of his who was living in Cuba at the time we were together. I believe I can help you, but I would rather talk to you first as this isn't a matter to be dealt over email.*

*Give me a call at your convenience.*

*Respectfully,*
*Vincent McCoy*

I retrieved my cell phone and dialed his number. A soothing professorial voice answered. "Mercedes?"

"Thanks for agreeing to talk to me," I said, my voice barely above a whisper.

"How could I not? I often wondered what had happened to Sarah Lee."

"Sarah Lee! Was that her real name?"

It was familiar but I wasn't sure why.

"Yes." He sounded baffled. "But you said you are her daughter. How could you not know that?"

"She used a different name in Cuba. Tania Rojas."

"Was it Tania? I'll have to look for—" He stopped.

"Did you know her?" I asked anxiously. "Her family? How can I contact them?"

"I have no idea where her family is. I didn't know her well either. In fact, I only saw her once, when she came back in—"

He hesitated. Despite his courteous messages, he probably suspected there was something fishy about me and my inquiries.

"In 1989?" I said.

"That's correct. What else do you know, Mercedes? I don't feel comfortable sharing anything else unless I see some proof of who you are."

"I have no proof of anything," I answered, discouraged. "Like I said, I just found out about my mother's death. I didn't even know her name until now."

"I'm sorry, but—"

"Wait! I have a letter from Rob where he mentions you! I mean, I have a photocopy. Will you consider it proof enough?"

He didn't answer right away.

"Let me look at it," he said at last. "Would you take a picture and send it on Messenger?"

I sent pictures of Rob's letter and envelope and the *Granma* article, and added the photo Candela had taken of me in front of the piano, hoping he noticed the family resemblance. *This is all I have*, I wrote. *I'm not going to ask my mother's family for money or anything. I only want to know who they are and for them to meet me if they choose to do so.*

Though I didn't believe in such things, I visualized the message going into the cyberspace surrounded by a golden light. It wouldn't hurt.

Half an hour later, a Messenger video call came through my phone. I fumbled with it, technology not being my strong suit. On the other side of the screen was a fifty-something gray-haired man. I waved awkwardly.

"Doctor McCoy?"

He waved back and held a picture in front of the camera. A tall blonde was sitting at the Villa Santa Marta piano with a little girl on her lap. There was no mistaking. My mom and I had the same blue eyes and slightly square face . . .

"You are Sarah Lee's spitting image!" he said. "And then the piano, still looking the same after all these years!"

"That's her!"

I wanted to reach through the screen and touch my mother's face. This was the first clear picture of her I had ever seen.

"What happened to your mom?" Doctor McCoy asked.

I decided to stick with the short version of the story. "No one knows exactly. There's an investigation going on."

"This must be very hard for you."

"Yes, it is . . . Now, these pictures, how do you have them?"

"Sarah Lee and Rob wrote to each other often. She also sent color film to develop here, but he didn't have a chance to mail the last pictures back to her. By that time, he was very sick."

"He died young too."

"AIDS."

"I am sorry." I allowed a respectful pause before asking, "So Rob and my mom were good friends?"

"Oh, yes. Like brother and sister. I remember how happy he got when her letters came—some through regular mail, directly from Havana, and others from Canada, Mexico, Eastern Europe . . . They talked on the phone too. But he was very protective of her. She didn't want her family to find her whereabouts, and he went to great lengths to honor her request."

That didn't bode well.

"Why was she hiding?" I asked.

"She was on probation."

I held my breath.

"What had she done?"

"Nothing too awful." He chuckled. "Sarah Lee and Rob went to El Salvador in a gap year. When they came back, she became active in the Sanctuary movement and was caught smuggling a Salvadorean family across the Tijuana border. She didn't go to jail on account of her age and the fact that the operation was done through a human rights group, but still, she wasn't allowed to leave the country. So she was, technically, a fugitive."

I retouched once again my mental image of Tania-Sarah Lee.

"Was she—a wild girl?"

"Goodness, no! She wanted to save the world. Her family was very conservative, which in turn made her rebellious. She even joined a 'Marxist group.'" He smiled. "As I said, I didn't know her well, but she seemed like an idealistic kind of person."

Dolores had been right. In the picture that Doctor McCoy was still holding my mother looked serious, pensive . . . and painfully young.

"Why did she go to Cuba?"

"Rob belonged to a San Diego group that campaigned against the embargo. He once traveled to Havana, and Sarah Lee went with him."

"But you said she couldn't leave the country."

"They didn't fly out of San Diego, but crossed the border on foot and boarded a plane in Tijuana. Rob returned after a few days, but she had met your father and stayed. It was love at first sight, Rob said. He wanted to go back, but then got sick and—"

His voice ran down.

"I figured that when she finally came back, someone would tell her about Rob. I was surprised she never contacted me. Then I graduated, moved to New York and . . . life went on." He stopped and let out a big sad sigh. "I will be happy to mail all these letters and pictures to you."

"Thanks, Doctor McCoy. I can't tell you how much I appreciate it."

"Oh, please. I'm sorry I didn't try to find Sarah Lee. But I didn't know how. And it was a hard time for me as well."

The creases around his eyes grew deeper. He looked, all of a sudden, like a much older man.

"Do you have any idea of how I can contact her family?" I asked shyly.

"No, but I will look for Rob's friends from San Diego. There has to be somebody out there who knows how to get in touch with Sarah Lee's folks, if they are still around."

After we hung up, he emailed me the photo of my mom and me by the piano and a few shots more. My parents appeared together in several, looking happy and very much in love.

# CHAPTER FIFTY-SEVEN

*December 15th, 1989*

*There isn't much I can write at this point, but we will get together soon. I am so looking forward to spending time with you, my friend. A long time!*

THE JOSÉ MARTÍ INTERNATIONAL Airport was quiet. Only a handful of people were inside the fish tank—a glass-walled waiting room reserved for departing passengers. On the other side, Sarah hugged Valentina and Carlos and suppressed a sob.

"There, there, Jackie O," Valentina said, squeezing her harder. "We'll meet again someday. Call me as soon as you get home. You have my number, don't you?"

"I've memorized it."

"Good for you."

It was December 17th. Valentina had gotten her two Russian passports, one issued to Olga Ivanova, with Sarah's picture, and the other to Galina Ivanova, with Mercedes's. But they hadn't been able to buy tickets yet. All the Aeroflot flights were booked until January.

"My contact will let you know if someone cancels," Valentina whispered. "Fifty dollars, remember? Don't let him con you into giving him more money!"

Sarah nodded and made an effort to smile. She managed to keep a brave face, but when the couple went through security and entered the fish tank, she broke down crying, gripped by the premonition that she would never see them again.

IT WAS A DONE deal. They were leaving tomorrow. The Aeroflot employee (who did ask for more money) had found two seats in the Havana-Moscow flight for December 23rd. Which was perfect, because Joaquín had already mentioned he had to go to work that day, even though it was a Saturday.

The plane would stop to refuel at Gander Airport in Newfoundland, where Sarah and Mercedes would get off. There was a special stopover area designed for passengers that wished to be admitted as refugees. Canadian authorities were used to it since they received dozens of asylum-seekers every year.

"All you have to do is show them your American passport, Jackie O!" Valentina had said. "You'll be home before you know it!"

Sarah wiped at her eyes. She missed her friend and the easy way she had of solving every problem that came her way. Speaking of friends, soon she would miss Lo too. And Joaquín, whom she still loved. She would even miss Villa Santa Marta!

She opened the first dresser drawer and took out her American passport. Under it was the marriage certificate. Sarah studied her signature, remembering her wedding day that now seemed so far away. She wasn't Tania Rojas anymore, and she would miss her too.

Joaquín would be furious when he found out—oh, he would probably destroy all her pictures and everything that could remind him of her. He would feel betrayed, and not without reason. He'd be sad too because he loved his daughter. And he loved *her*. Yes, he would be devastated. But she couldn't stay, not with the threat of a civil war looming. News of the

Romanian protests had reached Havana despite the censorship. Even Lo knew about what had happened in Timişoara! Sarah shuddered, recalling Joaquín's comments about taking the tanks to the streets. She was also sick and tired of shortages, blackouts, the ever-present surveillance . . . It wasn't just about herself. Mercedes deserved better.

*Easier to ask for forgiveness than permission, eh?*

*I don't need his permission to take care of my daughter!*

A tear fell on the marriage certificate. She couldn't take it. Carrying two passports with different names and nationalities was enough of a risk. (What if they searched her at the José Martí Airport?) But she didn't want to leave it within Joaquín's reach either. It was a symbol of the commitment they had once made. Her fleeing didn't necessarily mean the end. Once she was safely at home, she would call Joaquín and—

Inspiration struck her. She clutched the paper against her chest and got out of the room. First, she passed by Mercedes's. The girl was sleeping in her cradle. Sarah arranged the sheets neatly around her and tiptoed to the library, where she knelt by the tallest bookshelf. She had hidden the Russian passports and the plane tickets in the place where she least expected Joaquín to look. She retrieved them, folded the marriage certificate, kissed it and put it inside the *Secret Doctrine* pages.

On the desk was the leather pouch she had bought at the *diplotienda*. The words *Viva Cuba* had an ironic tinge at the moment, but the pouch was the right size for passports and tickets. Now all she had to do was wait until the next day and leave immediately after Joaquín had gone to work. The flight would depart at noon. Her backpack was ready, hidden in Mercedes's armoire. She only carried one set of clothes for herself, three for her daughter and the piece of paper with the Barbeitos' friend's address.

Joaquín didn't suspect a thing. He was still staying late for meetings, military practices and whatnot. That morning, he had told her he wouldn't be back until nine or ten. Thank God, because it was so hard to face him and pretend . . . Sarah looked up and met the fiery eyes of the lady in the pillbox hat. That *bruja* who, for all she knew, could have actually cast a circle of protection around the house.

"*¡Qué guanajería!*"

The word didn't sound funny anymore. In more than one way, she had been a turkey, a *guanaja*. Or maybe she had been just naïve . . .

Sarah glanced out the window to the backyard below and spotted two mangoes on the ground. Great. Now she could make a smoothie for Mercedes. There was one can of evaporated milk in the cupboard. She left the library, taking the leather pouch with her.

In the kitchen, she set the food processor on the counter and the leather pouch on the table. (She would put it in her backpack as soon as she went back upstairs to wake Mercedes up.) She opened the can, mixed the milk with water and went outside to get the mangoes.

The wind whistled around and shook the boughs of the trees. The first mango was rotten. The other was still green. And there was no place to buy more, or any kind of fruit. On a tropical island. Oh, she was so done with it! She threw the useless mangoes on the ground.

With some luck, they would be home in time for Christmas. She imagined Mercedes's amazement as she tasted her first pumpkin pie, sipped hot chocolate, smelled a Fraser fir, crawled under the tree to discover the gifts . . .

Sarah smiled. Her parents would be shocked at first, but they would get over it as soon they looked into the girl's limpid blue eyes. Her mother already suspected—and her father would melt. She had always been a daddy's girl, and now she would be back with a mini-her in tow. They would be a little tight at first, squeezed in the Pacific Beach cottage until she moved on her own, but there was space for a cradle in her room if she took all that surfing stuff away . . .

A noise startled her. It couldn't be Joaquín. Too early for him to arrive. Or not so early? It was the ashen hour, that peculiar time of the day when night hadn't fallen yet but you couldn't see the edge of things, when the whole world seemed to have gone underwater.

She heard Joaquín's voice. The kitchen door opened, and out he walked. His face was red with rage. In his left hand, he held the passports and the tickets; in his right hand, the Makarov.

# CHAPTER FIFTY-EIGHT

The sound of waves crashing on the nearby shore woke me up at seven-thirty in the morning. I recognized the Airbnb room where I had spent the night. It was in Pacific Beach, the San Diego neighborhood where my mother grew up and spent most of her life, except for her Cuban years.

Doctor McCoy—or Vincent, as he asked me to call him—had found a missing persons website with a page devoted to her.

*Sarah Lee Nelson*
*Last seen: San Diego, California, December, 1985*
*Date of Birth: March 7, 1967*
*Place of Birth: San Diego*
*Hair: Blond*
*Eyes: Blue*
*Height: 5'9"*
*Weight: 125 pounds*
*Race: White*
*Presumed to be in El Salvador*

It included three photos: a teenager with long blond hair wearing a Che Guevara T-shirt, a close-up of a smiling young woman and a group picture of surfers. Sarah Lee was in the last row, leaning on a surfboard. She looked so innocent that I wished to time travel in order to protect her, warn her, tell her she needed to stay home. Even if that meant I wouldn't be here now.

Below was a computer-generated image of her as an adult. We didn't look as much alike as I had expected, but the family air was undeniable. The page was dated 2006. Her parents had been looking for her all these years, hoping against all hope.

*La esperanza es la ultimo que se pierde.*

Their contact information was on the website. The phone number didn't work, but the address, according to the Pacific Beach White Pages, was still the Nelsons' residence.

Vincent had sent me my mother's letters to Rob and the last pictures he had developed for her. I devoured the letters in one sitting. A detail struck me as odd, and I called him again.

"There's a big jump in time in their correspondence, from January to September 1988," I said. "Do you know why?"

"Rob was already very sick and he didn't write much then," he answered. "I imagine she stopped writing too. But many letters from her got lost as well. He found out when they started talking on the phone. Maybe the Cuban surveillance system intercepted them. Or someone else."

My father, I thought.

I went back to the pages, crying over my mother's careful penmanship. I grieved for her, but the process felt backward, like a movie shown in reverse. By reading the letters and staring hungrily at the photos, I got to know Sarah Lee. I saw her change from starstruck girl to mature woman, from a child herself to a mother, from idealistic to disillusioned, all the while coming to terms with the realization that we would never meet.

THE AIRBNB WAS ONE block from the Nelsons' cottage. My first evening in California, I spent a good hour walking by the white fence and the little garden where my mother probably sat so many times, watching the ocean and dreaming of exotic places.

Like Cuba.

I had wanted to talk to my grandparents immediately, but by the time I arrived it was too late for strong emotions, considering they were over eighty. But the way had been paved. Vincent had already given them a heads-up. He didn't want for me to have to tell them that their daughter was gone.

Or was she?

Vincent had also mentioned something that made me reconsider my religious beliefs, or lack thereof.

"When Rob was on his deathbed, he suddenly opened his eyes and said, 'Sarah Lee! Here you are!' I looked around, expecting to see her, but we were alone in the room. Then he slipped into a coma and died. I've always wondered what that was about." He paused and his voice cracked. "It was one reason why I kept all the letters and pictures. That, and because Rob was my first love."

So maybe my mother had been there to welcome her buddy to the other side. And maybe she had been around me all those years in Villa Santa Marta. She could have been the one who haunted the house, not María Estela. Or they might have met in the otherworld. I was open to all possibilities. There might be an astral plane after all.

FOR THE FIRST VISIT to my grandparents, I chose a simple white dress and brown leather sandals. I also put on a silver chain with the locket, now cleaned and restored. The letters and pictures were in my purse. I hoped all that helped me establish my identity. Though, judging by the photos, I had Sarah Lee Nelson written all over me.

I set out to the cottage. The ocean was a spectacular blue.

The coffee shops and quaint stores alongside the street looked charming, even when still closed. The hustle and bustle of Miami was conspicuously absent. Honestly, I didn't miss it. Of course, I wouldn't live so far away from Mamina, and all my friends and my job were on the other coast, but I had already decided to spend more time in San Diego if my grandparents asked me to.

They had probably gone through their own grieving process, their extended heartbreak shaping them as it was beginning to shape me. The fact that they had stayed in the same house meant they were still, somehow, waiting for their long-lost daughter to come home. That wouldn't happen, but they would get *me* instead. I felt the locket pulsating against my throat as if it had a life of its own.

A wave crashed on the beach. A couple of surfers rode it, their fit bodies silhouetted against the sky. I imagined Sarah Lee doing the same, happy and carefree.

When I looked at the house again, the front door was open. A white-haired woman stood at the threshold, holding a tall man's arm. They came out and their eyes widened as I rushed toward them under the dazzling California sun.

## Acknowledgments

Thanks to my wonderful editors Yezanira Venecia and Taz Urnov. You made this book possible. *¡Mil gracias!* Thanks to my dear friends Raquel Troyce and Marisela Fleites-Lear for reading earlier versions of the novel and offering ideas and recommendations. Marisela, you helped me avoid more than one Cuban faux pas. *¡Gracias a todas!*